DATE
WEEK

OTHER TITLES BY TED FOX

Schooled

DATE WEEK

a novel

TED FOX

LAKE UNION
PUBLISHING

Published by Lake Union Publishing, Seattle

www.apub.com

Amazon, the Amazon logo, and Lake Union Publishing are trademarks of Amazon.com, Inc., or its affiliates.

ISBN-13: 9781662514531 (paperback)
ISBN-13: 9781662514524 (digital)

Cover design and illustration by Liz Casal

Printed in the United States of America

For Jenny.
Clearly.

NOW

"I can't believe you did this."

She's sitting at the room's desk, but with her back to it, her body facing the king-size bed, the larger of her two bags still open on top of it from when she pulled out her clothes for dinner.

"You would've done the same for me," he says, hoping for the best while squatting down in front of her and grabbing her hands. "Well, maybe not the same. You're more creative *and* more levelheaded than me, which is kinda crazy when you think about it. But you know what I mean."

He's anxious and rambling, waiting for her to say something else. Embrace him. Berate him. Absolve him. Something.

Their TV is on mute on the hotel-guide channel, and the quiet reminds him of playing high school basketball, of all things. Junior year, he had a potential buzzer-beating shot to win sectionals, and he still remembers all the sound being sucked out of the gym as he watched the ball arc through the air toward the rim.

He just hopes it ends better this time.

SEVEN DAYS AGO

Chapter 1

Will Easterly was not the kind of guy who spent a day off painting a room because he was just that handy.

To feel confident and capable as a self-sufficient 34-year-old, one who might someday prove adept at being responsible for something more than choosing between Thai and Italian for dinner? Maybe. To occupy his mind with something other than the major life change on the horizon that he felt woefully unprepared for?

Absolutely.

And that was how he came to find himself rolling the walls of the second bedroom in the apartment that third Friday in June. He and his wife had picked the color together, a shade cheekily named Can of Green Gables, but the fact that Will was going to have the room done when she got home from work was a surprise.

Not as big a surprise as seeing that plus sign on the pregnancy test she had taken three months earlier. But a surprise nonetheless.

Because when it came to making things look good, you usually wanted Rachel Armas around.

A graphic designer, she worked in the communications unit at a university, not because she was particularly passionate about higher education but because the school was near where she grew up outside Chicago, which meant she could live with her parents that first year after college to save money before she got her own place. (Will had followed her to the Windy City another 18 months after that.) Now she had the combination of earned experience and natural-born talent that could take her anywhere, and yet she was still designing departmental newsletters and posters for lectures that would be attended by 10 people.

When the two of them had graduated from the University of Michigan, Rachel had actually had another offer, a paid internship at an art gallery in New York City. She had been so excited, and he had been excited for her—and himself since he had lined up his own internship in Philadelphia, only a couple of hours away. He had been convinced she was taking it up to the moment she hadn't. When he'd asked her why she'd changed her mind, she'd just brushed it off and said it was too impractical. Not until they were living together had she told him it had been her parents who'd talked her out of it and she wished she could do that decision over.

A philosophy professor told me he needs me to "Photoshop something that conveys the rationality of belief," she'd texted Will one day at lunch a couple of weeks ago. He'd just gotten done talking with his own boss—Will was one of the main IT people at his company, and apparently they didn't teach you how to turn off your vacation out-of-office email at CEO school—and he'd responded to Rachel with a GIF of a cat punching a stuffed tiger repeatedly in the face.

This—this is why I married you, she'd replied. You get me.

So what're you going to do? Every time they talked about something like this, he wondered if she was questioning her decision to play it safe a decade earlier. It pained him to think about it.

Ehh I don't know. Probably just put some old guy under a tree looking depressed.

Sure, Can of Green Gables had been a joint decision—well, maybe 80 percent Rachel, 20 percent Will—so he wasn't going completely rogue. And it wasn't like she had actually said anything about waiting to do it together. Then again, this was going to be the baby's nursery, their future daughter's or son's room. Forget that *daughter* and *son* still sounded like relationships that should be reserved for people who didn't have a Dave & Buster's rewards card in their wallet. That was a given.

But priming and painting the nursery without Rachel? Again, it would be a total surprise, and not necessarily one that would be met with enthusiasm. Will could try to play it off, pretending he didn't think the paint fumes would be good for her, but he could already see the look on her face when she shot that down. It was the look she'd given him their sophomore year on the quad at Michigan when he'd first asked her out.

He may have had a hacky sack on him. In retrospect, he couldn't blame her for saying no.

So why in God's name had he started painting that room? Short answer, manual labor was an effective distraction.

From worrying about the baby being healthy, of course. But also about him and Rachel. He told himself that a miscarriage or any other worst-case scenario could never get between them. And mostly, he believed it. But in the corners of his consciousness, which he visited at 2:00 a.m. when he traded sleep for all the uncertainty awaiting him as a dad, his brain would sometimes remind him that he and Rachel had never been tested in that way, so how could he really know? How could he be sure they could survive *not* becoming parents now? And once he went there, it was a short jump to a different catastrophe:

What if he lost her in the process? Not their relationship. *Her.*

He had, in fact, seen a story about maternal mortality rates that Friday morning. It'd jarred loose those 2:00 a.m. thoughts straight into his first cup of coffee and threatened to send his brain into a tailspin. So, too, had the dream he'd had the night before. In it, Rachel had gone to the hospital to deliver, and the doctors had told them they were sorry, but if there had ever been a baby to begin with, they'd lost it due to a lack of this one piece of critical knowledge. When Will had asked what it was, he couldn't understand their response, and he'd started awake in a cold sweat in the spot where he'd dozed off on the couch.

It was only after he was done priming and on the last wall with the initial coat of paint that it occurred to him that a superstitious person might view his doing this when Rachel was still five months away from her due date as a needless tempting of the Fates.

A shiver went down Will's spine, and he did the only thing he could think of: he went to his happy place.

He cranked the T. Swift.

Perhaps not an entirely unexpected move coming from the guy who'd used his senior yearbook quote in high school to parrot a Rascal Flatts lyric. He saw the pop-country continuum to Taylor, anyway. Rachel, however, who had been laughing for a good five minutes upon discovering his passion for "Bless the Broken Road" while helping him unpack boxes when they moved in together, did not appreciate the connection. She immediately turned serious and told him that if he ever compared Taylor to Rascal Flatts again, he'd be waking up to Rachel's perpetually expanding The-Gift-That-Is-TS playlist every morning for the rest of their lives.

Rachel had meant it as a joke, but she'd loved the idea so much she'd done it regardless. Almost a decade later, the playlist was still going strong far more mornings than it wasn't. Which was fine with Will. He'd always liked Taylor—although maybe not to the point of finding a Rascal Flatts comparison blasphemous—so he had no regrets.

The same couldn't be said of his soft spot for would-be romantic gestures.

Sometimes he got it right, like his and Rachel's first Christmas as a couple. It had been junior year. Rachel was a voracious reader, and he'd set up a scavenger hunt for her at a local bookstore, where the clues had taken her to five books on her to-read list and then ultimately to him in the café, where he had been waiting with her favorite latte and that week's earnings from his tutoring job to buy the books with.

But other times? Less successful.

For instance, right before graduation, he had gone to Build-A-Bear and made a bear. With a recording of his voice saying "I love you."

In 15 languages other than English (most of which he had no business attempting).

Culminating in him sappily declaring, "No matter how you say it, I love you, Rachel Armas."

He'd led her to it with rose petals sprinkled throughout her apartment.

"Oh wow," she had said, taking his hands. "Okay. We're going to set aside that that teddy bear is the most chillingly creepy thing I've ever seen and focus on this: I love you, too, Will. So much. You are amazing, and we're great. Graduation isn't going to change that. I need you to trust that that's true."

He'd nodded, still not quite able to shake the feeling that she'd eventually move on from him once they didn't have a college campus to keep them together. She stood out from the background hum of life, unlike anyone he had ever met. He was smart, had been described on more than one occasion as "almost impossibly kind," and was not unattractive—she'd even convinced him to pose for her for a nude drawing assignment—but he felt like the world was destined to open up for her in a way that would be inaccessible to him.

And yet somehow, here they were.

"Ah, when did we get so old, Taylor?" he said to the wall as he worked on spreading out a drip to the undeniable banger that is "22." "Well, not you. You're flawless. But me? How am I going to be a dad? I can't even keep paint off the baseboard. Crap. There is paint on the baseboard. And the floor! There is paint on the baseboard and the floor! Okay—nobody panic!"

It was odd advice, given he was the only one there, but in a weird sort of way, it helped. He liked having such a defined task in front of him: remove the paint from where it wasn't supposed to be. He discovered it came off pretty easily with a little bit of scrubbing, and he guessed that had something to do with it being water based.

"Sounds plausible at least," he said to himself.

It was a warm day, and with the air conditioner off because of the open window, the sweat was beading up on his forehead and back as he crouched close to the floor. But he didn't mind. He felt like maybe he had stumbled onto something, like maybe this was the secret to parenting. Not the scrubbing itself—although based on the horror stories he'd heard about diaper blowouts, who knew—but this whole focusing on the little thing right in front of you and not getting overwhelmed by the enormousness of the entire project (i.e., raising a child to adulthood).

Because while Rachel's pregnancy had come as a shock and Will felt completely overwhelmed by it at times, he also hoped that raising a child together, *their* child, would only bring them closer. And how awesome was this baby going to be if she or he grew up to be anything like his wife? So creative. So talented. So caring.

So what if he was stress rollering a nursery and finding that maybe there was something to that paint-fumes defense after all? Rachel being pregnant was still a good thing. An awesome thing.

"I wonder if I have the shoulders to pull off a BabyBjörn," he said, standing back up, his body literally lifting with a renewed sense of optimism as he crossed the hall to open a second window and get a better breeze going. He was thinking about baby names—Rachel really liked Lane for a boy or a girl, but he was worried about the potential for all the stay-in-your jokes—and just putting on the finishing touches of that first coat when he heard Rachel's voice behind him in the doorway.

"Babe?" she said.

Will jumped, startled. It was only 4:00 p.m., meaning she was home from work a couple of hours before he expected her. Maybe she'd left early because they'd both taken the next week off—their annual Week of Nothing, when they allowed themselves to revel in being as lazy as they wanted—and she was just ready to start vacation. He'd taken the whole day for the same reason.

In any event, this was the moment of truth. He wished he'd had a chance to get the second coat on to bring out the full luster of Can of Green Gables, but overall, he was pleased with his handiwork.

"Now, keep in mind," he said, turning around and narrowly avoiding stepping in the paint tray in the process, "I still have one more coat to do, but . . ."

He stopped. Rachel was crying. His heart sank.

"Look, I know it's not perfect," he tried, "and I should've waited for you. Crap. I'm sorry, Rachel, I wasn't—"

"No," she said through her tears. She was barefoot but otherwise still dressed as she had been when she'd left that morning. "No, it's not that. The room looks great."

"Okay, now you're freaking me out because I would've believed *okay* or *not bad*, but not *great*."

That was the kind of thing that normally would've made her laugh, and she tried to muster one, but nothing came out.

Will's mind began to race, his painting-inspired parenting platitude a distant memory, and he began to panic for real. What was going on? Oh God.

It was the baby. Something had happened with the baby. That had to be it. Why else would she be so upset? And she'd come home to tell him, only to find him in the midst of painting the nursery for the child they would never have. *She* would never have. All because he'd been freaking out about the pregnancy and gone looking for something to do—something that, even as he was doing it, he had thought could be a jinx.

He noticed that she still hadn't stepped into the room, which now would be an ever-present reminder of loss, and instantly felt sick to his stomach.

"Hey, what's going on?" he said as he rushed over to her and took her in his arms. She kept crying, now into his shoulder, the purple highlight in her otherwise jet-black hair pressed into his chin.

"Rachel, I need you to talk to me," he said after another 10 or 15 seconds had passed, hearing his own voice starting to catch in his throat. "You really are freaking me out."

She sniffed loudly. "It's nothing. I'm being stupid."

Will felt himself exhale.

He was upset that she was upset. Clearly. But she'd never be so dismissive of a problem with the baby. And he was pretty sure this also meant no one had died. He just had to give her time to regroup. That he could do.

Rachel kept hugging him for another minute or so before letting go. He took a step back into the room, and she followed.

"You said you've still got a coat to do, right?" she clarified, scanning the walls. "Because it's a little uneven by the window. And over in that corner."

"There's the woman I love."

She did succeed in laughing this time and wiped her eyes with the back of her hand. She had on a sleeveless blouse, so the arm motion drew his attention to the tattoo on the underside of her right forearm. It was a Georgia O'Keeffe quote, written in script: "I believe that to create one's own world in any of the arts takes courage." Will had gone with her both when she'd gotten it and the first time when they'd known her parents would see it, at a dinner at Morton's steakhouse in the city.

Rachel had done it knowing they'd disapprove. Despite having talked about wanting that tattoo since college, she'd waited until she was 25 to get it, understanding that inking those words on her body would represent an unerasable rejection of her parents' sensibilities. And yet she'd hoped that somehow it would make them finally see her for who she was, who she'd become.

"But it's not . . . *permanent*, right?" her mom had asked upon discovering it when Rachel rested her arm on the table after they'd ordered the appetizers.

"Well, it hurt like hell, so I hope so."

Her dad had frowned before dipping his eyes back down to the menu. "That never would've flown in a boardroom," he'd said under his breath but still loud enough for everyone to hear. When she was in college, her parents had pushed her to major in something like economics, with an eye toward law school or getting an MBA. They'd never gotten over her choosing the arts, and if her decision to bail on the gallery position had been her way of belatedly appeasing them, the tattoo was meant to signal she'd made a mistake not going to New York.

Will had started to object to her dad's comment, but Rachel had squeezed his hand under the table and subtly shaken her head. Not worth it. They'd proceeded to move their way through an awkward dinner, and then they had driven home, laughing about her parents' infatuation with the television show *Blue Bloods* and planning what they were going to watch that night. She hadn't seemed to want to talk about the tattoo, so Will hadn't brought it up. It hadn't been until he'd almost been asleep, their bedroom dark and quiet, that her voice had come almost out of nowhere, no louder than a whisper.

"Nothing ever changes."

He'd put his arm around her, and she'd started to cry. Eventually she'd fallen asleep, and then he had too.

Now here they were again, and he wondered if, like that time, her parents had done or said something.

Rachel took a deep breath. Despite that laugh about her reaction to his painting, she still looked sad.

"So," she said, "I basically got offered my dream job today."

Will couldn't hide his confusion. "You basically got offered your dream job today?" he repeated.

"Uh-huh."

"Okay. But isn't that, like, a good thing?"

"It would be"—she sighed—"if I weren't about to have a baby."

Chapter 2

"Do you remember me talking about Rochelle Simmons?" Rachel asked.

"Rochelle—is she the woman from Creative Vices?"

"The founder, yes."

Creative Vices was the Los Angeles–based marketing agency behind some of the most creative advertising and public service campaigns (and the corresponding viral memes) of the last five years. Rochelle had visited the university's graphic design department to give a guest lecture a year before, and Rachel had stayed in somewhat regular touch with her over LinkedIn and email ever since. That had led to Rachel sharing her portfolio, which included both designs and original artwork, and Rochelle had told her it was as good as anything she'd seen.

"She has an opening for an associate creative director," Rachel said. "I've seen her posting about it for the last month, so I checked it out, just out of curiosity. It's a way bigger job than what I'm doing now. So I kind of put it out of my mind. Which was easy since I wasn't exactly looking to move us to California in the first place. But then she called this afternoon to ask me if I'd consider applying, because they're scheduling interviews, and she's not excited about any of the candidates they have. She thinks I would be perfect for it and wants to fly me out a week from Monday."

Rachel sat down on the window seat, careful not to rest her legs against the paint below in case it was still wet. The sun was streaming in from behind her, making it hard for Will to read her expression from his spot across the room, where he was putting the lid back on the can of paint.

"I agree with her: you would be perfect for it," he said. "So I'm still not seeing how this is a problem. I mean, my job is basically remote at this point, so I'm sure I could make that work." He wasn't completely sure, but that was a detail for later. When Rochelle had written her about the portfolio, Rachel had called him sounding like she'd won the lottery. Will hadn't heard her talk about her work like that in a long time. "And isn't this why you've kept talking to her? To maybe get a shot at something like this?"

"Well, yeah, but it was a lot less real then. She needs an answer by the end of the day. Like, today. She's on vacation next week and wants the interviews set before she goes so they can wrap this up when she gets back."

"And?"

"And it's LA. *An entirely new career in LA*. I've never even been west of Denver."

"Why do you think it'd be an entirely new career? You've been doing this kind of stuff for years now."

Her laugh came out as more of a snort. "Comparing marketing communications at a university to marketing at an *Adweek* Agency of the Year is like saying a Yorkie is basically the same thing as a wolf."

"Uh, no offense, but the whole crippling self-doubt thing is kinda my vibe, not yours," Will said, hoping to elicit a smile from her. Joking or not, he wasn't wrong, though he came by it honestly enough. His childhood and adolescence had often left him wondering where he fit in. Like on the first day of 10th grade, when the girl he'd had a crush on since freshman year greeted him enthusiastically at their lockers, and he thought maybe he'd have a shot at taking her to homecoming—until he overheard her and a friend laughing about his clothes that same morning. Asking girls to dances was not his thing after that. But to be fair, Will's denim vest had been objectively awful, and the girls couldn't have known just how vulnerable he was to feeling rejected.

"Don't do that," Rachel said, all too aware that Will's insecurity stemmed from his relationship (or lack thereof) with his father. Will and Rachel were each the first person the other had ever really opened up to about their complicated relationships with their dads—and in Rachel's case, with her mom also. "I hate when you downplay what he did to you."

"My point is," Will said, taking the spot next to her on the bench seat, "there's no way you'd not be great at this. Rochelle obviously thinks so too."

"That's very sweet, thank you. Misguided maybe, but sweet. But you seem to be forgetting the part where we'd have to move across the country. I can't have this baby two thousand miles away from home." She had just gotten the faintest hint of her bump, and she rubbed her stomach instinctively. "I mean, my parents are my parents, but they're also still my parents."

"That sentence was like an out-of-body experience."

"Word salad, I know. But does it make sense?"

"It does," he said. "But it's not like we go over to their house every Sunday for dinner or anything. When was the last time we even saw them?"

"The last time *you* saw them was when we told them I was pregnant. But they've been making more of an effort with me. Mom's even come to campus to have lunch with me a few times."

"Why didn't you tell me?"

"I don't know. I guess because I haven't quite known what to make of it. It's like they get me more now that I'm pregnant—like I finally make sense to them. And on the one hand, that drives me absolutely crazy. But on the other, it feels kinda . . ."

She trailed off, and Will knew she was tearing up again.

"Nice?" he offered. His dad had basically been out of the picture since he was eight, so he was no stranger to yearning for a parent's attention.

Rachel nodded. "And it's not like we couldn't use the help when the baby comes, right?"

He thought of how his own brewing panic was the reason they were sitting in a two-thirds-painted room and knew she had a point. Unlike with his dad, he had a great relationship with his mom, but she lived several hours away in Ohio. And his heart hurt when he thought the obvious person for them to call on would've been his aunt Katie, who had been like Will's second mom and had moved about 45 minutes west of him and Rachel not too long before they'd gotten married. But Katie had died suddenly from a pulmonary embolism a year earlier, leaving his mom without her sister and Will without a role model he'd come to rely on.

"Plus there's my sister," Rachel continued, "and the miscarriage, and I know they've been trying again, and it's not working, and her marriage is a mess, and . . ." She was crying harder now. "And I want to be there for her, but I feel like me being pregnant is just making it harder on her. So I already felt guilty about that, and now I'm . . ."

She stopped because the sobs started shaking her whole body. He pulled her in for another hug, and her next sentence came out in fits and starts between breaths.

"Now . . . I'm . . . *complaining* . . . about not being able to take a *job* . . . because I *am* pregnant . . . and I feel like the most ungrateful . . . self-involved . . . person ever."

It was one of those moments that called for just the right words, and he found it far easier to summon them on her behalf than trying to reassure himself, as his dad's rejection didn't hold nearly as much sway outside of Will's own head.

"Our second date. We went to the botanical gardens. Have I ever told you why I picked that?"

He felt her shake her head slightly on his chest.

"When I'd picked you up for our first date—Buffalo Wild Wings, because I had no clue what I was doing—I had seen that painting of orchids you'd done. So for date two, I thought Matthaei Botanical Gardens. They had flowers. They had art. It was perfect."

He paused for effect. Rachel leaned back from him, but he kept his arm around her shoulder.

"And then came the coleslaw," he said.

She hiccuped a small chuckle.

"You'd think after seeing you order a salad with a side of fries at friggin' *BW's*, it would've at least crossed my mind that you *might* be a vegetarian. But no. I went to that deli on my way to your apartment, confidently ordered one roast beef sandwich and one turkey sandwich, and then, being the gentleman that I was, presented them to you on a picnic blanket and invited you to choose. At which point you told me you *were* a vegetarian, but that it was okay, you would just eat the coleslaw."

"You looked like you wanted to crawl under the nearest bench and die," she said. "I felt bad for you."

"Oh, I was mortified. But you were super nice about it. Even after that bee proceeded to sting you, and your finger swelled up to twice its normal size."

"It wasn't *twice* its—"

"Nevertheless," Will pressed on, raising his free hand to signal this was his tale of woe to tell, "you soldiered on, right through my awkward attempt at a good night kiss that, instead, resulted in me patting you on your back. Like I was your uncle hugging you at a funeral."

"I don't even remember that."

"Of course you don't. Because you were about to get violently ill as a result of food poisoning from the tainted coleslaw I force-fed you."

She grimaced at the memory as she moved from under his arm and tested the wall lightly with her index finger to see if it had dried. Deciding she was in the clear, she rested her back against it and put her feet up on his lap, the indentations from her sandals not yet faded from her skin. It was still a little early in the pregnancy for her feet to be swelling from the baby, but they had always done so in the heat, and he knew she was worried about what they would feel like by the end of the summer.

"Between the hacky sack on the quad, the Buffalo Wild Wings, and that disaster of a second date, I just assumed I'd never hear from you again," Will said, massaging her soles.

"Ha, I was not so easily deterred."

"And do you remember what you said to me when you called?"

"Honestly, no," Rachel said.

"You said, 'You should probably let me plan date three.' Then you laughed. *Laughed, Rachel.* I was stunned. 'There's going to be a date three?' I asked. And you said—and I'll never forget this—'I like you, Will. You're you, and you let me be me.'"

She managed an actual laugh this time. "I had a real way with words."

"You did, actually," he said. "And that's the reason I'm telling you all this. Because you, self-involved? Rachel, people who're self-involved, they don't see people like me for date three. Especially not at twenty years old, and especially not when I know for a fact you had plenty of other options. You are the most genuine, thoughtful, caring human being I've ever known."

Her face was serious again, and she looked out the window. "Well, we'll see, won't we?"

"What do you mean?"

"I've never taken care of a baby. Neither of us have. What if I'm terrible at it? What if I'm so sleep deprived I don't hear her or him crying in the middle of the night? What do I do if he or she has a fever? What if I try to breastfeed, and I can't?"

"Do you want to breastfeed?"

"I don't know!" she said, turning back to him, exasperated. "My sister's the one who's always been into this stuff, but she doesn't get to be a mom. Meanwhile, I don't even have an opinion. But everyone acts like I'm supposed to. The only thing I do seem to know is that apparently

I'm going to blame my baby for getting in the way of my career. Real mom-of-the-year material there."

"That's not what you're doing."

He thought about telling her he was scared, too, but it didn't seem like what she needed to hear. Not then, anyway. He also didn't like that she seemed to be falling back into that trap of shelving what she really wanted because of what other people might think.

Rachel leaned toward him and put her hand on his cheek. She smiled.

"I love how supportive of me you are," she said. "That was one of the things I could tell from the beginning. But it's just not the right time. I can't take all this on professionally while also trying to figure out how to be a mom, with no one for us to ask for help. I'm not going to do that to the baby, and I'm not going to do that to us. Sometimes the boring job is the right job."

Sometimes the boring job is the right job.

Will heard that sentence, and it was like the smoking gun attesting to the fact that she felt she was at a professional dead end. And who knew? Maybe she was bored with other things about their life. It made him queasy.

"I really do think that together, we could handle this," he said, his own doubts about parenting thousands of miles away from anyone they knew no match for his desire to make sure she didn't grow unhappy with their circumstances. "All of it."

"What? The job? California?"

"Yeah."

"Will," she said, hands on both his cheeks now, "I want you to listen to me on this. I know being an awesome parent is as important to you as it is to me. And I don't feel like I can be that in Los Angeles right now. I'll get over it. So I need you to also. Okay?"

"But—"

"Will. Okay?"

The sun gave her entire face a warm glow, but there was no mistaking the sadness in her eyes.

"Okay."

"Okay," she repeated. She swung her legs back down to the floor and stood. "Now if you'll excuse me, I'm going to go write Rochelle back and tell her no in the most artful way possible, and then I'm going to kick off my Week of Nothing by allowing myself to wallow a bit longer in the privacy of a bubble bath. Can you pick us up something for dinner?"

"Sure. I wanted to go out and get a new roller cover for the second coat, so I can do both. Any preference on food?"

"You surprised me once today. I'll bet you can do it again. Just be prepared to binge some reality TV when you get back. The shamelessness of *Date Me Now!* is a balm to my soul." She disappeared out the door and down the hall before calling back, "On second thought, get whatever you want. This is an ice-cream-straight-from-the-container night. Don't judge me."

He wouldn't. Not only because he wasn't a jerk, but also because she'd just given him another idea altogether.

Chapter 3

Going to Lowe's just to get a new paint roller cover is a bit like taking a Hummer pretty much anywhere: overkill. The aisles are so large and there's so much *stuff* that the express lanes would be better served measuring gross tonnage than the number of items in your cart.

But Will was headed to the one in Lincolnwood anyway because he needed the drive time to think. He didn't remember Rachel crying that night in bed after she'd shown her parents the tattoo just because it had been an intimate moment. He also remembered it because Rachel hardly ever cried, and never about anything to do with work, which was in direct contrast to what he'd just witnessed. Even when her boss's boss had come down on her hard over something she'd done for the president's office that she hadn't cleared with him first, ranting and raving about how she was out of line, wasn't a team player, etc., etc., she'd been unfazed. Her retelling of the incident had been dispassionate and a little bemused, all the way through to her wrapping it up with, "So anyway, confirmed he's a dick. What do you want to do for dinner?"

No, to elicit the kind of emotion she'd shown about Creative Vices, whatever it was really had to mean something to her, get at the core of who she was. That was why he was so concerned to see her just brushing it aside.

He was still preoccupied when the screen on his dash lit up with a call from his mom. She'd already called around noon from the Apple Store to ask his opinion on whether she needed a new iPad. Getting two calls in one day was unusual, so he didn't think he should let it go to voicemail, even if his mind was elsewhere.

"Hey, Mom."

"Hi, Willie Will." She'd called him Willie Will since he was a baby. "I'm sorry to bug you again. Is now a bad time?"

"Oh no, you're fine. Just on my way to get some painting supplies. What's up?"

"Right. How's that going? Was Rachel surprised?"

Will thought about how to answer that. "Yes and no? She seemed happy with it, but she had a lot going on at work today, and that kind of dominated the conversation."

"How's she feeling? People will tell you the second trimester is easier than the first, but I always say, there's no *typical* in pregnancy."

"Yeah, she's feeling pretty good right now," he said, rolling up to a stop sign. "Physically, at least. It's all just a lot sometimes, you know?"

"Oh, I remember that feeling. Make sure she doesn't feel like she's in it alone. Trust me, I . . . well . . ." More than 25 years after his dad had left, his mom still avoided talking about him whenever possible. She didn't know eight-year-old Will had listened to their final fight from the other side of their bedroom door. "You're giving her what she needs, right?"

"I mean, yeah, I'm doing my best."

"Now I'm talking about *everything*, Willie Will. Just because a woman is pregnant doesn't mean she doesn't still have certain *needs* that have to be met. Do you understand?"

"Uh-huh."

"In fact, she may need to feel desirable in that way now more than ever."

She was really doing this, wasn't she? *"Mom."*

"I'm talking about sex, dear."

"Yeah, I got it. And I don't think you're allowed to call me Willie Will while giving me sex advice."

"Oh, it's fine," she said, laughing. "It's just a part of life—a beautiful, wonderful part."

It was hard to pinpoint precisely when it had started, but sometime after Will had graduated from high school, his mom had undergone what you might call a sexual awakening and truly embraced her single life. She had gotten married young and hadn't really dated at all while Will was growing up, so he was happy to see her so happy. The first time she'd mentioned having sex on a blanket at a Billy Joel concert, though, he'd had to instill some conversational guardrails.

"Was there a particular reason you called, Mom? I mean other than to discuss my sex life?"

"Ah yes. I got the new iPad, but now I can't set it up because I don't know my Wi-Fi password. Because *someone* made me change it from something that was easy to remember the last time he was here."

"Yes, I did. Because *internet* was not a good password. I'll text it to you."

"Not while you're driving."

"No, when I park."

"Good. Thank you. All right, I've gotta go. I've got a date."

"Make good choices, Mom."

She laughed again. "No promises. I love you, Willie Will."

"Love you too."

They hung up. Conversations with his mom were often an adventure, but he'd be the first to tell you she knew what she was talking about. And she was right: he wanted Rachel not just to know but to really feel that whatever he could do to be there for her, he would. That meant showing her that she had every right to be bold and that whatever hesitations she might have could be overcome by radical faith in one another.

It also meant downplaying his own fears about parenthood to make sure they didn't complicate things even further.

And in a weird way, *Date Me Now!* had given him the road map to do all that.

The show had long been Rachel's reality TV comfort food, and he'd been watching with her for as long as they'd lived together. It could be skeezy, as is to be expected when you're working from the premise that a couple of dozen people will aggressively vie for each other's affections five minutes after meeting. And the exclamation point in the title was simultaneously confrontational and desperate.

But, man, could they put together some dates.

And now that Will and Rachel had a week off from work, what was to stop him from reminding her how incredible and how adventurous she was by doing the same?

Taking her on the epitome of a *Date Me Now!* date wasn't feasible. He couldn't, say, whisk her off to a glacier for lunch and then have them grab a hot-air balloon to the Icelandic Opera in Reykjavík, sipping 50-year-old port as they soared through the indigo sky, recounting the *noble purpose* (a past contestant's now-iconic explanation for his motivations) that had brought them there.

For one, they didn't live near any glaciers—although there had been a ski hill in college, rumored to be a former landfill, which was only a five-hour car ride away—and they certainly didn't have the budget to fly to any (not if they hoped to send this kid to college, anyway). Also a hot-air balloon ride would run counter to their well-established heights embargo, put in place after Will hyperventilated while looking down in the glass balcony at the Sears Tower Skydeck. And as much as Rachel enjoyed the show, *Noble Purpose* was the name of the fictitious yacht she liked to say offered nonstop service to Doomed Pickup Line Island.

But still. He had a week. He had a car. He had never shied away from showing Rachel he loved her in . . . nonsubtle ways.

It was too perfect. Five dates. Five cities. He could do this. He could make her remember they weren't boring.

When Will got excited about something, he fell hard for the idea, and he was already so caught up in what this might look like that when the light he was stopped at turned green, he didn't notice until the guy behind him honked. He waved his apology into the rearview mirror and accelerated, reviewing the parameters he would have to meet to make it all work.

That they would drive was a given, mainly because of the cost but also because flying would just complicate everything. He didn't want to spend half their time in airports or trying to get to and from them. Plus they'd always been good road trip partners, even more so once he'd admitted he was never going to beat her at the alphabet game. (The letter *j* is an endangered species on American highways, and Rachel had an uncanny ability to spot them first.)

"So it has to be the Midwest," he said to himself, turning off the podcast that had started playing after he'd talked to his mom and that he hadn't heard a word of. "Or Midwest adjacent. And the dates have to mean something to her. They need to be special."

A native Ohioan, Will knew the words *Midwest* and *exotic date locale* weren't necessarily natural companions. Right on cue, he saw a billboard on the left side of the road advertising a restaurant in the Wisconsin Dells called I Plead the Fish, featuring its "World-Famous Flamethrowin' French Fried Flounder!"

"I know you're bummed about this whole job thing, Rachel," he joked to the empty car, "but it's nothing some fish puns and deep-fried alliteration can't fix!"

Wisconsin did have Milwaukee, though—and that might be something. It wasn't even an hour and a half away. And Will was pretty sure there was a T. M. Clemens house there. Clemens was the architect Rachel had written her thesis on at Michigan, and she'd taken Will on the guided bike tour of several of Clemens's buildings in Chicago like a week after they'd moved in together, when she'd been going through a brief I'm-going-to-start-my-own-firm phase. (That had ended when she'd accepted a promotion at work that she didn't really want but deemed the mature thing to do.) He could swear Rachel had mentioned something about Clemens in Milwaukee too. There was also Summerfest, this huge outdoor concert series they had talked about going to for a few years but had never actually gone to.

As he flicked on his signal to turn into the Lowe's lot, his pulse quickened with the possibilities. He parked and, after texting the Wi-Fi password to his mom, immediately began googling. Yes! There was a Clemens house in Milwaukee! And it was open for tours . . . on Saturdays.

Here was the first glitch.

It was Friday. The last tour time was 2:00 p.m., in just over 20 hours. Rachel was currently in the bathtub in their apartment, and he was sitting in his RAV4 at a Lowe's, in flip-flops and a paint-splattered Nirvana T-shirt.

Not exactly road ready.

The early evening was still hot, so he turned his car back on momentarily to put the windows down. When he got in modes like this, the prospect of something exciting starting to take shape just beyond his grasp, obstacles didn't make him panic. It was the opposite: they made him work that much harder to find an answer. He almost enjoyed it. Rachel was the artist; his creativity came out in the way that he believed if he just thought about something hard enough, he could figure it out.

It made his inability to picture himself as a successful father all the more unsettling. The man who should've been his role model in that regard—his dad—told his mom on the way out that maybe things would've been different if they hadn't had a kid. Years later, Will would come to question whether he'd actually heard that at their bedroom door or he'd just convinced himself he had. By then, it almost didn't matter. And either way, he'd be flying blind on how to be a dad.

But he could figure out Milwaukee.

He was also having this dawning recognition of Nashville as their final stop. Growing up, Rachel had ridden horses and listened to Dolly Parton and other women country artists while around the barn, and she loved them for their tenacity in the face of rampant sexism. There was something about musicians following their hearts to that city that he thought would get her thinking big again.

Maybe even thinking about Creative Vices again.

Things like a cross-country move or the distance from family, while intimidating, didn't have to be deal-breakers. Sometimes they were just the tax you paid in order to have dreams. And Will and Rachel were going to still need two incomes after the baby came, so what was the difference between day care in Chicago and day care in LA? Better weather?

It was an interesting thought. So was the idea that there might still be time to get Rachel there for an interview.

Will caught himself.

"No," he said, putting the windows back up. Not trusting where his train of thought was headed, he forced himself to stuff the phone back in his pocket, get out of the car, and begin walking into the store. She'd told him to let it go, and he would. He had to. It was her career, not his. Supporting her didn't mean he got to tell her what to do. He believed that with every fiber of his being. This week would just be about the two of them and showing her that while they were about to be somebody's parents, they would always be so much more than that. More fun than that. The trip couldn't be about anything else. Will knew that.

He just wished she hadn't ruled out the interview so quickly.

Because she did this sometimes, hunting for reasons why the thing she wanted wouldn't work because going after it might initially be uncomfortable. It wasn't just in her career. Take the tattoo, for example. Once they'd moved in together, it had taken him over a year to convince her that her parents would eventually get over it—and more importantly, who cared if they didn't—before she finally made the appointment and went. And despite that night when she'd cried in his arms in bed, she had never once expressed regret over that decision, unlike with New York and the art gallery.

Too bad Rochelle hadn't given them more time.

The automatic doors slid open, and his mind went back to Milwaukee. The tight timeline notwithstanding, it made sense to start there. If he had any hope of getting Rachel excited enough about this trip to abandon the Week-of-Nothing tradition and leave on practically zero notice, he needed that first stop, the one that would get them moving, to intrigue her while still being manageable. The Clemens house and Summerfest would accomplish that, and a total of an hour and 20 minutes on the road was all it would take to get them there. He would pitch the week itself as "Why sit around and watch *Date Me Now!* when we can do a budget-conscious kinda sorta imitation of it?"

Okay, so he could work on the pitch. It also wouldn't hurt that the alternative would be a staycation filled with Target runs and asking each other "Does this still smell good to you?" when pulling containers out of the fridge.

Provided she said yes to going, that left only one problem: a little detail known as Lake Michigan. After getting distracted by the ceiling fans—they needed one in the baby's room, along with an electrician to install it, and an entire squadron of them were hovering over him like white, wood, and brushed-nickel helicopters—Will considered the geography.

Lake Michigan was one of the largest lakes in the world, with Milwaukee on the western shore of it. But where did you go after that? Every other place he was thinking of (Ann Arbor to revisit their college campus?) was well beyond the lake's east side. Maybe there was a ferry they could take across to Michigan, and maybe that ferry would let them take their car. But that was all moot because while Will did not do well with heights, Rachel didn't do well with boats. She had gone on a cruise with her family when she was 10 and had sworn she would never willingly sail so far from land ever again, proclaiming to anyone onboard who would listen, "Everyone said the *Titanic* was safe too."

Will was puzzling through this when something on the shelf caught his eye. It was a box containing the same model of ceiling fan as one of the ones whirring overhead. He'd noticed it because of the 25-percent-off sign in front of it. Then he noticed the words on the side: "The Evening Breeze. Part of the Mackinac Island Collection."

Mackinac Island. He'd heard of that. It was a resort area. And it was right by the Mackinac Bridge, right? The thing that connected Michigan's Upper and Lower Peninsulas?

Will got his phone back out, brought up his map app, and punched in Milwaukee as his start point, Mackinac as the end. There it was, a route right up the west side of Lake Michigan and through the UP. Six hours, give or take.

He put his thumb and index finger on the screen and spread them apart to zoom in on Mackinac. Okay. There didn't seem to be any bridge to the island, which meant they were probably dealing with another ferry situation. Not to worry. It wasn't a cruise. It had to be 15, 20 minutes tops. Rachel would be fine with it. Probably.

"Yeah, I'm gonna need to find a sweet hotel," he said, closing his screen and heading for the paint section.

Nevertheless, he was feeling good. Chicago to Milwaukee. Milwaukee to Mackinac Island. Mackinac Island down the Lower Peninsula to Ann Arbor. Ann Arbor to . . . somewhere. And somewhere to Nashville. He'd come up with all that in under an hour, and he was confident he could flesh out the rest if she said she was in.

No. *When* she said it. She needed a chance to focus on something other than the baby, something other than all the unknowns that came with pregnancy and impending parenthood. He had a hard time admitting it, but he needed that, too, and he couldn't help but feel a certain urgency to make this trip work because he didn't know the next time they'd get to have an adventure like this, just the two of them. If he could seize this moment, make the week into something unforgettable at the drop of a hat—what Aunt Katie would've called "taking the bull by the balls"—it would signal to Rachel that they were the authors of their story. Not her parents. Not his dad. Not some mommy blog or a stable but stale career.

Them.

He found the roller covers after only two wrong turns—two fewer than two days before—and paid before shifting his attention to what he was going to get himself for dinner. By the time he was unlocking his car, he'd decided on Chipotle and was about to open the app to place his order, but there was a little light continuing to blink in the back of his brain that was proving impossible to ignore.

So rather than opening the app, he pulled up his text thread with Ali, his best friend since Michigan and the one who had made him realize you don't take someone you like to Buffalo Wild Wings on a first date. Their texts were an ongoing dialogue, rivaled only by Will's thread with Rachel.

Scenario: Your wife turns down an interview for a job she clearly wants after the company's founder personally recruited her for it.

Ali's text-response times were the stuff of legend. Once, when Will was living in Philadelphia for the internship, he had written Ali from his desk at 8:15 a.m. to ask him which Muppet their freshman-year history professor had called "a mouthpiece for the establishment." As soon as he did, he'd remembered Ali was in California on vacation and three hours behind him. That was when the answer had come through.

Sam the Eagle. He wasn't wrong.

Sure enough, before Will got his key into the ignition, Ali had responded.

Okay . . .

Would it be acceptable, Will pecked out, under any circumstances, for you to intervene under false pretenses without telling her?

No.

Will tried again. What if it wasn't just a job she wanted but her literal DREAM job?

No.

What if you were afraid she was going to regret it forever but the window was going to close before she realizes it?

No, Ali typed back for the third time.

What if . . .

Will sent that last *what if* on its own to buy himself a few extra seconds to come up with such a compelling argument that it would convince his friend to give him the green light.

No, Ali wrote.

You didn't even let me finish that one, Will replied.

The answer is always no.

Are you sure?

Yes.

Will sighed to the interior of his car. Yeah, you're right.

You're going to do it anyway, aren't you?

Will immediately typed No of course not. He had known the answer before he'd texted Ali. Part of him had been hoping his friend knew of a moral loophole that would allow him to do it without simultaneously being the embodiment of some sort of strange the-man-knows-best antifeminism. But he knew such a loophole didn't exist. The whole thing was a terrible idea.

And yet 30 seconds later, No of course not was still staring back at him, unsent.

SIX DAYS AGO

Chapter 4

Will glanced down from their bedroom window to the street in front of their building and then walked out into the hallway.

"If you had any lingering doubts about this trip," he said to Rachel, who was in the bathroom blow-drying her hair, "you can put those to rest."

"What?" she asked, switching it off.

"I said if you were still unsure about doing this, the universe has given us a sign."

"Really? I didn't hear you say the word *universe*."

"I thought you didn't hear me say anything."

"I would've heard something as cheesy as that," she said with a smirk.

"Ha ha ha. Well, I guess you *don't* want to know, then, that the spot right outside the front door is open." They both parked in a lot behind the building, the limited street parking eluding them like sobriety at Mardi Gras. The space in question belonged to a 75-year-old man who never left his apartment and never moved his 1991 Mazda Miata.

"Wait—Filbert's spot?"

"Uh-huh. Which means packing the car just got way easier. I know it's only, like, three bags, but you gotta admit—"

"Will."

"Yeah?"

"Filbert's spot is open. Why the hell are you still here talking to me? Go!"

"Good point," he said, turning and jogging toward the kitchen to grab his keys as the white noise of the hair dryer started up again. It was 9:30 a.m. on Saturday, and Filbert had probably run out for breakfast or coffee or maybe some Turtle Wax. The man's car was parked outside 12 months a year and had lived through more than 30 Chicago winters, and yet it continued to sparkle like the middle-aged impulse purchase it surely once was.

Will descended the stairs and emerged from the building's entryway, happy to confirm that Filbert had yet to return and no one else had grabbed the spot. They wouldn't be using it for more than a few minutes, but he felt like he'd almost willed it into existence, not unlike the trip itself. When he'd gotten home the night before and launched into his pitch, even before removing the foil cover from his burrito bowl, Rachel had been skeptical. She'd been on the couch, already in her pajamas, wondering aloud whether she could rewatch all six seasons of *Schitt's Creek* over the course of the coming week once they were caught up on *Date Me Now!*

"Not that I don't think that would be an admirable pursuit," Will had said, a nod to the fact that approximately 50 percent of their text exchanges involved at least one GIF from the show, "but when's the next time we'll have a chance to do something like this?"

He'd realized he'd come in too hot and hoped that if he could downshift into appearing playful, she wouldn't pick up on just how invested he already was in her saying yes.

"When's the next time we'll have a chance to do something like *this*?" Rachel had said, stabbing her chocolate chip cookie dough with an oversize spoon. "I hate to say it, but Week of Nothing's days are numbered with a baby. And it also feels a little too on the nose. Like we'd be *trying* to be spontaneous, you know?"

"Sometimes spontaneity needs a little bit of a nudge. Especially in the Midwest."

"Not to mention we're a little old for *Date Me Now!* cosplay. I like sleeping in our own bed. That memory foam has been the MVP of this pregnancy so far."

"C'mon, who *doesn't* want to walk around some fancy old house designed by an architect whose genius was an existential threat to the fragile male ego?"

At that, she'd laughed. And he'd known he had her.

"Let's do something better than general admission for Summerfest," she'd said after officially agreeing. "Just because it's outdoors doesn't mean I want to sit on a lawn chair the whole night."

"I thought you and I could just channel my mom at Billy Joel," he'd said with a wink, plopping down next to her on the couch.

"One, gross. Two, I did that once in college. It's overrated."

"What? Sex at a concert?"

"Yeah."

"With who?"

"It was before I met you."

"Who was it?"

"I don't see how that's relevant," she'd teased. He'd gone quiet for a second, so she hit play on the remote.

"No way," Will had finally said. "You're messing with me."

"Sure, I am, sweetie," she'd said and patted him on his knee. "Sure, I am." He'd stared at her, and she'd just arched her eyebrows.

"I'm both incredibly attracted to you and wildly insecure at the moment."

She'd laughed over *Date Me Now!* "Perfect—just like the guys on the show. Now shh—this improv date has dumpster fire written all over it."

After he'd finished eating his dinner and bearing witness to said dumpster fire—a joke that insinuates if you strike out with your date, then you'd like to sleep with her mom is never going to break in your favor—Will had opened up his laptop and begun researching and making some purchases. The week having been his idea, Rachel had been content to let him handle the planning, save for her thoughts on the concert tickets and a request regarding the *somewhere* stop between Ann Arbor and Nashville, which had become Lexington, Kentucky. Will had suggested it because of her history with horses—she'd always talked about how free she'd felt when riding—and she'd reminded him that while she did indeed love them, she didn't necessarily have a high opinion of horse *racing*, so he should pick what they'd do there accordingly.

Thanks to the resale market, the concert piece had been easy enough to handle. At that time the next night, they would be seated in the pavilion venue, row *X*, seats one and two—which hadn't sounded great at first but were surprisingly close to the stage—in real seats, under a roof, and right on the aisle. It wasn't the festival's main stage, and Will didn't know Gretchen Grayson, the evening's headliner, but Rachel did and liked her, informing him that Grayson had left her first label because she'd had limited creative freedom there.

"Not that I can relate or anything," she'd added, only reconfirming how stifled she was feeling at work.

They'd gotten that show plus the ability to check out most of the other stages, all for only about 20 dollars over face. Lexington had taken a little more work, but with some searching, he'd found a farm that was part of a racehorse-adoption program and that was hosting a charity horse show the following week.

"That actually sounds awesome," Rachel had said when he showed her the website.

He'd clicked and bought those tickets, checking them off his list along with the Milwaukee to-dos, which also included the reservations for a Clemens house tour and a Milwaukee hotel within walking distance of the Summerfest grounds. He'd then turned his attention to the hotel for Mackinac Island, stop number two, and had let out an audible "Nooo" upon seeing the prices for the Grand Hotel, which was apparently the island's flagship resort.

"What?" Rachel had asked.

"Huh? Oh. I . . . uh . . . I just can't believe Brandt brought up his ex this soon. Episode two? C'mon, dude."

"Um, it's because he's totally there for a *noble purpose*, Will." They'd both laughed, and he'd gone back to his computer, more vigilant about working in silence. And despite the Mackinac complication, by the time he'd crawled into bed next to Rachel around midnight, he'd had their full itinerary more or less booked and locked into place. When they'd woken up Saturday morning, Rachel hadn't shown any hints that she was just humoring him and had seemed legitimately excited about the week ahead—so much so that she was waiting for him on the sidewalk, a large smile across her face, when he pulled up to the front of the building and parked in Filbert's spot. She looked like someone fully ready to embark on a road trip, except her hair was still damp, and only one of her two bags was over her shoulder.

"I have to go back up," she clarified when she saw the confusion on his face as she opened the passenger door and tossed the bag into the back. "I just wasn't about to lose this spot."

"What were you going to do if he came back, arm wrestle for it?"

"No, I was going to tell him you were moving the car here so your pregnant wife wouldn't have to walk so far."

"You don't think carrying your own bag down three flights of stairs undercuts that argument?"

"Doesn't matter. Arguing with a pregnant woman isn't allowed in this country. It's a real plot twist from the rest of our lives."

She winked at him, and a spark passed through Will's body. This was not the Rachel who'd come home from work crying the night before. This was his wife, the woman who had gone straight up to Rochelle Simmons after that lecture and made such a strong impression in their 20 minutes together that Rochelle was now recruiting her from the other side of the country. This Rachel, she was optimistic. Unflappable. A powerhouse.

And they hadn't even gotten on the road yet.

They walked back up the front sidewalk, hands linked loosely together.

"You know," she said, letting go and moving ahead of him at the base of the stairs, "it occurs to me that we're doing pretty good on time this morning, and that maybe we have *time* to do something *else* before we leave. We are on vacay, after all."

Will stared at her from behind, five feet of curves in a dark-blue tank top and a pair of lightweight joggers with just a hint of cling to them, and he hoped she meant what he thought she did.

"You mean . . . ?" he asked.

"Yes. But before you get too excited"—she stopped on the landing and looked back at him—"I was kinda hoping this one could be about me." She ran her fingers through his hair and exaggeratedly pursed her lips, and his heart beat faster. "On account of me having such a rough day yesterday and everything. Is that okay?"

"Well, I don't want you to feel sad," he said, his voice barely escaping his throat. He was transfixed by the way she wanted him. In some ways, it was more of a turn-on than sex—which was why he was working so hard not to imagine his mom saying how proud she was of him.

Too late.

Fortunately, the way Rachel grabbed his hand again and led him the rest of the way up to their door and into the apartment made everything else obsolete. They never even made it into the bedroom.

When they were done, Will crawled back up and lay next to her while her breathing returned to normal.

"I'd say this trip is off to a promising start," he said.

"I'd say so. And please know that your generosity will not go unrewarded."

"Does that mean sex at the concert is back on the table?"

"Ha. No. But I haven't entirely ruled out the botanical gardens when we're in Ann Arbor." He'd made sure a return to the site of their memorable second date was on their list.

Will's whole body felt tingly. "I know you're joking, but I'm still not sure what I did to deserve you."

"Considering what you just did without expecting anything in return," she said, sitting on the area rug in front of the TV and retying the drawstring on her pants, "I think you may have that backwards."

Rachel's phone dinged from the kitchen table. She kissed him on the cheek and then got up to retrieve it. Will stood, too, ready to go grab her other bag and his own oversize duffel, but when he saw how intently she was reading her screen, he lingered by the couch.

"Something going on?" he asked after a few more seconds had passed.

"No. Just an email back from Rochelle."

"What did she say?"

"You know, 'Too bad, thanks for letting me know,' et cetera."

"That's it?"

"Here, you can read it if you want," she said, extending the phone toward him on her way back to the bathroom. "I'm gonna finish drying my hair."

Will started reading as she flipped the blow-dryer back on. She and Rochelle had gotten to know each other well enough that Rochelle didn't even bother with a salutation.

Damn. I understand. But I'm not going to pretend like I'm not disappointed. For what it's worth, I really do believe you're ready for a new challenge, even if it's not with us. They don't know what they have in you there.

Alright. I'm headed offline for a week. We'll see how long that lasts. —RS

He read it again. In his experience, a potential employer didn't talk like that to just anyone. Or to anyone, period.

When she'd handed him the phone, Rachel hadn't said anything about Will also reading *her* email declining the interview, but she hadn't said anything about him *not* doing it, either. Now the header line was staring him in the face. And with his curiosity too much to resist, the scales tipped in favor of him telling himself she wouldn't care. This required him to ignore that that opinion had at least a little to do with the continued noisy static from the hair dryer ensuring she wouldn't be appearing next to him unexpectedly.

Hey Rochelle—

First off: Wow. This sounds like an INCREDIBLE opportunity, and I'm so flattered that you thought of me for it. Your faith in my abilities, not to mention your continued mentorship, mean a lot.

Unfortunately—and reluctantly—I'm going to have to pass on the interview. This isn't the kind of thing we as women are supposed to admit, but here goes the brutal honesty: I'm just having a hard time wrapping my mind around making such a huge change while also being pregnant.

I know you haven't actually offered me the job at this point, but I don't want to waste your and your team's time interviewing me, etc., if I feel like I wouldn't take it even if you did.

Thank you again, and best of luck with the search. Anyone would be lucky to work with you.

—Rachel

Now Will's eyes scanned back over his wife's words, several of which popped out like neon signs. Unfortunately. Reluctantly. Incredible (in all caps).

Coming from somebody else, this email would be exactly what Rachel had said it was: an artful way of saying no to someone you respect. But he knew Rachel. She was not an all-caps typer, and a phrase like "Anyone would be lucky to work with you" was not one she'd throw out just to be polite. Although she'd cried telling him about it, it was possible she wanted this job even *more* than she was letting on but was too nervous to put herself out there.

He felt like he'd seen this movie before. The procrastination on the tattoo. The fleeting image of her own business. The art gallery, which had been coloring her perception of her job for over a decade.

Will pictured a couple of years in the future, Rachel trudging off to campus in a foot of snow to go to a job she'd long since outgrown, her creative ambitions limited to admiring the scribblings of their two-year-old.

He had no doubt that she would love that baby madly and be an amazing mom. He was positive she would never blame him for her career not taking shape how she'd envisioned. They'd settled near her family, not his, and he'd tried in the very limited amount of time before she'd had to reply to Rochelle to convince her to take the Creative Vices interview. But Rachel had been adamant, and there was only so much you could do in one conversation.

Even so, standing there in their little two-bedroom apartment, on a sleepy side street thousands of miles away from the Southern California sun and the type of job she'd dreamed of, he couldn't help but worry that a life with him would start to feel small to her. Not that she would ever say that or maybe even consciously think it. Rachel's commitment to him was the tightest bond he'd ever known.

He just never wanted it to start to feel like an obligation.

But you feel what you feel. And Will was unsure whether a future in the Chicago suburbs would feel like enough for her.

Whether he would feel like enough for her.

The hair dryer stopped, and he instinctively turned the phone screen off and walked it back to her in the bathroom, setting it on the counter next to the dish where she kept her rings.

"It's a nice note," he said.

"Yup," she said, putting her toothbrush in her toiletry bag.

"But it still doesn't change anything for you?"

45

"Nope." She picked the phone up. "People say all kinds of stuff at the interview stage. It doesn't mean anything."

"I don't know. Last night at least, it sounded like you felt like she'd done everything but officially offer it to you."

"I was upset, so it's *possible* I was exaggerating a bit for dramatic effect."

Will didn't entirely buy that answer. "I think you may be exaggerating *now*. Like, in downplaying how interested she is in you."

Rachel looked like she was about to say one thing but then pivoted to another.

"What does it matter? Even if I had changed my mind—which I haven't—I already turned it down. Rochelle's on vacation. I'm on vacation. It's a done deal."

"I'm sure it's not *done*, done."

"Yes, it is," she said, an edge entering her voice before her face softened again. "And that's already more work talk than I wanted this week. In fact, I'm taking my mail app off my phone entirely for the next seven days. I'm all yours, baby."

She smiled at him, and he thought for approximately the millionth time in his life that there wasn't anything he wouldn't do for her.

"Okay," he said, dropping it. "I'm going to get the rest of our stuff. Meet me down at the car?"

"Be there in five."

Will went to their bedroom, grabbed the bags off their bed, and headed to their front door, something from Rochelle's email back to Rachel now stuck in his mind.

There was someone else cc'd on it.

He didn't know who bleon@creativevices.com was. But five minutes felt like enough time to figure it out.

Chapter 5

If Rachel hadn't been pregnant, it would have been overwhelmingly likely that Will would've found a way to wind their route through Sandusky, Ohio, so they could go to Cedar Point. Pretty ambivalent toward his home state as a whole, he would go to odd lengths to defend the greatness of the amusement park known as "the roller coaster capital of the world." Trips to Cedar Point weren't just a staple of his growing up, a long weekend on Lake Erie being far more affordable for his single mom than a Disney vacation, but he'd also spent the summer between his freshman and sophomore years at Michigan as an operator on the Gemini, a two-track wooden coaster dating from the late 1970s. A not insignificant part of that job involved telling riders to enjoy the rest of their day at "America's Roller Coast" approximately 20 times an hour.

"I thought you said it was 'the roller coaster capital of the world,'" Ali had said when they were back on campus recounting what they'd been doing over the previous three months.

"It is," Will had replied with an unmistakable trace of reverence in his voice. "It's both. It has *two* nicknames. Crazy, right? That's how sick the coasters are."

"*Sick* coasters?"

"Totally."

"Maybe keep that to yourself when we try to talk to girls."

Will's love of aggressive thrill rides may have been a conversational liability when speaking to a fledgling romantic interest, but it was downright useless once that person had married you and you were trying to plan things for her to do that wouldn't violate the restrictions imposed by pregnancy. That meant the closest Will and Rachel would get to an amusement park on this trip was driving by Six Flags Great America before they'd even crossed the Illinois-Wisconsin border. It was impossible to miss, right there off I-94, and seeing it prompted Rachel to tell a story about her and her friends going there the day after prom.

"Seth rode the Superman roller coaster like five times," she said while opening a box of Dots, inexplicably her road trip candy of choice. "After the last one, I literally had to help him walk to a bench."

The mystery man Rachel may (or may not) have had sex with at a concert in college was one thing. He existed almost entirely without context, which made him hard to picture and therefore easier to forget. But Seth? Will had heard a lot about Rachel's high school boyfriend over the years, such that Seth, or the idea of him, had taken up permanent residence in Will's mind as Rachel's first true love and some sort of standard he'd forever be competing against.

It also didn't help that they had run into Seth at a Cubs game a couple of years earlier, and he'd been reminded that Seth was basically a slightly older, more believable Timothée Chalamet.

"Superman," Will said with a mirthless laugh as he changed lanes to pass a semi. "Please. I once rode the Mantis *nine* times in three hours. That was a *standing* roller coaster."

"So you've told me. On multiple occasions. What was that place called again? Cedar Grove?"

"Cedar *Point*. Cedar Grove sounds like a cemetery."

"Seems fitting. Given how harrowing your experience there was, I think we should be thankful you made it out alive."

"Well, that was the day I learned to never underestimate a crotch harness. I'm actually surprised I was able to get you pregnant."

Rachel kicked off her sandals and put her feet up on the dash, her toenails freshly painted in a purple that matched her highlight. "This baby really is lucky to have us. You're not getting these kinds of life lessons in school."

In reality, Will thought about that a lot—not the crotch-harness thing, because that would be strange, but generally, what kinds of lessons he, as a dad, would be entrusted with imparting. It's not like anyone could really tell you. Take God, for instance. Will knew he wasn't an atheist, but he also knew he and Rachel weren't religious. So what was the right thing to teach someone else? Did you just act like you believed all the stuff that you didn't until your kid was old enough to hear you admit you'd just been going through the motions? That didn't seem right. But neither did offering nothing on the subject.

His excitement about becoming a dad had been tempered by questions like these ever since they'd begun talking about the potential of having children, long before Rachel had gotten pregnant. There was a part of him that knew two things could be true, that you could feel both anticipation and fear. It wasn't unlike how he both wanted Rachel to be able to read his mind about his anxieties and was also grateful she couldn't, because he didn't want to burden her with them. Because he was embarrassed, maybe even ashamed by them, sometimes worrying that not knowing what to do meant he'd be no better at all this than his dad had been.

But she was doing all the work carrying that baby, not him. His job was to support her in that and wrestle with his demons on his own time. Which meant that anytime Rachel started to steer the conversation toward this or that insecurity about the day-to-day, practical realities of becoming a parent, Will pushed down his desire to voice his own worries and shifted into cheerleader mode. Wanting her to focus on the fun they were going to have on this trip only exacerbated that.

"On the subject of school," she said once they'd crossed into Wisconsin, "have you thought about that at all?"

"You mean for our child who will think twice before ever buckling her- or himself into a nonstandard roller coaster car?"

"That's the one."

"Don't we have some time?"

"Fair point." She was quiet for a few seconds. "What about day care then? What do we even look for? Should we be looking now, or do we wait until the baby is born?"

Will had no idea and wanted to say that maybe they could ask their pediatrician. But they didn't have one of those yet either. And there were no answers to be found out there on the open road, where it was just them and, off to their left, the Mars Cheese Castle, another I-94 landmark that looked exactly like it sounded.

"I mean, I guess it wouldn't hurt to get started," he said.

"Yeah. Maybe I could ask Alicia. Her boys are eight and six, but at least she did all this somewhat recently."

Alicia was one of the writers in Rachel's office. Rachel routinely found her exasperating—you did not want to get this woman started on the Oxford comma or her passion for her Peloton—but she did have a combined 14 more years' experience raising kids than they did. Will was grateful to Alicia in that moment for allowing him to not have to dig too deeply into his lack of knowledge on the subject of day care—one his dad would've been similarly worthless on—and make it easy to feign confidence.

"See?" Will said. "We got this."

"I don't know if picking the brain of my so-called gluten-free coworker who was definitely eating a Panera bread bowl Thursday qualifies as us *having it*, but I appreciate the sentiment." Rachel got a thoughtful look on her face. "Ooh, Panera. That sounds good. What time is our tour again?"

"One," he said, looking down at the clock. (There hadn't been any spots left on the two o'clock tour.) It was a few minutes before 11:00 a.m., and they were a little over half an hour away. "So we can definitely eat first."

"Awesome. I heard they have a grilled mac and cheese sandwich now, which sounds both ridiculous and like it's about to be the best meal of my life." She pulled her feet back down and readjusted in her seat. "Oh—I know what I forgot to tell you. So, this Clemens house?"

"Yeah?"

"She considered it her least successful design."

"What do you mean?"

"I sort of remembered reading about Milwaukee when I was doing my thesis research, so I looked it up last night after I got in bed. She called it the Milwaukee Mistake. Never even finished the interior. She sold it to this family who ran a funeral home there for like fifty years."

"A funeral home?" Will asked. Erstwhile mortuary didn't scream *fun road trip*. "Not quite what I was picturing when I suggested it."

"I know, but these volunteers are working on restoring it to look like other things she was designing at the same time. I think it's actually kind of inspiring."

"Oh, yeah, well, that's what I was going for."

Rachel laughed. "Where are we staying?"

Provided they weren't at sea, Rachel was not at all picky about accommodations. When everyone else, including Will and Ali, had been headed to beaches for spring break, she and her roommate spent a week hiking and sleeping in a tent in the Appalachian Mountains. The only reason he'd been looking at the Grand Hotel in Mackinac was because he wanted their stop there to be memorable, not because Rachel had a real thing for concierge service. But on the heels of the least-successful-design conversation, it would've been nice if the hotel didn't have a number in its name.

"Uh, it's called 3W Suites," he said, grateful that it at least wasn't a chain. "It's in this neighborhood called the Third Ward, and there's supposed to be all these awesome restaurants."

"Sounds great."

"Plus it's walking distance to Summerfest."

"Babe, you don't have to keep selling me. I'm showered, I'm not in pajamas, and I'm not ordering something on DoorDash. With all due respect to the Week of Nothing, this has already wildly exceeded my expectations for today."

She smiled at him, and he was about to ask her what she thought she might be in the mood for at dinner—there was an Italian place that had caught his eye, but he didn't know if pasta was the right energy before a concert—when her phone dinged with a text from her sister. Rachel had texted Isabel and their parents that morning to tell them that she and Will were hitting the road for a week. Rachel and her mom had been planning to go shopping for baby clothes at Old Orchard on Tuesday or Wednesday, and her mom had been thrown off by the idea of this last-minute trip getting in the way of that. No fewer than three times, she'd reminded Rachel to pack her prenatal vitamins, while cautioning her not to stay out "until all hours," a turn of phrase that prompted Rachel to mutter that she sounded like a grandma already.

Isa, as Rachel (but not their parents) called her, was just responding to that first text saying they were going on the trip.

"My sister says she's jealous and that the last thoughtful thing Owen did for her was buy them a couples' package for one of those sensory-deprivation tanks for Valentine's Day."

Will's face wrinkled. "Odd choice. For several reasons. Including her claustrophobia."

"Yes, it was. And you know that, but somehow her own husband doesn't."

"Well, comparing Owen to me really isn't fair. It's like saying Nicholas Sparks is no Jane Austen."

"You're Jane Austen here?"

"I think that's pretty obvious."

"Because I have to say, spur-of-the-moment"—Rachel gestured out the window just as they happened to be passing a large, indeterminate piece of roadkill next to an orange construction barrel—"maybe-not-romantic-right-this-second-but-in-general-fanciful type of getaway? It's a little *Notebook*-ish."

"How is this in any way like *The Notebook*?"

"It's not. But it's the only one I've seen."

"Uh, false. You *sobbed* at that one with Miley Cyrus too."

"Oh, right," she said, looking wistful. "*The Last Song*. And so did you, by the way, Mr. Tough Guy."

"Yeah, but I get emotional over everything, so it's less embarrassing."

"Mmm, is it?"

"Yes, it—crap."

"What?"

"My phone," he said. "I think it just slipped out of my pocket and fell between the console and my seat."

"On it," she said, reaching over and starting to fish around with her hand. He didn't think much of it until she pulled the phone out a few seconds later and caught a glimpse of a text on the screen.

"Why is Ali asking if you came to your senses about the thing with my job?" Rachel said as she handed the phone back.

She was looking at Will with an expression that was somewhere between curious and suspicious, waiting for an explanation as to what exactly this text was referencing, and he was doing his best to keep the car out of the ditch that his brain had already metaphorically careened into.

"Oh, I . . . uh . . ." She'd called her job boring. Had he just been supposed to ignore that? What would she think in another year or two? "I told him about the Creative Vices thing, and how it was in LA, and that I didn't think moving would be that big a deal but you did. He told me to listen to you."

Will tried to assuage his guilt by telling himself it wasn't a total lie: Ali *had* told him to listen to her. Will just happened to be doubling down on that and purposefully misleading his wife about the true extent of his and Ali's conversation. And leaving out the part where he'd gone on the Creative Vices website earlier that morning and figured out bleon@creativevices.com was Rochelle's assistant, Beatriz, who was likely in charge of scheduling interviews.

His stomach churned against his will.

"This sounds a lot like work talk," she said.

"This was last night. It was before the work-talk embargo took effect."

"All right," she said, unable to completely hide her skepticism. "As long as you're not getting ideas. I still remember the look on my parents' faces when they forced me to apply to the University of Chicago, and then I didn't get in. I think that was their first inkling I wasn't going to be a lawyer. Unmet expectation is that much worse when it's thrust upon you."

"What's that from, the Declaration of Independence?"

Rachel laughed, but it felt ill-gotten to him since the joke was aiding in covering his tracks. He was like a magician who'd traded sleight of hand for being a shady spouse.

Still, it had worked. Because the next thing he knew, they could see the Milwaukee skyline. Soon thereafter, he was easing the car down the exit ramp into the city in pursuit of Panera and a macaroni and cheese sandwich. Rachel alternated between speculating how the sandwich would hold up when dipping it into the tomato soup she was also going to get and whether their baby would grow up to be an indie-pop fan after attending a concert in utero.

"I mean, it's possible, right?" she asked. "Or at least not impossible?"

"No, not impossible," Will said.

He was answering her question. And in doing so, he was also offering up a silent prayer for what the week ahead might accomplish.

See? he said telepathically to their future child. *Not an atheist.*

Chapter 6

Any doubts that had crept into Will's mind about the Milwaukee Mistake evaporated as soon as they walked into the house. And actually, it'd happened even a little bit before that while they were ascending the stairs of Clemens's trademark S-shaped front porch and Rachel reminded Will, a tinge of expectation in her voice, that the architect had referred to this space in her homes as "the river bend."

"You weren't supposed to carry the troubles of the world back across with you when you came home at night," she'd announced when they'd reached the top and were taking it in. Her delight at that, though, was quickly eclipsed by what she saw inside.

"Look at all that natural light," Rachel marveled in the direction of the bank of windows while stepping into the living room.

To Will's eyes, the space looked like a DIY project still in need of a lot of doing. The hardwood floors were scuffed and battered, the walls were white and largely bare, and he was pretty sure the windows that had captured Rachel's attention were still in need of framing. The only reason it was *pretty sure* and not *all-the-way sure* was because he was the type of person who got nervous painting a nursery and wasn't altogether confident he knew what a window frame was in the first place. Regardless, he knew they didn't look like they would at the end of the restoration, and that made Rachel's excitement over being there all the more endearing.

The only pieces of furniture in the living room were a dozen or so decidedly *not* period-specific chairs set up facing some framed Clemens archival prints on easels, the area in front of which the docent would presumably use to talk to them once the tour started. The night before, Will had paid the 15 dollars for their two tickets but thought he should see if they needed to check in somewhere. He was about to tell Rachel that was what he was doing when a motorcycle roared by on the street and momentarily drowned out all noise around them, so he left her to her examination of one of the prints and headed down the narrow hallway farther into the house. At the end of it, he could see an older woman with a small cashbox and a credit card reader sitting next to a table with a spread of brochures.

"Welcome to the T. M. Clemens Milwaukee historical site," she said cheerily when he reached the back room where she was set up. Now that he was in there, he saw a second woman seated at the other end of the table.

"Thanks," Will said to the woman who'd greeted him, while nodding a hello to the other. The latter was younger, and her hair and glasses made him think of Aunt Katie. God, he missed her. She used to take him to the movies every weekend from the time his dad left until he was 12 or 13. As he'd gotten older, he'd realized his aunt had done that as much for Will's mom as she had for him, just a way to give her sister some time to herself each week. To know that there were people who still loved the two of them that much—it didn't make up for what his dad had done, because nothing ever could, but it made Will even more grateful for his aunt and that time they'd had together. She'd never had kids of her own and yet had been such a natural with him that she easily could've passed as his mom. He wondered whether he'd have even half of those instincts when it came to his own daughter or son.

"Do you have a reservation?" the first woman asked.

"Yes. It should be under Easterly? For two?"

"Easterly—yes, there you are. You're all set. Henny here will be leading your tour. She'll meet all of you in the front room in a few minutes."

Henny smiled at him, and the resemblance to his aunt grew even stronger.

"My wife was right," he said. "The amount of natural light in here is amazing."

"You bet," Henny said. "Clemens put windows all over the place. She called them 'our portal to understanding the world.'"

"She really liked a turn of phrase, didn't she?"

Henny chuckled. "Indeed, she did."

And then before Will knew why he was saying it: "You know, this is probably going to sound weird, but you really remind me of someone."

"I do?"

"Yeah. My aunt Katie."

"Well, I hope that's a good thing," she said, laughing again.

"Oh, absolutely. She was the best. And she actually volunteered at the historical society in our town. She would've loved this place." Henny picked up on his use of past-tense and conditional verbs, and he was suddenly stuck in that limbo of how much to share with a stranger about his aunt's death when the only reason for doing so was to add context to their small talk. Well, that, and he didn't want Henny to misread his comparison as some sort of comment on her age. His aunt had only been 61 when she died.

In the time he spent thinking through this, it hit him again how much he would've liked to talk to Katie about his fears around becoming a dad.

"She, uh, passed away a year ago," he added. "Kind of out of nowhere." He paused. Now it sounded like he was telling this poor person he'd met 30 seconds before that she could drop dead at any moment. "I mean, it was unexpected. Because she was still pretty young."

Will had no idea if he was making it better or worse. Fortunately, Henny just smiled an understanding smile at him.

"I'm sorry to hear that," she said. "She sounds like she was a great lady."

He smiled back, and relieved to have been let off the hook of his awkwardness, he gave a little half wave goodbye and headed to find Rachel. It didn't take long because he could hear her pretend laugh—the one where you oversell how funny you think something is because in reality you don't find it funny at all, but you can tell the other person is expecting some kind of reaction—from down the hall. When he reentered the front room, the laugh immediately made sense.

Rachel was sitting down now, right next to a couple attempting to manage a toddler and an infant. Whether she had ended up in this spot by choice or by chance, Will didn't know, but he was positive that she would've been banking on this couple being far too preoccupied with their kids to strike up a conversation with the partially purple-haired woman one seat over.

She had been wrong.

"This is Ronald and Gwen," Rachel said as Will took the seat on the other side of her. "They're from Bartlett, and these are their kids, Ronnie Jr. and Felicity. Gwen was kind enough to be giving me recommendations on nursing bras"—Rachel turned like she was getting something out of her purse so only Will could see her face, where dismay and/ or disbelief appeared to have enlarged her eyes to twice their normal circumference—"even though I told her it really wasn't necessary since we just met two minutes ago."

"Oh, I don't mind," Gwen said, shooting a look over Rachel's head straight to Will, a smile plastered across her face. "We mommies have to stick together!"

"And Gwen is an expert," her husband bragged. "I mean, breastfeeding two babies at once? I don't know how she did it!"

Will looked at Ronnie Jr., who was around three and currently attempting to scale a radiator, and Felicity, who wasn't doing much of anything. That made sense since she couldn't have been more than six months old. What didn't make sense was how their age gap translated to a period of time when they both would've been breastfeeding.

It seemed he was unsuccessful at hiding his confusion.

"Ronnie Jr. breastfed until he was two and a half," Ronald clarified. Like that was a thing you heard every day from a guy on a T. M. Clemens tour.

"Is that . . . typical?" Will asked, doing his best to suppress his mounting sense of horror.

"Not really," Gwen said. "We like to say he's a real boobs guy!"

"Did you hear that, Will?" Rachel said, still pretending to riffle through her purse. *"Ronnie Jr. is a real boobs guy!"*

Ronald and Gwen began to cackle, and it was now Will's turn to bust out his fake laugh.

"Sounds like we have a fun bunch today," tour guide Henny said, gliding into the room and causing everyone to quiet down.

"Oh, thank God," Will muttered under his breath as Rachel gratefully gave up the hunt for whatever she had never been looking for.

Henny started by asking where everyone was from. There were 11 adults plus the two kids, with Rachel and Will and the overly enthusiastic breastfeeding brigade all hailing from Illinois. And yet their tiny group still managed to represent not only three other states—an older couple from Michigan, a younger one from Iowa, and a middle-aged guy from right there in Milwaukee—but also another continent, the mother-son expat duo from São Paulo saying they'd worked a day trip to Milwaukee into their visit to Chicago. They were a family of architects, which made their traveling thousands of miles to end up on this 1:00 p.m. tour across the street from a vape shop feel a little less random.

While they were still doing introductions, the baby began crying, so Gwen quickly transitioned into feeding her—and under a cover-up, no less. Even after his conversation with Gwen and Ronald, Will was impressed by just how seamlessly she did this, simultaneously attaching a human being to her body, quieting said human down, and continuing to listen to Henny as she went around the room. It kind of made being a dad look like a cakewalk by comparison, although Ronald was getting red in the face from the exertion of trying to keep Ronnie Jr. from climbing out an open front window.

Will felt his phone buzz inside his pocket. He slid it out a couple of inches to read the text.

Frankly SHOCKED I can't see Gwen's bare breast right now, Rachel had typed from right next to him. He glanced at her, and her face was so unassuming, despite having sent that, that he had to play off a snort as a cough.

Impressed by Gwen or not, he sensed an opportunity to calm some of Rachel's doubts.

I think the last few minutes make a compelling case on behalf of NOT breastfeeding, he wrote back.

He saw Rachel peek at her screen and the corner of her mouth curl ever so slightly into a smile as she hearted his text.

Henny began her presentation, referencing both the framed prints behind her and a binder with photo sleeves that she'd carried in. Despite working in IT, Will had sort of a love-hate relationship with technology, and he found the analog nature of the experience kind of refreshing.

They learned that everybody who worked there was a volunteer and that they still needed to raise around a million dollars to finish the restorations. Henny explained that what they'd be seeing was the prototype for a much larger house Clemens had gone on to build for the governor of Michigan a few years later, one that had become synonymous with her design aesthetic.

"Now as you may know," Henny said over the noise of a diesel pickup idling outside, "Clemens didn't think much of the house we're standing in right now. What you may *not* know is that she did say if it weren't for the mistakes she made here, she never could've built the Michigan house. And as far as I'm concerned, this place is pretty special all on its own."

Rachel nodded along with everything Henny was saying, clearly enjoying herself. Will smiled.

It was at this point that it became a walking tour, and the group stood up to follow Henny to check out the kitchen. Everyone except Gwen, that is, who stayed behind in her seat to finish feeding Felicity. Rachel seemed eager to both put some distance between herself and the family and see the rest of the house, and Will had to hustle to keep up with her. He wondered as he did if she was thinking about how something as simple as listening to this talk got infinitely more complicated with small kids in tow. He was. And even noticing it kind of seemed like complaining. He felt guilty about that. Because complaining is what his dad would've done.

Will had a memory from when he was probably five or six of going out to dinner with his parents and them not being able to sit in the bar because of Will and having to wait like 45 minutes for a table as a result. His dad had carried on about it all the way through the meal.

"Why should we have to wait just because we've got a kid?" he'd said more than once. "It's not like I'm going to ask them to make him a cocktail."

His dad's anger had been mainly directed at the host and waitstaff, but it had made Will feel like he'd done something wrong just by being there. Could he be that unaware with his own kid? Would he make her or him feel the same way without even realizing it?

He tried to shake it out of his head and shift his attention back to the tour, but that proved easier said than done. As they were all crowding in to hear Henny point out some of the finer features of the small yet highly functional kitchen, Ronnie Jr. grabbed his Thomas the Tank Engine T-shirt and began shouting "Time for Ti-mis! Time for Ti-mis!" as loudly as he could.

Ronald, who was trying to hold his son's hand as he squirmed to get free, initially just tried to ignore it, a bold flex given that his child was literally harder to speak over than the motorcycle had been. When it was clear that wasn't working, he squatted down next to Ronnie Jr.

and attempted to reason with him through a strained smile. Will had no idea why Ronald didn't walk him out of the room. Henny had to stop her talk entirely, and no matter how much solidarity Will tried to muster for Ronald's plight, at some point, the adult subjecting his three-year-old to a tour of an old house where people are trading knowing glances about sconces ceases to be a sympathetic figure. It wasn't until Ronald offered to buy Ronnie Jr. a new train when they were done that the boy quieted down.

Their group moved into the room with the cashbox, which had been the dining room, and while in transit, Will decided to roll the dice and try on dad voice in an attempt to show himself—and by extension, Rachel—that he was not his dad and was ready to handle situations like this.

"You know, I used to watch *Thomas* when I was little," he said to Ronnie Jr. He had hardly any experience talking to kids and was going for approachable but confident. It came out like the Kool-Aid Man mixed with an electric toothbrush. Rachel gave him a strange look, and he shifted back to his normal delivery. "Uh, who's your favorite train?"

"Gordo," Ronnie Jr. replied without otherwise acknowledging him.

"That's what he calls Gordon," Ronald said.

"Oh, sure," Will said. "I remember Gordon."

More specifically, he remembered that Gordon was indisputably the biggest asshole on the island of Sodor, which kind of explained a lot about the preceding five minutes.

"Did you know George Carlin was the narrator on *Thomas* when we were growing up?" he tried with Ronald. "Crazy, right?"

Ronald had the same reaction to this that Rachel had had to Will's sounding like a deranged, talking pitcher of red drink. "Who's George Carlin?" he asked.

"You know, the comedian?"

Nothing.

That was enough chitchat with Ronald and Ronnie Jr.

"So, everyone talks about Clemens's front porches because of the river bend," Henny said. "But if you look out the windows here, you'll see a large back porch, too, that she envisioned as being able to sleep an entire family. And you might be wondering: Why? It's not like the Upper Midwest is ideally suited to indoor-outdoor living. Well, turns out fresh air *is* pretty desirable when there's tuberculosis everywhere like there was back then. And on a related note, you might want to hug a scientist and say thank you for vaccines."

Will thought of his aunt again. She'd been a high school chemistry teacher, and she'd made him swear up and down that if/when he and Rachel had kids, they would have them fully vaccinated. Once he'd assured her that they would, she'd shaken her head and said, "It's just those antivaxxers—they're like flat-earthers but without the whimsy." The memory made him happy and sad at the same time. It was one of the last conversations they'd ever had, just a few months before she'd died.

"All right," Henny said, "we're going to walk back through the house to the staircase so we can check out the second story. Mr. Fiesterly, lead the way."

Will liked Henny too much to care that she'd screwed up his name, so he started their retreat from the dining room. And as much as he wanted to believe that she'd chosen him due to some sort of unspoken cosmic connection via Aunt Katie, the truth was that after Ronald and Ronnie Jr., Will was closest to the door, and father was now busy arguing with son about whether he needed a diaper change. That porch may have been designed to combat tuberculosis, but it would've been no match for the fresh hell coming out of Ronnie Jr.'s pants, incriminating evidence that the three-year-old continued to deny at all costs.

The smell reached Rachel a second or two after Will, and she slid past Ronald and Ronnie Jr. to rejoin him and make their escape. True, they were fleeing a full diaper like it was one of the undead, but in their defense, zombies at least had the good sense not to be Gordon people.

There was no point in suffering for someone who was already a lost cause, especially when that someone shared zero of your DNA.

"They may need to go back to breastfeeding," she whispered to Will when they were several steps in front of everyone else. "Because whatever that kid is eating now does *not* agree with him."

"I think my eyes were about to tear up."

"Don't judge me," she continued, leaning in even closer and slipping her fingers through his as they approached Gwen burping Felicity. The two of them were at the spot where the hall emptied into the front room, the baby staring Will down over her mom's shoulder as he and Rachel approached. "But if our child ever smells like that, I don't know that I'll be able to love it anymore."

Rachel gave his hand a loving squeeze, and his lips parted for what was about to become a chuckle. Which was really too bad.

Not because her joke wasn't funny. It absolutely was, in that deadpan, slightly twisted style that was Rachel's specialty, and it eased some of the pressure he'd been feeling using Ronnie Jr. as a litmus test for his parenting instincts. It was just that little Felicity—perhaps in a show of solidarity with her brother, perhaps acting on behalf of every baby everywhere who had ever been insulted by a grown-up—took it upon herself at that precise moment to let loose a torrent of projectile vomit so vile it made Ronnie Jr. smell like a florist. Given the proximity of the baby and the narrowness of the hallway, Will never stood a chance.

And once someone's vomit has passed through your parted lips and into your open mouth, it really is impossible to never not taste it again.

Chapter 7

America's Roller Coast had had a water-flume ride. A big one. One that Will had never set foot on. Not because he was scared of it. But because he couldn't imagine anything more unappealing, more revolting, than getting drenched and then standing there soaked through your shirt, drip-drying in amusement park swamp water.

What a quaint notion that had been.

"The bedroom at the top of the stairs," came Henny's voice from somewhere behind him, "you'll see that it . . . oh. Oh my God. Mr. Fiesterly, are you . . . how . . . what happened?"

Will wiped some of the semidigested breast milk off his face, wishing he could do the same with what had gone down his throat.

"Bit of an accident," he said weakly.

"Felicity's my burper!" Gwen added brightly, dabbing delicately at her daughter's mouth with a cloth while seeming unfazed by what had just shot out of there. Will was too traumatized to respond, but Rachel was done humoring this family.

"Um, are you going to apologize to my husband or what?" she asked.

"I mean, I'm sorry he got in the way," Gwen said, unafraid to look offended at the question. "But it's just a natural part of life. You'll understand that soon enough."

"How someone can think their baby is so friggin' special that it gives them a free pass to abandon any semblance of responsibility to the rest of society? No, I don't think I'll ever understand that."

"Ladies, let's all just calm down," Ronald said. Will hadn't noticed him and Ronnie Jr. brush past him, and he remembered a simpler time when the most disgusting thing in his life was an awareness of the toddler's dirty diaper.

"Excuse me, guy I met thirty minutes ago," Rachel said to him. "Did you just tell me to *calm down*?"

Even in his . . . compromised state, Will was filled with appreciation for what a badass his wife was. And not just because it was his back that she had. It was more how self-possessed she was, even when he knew her adrenaline had to be flowing. She might play it back later, analyze how she felt about the situation after it was over, but he admired her ability to not let herself or those she cared about get pushed aside. It was a trait that he knew would make her a great parent and one that he worried he lacked.

"I didn't mean . . . ," Ronald started before trailing off. His face said he knew he had miscalculated once and that he had no interest in going two for two. He turned to Gwen. "Maybe we should just go. Ronnie Jr. needs a diaper, and I don't think he was going to last much longer even if he didn't."

Gwen—who for some reason hadn't stopped burping the baby even though there couldn't possibly be anything left inside of her—had traded her carefree glow for cool disregard, which she trained on both Rachel and Will as she spoke.

"Fine. I don't want to spend any more time around these Judgy McJudgersons anyway."

"Was that supposed to be an insult?" Rachel said. "You really should try reading something that's higher than a preschool level, Gwen."

The woman of the couple from Iowa mouthed a "Damn," and the mother and son expats traded glances while pretending to be distracted by something in the kitchen. Gwen's cheeks reddened, and she turned with Felicity to follow her husband and son, who were already halfway out the door. For a moment, Rachel and Will both forgot that he looked like he'd been slimed by a hagfish—she because she'd vanquished a woman who gave unsolicited nursing-bra advice, and he because he was dumbfounded by the fact that they'd really left without apologizing.

"Well, since they wouldn't say it," Henny said, "*I'm sorry* that happened. If there were ever a case for an exception to our no-public-restroom policy, I'd say this is it."

Rachel fully took in the extent of the damage to what had been Will's favorite Michigan T-shirt for the first time. She was concerned for his well-being, although he wouldn't have blamed her if she concluded that she could never kiss him again.

"I can't believe this," she said, careful to touch the arm that *didn't* currently have breast milk drying in its hair. "I feel so bad for you."

"It's all good," he lied while fantasizing about self-immolating. Then, to Henny: "I do think I'll take you up on that bathroom offer, though."

"Of course. Now unfortunately"—she cringed a little—"it's not in this house. You'll need to walk down to the end of the block to the building that looks like an old convenience store, which is our gift shop and visitor center. That's where the tour ends, so we can meet you there. I'll let them know you're coming."

Walking down the sidewalk covered in vomit—he hadn't done that since that spring break trip with Ali when Will had had three too many Hurricanes. But he had been 22 and in Key West. In a way, it would've been like he hadn't gotten his money's worth if he *hadn't* found himself in such a state at some point over the course of that week.

Okay, so it had never been like that. It was gross back then too. But knowing this was the first and almost assuredly not the last time he'd be covered in baby vomit put him right back to wondering if there was any way he could possibly be prepared for what was coming, if Rachel would still think the boring job was "the right job" once barf became a regular part of their lives. It felt like Felicity had spewed a spotlight onto his insecurities, making them harder to hide.

Shuffling down a leafy city street sober at 1:30 in the afternoon was also just a little more conspicuous than being drunk outside the Sloppy Seagull at 4:00 in the morning.

All was not lost, though. He could see his car in the distance, sitting right outside the visitor center that was his destination, and he realized that what 40 minutes earlier had just been a good parking spot now held the promise of a change of clothes and his toothbrush.

A baby on this T.M. Clemens tour just went all Sloppy Seagull on me, he texted Ali while he walked. Ali had seen Will at his best and at his worst—not just times like in Key West, but real stuff, too, like when it hit Will 15 minutes before his wedding that his dad, who hadn't RSVP'd, really wasn't going to show. Will broke down in the back of the church, and it was Ali who had been there to hug him and remind him that he was marrying Rachel and nothing else that day mattered. Theirs was one of those rare friendships where you didn't have to be afraid to look stupid in front of the other person, and Will loved Ali for that.

You still haven't answered my question, Ali wrote back before Will had taken another 10 steps. Also: What the hell are you talking about?

Right. Will owed him not one but two explanations.

First there was Rachel's job situation, the subject of that ill-timed text on the drive. While the speed of Ali's responses made you wonder if they'd been in progress even before you sent your message, Will had no such reputation, so he'd taken advantage of that to postpone formulating his answer to his friend's question. That had meant stuffing his phone into his pocket, giving himself over to Rachel's enthusiasm about the macaroni and cheese sandwich—a delicious decision, to nobody's surprise—and then suggesting they use her phone to navigate across the city, which would keep his out of sight and offer extra insurance against any more close calls.

He didn't feel good about it. But no worse than when he'd tested the definition of a lie with Rachel in the car.

Beyond all that, Ali had no idea about the trip itself, which Will had never gotten around to mentioning the night before.

I convinced Rachel to use our vacation to take a spontaneous road trip. Five cities in the next week, starting in Milwaukee. Hoping it cheers her up.

About the job? Ali asked.

Yeah.

Can I assume that means you've moved on from trying to figure out a way to intervene there?

Will unlocked the car but stopped short of opening the back door, weighing how much to divulge.

Define "intervene," he sent back.

I knew it. Let the record show I tried to warn you.

Duly noted, Will typed after fishing his toiletry bag and a fresh Michigan tee out of his duffel. That his mid-30s wardrobe still bore a striking resemblance to how he'd dressed as an undergrad felt like almost as big of an indictment of his fitness to be a parent as the Dave & Buster's rewards card.

Almost.

Do me a favor though, he continued. It's close quarters in the car, so no more unsolicited texting about how I may be destroying my marriage.

Got it. Trying to keep that spark alive, right?

Something like that, Will said, forcing himself to sound breezy and irreverent, like it would keep the fire he was playing with from blazing out of control.

He added a reusable shopping bag to his load before locking the car again and heading up to the visitor center. His plan was to strip off the stained shirt, completely soak it, and then store it in the shopping bag until they got to the hotel, at which point he would take a shower set as close to boiling as humanly tolerable and use every last ounce of the tiny bottle of shampoo on both him and his beloved crew neck.

The center was currently empty save for a much older man sitting at a table with his own cashbox and card reader.

"Jiminy Christmas," he said, sizing Will up. "Henny wasn't kidding."

"No, I'm afraid she wasn't."

"Bathroom's back there," the man said, jerking his thumb over his shoulder. "Although you may need an exorcist."

Will laughed out of surprise as much as anything else. He hadn't expected an octogenarian working a T. M. Clemens gift shop to be so quick with the one-liner.

After pushing open the door with the NOT A PUBLIC RESTROOM sign, Will set his toiletry bag down on the little sink and unzipped it, deciding he'd start with everything above his neck before moving on to the shirt. Because his bottle of bodywash at home was big, he hadn't packed any, choosing instead to rely on the complimentary offerings at the hotels, so all that was available to wash his face with was some Dial hand soap. He eyed it reluctantly but only for a second.

"Let's do this, Citrus Sunburst," he said, pumping the foam into his hand and proceeding to scrub his pores with the vigor of a man auditioning for a job at a day spa. With his eyes closed, he tried to distract himself from the grittier details of the cleansing task at hand, and his mind drifted back to Aunt Katie and something she'd once told him about his dad.

She'd taken Will to see the first *Harry Potter* movie, which stood out in his mind not only because he and Emma Watson were the same age and he'd proceeded to develop a massive crush on her, but also because it was November 2001 and his and Katie's first trip to the movies after 9/11. He had gotten very clingy to his mom following the attacks, so it took a while to convince him to leave her for anything but school.

There had been a baby crying two rows in front of them from the moment the coming attractions started. If Will knew next to nothing about babies at 34, he'd had absolutely no clue at 11, but from the sound of the cries, he'd been able to tell this one was little. *Really* little. By the time Hagrid apparated on that rocky island on Harry's 11th birthday to inform him that he was in fact a wizard, Katie had had enough and leaned forward.

"You know, your baby seems pretty upset," she'd said, making no attempt to whisper.

"So?" the mom had fired back, equally loudly, her baby now up on her shoulder just like Felicity had been on Gwen's. "What do you want me to do about it?"

"Maybe take her outside? Or, you know, don't take an infant to the movies in the first place?"

"So I'm supposed to rearrange my life around my kid's schedule? You need to mind your own damn business."

Will remembered his eyes going wide. There was a somewhat legendary, perhaps slightly apocryphal story in their family about a bar fight Katie had gotten into in college when a drunk sorority sister had made the mistake of calling her a word that she shouldn't have. Had her nephew not been sitting there in the movie theater and the woman not been a young mother, there would have been a nonzero chance that a new chapter would've been added to that legacy. As it was, Katie had just sat back in her seat and tried to process what she'd heard. The baby had eventually quieted down—not until Harry, Hermione, and Ron reached Hogwarts, though—and the rest of the movie unfolded without incident. When it was over, he and his aunt had been sitting there, talking about the climactic scene with Voldemort, and the woman had muttered something as she walked out. Will hadn't been able to hear it, but he'd guessed it wasn't that far off from what had been said that night in the bar.

"Your child is lucky to have such a caring, *committed* mother," Katie hollered after her. Under her breath, she added: "What a . . ." She stopped and looked at Will. "I'm sorry. Your aunt shouldn't let people rile her up like that."

"It's okay." And then, because he was 11 and looking to expand his vocabulary of expressions that could get him in trouble: "What was that word she used again?"

"Nice try. I was actually talking about before. When she said the thing about not rearranging her life. It reminded me of something your . . ." She checked herself again and took a different, sufficiently vague approach. "Some parents just don't get it, is all. But, hey, at least that baby didn't puke on us or anything."

Will couldn't remember if he'd consciously made the connection that "some parents" referred to his father right then or not. But on those few occasions when Will put himself out there and reached out—his high school graduation, when his dad had been "too busy at work" to come, or graduation from Michigan, when he had been "already going to Hawaii," or Rachel's and his wedding, when his dad's absence had brought him to tears—that day at the movies came back to him. Will hadn't tried contacting him since they'd gotten married, and he didn't know if he ever would again. Not even to tell his dad he was going to be a grandpa.

But no amount of distance could put to bed Will's fear that he'd inherited some sort of terrible dad gene that was just waiting for the opportunity to be exposed.

We're almost at the gift shop, so get your clothes on, Rachel texted him.

Ha ha ha, he wrote back, although having gone straight from washing his face to brushing his teeth to soaking and wringing out the soiled shirt, he did find himself standing there bare chested at the moment.

You should know I contemplated drinking that entire bottle of hand sanitizer near the door, he typed after slipping the new, clean shirt over his head.

Look at it this way: It's not like our baby will be able to do anything worse to you than this. It can only go up from here.

Her last sentence froze him for a second. There were all kinds of ways it could go down. Vomit was gross, but vomit was also nothing. What about pneumonia? What about SIDS? Hell, he'd just heard somewhere that honey was fatal to infants. Honey? Really? What else didn't he know?

"All proceeds from the store go straight to the restoration project," he heard Henny say to the group as they were walking through the front door. "But there's also one last piece of the tour to show you in here."

She saw Will reappear from the bathroom. "Ah, good to have you back, Mr. Fiesterly. You look good as new. All right, all, let's head to that display case over there."

Rachel let everyone pass by, and Will rejoined her at the back of the group.

"I think Henny kinda likes you, Mr. Fiesterly," she said quietly, unable to contain a wink-wink of a smile.

"Don't say that," he said, still distracted. "She reminds me of Aunt Katie."

"Oh wow. I can *totally* see it."

Once they were all gathered around and peering down at the case, Henny explained what they were looking at: Clemens's original blueprints for the Milwaukee Mistake, dated April 1922. The house in the drawing was referred to as the Crawford, her husband's name, a loving gesture to the man who had acted as her business manager and who had frequently stood in for her at meetings with men who wouldn't have worked with her if they'd known T. M. Clemens was a woman. He'd even pretended he *was* T. M. Clemens at times. It had been during the construction of the Milwaukee house that she'd discovered he'd been stealing large sums of her money to carry on affairs with a variety of mistresses. Henny said many scholars had come to believe that this, and not the house itself, was the true reason Clemens had abandoned the project and called the house a mistake.

"It's an awful story," she added, "but it also can't take away from the beauty of what she did here. I think there's a lesson in that. And in being really sure the people who say they love you mean it."

Will looked down at Rachel. She loved him. He knew that.

It was everything on the horizon that scared him.

Chapter 8

To their surprise, on a busy concert weekend, they were able to get into the hotel early, which gave them a couple of hours to relax and, in Will's case, disinfect. He had hardly set their bags down when he retired to the bathroom to scrub that shirt within an inch of its life.

"It's a little touch and go," he said after he left it hanging over the towel rack, "but he's convalescing nicely."

"That's a relief. You referring to a shirt as *he*, not so much."

"What can I say? We've been through a lot together."

Rachel got a book out of one of her bags. "I'm gonna go down to the pool and read for a little bit. Do you want to come with?"

"Nah, I think I'll just hang out up here and take an actual shower. The hand soap at the visitor center, while lovely, had its limitations."

She went to kiss him on her way to the door but, thinking better of it based on what he'd just said about his current hygienic state, opted to pat him on the arm instead.

Alone in the room, Will went to retrieve his clothes for the concert from his bag. The one where Rachel had packed her book was still open, and inside it he saw a tote that he hadn't realized she'd brought with them.

It was from the Art Institute of Chicago and featured the famous Georges Seurat painting *A Sunday on La Grande Jatte*. The painting was huge and the focal point of the room it was housed in, and whenever Rachel and Will went to the art institute—which was at least five times

a year—she always made a point of sitting in that room for several minutes or more, soaking in the painting. The third or fourth time they'd
done this, he'd asked her why she kept coming back to that spot, and
she'd told him a story about going there for the first time on a field trip
in the seventh grade.

"I don't really know how," she'd told him, "but when I saw that
painting, I knew that I wanted to be some sort of artist. It's like I found
myself in there."

Rachel didn't usually say a whole lot about the painting after they'd
gone, but just looking at it seemed cathartic for her, like she was recon-
necting with an elemental part of who she was.

When Will had been planning to propose, he'd known he wanted
to do it there. The only problem had been that Rachel had had no interest in a public proposal, and despite his best efforts, he hadn't been able
to arrange with the museum for a way to pop the question in front of
the painting while also ensuring no one else would be around.

So one Saturday, he'd rolled the dice.

Most often, they went to the art institute in the late morning, but
he'd suggested they go out to lunch downtown beforehand and successfully pushed them back to early afternoon. That had put them in the
Seurat room around 4:00 p.m., and Rachel had been ready to go by
4:15, but for his plan to work, Will had needed them to still be there
when the museum closed at 5:00. So he had stalled in the gift shop for
45 minutes, claiming he was looking for a birthday gift for his mom.

Rachel had seen Will agonize over picking the perfect present
before and didn't grow suspicious, although she had clearly been ready
for him to wrap things up after 45 minutes of browsing. Which he'd
done—only to discover when he went to pay that he'd lost his wallet
somewhere in the museum.

He hadn't, of course. But that's what he'd told the cashier, who had
told the head of security, who had reluctantly given them 10 minutes to
go back in and look, but only because Will had said he was sure it must

have fallen out when they were sitting down by the Seurat and because the guy had said Rachel reminded him of his daughter.

When they'd gotten to the painting, Rachel had immediately gone for the bench they'd been sitting on and felt around in the space between the back and the bottom cushions. She didn't find a wallet.

But she did find a box with a ring in it.

When she'd turned around, Will had been on one knee. She'd been so surprised that her hands had gone to her mouth, and the box had fallen to the floor. He'd picked it up without taking his eyes off her, opened the lid, and asked her to marry him. Her hands still covering her mouth, she'd nodded yes—in front of *A Sunday on La Grande Jatte*, on the very spot that had triggered her love of art, without another soul around to witness it. It hadn't been glamorous or over the top, but it had been distinctly Rachel. She deserved a story like that, and she deserved to be with someone who would do everything in his power to make sure it happened.

Will hadn't known what he would've done if the security guard hadn't let them back in or if, God forbid, someone had somehow discovered the ring in the hour between when he'd stowed it in its hiding spot and when they'd returned. It wasn't like he'd had a spare.

But he'd wanted her to find it there, the way she'd said she'd found herself all those years before. It had been worth the risk. He'd had to try. For her.

Didn't he owe her the same now?

If I just could've gotten her to take the interview, he thought and started to head to the bathroom. *Because it's not like I can accept it for her.*

He was just about to turn the water on when he asked himself if maybe he could.

Walking back out into the room, he proceeded to start pacing, an idea that had existed in some vague form almost from the instant he'd seen Beatriz's email address now coming into sharper focus.

It would be so easy. Neither Rachel nor Rochelle was checking email. But Beatriz presumably was. One email from him to her could change everything.

Of course he couldn't write to her as Rachel's husband. That wouldn't make any sense. Maybe he could pose as a corporate recruiter? Like Rachel had hired him to negotiate on her behalf, and she had changed her mind about everything and was now asking him to reach back out? He guessed that would be plausible, but it might raise some questions.

Ideally, the email would come from an account that wasn't his. It would come from Rachel.

Or short of that, at least look like it had.

Will took out his phone and pulled up the page where you can create a new Gmail. Rachel's name followed by their three-digit apartment number, and he'd have an address to send from. It'd be like Crawford Clemens with T. M., minus the financial fraud and philandering.

He stared at the screen and thought about what he was on the verge of doing. He switched over to his and Ali's texts and scrolled back to the night before.

The answer is always no.

Doing this would be wrong. Will knew that. He would be betraying Rachel's trust in a particularly flagrant way.

But.

What if it was a smaller wrong that served a greater good? What if it was the grand gesture that would give her everything she wanted and ensure their future was what she'd hoped it would be, a story so fantastic they'd pass it on to their grandkids someday when taking them for ice cream on the Santa Monica Pier?

His eyes went from the phone to the tote again. Its appearance had been a bit of a surprise not only because he hadn't seen her pack it but also because she hadn't used it in a long time, tucking it away in the closet and forgetting about it.

And now Rachel had gotten it out for the first time in forever, the day after Rochelle had contacted her about the job and she had cried telling Will all the reasons she couldn't do it.

There was every possibility it was simply a coincidence. But standing there, phone in hand, heart beating fast, sensing that this—this moment right here, in the quiet of this hotel room—would be his one and only chance to keep Rachel from looking back on Creative Vices with regret, Will felt like her choice of bag signified something else.

She wanted more. Needed more. Needed to have the kind of career that gave her the same feeling that had made her fall in love with art in the first place.

She'd called her current job *boring*, but he feared she'd been thinking about their entire situation, their whole life together, when she'd said it.

From what Will could tell, all the other candidates already had their interviews scheduled. This process was passing Rachel by, and with each minute wasted, it would get harder to try and reel it back in. Experiencing Clemens's designs up close again, going to a concert to see an artist who'd followed her creativity at all costs, going back to their college campus and revisiting a time in her life when she'd been immersed in her own art—he had to hope all that would inspire her in due time.

He just didn't have the luxury of waiting around until it had.

So he started typing.

Hey Beatriz—

This is Rachel Armas. I'm on vacation and off work email but had a question for you, which is why I'm writing from my personal account.

After sleeping on it, I've reconsidered. Can we still make the interview happen, or am I too late? If so, I'd be coming from Nashville, so I'd have to fly from there.

Thanks in advance.
Rachel

Will read it back, looking for any tells that might indicate to Beatriz it was someone other than Rachel writing to her. There was a lot going on in those six short sentences.

But it wasn't enough to keep him from hitting send.

Chapter 9

"I'll tell you what," Rachel said, the corners of her mouth stained with barbecue sauce. She'd gotten a fully loaded Impossible Burger with fries and couldn't stop raving about it. "If this were *Date Me Now!*, you'd definitely be getting the All-Access Pass tonight."

Will swallowed an enormous bite of cheesesteak, his own lips smeared with provolone. "I have to admit, I'm not quite sure this meets the standards of a quote, unquote *romantic* getaway. But it is getting the job done."

The concert was at 9:30 p.m., so they'd left the room at 6:30, hoping to grab dinner at a restaurant in the Third Ward. The first three places they'd tried each had hour-plus waits, which didn't seem at all unreasonable given it was a Saturday night during concert season. But Rachel didn't want to risk getting stuck somewhere and suggested they instead go in early, eat on the Summerfest grounds, and just sort of wander around listening to other bands until it was time for the show.

"Maybe we can try the Third Ward for brunch tomorrow before we leave," Will said as he reached for another napkin. "We're going to be in the car awhile, so it might be worth having an actual meal somewhere. No offense to your burger."

"Thank you for clarifying. Because a fake burger this good is a special thing, and you would've been sleeping alone tonight if you'd implied otherwise."

He thought about the email to Beatriz and hoped Rachel's joke wasn't actually some sort of foreshadowing of her kicking him out of their bed.

"Speaking of *special*," Will said, determined to change the subject in his own head, "have you ever noticed the opening act is always called a *special guest*?"

"What do you want them to say instead? 'Here's the person you didn't pay to see'?"

"Maybe just *the opener*? It's like everybody's afraid to admit it's a warm-up."

"But maybe *special guest* is what the special guests prefer."

He was about to tell her why he thought there was no way on earth that could be possible, but at that exact moment, there was such loud laughter from behind her that he got distracted. He looked over Rachel's right shoulder, through the throngs of people, and spotted the laughers: a couple about their age, both of whom were wearing what at a distance looked to be some type of VIP pass. And had it stopped right there at the lanyards hanging around their necks, everything would've been fine. But Will made the mistake of glancing up at their faces, which was when he realized the woman he'd never seen before was holding hands with someone he had.

It was Seth. As in Rachel's old boyfriend Seth.

Will quickly looked down at the last third of his cheesesteak, hoping that if he concentrated on it hard enough, it would mean that the eye contact he was scared he and Seth had just made was only a figment of his imagination. Or short of that, that Seth wouldn't register who he was, allowing Will to be both insulted that Rachel's ex didn't remember what he looked like and thrilled that they wouldn't be reliving their chance encounter at the Cubs game. He had enough on his mind without having to try to interact with the beautiful human from Rachel's past.

What Will hadn't noticed in all this was that Rachel had turned her head after he did.

"No way," she said. "I think that's Seth."

"Who?" Will said innocently, not taking his eyes off his food.

"Seth. From high school. That's so weird. You know? Because we were just talking about him?"

"Oh, right. *Seth.*"

In truth, it *was* odd for Will and Rachel to see him there so soon after talking about him. Despite the high school stories, Seth hadn't been an active part of Rachel's life in years, save for some happy-birthday texts and the like, and the two of them were even inconsistent about that. They hadn't had a falling-out or anything; it was just the normal drift that happens when you and most of the people you were close with at 18 go off in different directions and start the long process of becoming whoever you're going to be for the rest of your lives. Which explained why Rachel did not hesitate to yell out:

"Seth Sanders, the pride of Livingston High School!"

Seth looked her way, startled, before breaking into a huge grin, saying something to the woman he was with, and then leading the two of them over to where Rachel and Will were sitting.

"Rachel Armas, the Picasso of Palatine!"

Rachel stood to greet him, and they gave each other a huge hug. Will got up, too, but only because he felt like he had to, and steeled himself to appear friendly for when the man who looked like he'd just stepped out of a J.Crew ad disengaged his arms from around his wife. While he waited, he had the chance to fully register that Seth's date was as striking as he was, her flowy green dress perfectly complementing her hair as it cascaded to just below her shoulders. For her part, Rachel looked beautiful in a floral-print romper and sandals, and next to the three of them, Will was the designated driver on the Cool Kids' Trip to the Concert.

Rachel and Seth separated, and he thrust his hand toward Will.

"Will, great to see you again, man!"

His enthusiasm was palpable. And annoying. Even more so because he seemed to mean it.

"How's it going, Seth?" Will said, catching a whiff of cologne. Seth even smelled attractive.

"Ah, it's goin' great." He took a step back and put an arm around his companion. "And this wonderful woman is the main reason why. I'd like you both to meet my fiancée, Francesca."

"Oh my God!" Rachel exclaimed. "That's amazing! Congratulations! Oh, and hi, Francesca! I'm Rachel, and this is Will!"

They all four laughed, with the three meeting for the first time then taking turns awkwardly shaking hands. The requisite small talk ensued, and Will and Rachel learned what they probably would've already known if she were more active on Instagram: that the happy couple had met at a mixer for graduates of the University of Wisconsin Law School and gotten engaged just the weekend before. Will studied Rachel's reaction to all this out of the corner of his eye, and she seemed genuinely delighted for them, which made his mild yet nagging obsession over what she thought about Seth all these years later feel a little ridiculous.

After the story of the engagement, it was Seth's turn to ask what was new with them, and Rachel told him and Francesca that she was pregnant, setting off another round of *Oh my God*s and congratulations. Without a shared history, Will and Francesca were mainly spectators in all this, but he was okay with that because it made it much more difficult for their significant others to reminisce for too long.

"So, do you two have pavilion or main-stage tickets?" Seth asked as the conversation started to peter out. It hadn't even been five minutes.

"Pavilion," Will said, channeling his excitement that their interaction was almost over into socially acceptable anticipation for the concert.

"Hey, us too!" Seth said. There was something in his tone that made him sound like he'd just unraveled a plot twist on a prestige drama, and Will had a sinking feeling about what was coming next. "You two should totally come sit with us! My company rented out the private bar facing the stage, so we can hang out and catch up some more!"

"That sounds awesome!" Rachel said, undoing whatever incremental emotional growth her husband had achieved while standing there. "What do you think, babe?"

Will was ready. "I mean, would they even let us in? It's not like we have tickets to *that*, and I'm sure the space is limited."

"Oh, I think we'll manage," Seth jumped in. "I am a vice president, after all." He winked like he was making a joke. Mostly. There was about 15 percent *You knew that, right?* mixed in with it.

Perfect. The only thing Will wanted to do less than hang out in a club with Rachel's ex was hang out in a club with Rachel's ex after having called extra attention to the fact that the ex was pulling strings to get them in. Will momentarily entertained the idea of advocating on behalf of the seats he'd purchased, but he couldn't come up with a compelling case why they'd be preferable to a private bar, even if Rachel couldn't drink. No matter how deceptively good row *X* was, it was still row *X*, which by the very nature of row *X*'s could not be a VIP space.

"Sure, yeah," he said with markedly less enthusiasm than he'd said *pavilion*.

"Great!" Seth said. "I think it's actually open now, so we can head over."

He reached for Francesca's right hand with his left, and Rachel grabbed Will's left with her right, allowing them to walk four wide with Seth and Rachel in the middle, chatting away. Will imagined themselves posed like the cast photo of a *Friends*-style sitcom that he would henceforth refer to privately as *Reluctant Acquaintances*.

"So I gotta ask," Francesca said, leaning around Seth so she could see everyone. "Why 'the pride of Livingston'?"

"Well, as I'm sure you know," Rachel said, "Seth was quite the politician back in the day. President of the entire student body our senior year. Not that anyone really cared. I started calling him the pride of Livingston as a joke. He came up with Picasso of Palatine in response because of how much I liked art."

"You have to admit," Seth said with a sly grin, "you and I did have some fun in the student government office. If I'm not mistaken, wasn't our first kiss in there?" Rachel rolled her eyes, and he laughed, before looking at Will and adding: "Sorry, bro."

"Yeah, you seem real broken up about it," Will said, pushing out a smile. "But it's cool: I'm aware you two went out."

"Not just went out. I mean, we were each other's *firsts*—also in the student government office, ironically enough."

This time Rachel socked him in the arm, and he laughed again.

"I think that's enough about our dating history," she said. "These two don't want to hear about it."

"Oh, I'm just goofing around," Seth said. "Will knows that. Right, Will? I mean, he got you in the end, didn't he?"

At that, Francesca stopped and stared at him. She was smiling, but it was the kind of smile that warned you taking its continued presence in your life for granted would be a mistake. "Got her in the end? What am I? Your consolation prize?"

Had Will known the pilot of *Reluctant Acquaintances* was going to involve Seth squirming so much, he would've been happier about being cast. He could've done without the reminder that Rachel and Seth had slept together, though—she'd told Will that a long time ago—and finding out they'd been daring enough to do it on school grounds made him feel more than ever like she'd inhabited a completely different universe in high school than what he'd known.

"Frannie, c'mon," Seth said. "You know what I mean. It was high school. It's ancient history."

"Yes. It is. So maybe tone down your delight about it a couple of notches."

She didn't drop his hand, and they all resumed walking, but Rachel and Will hung back a few steps to break up their four-person phalanx and give Seth and Francesca some space. From behind, they could see him doing a lot of talking and her body language gradually warming back up to him as they picked their way through the crowds to the bar.

"He's just . . . ," Rachel said but didn't finish the thought.

"An ass?" Will offered after several seconds had passed.

Rachel laughed. "I was going to go with 'So much, sometimes.'"

"I guess I can't give him too hard a time. He is still clearly hung up on you after all these years. I mean, it kinda makes me wish that kid about to walk by him with the chili dog would just smash it into his shirt. But I get it."

"That's so not the case," she said, "and even if it were, he'd be out of luck. Because you're stuck with me. Unless I ever meet Barack Obama."

"Obama? Really? He's like sixty."

"Yes, yes, he is," she said, reaching her hand up to rub his back. "That happens, and you and I might have to have a difficult conversation."

Chapter 10

Their admission into the private bar was even more obnoxious than Will had imagined it would be.

There was the predictable initial confusion over him and Rachel not having passes, followed by Seth explaining they were *dear friends* of his. The woman checking tickets didn't seem to know what to do with this, and Will's hope that the whole thing might fizzle was briefly rekindled. But then a second woman with a clipboard came up and asked what was going on, and when the first explained it to her, clipboard lit up and said, "Oh, of course! Any friends of Mr. Sanders are friends of ours!"

That was bad enough. Until the woman at the entrance apologized for not just waving them through on her own, at which point Seth was perfectly lovely and understanding, exhibiting none of the entitled impatience that would've made it a little easier for Will to keep believing he had no redeeming qualities.

Rachel and Francesca went to get them a table, and Will and Seth headed to the bar for drinks. As much as he would've liked to have been intoxicated before settling in for whatever extended conversation they were now about to have, Will planned to only have a beer or two since Rachel couldn't drink.

"Can I get a Corona and a water?" he asked the bartender. "Actually, wait—can you do a virgin Bloody Mary?"

"A Virgin Mary? Yup, no problem. Is that instead of the water or the Corona?"

Will's brain skipped. You didn't have to be Catholic or even religious to not know what to make of Virgin Mary as a name for a cocktail.

"Uh, the water. It's for my wife. She's pregnant."

"Hey, congratulations, man. I'd say it's on the house, but open bar, so—you know. Congrats from your company, I guess."

"Oh, yeah, no, I don't work for . . . whoever this company is. I'm just friends with that guy down there." Will motioned toward Seth, who was ordering at the other end of the bar. "Well, not really friends, either. Just acquainted with him. Reluctantly."

"Good for you," the bartender said. "These people are tools."

Will put a five in the tip cup and took the drinks. He would've gone to the table by himself, but Seth got his two glasses of white wine at the same time and intercepted him by one of the three appetizer tables.

"So, do you live in Milwaukee now?" Will asked, determined to steer things into more superficial territory that did not involve Seth having seen Rachel naked.

"Nope, still Chicago. But we do a lot of business in Milwaukee. There's actually a good amount of clients in here tonight. Speaking of"—he ratcheted his voice up to megaphone—"Tony! Good to see you, my friend!"

It was the same kind of show he'd put on when shaking Will's hand earlier, only louder, and Seth and Tony dove right into talking about whatever it was they were going to talk about. There was something about a merger, and then something about pickleball, with Will immediately pushed into the role of conversational third wheel who served no purpose in standing there. He lingered a socially acceptable amount of time for Seth to acknowledge his presence in some way, but when that didn't happen—perhaps because there would've been no one around to acknowledge how gracious Seth was being—Will made the break he had intended when leaving the bar and joined Rachel and Francesca at the table they'd secured.

"Francesca was just telling me about her job," Rachel started, clearly relieved that it was no longer just the two of them. Judging by their body language, the conversation hadn't quite been effortless, and Will caught Rachel sneaking a glance at the clock on her phone before accepting the drink he was setting in front of her. "Ooh, a Bloody Mary. I haven't had one of these in years— and never one with without booze. Who says pregnant ladies don't go hard?"

"To motherhood and mocktails," Will said as he sat down next her.

"Cheers," Rachel said, clinking her glass to his bottle and then taking a sip. "Mm, not bad. Anyway, Francesca works in the Bulls' front office."

"Well, that's pretty awesome," Will said. "As, like, general counsel?"

"Basketball analytics, actually," Francesca said. "I have an MBA, too, and I was a huge Michael Jordan fan growing up, so it's kind of a dream come true."

Will spent the next 10 minutes peppering her with everything from questions about the efficiency of zone defenses to trade suggestions. He wasn't a die-hard Bulls fan by any stretch, but he had played basketball in high school, and he knew enough about the NBA to have more than a passing interest in how Francesca spent her days. Will got the sense that Francesca was happy to humor him, mainly because she loved her job but maybe also a little because the more they talked about basketball, the further they got away from the fact they were with people who had previously been with each other. Rachel also remembered that someone from her program at Michigan had gotten a job in the marketing department with the Cleveland Cavaliers, and it turned out Francesca had met that person earlier in the week because they had recently taken a job with the Bulls. The conversation fell into a nice little groove, no doubt further aided by the fact that Will and Rachel were not the type of people to ask someone they'd just met for tickets to a game.

When things did finally hit a natural lull, they sort of looked around and collectively noticed that Seth still wasn't back.

"There he is," Francesca said after a few seconds of scanning the room. Seth had moved on from Tony and was now the focal point of a circle of people, all of whom were enjoying themselves immensely. "I swear that man has his own gravitational pull. People are just drawn to him."

Will anticipated Francesca would be exasperated by this. Sure, the vibe around their table had loosened up considerably, but there was no getting around that Seth had pulled together his solar system of admirers by leaving her with two people she hadn't known an hour earlier—one of whom he'd slept with. After a particularly long line for the bar at Will's office holiday party several years before, he and Rachel had made a pact that going forward, if either of them was left on their own with the other's coworkers for more than seven minutes, the offending party would be given back-to-back weeks of laundry duty (they typically alternated). Case in point, neither of them worked with Francesca, but he had been watching the clock while waiting on that Virgin Mary (still awkward) just in case. The similarities to what Rachel had come to refer to as the 14-Minute Scotch Affair had been too much to ignore.

But with Francesca and Seth, it was the opposite. She seemed positively enchanted by the way he was the center of everyone else's universe. When he finally did rejoin the three of them, he slid in right next to her, and she wasted no time getting her hand on his knee. Despite the hiccup on the walk over, they appeared completely at ease beside one another—something that you'd think would be a prerequisite for two people getting married but often isn't. That was one thing Will wasn't jealous of because he and Rachel had always had it. He reached out and grabbed her hand to remind himself of that.

"All right," Seth said. "Catch me up. What did I miss?"

"Well, I played it cool and totally did *not* ask Francesca a million questions about her job with the Bulls," Will said, causing them all to laugh and Seth to kiss his fiancée on her forehead.

"And I was about to say how much the wine you're drinking *isn't* making me feel a certain kind of way and that in no way have I found this Bloody Mary lacking without vodka."

Everyone laughed again, and Will caught himself thinking, *You know, this is actually kind of nice.*

It lasted for a few seconds.

"I still can't get over that you're pregnant," Seth said. "It's so"—he turned to Francesca—"what's the word I'm looking for?"

"Huge," she said. "Life altering. I mean, when we talked about having kids, we pretty quickly figured out that cool aunt and uncle is more our speed. There's just so much to parenting, and how it changes every other aspect of your life. But to see the two of you jumping into it . . . I don't know. I guess what we're trying to say is, it's impressive."

"Hey, thanks," Rachel said. "For the record, we also would've accepted exciting, overwhelming, or abjectly terrifying."

"And it won't change *everything*," Will said, unsure if that were true but wanting to give Rachel the peace of mind of thinking he was unfazed by their comments.

Seth's brow crunched in concern, and he lowered his voice. "Speaking of, you're gonna keep working, right?" He asked it like he'd been up at night for years stressing over Rachel's career trajectory.

Will hated that Seth was acting as though his opinion should somehow count in this. He hated the pressure on Rachel to give the *right* answer that was implicit in the way the question had been asked. And he hated the implication that he might ever ask her to walk away from her work if she didn't want to because she was having a baby.

"Yup, that's the plan," Rachel said.

"Oh, good. Not that being a stay-at-home parent wouldn't be great. But I always imagined you with, like, a team of people around you, doing all this supercreative stuff."

"Ha, well, if that ever happens, I'll let you know. I mean, a university marketing communications office isn't exactly the NBA."

Rachel's face gave nothing away, but her fingernails were digging into the palm of Will's hand. He knew she was quickly losing patience with her employment status as the subject of conversation, which suggested to him that at least part of her was already second-guessing her decision to play it safe and not go on that interview.

"Are you going to find out what you're having?" Francesca asked before Seth could say anything else. "You know, ahead of time?"

"No, we want it to be a surprise," Will said.

"Wow," Francesca said. "That's so cool. I don't think I would ever have the self-restraint. It would drive me nuts."

Will understood. Because more accurately, Rachel wanted it to be a surprise; Will, on the other hand, was grasping for anything that would allow him to feel some semblance of control and would've welcomed knowing.

"If we *did* have a kid," Seth said, "I'd want to do one of those gender-reveal things. Like, hit a golf ball and have it explode pink or blue."

"I mean, I know you said parenthood isn't for you," Will said, "but I think it's really selfish to deprive the internet of such great original content."

That got a good chuckle, which covered up just how ludicrous both Will and Rachel considered these kinds of staged family "moments." Not to mention judging those who engaged in them was a lot easier than figuring out everything that would come next. Because where was the line between not giving a girl a doll just because she's a girl, but not going out of your way to keep her from playing with them either? Between not subconsciously defaulting into always giving a boy blue cups but also not weirdly insisting they always had to be pink?

Despite the final decision having been largely Rachel's, Will had actually been the one who'd first suggested Can of Green Gables for the nursery. But then, after she'd said she liked it, he had spent the next several minutes trying to talk her back out of it because he was afraid it was some subtle signal about what he hoped the gender of the baby would be. He'd argued it had meant he was leaning *girl* until he had zagged and said no, it almost assuredly indicated he wanted a boy.

"Then again," he'd said when he'd fully convinced himself it was a son he was after, "maybe when I saw the name on the can, I thought 'That's a girl's color.'"

"Babe?" Rachel had said.

"Yeah?"

"Go wait in the car."

She didn't get migraines, but she'd been pinching her forehead like she had one, and that image came back to him every time the circus inside his head threatened to pop out. Carrying a baby, worrying about her sister, dealing with her parents—and now negotiating her disappointment about this job—all that was more than enough for her to worry about. He wanted his presence to be a comfort, not a burden.

But that didn't change the fact that the more Will thought about it, the more it seemed like no matter what you did, from day one, you were steering your kid down a path toward a destination that neither they nor you would know how it fit them, if at all, until years later. That was an almost unimaginable responsibility, and one that he had qualified for not by proving himself particularly worthy or the best at this or that. No, the only credential he'd possessed was a functional reproductive organ. It was that dubious standard that had allowed his own father to become a dad. The man had given him half of his DNA and then disappeared into a new life somewhere in Florida, providing a convincing rebuttal to that bland parenting aphorism "It all just works out."

And if Will was avoiding articulating all this to Rachel, he certainly had no interest in trying with her high school boyfriend. Hence his relief when his remark about content for the internet caused a pivot in topics, even if it involved Seth leading them down a rabbit hole about the dance routine he and Francesca were learning for their wedding and planning to live stream. Some 20 minutes later, Will was stunned to find himself thinking the whole thing sounded kind of sweet and that he was experiencing genuine warmth toward them again, especially when he remembered he'd only had the one beer.

"The strangest part?" Seth said. "Frannie and I never realized we are the same exact height until the choreographer pointed it out. Like, we are both five-eight, on the dot. It's so weird how you can be with someone and not notice something you'd think would be obvious."

"Ha, no danger of that with us," Rachel said. She looked at her husband and reached up to ruffle his hair a little. "I've always kind of loved our height difference."

"Hey, get a room, you two!" Seth joked, and Will had never felt more pleased to be six-one.

"Actually, as it turns out, we have several," Rachel said. She told them that Milwaukee was stop one on a weeklong tour of dates that would ultimately land them in Nashville. Her excitement not only over the trip but also over how Will had managed to pull it together was unmistakable.

"I would one hundred percent watch that romantic comedy," Francesca said. She seemed authentically enthused by the idea of the whole thing. Seth, meanwhile, had started doing something on his phone before Rachel had even gotten them out of Michigan, but that didn't stop him from having all kinds of thoughts about the trip.

"Enjoy it while you can," he said. "You know, because once the baby comes, you won't get to do stuff like this anymore."

"Hold on," Will said, whatever warmth he'd felt from hearing ad nauseam about their stupid wedding choreography quickly receding. "Are you saying it's *not* advisable to take an infant on a long road trip?"

"Whoa, did I hit a nerve there, big guy?" Seth said it with a laugh, but Will could swear he saw a flicker in his eye, and Will knew that Seth knew he'd gotten under his skin.

Seth seemed fine with that.

Rachel was still holding Will's hand under the table, and she gave it a squeeze to let him know she was with him.

"Anyway," Seth went on, "you gotta talk to Ethan. He's one of my clients. He grew up in Ann Arbor and can tell you stuff to do there."

"We already have stuff to do there," Will said. "It's where we went to college. Remember?"

"Yeah, and I love that botanical garden," Rachel added.

"Sure," Seth said. "But there has to be something . . . more, right? I mean, no offense."

"Something more?" Will shot back. "You mean like a superhero roller coaster that's definitely *not* a pale imitation of a legitimate thrill ride?"

"Babe," Rachel said quietly.

But she needn't have. Because Seth just gave him a puzzled look before turning around and shouting, "Ethan!" A man several tables over looked up, and Seth motioned him over.

"Oh, so Ethan is *here*," Rachel said. She took a long slug of her drink. "That's terrific."

Seth missed her sarcasm. Or chose to ignore it. Otherwise, there was no way Ethan Chambers would've joined them for the next hour, especially considering that, in the first 60 seconds, he confirmed that he in fact hadn't grown up in Ann Arbor but rather in a town called Brighton that was like half an hour away.

"You know, the University of Michigan's in Ann Arbor," Ethan said. "But we all called it U of M."

"You don't say," Will said. "I really do feel like I know *more* about Ann Arbor already."

Seth and Ethan started talking about the time they'd seen the Rolling Stones together at the Detroit Tigers' baseball stadium—notably, also not in Ann Arbor—and were just recounting the parking situation when an all-women country band started to play, the last supporting act of the night. The rows down below the bar's perch were only about three-quarters full, but Will saw Rachel looking longingly at the stage while trying not to abandon all pretense of paying attention to the people chatting obliviously across from them.

"Rachel, what was the name of that history teacher we had?" Seth asked at one point.

"Huh?" Rachel said.

"You know, the one everyone used to call Cat Man?"

"Oh. Mr. Frisky."

"Frisky! Right! So classic. You gotta tell them the story about the time . . ."

Rachel cut him off. "I don't mean to be rude, Seth, but I actually wanted to hear this group."

"Who? The opener?"

It seemed like a fairly unnecessary question given how loudly he was talking to be heard over them.

"Yeah," Rachel said.

"Okay, suit yourself. I'll tell it. To be honest, I don't even know who the headliner is, let alone these people."

"The headliner is Gretchen Grayson," Rachel said.

Seth just laughed and once again appeared unfazed by Rachel's annoyance, gleefully regaling the table with the tale of the time he and some kid nicknamed Snuffy put a can of cat food on Mr. Frisky's desk. He told it with the verve of a thief reliving a bank heist.

Ethan was enthralled. Francesca was at least attempting to humor her fiancé. Will was wondering about the night that could've been if they'd just gotten a table at one of those restaurants and never spotted Seth.

And Rachel was not going to miss this concert.

"All right, I think we should head out," she said as Ethan finally (and mercifully) walked away a few minutes after the women had left the stage.

For the first time, Seth looked put out. "What? I thought you were going to watch the show with us."

Rachel stood, and Will rushed to follow. "No, I mean, this has been great," she said. "Really. I'm so glad we got to catch up, and so happy we got to meet Francesca. But Will got us good seats, and we haven't gone to a concert together in a long time—and it's like you said, who knows how long it'll be until we get to again." She put her arm around Will. "I know you two get it."

Will wished he could frame the expression on Seth's face.

"Of course we do," Francesca said before Seth could object. "And it was so great meeting you too."

They stood now, as well, and Rachel hugged goodbye with both of them. Seth extended his hand to Will like he had earlier, but Francesca went for the hug this time, and Will briefly panicked that she might say something about them coming to the wedding. But no invitation was offered, and after one more exchange of congratulations, he and Rachel were on their way to row X.

Finding their way to their seats through the crowd didn't leave a whole lot of space for chitchat. With the main event getting ready to start, the rows had filled considerably, and the music playing from the massive speakers above and around the stage mixed with a general buzz in the air. The backdrop of the stage itself opened onto Lake Michigan, although as you walked down the aisleway toward the seats, you could really see only the dusky sky, indicative of the setting sun. The lattice-work of the roof above them was awash in a mix of blue and green light, while the sides of the pavilion were completely open, allowing a refreshingly cool summer breeze to blow through. It was everything Will had hoped it would be when coming up with the idea the day before.

Everything except for the Seth detour.

"Thank you for getting us out of there," Will said once they had claimed their spots right on the aisle. Row X really was a misnomer. VIP or not, the seats were awesome.

"As if there were ever any doubt," Rachel said.

"I gotta admit, I had some doubts."

"You did? You thought I'd give up this with you to hear more about Ethan's microgreens start-up? Especially when we really don't know when we'll get to do this again?"

The joy he'd felt at her leading them away from Seth to the seats Will had bought for them was now tempered by the hint of melancholy in her voice as she said this. But for once, he didn't have to try too hard to minimize his own fears about the same thing because he was preoccupied by something else.

"No. But Seth—you were so excited to see him, and then to go to the bar. I don't know. If I'm being honest, I guess when he comes up, sometimes I feel like I can't compete."

"Seth? Really? Did you see him try to pop and lock at the table when describing their wedding dance?"

"But it's not that far fetched, is it? I mean, there was the student government office."

"Oh God. Look, I'm not gonna lie to you: the man is not unattractive. And the bouts of narcissism aside, he's a good guy. We had fun together. But tonight, I watched you turn what had been two women desperate to be anywhere but at the same table into a super enjoyable, albeit somewhat detailed, conversation about the Chicago Bulls. To me, it doesn't get any hotter than that. That's something he could never do. Could never be *bothered* to do. And besides, like I said at the table, I like my guys tall."

Will had read that Obama was also six-one, and he was about to make a joke about all the other similarities between himself and the former leader of the free world, but he never got the chance. The first notes were struck somewhere offstage, and the crowd erupted. Rachel stood right away, and when Will didn't immediately follow, she reached down her hand and guided him up so he was standing behind her.

"Most important," she said right into his ear as the stage lights came up, "Seth is not the kind of guy you sway with in the aisle at a concert on the lake. I've only ever met one of those."

The backing band began to play in earnest, and Will and Rachel were off, his arms wrapped around her, moving back and forth like they did when they danced together alone in the apartment. He didn't know what this week would ultimately have in store. But in that moment, it didn't matter.

Because in that moment, everything was perfect.

FIVE DAYS AGO

Chapter 11

When Will had fallen asleep in their hotel following the concert, the glow from the TV acting as a night-light, he'd felt good. The whole show had been great, as evidenced by the fact that when he'd asked Rachel if she wanted to sit down and take a rest, she'd just started singing even harder. Neither of them had sat once.

But he'd gotten something more too. Clarity, maybe, or the beginnings of it, when it came to that question he'd had about how to talk to their future kid about faith. Perhaps it was just about being aware of those things out there, like listening to live music with several thousand other people, that let you feel connected to something bigger than yourself, which in turn opened you up to both our shared humanity and the limits to what we, as humans, can fully understand.

Then there was the song Gretchen Grayson had dedicated to her two-year-old daughter, who, she informed the crowd, was asleep for the night on the tour bus.

"My ex-husband says I'm a bad influence," she'd said before she'd started playing. "I told him, 'God, I hope so.'"

The entire pavilion had erupted in cheers, and Will and Rachel had smiled at each other, the idea that being a good parent didn't mean being a perfect person seeming to hit them both as simple yet profound. It had been a warm, reassuring thought to drift off to.

Unfortunately, however, as is so often the case with the things that bring us comfort, 6:30 a.m. can make last night seem like a million years ago. Especially when you wake up to your wife talking hurriedly in her sleep. He was still groggy when he heard her say:

"I quit."

That's what Will thought he heard, anyway. It was surrounded by a lot of indistinguishable muttering, and he wasn't fully awake enough to trust that his ears had gotten it right.

Regardless, he was fully awake *now* and spent the next hour staring at the ceiling, thinking *Quit what?* while attempting to convince himself this further justified his recent engagement in some light identity theft.

"You awake?" Rachel asked at 7:30 a.m. when the Taylor Swift alarm finally rang, but not until Taylor had gotten through the first chorus. Rachel considered cutting her off any earlier to be a crime against nature and good taste.

"I've been up for the last hour trying to figure out how to teach our child to blow their nose," Will said. This was true too. It had been a real witch's brew of anxiety.

"That seems pressing."

"Like, how do you explain it to them? The only way to describe it is to say to blow air out of their nose, but that's like saying you have to breathe by breathing."

"Okay. No one teaches you how to breathe, either. So you just do it."

"Right. *You just do it.* But does blowing your nose work the same way? I don't think so. I think you have to learn how. Which means someone has to teach you. Ergo my concern. And if you don't learn, do you get, like, sinus infections or something?"

There was a pause while Rachel shifted under the covers so she could look right at him.

"You've really been thinking about this since six thirty?" she asked.

"Well, not the whole time. I was also thinking about the first night we ever spent together."

Also true. A lot can go through your head in an hour in the dark.

She smiled. "Halloween, junior year. I think I was ready like three months before you. Turns out all it took was a Princess Peach costume showing a non-Nintendo-approved amount of cleavage."

"If you'd known about my secret Bowser fetish, we wouldn't have made it past Labor Day."

"You know, you're incredibly lucky you found someone who knows what you just said wasn't serious."

"Fair point. But as great as our first time was—"

"Whoa," Rachel said, her nose crinkling skeptically. "Just great? I remember the look on your face afterwards. *Great* wishes it could elicit that kind of reaction."

Will pulled her in so she was right up against him, and she laughed as she hooked her right leg over his. He started to rub his hand gently back and forth over her leggings.

"Amazing," he said. "Fantastic. Life affirming. But in this case, I was actually thinking about the first time I slept over at your apartment. It was like one o'clock in the morning, and we had just finished watching *I Love You, Man.*"

"A criminally underrated film if there ever was one."

"Yes, your thoughts on Jason Segel are well documented. Anyway, we were both falling asleep on your couch, and when I got up to leave, you were like 'Why don't you just stay?' You were so out of it, I knew it wasn't about sex. It was about being near each other and not having to say goodbye. It felt . . . I don't know, thrilling. Like neither one of us wanted to be anywhere else in the world except there with each other. Is that corny?"

Rachel looked up at him from his chest. "A little. But it's also one of the most romantic things you've ever said to me. And that's saying something."

There was a flash in his mind, an impulse.

Ask her. Right now. Ask her if she's sure she doesn't want to at least take the interview.

But then Rachel leaned in to kiss him, with things progressing quickly from there, and his upright intentions vanished.

Now's not the right time, anyway, he told himself, his last thoughts before the feel of her completely overwhelmed him. *We've got this whole week first.*

Even after years of being together, when they were *together,* with hardly anything left to surprise them, they were just as focused on one another as they had been that first time on Halloween dressed as Peach and Obi-Wan Kenobi (the Ewan McGregor 2000s version). And in a hotel room where the only neighbors who might overhear you were people you'd never see again, if you ever saw them in the first place, that focus got a little . . . louder than usual.

Once things had quieted down, they lay back next to each other in a swirl of sheets. He reached out and rested his hand atop her wrist, but they remained quiet for a minute or two. Based on everything he'd ever read or heard, becoming parents wasn't typically a boon for any couple's sex life. So while he hoped she'd still look at him the same way after the baby arrived, the possibility that she wouldn't scared him a little.

"Well, I don't know about you," Will eventually said when he'd put the lid back on those fears, "but I thought that was *great.*"

Rachel pulled her pillow out from under her head and whacked him with it. "I'm taking a shower. And then I was promised brunch."

Will pushed the pillow off his face wearing a big grin, and she kissed him on the forehead before climbing out of bed and walking noiselessly across the carpeted floor toward the bathroom.

He unplugged his phone on the nightstand. He was going to see if he could put their name in ahead of time at any of the restaurants he'd looked at. At least that was his intention. Checking the phony email he had created for Rachel right after they'd been so intimate with one another somehow felt dirty. Besides, there'd been nothing when he'd looked when he went to the bathroom at the concert or when they'd gotten back to the room afterward, and now it was still too early on Sunday morning.

But he couldn't help himself. Which was why he saw Beatriz hadn't written back that morning.

It had been late Saturday night, California time.

Hi, Rachel—

So glad you wrote when you did—I think we can still make this work. I'll send you more details on Monday.

Thank you!
Beatriz

"Forgot the shampoo," Rachel said. Will hadn't noticed her reemerge into the little foyer area by the door and was startled enough to drop his phone into the comforter. The room was so dark from the hotel-grade curtains that she couldn't see his surprise or the guilty look on his face. "Oh, and I'm feeling waffles this morning, so please bear that in mind."

"Will do," he said, picking the phone up as she went back into the bathroom and shut the door. Until Beatriz had responded, what he'd done hadn't quite seemed real. As an IT guy, he knew that the amount people talked about email "eating" the messages they were either supposed to have sent or received grossly overstated how often this actually happened. And yet spam filters did exist, and if his email had been intercepted by Beatriz's, it would have been like he'd never sent it.

But once he knew she'd read it, it would make Rachel look bad if "she" *didn't* respond.

Rachel, who had been talking in her sleep about quitting what he could only assume was her job at the university.

He'd made his decision, and there was no escaping what he'd done now. His only option was to make it work.

Will waited until he heard the shower turn on before tapping out a quick response, as his wife, saying Sounds great—thank you.

Then he hit send and told himself not to look back.

After waffles at a place in the Third Ward and a CVS stop to load up on snacks, which went in the suddenly and weirdly significant Seurat tote, they left Milwaukee and headed for Mackinac Island. Under normal conditions, they would've crossed from Wisconsin into Michigan just inside the three-hour mark. However, they hit construction in the form of an extended lane closure and were about an hour behind that schedule.

"Where are we?" Rachel asked, having nodded off listening to an NPR podcast while they were stuck in traffic. "Is this the Upper Peninsula?"

"No, not yet," Will said. "But we're really close. And that's not just the GPS and the road signs talking. There was a billboard a minute ago for a motel with fish-cleaning stations, so I think it's safe to say we've left the trappings of big-city life far behind."

Rachel stretched her legs out from under her and put her feet back on the floor. "Progress, thy name is fish guts," she said with a sleepy smile.

They rode along in silence for several minutes as she continued to wake up, driving through Marinette, Wisconsin, and then crossing over a bridge and officially entering Michigan through Menominee.

"I have to admit I'm disappointed it's the same welcome sign as it is at the Ohio-Michigan border," Will said.

"Well, it is the same state."

"I know. But this feels like it should be more of a . . . a big to-do. Certainly a bigger to-do than what I can get outside Toledo."

"I think it is. Look at that view."

Rachel was right. Lake Michigan, specifically Green Bay, was outside of their windows now, and as they left the town on M-35, it became a rolling landscape off to the right of the car, jutting up disconcertingly close to the two-lane road at some points and then disappearing behind the tree line at others. It felt like they were passing through a nature preserve, just one with beach houses and cottages scattered here and there. Even the roadkill seemed majestic thanks to what they were pretty sure was a bald eagle diving down to scavenge it.

"Well, cell service is gone for the time being," Rachel said. "You wanna play the alphabet game?"

"Sure. But only because there are basically no signs anywhere on this road, and you can't claim victory unless you make it through *z*."

"*A* in *lake*," Rachel said without hesitation, pointing to the TIMMONS FAMILY LAKE HOUSE sign below what was presumably the Timmons's mailbox.

"This may have been a bad—" Will started. "Ooh, *a* in *place*, on that street sign."

"Nice. Hey, you know another thing I really loved about the concert? The way she talked about being a mom. Like, if she can be a touring musician and figure it out, I'm sure we can figure out day care. Maybe that sounds fan-girly, but it made all that's coming seem a little less intimidating."

Will smiled like he had in the stands the night before, not just because of the memory of that moment but also because Rachel sounded like someone rediscovering her confidence.

"*B* in *Escanaba*," Rachel said. Escanaba was the next main town they'd go through, and sure enough, there was a sign telling them it was 34 miles away. "I also got some ideas for my next tattoo."

He looked over at her, surprised. "I didn't know you wanted another tattoo."

"I kind of like the idea of having one on the inside of my left arm, but I've been coming up empty on inspiration. Until last night. She had that logo with the vines growing through her initials? Something like that, but maybe with flowers. I'd have to draw it to know for sure."

"Love it," he said, squeezing her hand and patting himself on the back once more for pushing her to get the first one. "Hey, while we're in Ann Arbor, maybe we could go to that place you wanted to try when we were in college."

"*C* in *Carters*."

"Damn these mailboxes!" Will said, which made her laugh.

"I love that idea," Rachel said, "but when my doctor saw my other one, she got this real disapproving look and made a point of telling me that it's not that pregnant women *can't* get tattoos, but she wouldn't necessarily *recommend* it. Now, as you know, normally with tattoos, I'm all about drawing the ire of my elders. But when it comes to the baby being healthy, I don't want to take any chances."

Will didn't know enough about tattooing to understand what the specific risks would be, or even if they were that significant. But he still felt like he should've known better, and just hearing the phrase "baby being healthy" began to take his mind down that path of what would happen if he or she wasn't, or if something happened to Rachel during birth. Again, he was short on specifics, the image he was imagining hazy, but it's often in the haze that foreboding and fear do their most effective work.

"*D* in *Dolly's*," Rachel said as a small bar wedged between the road and the water appeared in front of them. It was the first business they'd passed in miles.

"Maybe we could go back to Ann Arbor after the baby is born," Will said, trying to push through whatever he was picturing. "You know, so you could get the tattoo then."

"Yeah, that's an idea. Although it seems silly to go all that way just for that. Too bad it won't work this week. That would've been really cool."

Her mild disappointment coupled with the grip of his grim imagination called for something unexpected to combat them both.

Will glanced at her.

"Or," he said, dragging the one syllable out for dramatic effect.

"Uh-oh. I know that face. That's your I-have-an-idea-that-my-wife-is-going-to-roll-her-eyes-at-for-legitimate-reasons face."

"What if *I* get a tattoo at that place while we're in Ann Arbor?"

"You? Babe, no offense, but you can't look at the needle when you get your flu shot."

"First of all," he said, resting his wrists on the steering wheel and making a one with his index finger, "*B* in *bar*."

"From the Dolly's sign?" Rachel asked incredulously. "No. Disallowed."

"What? Why?"

"The sign is no longer in view, which violates the most basic rule of the alphabet game. Plus I already took the *d* from that sign, and you know how I feel about double-dipping."

"These are special M-35 rules on account of the fact that neither one of us will be able to finish before we get to Mackinac."

Rachel thought about that for a second. "Wanna make it interesting?" she said.

Will knew her mischievous smile meant there was a good chance he was going to come to regret this, but he couldn't resist her. Particularly not when she was clearly enjoying herself and the trip.

"What do you propose?"

"If I can get through the entire alphabet before we get to the hotel—playing by the real rules handed down to us by the alphabet-game gods, not your made-up blasphemy—then not only do you have to get the tattoo, but I get to pick what it says."

"Okay," he said, thinking out loud. "My *second of all* was going to be that I totally watched the needle at my last flu shot, so I think I'm more than prepared for the pain."

She smirked. "Sure you are."

"And in terms of you picking, you'd have to live with me having gotten whatever it is, so I'm fine with that. My only condition is that it's text only, so no pictures of, like, that bald eagle eating a squirrel."

"Agreed."

"And what do I get if you lose?"

She leaned across the center console and put her hand on the inside of his thigh. "Remember when I said I hadn't ruled out sex in the botanical gardens, and you assumed I was joking?" she whispered in his ear.

He swallowed hard. "Uh-huh."

"If I lose, it turns out I wasn't." She kissed his earlobe, and it took a heroic act of concentration for him to keep the car steady behind a pickup that looked like it belonged in a monster-truck rally.

"Deal," he managed to say.

"Oh, and, Will?" Rachel was still whispering.

"Yeah?"

"*E* on that truck's license plate," she said with a laugh as she pulled away.

Somehow in the midst of seducing him, Rachel had clocked another letter, a testament to just how likely it was Will was going to lose the bet and have to count on his wife's aversion to permanently and embarrassingly defacing the person she woke up next to every day. Given they were both distracted, it took them an extra beat to notice what else was on that truck, plastered prominently in its back window: a decal evoking a stick figure family, except the parents were a pair of assault rifles and the kids were three handguns. It was right next to a Jesus fish.

"Well, this took a depressing turn," Will said. "I mean, beyond my impending defeat."

Rachel sighed. "Just another day in the USA."

The conversation around guns had always boggled Will's mind a little bit. He didn't begrudge someone wanting to own a rifle to go hunting, but the argument that the Second Amendment gave people unfettered access to assemble their own armories seemed a particularly egregious violation of common sense. Nobody was making the case that civilians should have tanks and fighter planes (well, a few probably were), so how could anyone possibly think giving them automatic weapons was a good idea?

But as upsetting as it all was, it was too easy to feel like it was removed from his reality—until he knew he'd be a dad. Now every school shooting and lockdown drill he read about left him feeling like they'd miscalculated in thinking they could ever provide a kid with something resembling a childhood.

It was a lot to hang on one truck, whose plate was from out of state. And even if it had been local, it was still just one person's opinion. It would've been unfair to take it as speaking for an entire region.

Yet an uneasy silence fell over the car, exacerbated by the intermittent cell service. They were still in a dead zone, which pointed to the ways the alphabet game and their flirtation could give way to some truly unsettling circumstances within a matter of seconds.

"What do you think someone does if their car breaks down on this road?" Will asked, purposefully redirecting from the truck's decal and framing his question to be about some unknown third party rather than him and Rachel so as to keep the thought exercise from hitting too close to home with their current situation. "I've seen, like, one gas station this entire stretch, and assuming there's no phone, what's left? Walking up to someone's house and asking for help?"

"I guess so, yeah."

"Can you imagine that? Rolling the dice on who answers the front door and their views on firearms and/or trespassing? I'm stressed just thinking about it."

"Me too. And we're white. There's a lot less *Get Out* potential for us."

Will didn't know what to say to that. Because what was there to add? There were things that their son or daughter would one day ask about, and they'd have to try to answer to the best of their ability, knowing full well as they did that those answers would be unsatisfactory, never fitting neatly into a Disney movie–style resolution. It was different from wondering how you'd answer the God question. Because for all the advantages this country brought—and to be sure, Will knew there were many—these types of issues surfaced a sense of despair in him about the state of society and their kid's safety as a part of it.

He supposed he could've said *that* and shared more with Rachel about how nervous he was that he wasn't up to the challenge of parenting—you know, in terms that didn't involve tissues and boogers. He'd in fact felt himself edging up to that line just a minute or two earlier in the wake of seeing the truck.

But he couldn't bring himself to get the words out. He knew that might've made it easier, wrestling with the darkness together rather than letting it fester alone.

He just didn't know how to say he was scared their child might go to school one day and not come home and still tell people he was excited to be a dad.

They both watched the trees flashing by on either side of the road for a while. When they passed a homemade sign advertising fireworks for the upcoming Fourth of July holiday, Rachel didn't bother to call out the *f*. Will didn't think she'd given up on the game. If he'd had to guess, she just needed some time before she was ready to play again. It was a shared sentiment.

He reached for her hand, and they drove on.

Chapter 12

Taco Bell never tastes better than it does on a road trip. And when you're trying to regain the enthusiasm you had before the bumper sticker on a pickup truck pierced the joy of your vacation bubble, a crunchy taco made from Doritos can be downright magical.

"Fun fact," Will said, trying to lighten the mood as he wadded up the paper from taco two and prepared to unwrap taco three. It was late afternoon, and the dining room was empty except for the two of them. "That summer I worked at Cedar Point, a few of us went to the local Taco Bell, and they challenged me to chug a sixty-four-ounce mix of ten different fountain sodas in a minute and a half or less."

"And?" she asked.

"Eighty-eight seconds."

"Wow. I don't know whether I'm turned on or repulsed. What did you get for doing it?"

"They were supposed to cover my Taco Bell for a month. Of course, after I proceeded to throw up my Mexican Pizza through my nose, I never went back. Until today."

Rachel set her cup down abruptly. "Hold on. Are you saying this is the first time you've had Taco Bell—*since we were in college?*"

"That is what I'm saying."

"Oh my God. You think you know a person."

"Yeah, I'm not proud of it."

"So is this the best moment of your life right now? And rest assured, I'm not fishing for you to say it was our wedding or something."

"I'm eating a taco that's a large part Dorito, so I'd have to say yes."

"Not since college," she muttered as she stood to go to the bathroom. "Man."

While she was gone, Will decided to restart his phone, which still seemed to be glitching even though they'd reemerged from the wilderness. Once it turned back on, he got a text from his mom that she'd sent an hour before but that hadn't come through.

> You and Rachel should try a couples yoga class. There's one at my studio for people who are expecting, so I'm sure you could find one by you.

Will had written her from the CVS after brunch and said he was worried because Rachel had been talking in her sleep (he hadn't shared about what). He weighed his mom's suggestion for approximately half a second.

> Thanks, but I don't know that we're "couples yoga" kind of people.

He'd started searching for things for him and Rachel to do in Nashville back at the hotel in Milwaukee but hadn't found the right fit, so he picked it up again as he waited to see if his mom would write back. While he was driving, it'd occurred to him to try googling "Taylor Swift Nashville" and just see if anything interesting came up.

After a little scrolling through the most obvious results, he thought he'd found what he was looking for.

"All right," Rachel said, returning to the table, "let's get this show on the road. I'm about to show you how the person driving can still dominate the alphabet game."

Her words were playful, but Will could still sense in her tone some of the tension from the car. He felt it too. But this seemed like an opportunity to show that he could be a steadying force for them both— the kind that could let her tackle a new job in California even with all the other changes in their life.

"That remains to be seen," he said as he stood to carry their tray over to the trash. "Hey, what do you think of this for Nashville?" he asked, handing her his phone.

She read from the web page, her voice rising and expression brightening as she did. "'Join us on our rooftop bar on the last Saturday of each month for Swift Saturdays. All Taylor. All eras.'" She looked up at him and let out an exaggerated gasp. "'Costumes encouraged.'"

He laughed. Despair was no match for Taylor. "Is that a yes?"

"It's not only a yes, it's whatever the opposite of a hard pass is."

"A hard yes?"

"We'll keep workshopping it. In the meantime, I'll figure out what we're wearing."

"To be clear, I'm committing to going, not to the costume part."

Rachel gave his phone back to him. "We'll see."

"I'm serious, Rachel," he said, basking in the success of his plan to make her feel better as they walked out the door into the sun and toward the car.

"Uh-huh."

Successful or not, he really had no intention of wearing a costume, and he was about to repeat that when he was interrupted by his mom texting back about his rejection of couples' yoga.

You don't know what you're missing. :) Where are you now?

Just leaving a Taco Bell in Escanaba, Michigan.

She emphasized his text. Back on the horse—good for you. Love you. Drive safe.

Love you too.

"My mom thinks we should do couples' yoga for expectant moms," Will said once he and Rachel were in the car with her now behind the wheel.

"Ha—what did you say?"

"I told her I thought it was a fantastic idea."

"You're either lying or need to get busy impregnating someone else."

He put his hand to his chin like he was really mulling over women who might want to sleep with him.

"You know, it's not polite to tease a pregnant lady," she said. "I'm afraid I'm going to have to take the *g* in *morning*"—she pointed at the Taco Bell window—"as a penalty."

"What?!" he exclaimed in faux indignation. "You already took the *f* in *breakfast* from the same sign! You can't double-dip! What happened to playing by the 'real rules handed down to us by the alphabet-game gods'?"

"'Alphabet-game gods'?" she said, playing dumb. "Now you're just making things up."

They pulled out of the parking lot, their next stop a reasonably priced hotel on the beach in St. Ignace, which was right across the water from Mackinac Island. They had crossed from the central to the eastern time zone before they'd gotten to Escanaba—with Will silently hoping that the road sign proclaiming that transition contained the only *z* in the Upper Peninsula—and had a little over two hours to go. He still hadn't broached the subject of the ferry ride to the island with Rachel. If all else failed, and she really didn't want to get on the boat, there were beach chairs and a firepit plus a casino down the road, so he was confident they'd have things to do. He just couldn't tell his mom they'd missed the Rick Springfield show at the casino by one weekend. She'd be devastated.

About 20 minutes into an audiobook, they had left Escanaba behind and passed through another town called Gladstone—Rachel racking up nine more letters to his six in the process—before seemingly going back off the grid. The prospect of Will getting that tattoo was becoming more real, and it was true she had knocked out the notoriously difficult-to-find *j* before they'd made the foreboding transition back to two-lane roads, but all hope wasn't lost. She was on *q* now, and when he'd looked at the map while they were eating, he'd seen that Hiawatha National Forest was on their horizon. He figured all they had to do was make it there, and she'd be looking for that *q* forever.

What he didn't count on was the rural roadside marijuana dispensary.

"You gotta be kidding me," Will said, commenting on the sign before she did and knowing full well that, needing an *h*, he was powerless to do anything with it.

"What's that?" Rachel said. "Oh yes, I believe I *will* take the *q* in *Cannabis Queen*."

"Seriously, what are the odds? And more importantly, why is your turn signal on?"

"Bathroom. Pregnancy bladder, and who knows the next time we'll see somewhere we can stop. Plus I want to get their opinion on where you should get your tattoo. I'm thinking butt cheek, but I'm open to suggestions."

She eased the car into the gravel lot and parked in a spot right outside the door. The only sign that they weren't alone was a dusty Ford Fusion with a parade of Grateful Dead bears on it a few spaces over. He looked around at the impenetrable tree line and thought back to a true-crime documentary he'd watched once where marijuana farmers living in remote locations had these huge stockpiles of weapons to protect their crop. And possibly to hunt Sasquatch.

Glancing at Rachel's stomach, he pictured telling their child the world was a great, sensible place to live and to just ignore him as he researched options for them to relocate to Mars.

"Maybe I should go in with you," Will said. He wasn't crazy about her going alone, and that was a good mask to get him out of the car and away from the existential dread he experienced every time he remembered one of those marijuana farmers had been elected to Congress.

Seriously. Humans. What?

"Nah, I'll just be a minute," Rachel said as she unbuckled. "Besides, any place whose logo is the queen of hearts doing a bong rip has too much whimsy to be scary."

She left him the keys, and he leaned over to roll down her window before doing the same with his. The weather since they'd left Chicago had continued to be on the cool side for summer, especially now that they were as far north as they were, but it still wouldn't take long for the late-afternoon sun to make a closed-up car feel stuffy. Without cell service to distract him, he took a deep breath and listened to the sounds of the birds and tried to appreciate the view around him. They were inland enough that you couldn't see Lake Michigan, but it was a beautiful landscape nonetheless. No wonder the queen looked so relaxed.

Well, that, and the weed.

Will found himself staring at the sign. He wouldn't have called it a trigger because trigger implied trauma, and trauma was something horrible and gutting. It was just that word. *Queen.* It had this ability to take him back to one of the more indelible moments of his childhood, which was kind of a weird thing to be true for a kid from the States who grew up with little to no awareness of the royal family.

It was a Wednesday night near the end of second grade, and his dad had surprised him by telling him they were going to play hooky the next day so he could take Will to his first Cincinnati Reds baseball game.

It would be just the two of them. It was never just the two of them. Will had hardly slept that night because he'd been so excited.

They'd left first thing Thursday morning, and when they got to Cincinnati, his dad had announced, "Welcome to the Queen City!"

"Why do they call it that?" Will had asked.

"I don't know."

"Do you think it's for the queen of England?"

"I'm not sure."

"Why do they give cities nicknames anyway?"

"God, I don't know, okay?" his dad had said, starting to lose his patience, his voice sounding like it had that night at the restaurant when they couldn't sit in the bar. Even at eight years old, Will had been aware he'd been peppering him for the entire drive.

His cheeks had reddened. "Sorry, Dad."

"It's okay. Just, do you always have to ask so many damn questions? It's obnoxious."

Will had resolved then and there to not ask another question for the rest of the day. And he hadn't. They'd watched the game, they'd eaten hot dogs, his dad had taught him how to keep score. They'd laughed together and cheered together and even booed together at a particularly terrible strike call. When they'd gotten home late that night, Will fast asleep in his booster seat, his dad had carried him to bed. It was the best day of Will's young life.

Two weeks later, his dad was gone for good.

When that happened, Will's mind had gone straight back to their day at the ballpark, the one and only extended father-son time they had ever spent together. Everything had gone so great. They'd had so much fun. Except for when he'd asked his dad why they called Cincinnati the Queen City. To an eight-year-old Will, the conclusion was inescapable: his dad had left because he'd asked too many questions. Because he was obnoxious.

On the verge of becoming a father himself, Will didn't still believe that, of course. Not literally, anyway. Because deep down, he did still feel like he was what had driven his dad away, and that it had happened when he'd least expected things to go wrong. He knew he carried that with him. He knew it represented something horrible and gutting. He'd just never thought of it as trauma.

"Well, that was a delight," Rachel said, getting back into the car.

"You sound sincere, in which case their restroom exceeded all my expectations."

"Okay, so, confession." She turned in the driver's seat to face him, and it was then that he noticed she was holding a small brown paper bag. "I didn't actually need to go to the bathroom. I stopped to buy edibles."

"Can you take those when you're pregnant?"

"No. Well, I don't think so. Who knows. But they're not for me. They're for you."

Chapter 13

Will looked at her suspiciously. They had both smoked occasionally at parties in college, but neither had done it since, nor had they experimented with marijuana's suddenly socially acceptable cousin, the gummy.

"As soon as you said you were going to get a tattoo, I thought we should get you one to take beforehand," Rachel explained. "You know, to help ease your nerves."

"I didn't say I *was* going to get a tattoo. It was part of a bet, and you've still got a way to go."

"Oh, please. We both know it's happening. I'm unstoppable."

"So you say. But you still didn't need to stop here. I seem to recall Ann Arbor embracing weed long before all these other places started making it legal."

"That's true. But I decided to stop here," she said, pulling the pack of 10 out of the bag, "so you could take one right now. While we're driving."

"Excuse me?"

"C'mon," she teased him. "You're the one who said we don't know when we'll get to do stuff like this again. And when are you ever going to have the chance to take an edible in the car after we have a baby?"

"That wasn't exactly an item on my bucket list." He took it from her. "Although I'd be lying if I said I'm not a *little* intrigued."

What intrigued him was how happy this seemed to be making her, like they had somehow been transported back in time to when they had been younger and had had far fewer responsibilities.

"Of course you're intrigued," Rachel said. "It's a brilliant idea." She ripped open the resealable package and dropped a gummy in his hand. It wasn't much bigger than one of her Dots and was covered with flecks of sugar.

"Are you sure you're not doing this just so I'll be too stoned to tell whether you actually make it through z?"

"Possibly." Rachel's entire face seemed to twinkle with anticipation, and he knew resistance was futile.

"What the hell," he said, going to pop it in his mouth.

"Whoa, hold on," she said and grabbed his wrist. "This is ten milligrams, and the guy said since it's your first time, you should only eat half. Or even less. I still remember how loopy you got when you overdid it in college."

"Isn't that the whole point of getting high?" he asked as she let go. "Getting 'loopy'?"

"Hey, don't air quote me. And yes, it is, but you got, like, paranoid a couple of times when you smoked too much. Like when you thought that dog was a wolf and it was hunting you. We're just going for mellow. Like you're buzzed at a wedding or something."

"That dog was aggressive."

"That dog was a twenty-pound cockapoo."

"Look, if I'm going to do it, I'm going to do it. I mean, I'm not that old."

She laughed. "All right. Don't say I didn't try to warn you."

"Noted," he said, beginning to chew.

"How is it?"

"Pretty delicious, actually. Fruity."

He swallowed as she put the car into reverse. They started the audiobook again, and despite the package's promise that the gummies were fast acting, 15 minutes later, he was still tracking plot details and watching a seemingly infinite abundance of trees whiz by their windows just as he would've had he taken nothing. Rachel had managed to pick up an *r* and an *s* on two different HIAWATHA NATIONAL FOREST signs, which was also a bit of a buzzkill.

"I don't think it's doing anything," he said when the chapter they were listening to ended.

"It will."

Will picked up the bag again and studied it. He and Rachel had been together almost 15 years, they were about to have a baby together, and yet his urge to want to entertain her, to make her feel like their life defied the ordinary, was undeniable.

"I don't know," he said. "I could just have a high tolerance. It's not like I'm actually smoking anything."

"Everything I've ever heard or read about edibles says it will kick in. So did the guy at the store. You just have to give it some time."

He pulled the two sides of the bag apart at the resealable strip. "If I take a second one, will you give me editorial control over the tattoo?"

"One, that's a terrible idea. And two, not a chance."

"Eh, you're driving, and I'm sitting here doing nothing. What's the worst that could happen?"

And before she could stop him, a second 10-milligram gummy disappeared between his lips.

Rachel gave him a side-eye. "Well, this should be interesting."

"Just don't get your hopes up about skating by on the back end of the alphabet. Because I am *on* it."

"Can you get *on* the snack bag and pass me some of those peanut butter crackers?"

"Aren't you afraid you'll be depleting my supply for when the munchies hit?" he joked, turning in his seat so he could get to the Seurat tote in the back. After several seconds of digging around, he found the crackers, opened the plastic sleeve, and handed them to her.

"Thanks," she said. "Now can you restart the chapter? I didn't hear the last couple of minutes on account of your questionable decision-making."

Will backed the audiobook up and glanced at the RAV4's clock as he did it. 4:44 p.m. *Triple fours,* he thought for no reason in particular. He then resumed listening and taking in the scenery.

It was 4:53 p.m. before he spoke again.

"Rachel," he said in a loud whisper through gritted teeth.

"Uh-huh," she said, clearly bracing herself for whatever was about to come out of his mouth.

"I don't mean to alarm you," he said in a serious tone, "but I think that motorcycle may be headed right for us."

"You mean that motorcycle stopped on the shoulder on the other side of the road?"

"Oh God—you see it too. I was hoping I was just imagining it. Okay. Stay calm. Preparing evasive maneuvers."

Will rolled down his window and quickly unbuckled his seat belt so he could stick his head out like a dog.

"What the hell are you doing?" Rachel shouted over the suddenly amplified road noise.

They blew by the Harley and its owner checking something on his cell phone, and Will pulled his head back in. "Uh, saving our lives. It passed right through us. Didn't you feel it?"

"Feel what?"

"The draft of a cold breeze."

"Your head was out the window, Mr. I Don't Think It's Doing Anything. And the feeling-a-draft thing is for ghosts, not motorcycles."

"Wait." He stared at her. "I need you to be honest with me right now."

"Okay: yes, I am honestly regretting my decision to buy you edibles."

Will didn't have time for regrets. "Do you think it was . . . a ghost rider?" His voice dropped, and his tone got even more serious than before. "Like the Nicolas Cage film *Ghost Rider*?"

"What I think is that you need to close your eyes and just try to relax."

To his credit, he did close his eyes. Whether he relaxed was subject to interpretation. But he did feel less fearful about parenting for the time being.

"Do you believe in the multiverse, Rachel?"

"I believe I'm not going to hear any more of this book right now," she said, turning the sound system off.

"Like, do you think there's a universe where I'm having Doritos *right now* instead of at that Taco Bell?"

She wanted to be too annoyed to smile, but she couldn't help herself. "Why don't you tell me what you think, Will."

"Thank you for asking. I want to believe it's real. I mean, I want our son or daughter to live in a world where it's real. Because can you imagine? Two planes of existence, coexisting, in a perfect harmony of existence, where I'm eating Doritos—what's the word that's like *thrice* but means two times instead of three?"

"Do you mean *twice*?"

"Right. *Twice.* So clever. And think of it: twice the Doritos. I'm . . . I'm overcome with the sense of possibility."

"Are you crying?"

"It's just so beautiful, Rachel," he said, legit sniffling. "Behold, I've gazed upon the face of the Lord, and lo, he said unto them, nacho cheese . . . is . . . good!" He put his hand on her stomach. "I can't wait to tell the baby the news."

"You know, if they had taught us about nacho cheese in Catholic school, I might be more religious today. I've got some barbecue chips in the bag if you want them, though."

He moved to return to the tote. She was about to tell him he could open his eyes for this part since he had forgotten to do so and was groping emptily at the air, but he froze suddenly in the opening between their two seats.

"Everything okay there?" she asked.

"Right as rain," he said—because, pot. "Hey, you know what I wish?" His eyes were still closed as he asked the question.

"What's that?" Rachel said, once again unable to resist.

"That we could have the baby shower . . . *at Hogwarts.*"

"Like, at Universal Studios?"

"No, the *real* Hogwarts."

"There isn't a *real* Hogwarts."

Will's eyes popped back open. "But there is! How soon you forget the multiverse!"

"Ah, right. I do have a habit of doing that."

"We'd invite Dumbledore. Obviously. Harry and Hermione—but not Ron, he'd just make it about himself. Mario and Luigi."

"Wrong franchise, babe."

"Oh, it'd be a crossover sort of affair. It is *our* baby, after all. So Scorpion and Sub-Zero too. And I cannot stress this last part enough: every last Sasquatch we could find."

"Sasquatches, got it."

"Indeed." His voice got serious. "They owe me after everything I've sat through for them."

Will reset himself in his seat. He promptly engaged the dashboard in a staring contest.

"I still don't think it's doing anything," he observed after a good 30 seconds.

"Yeah, you know, I think you might be right," Rachel said, reaching over with her free right hand and grabbing the bag of gummies off his lap while he wasn't looking. She then transferred it to her left hand and stuffed it down in the storage compartment on the driver's door.

"Like, I don't think I've ever thought this clearly in my entire life," Will continued. "Picture it: our child, *our progeny*, will carry pieces of us both beyond our mortal limits. How wonderful. It's like I can see the concept of time. Have you ever *seen* time, Rachel?"

"I can't say that I have. But I do see a *t* on another HIAWATHA NATIONAL FOREST sign."

"Curses! Promise me you won't make me get this blasted tattoo on my buttocks."

"I think now that you've referred to them as buttocks, I'm morally obligated to do so."

For the second time in a matter of minutes, Will undid his belt, except now he got down on the floor and knelt. Or what passed for kneeling in the front seat of a moving compact SUV.

"Um, what is happening?"

"Rachel, I beseech you," he said, donning an English accent and clasping his hands in supplication. "Mar not my hindquarters. Promise me."

"This isn't safe. You need to get back in your seat."

"Not until you promise me!"

"Fine—I promise not to make you get the tattoo on your butt. Happy?"

"Huzzah!" he cheered before noticing he was stuck. His right shoulder had gotten wedged under the glove compartment, and he was having trouble extricating himself.

"Your beauty . . . ," he huffed, "is exceeded only by . . . your wisdom . . . which is exceeded . . . only by your . . . oww! . . . mercy. Ah. There."

When he had buckled himself back into his seat, Will looked at Rachel longingly.

"Psst," he said.

"Hi there."

"Want to know a secret?"

"Do I have a choice?"

"I'm the luckiest guy on earth. My wife is awesome. And she's going to be an awesome mom."

Even through his cloud, he could see this meant something to her. Maybe because he was too far gone for it to be anything but sincere. And he wasn't done.

"Just don't tell Rachel I got high without her. She'd be *so* pissed."

FOUR DAYS AGO

Chapter 14

Rachel considered the ferry as it pulled into the dock. Setting aside the obvious fact that it wasn't used for fishing, Will thought it bore a passing resemblance to the boat from *The Perfect Storm*, a detail he chose to keep to himself.

"So it's this or video poker at ten o'clock in the morning on a Monday?" she asked, eyes still on the ferry.

"I think they also have a hybrid version of craps," Will said.

"But we missed the 'Jessie's Girl' guy?"

"Rick Springfield, yes. By a week."

"Well, congratulations, babe," she said, looking up at him from behind a pair of aviators, the sun of a cloudless day dancing off the water behind her. "I think you've found the one scenario in which I'd choose boat."

She was smiling, so he knew she was playing up her hesitation some for his benefit. When they'd had coffee on the balcony outside their second-floor room that morning, they could see Mackinac Island on the not-too-distant horizon. It had been the perfect moment to break it to her that there was no bridge out there, as the island's proximity to the mainland combined with the calm and clear conditions had made it easy to see that this boat ride would be nothing like a cruise. Will could tell when he told her that Rachel wouldn't be looking forward to the ferry, but it also hadn't seemed like she'd thought it was that big of a deal. She had been far more invested in telling him about how, when they'd checked in the night before and discovered their TV was stuck on one channel, he had insisted that she not call to get it fixed because it had been airing the '70s classic *Smokey and the Bandit*.

"*Smokey and the Bandit?*" he had said, blowing on his latte. "That's weird. Burt Reynolds, right?"

"Yup."

"Huh. I've never even seen that movie."

"So you told me. But you were very high. And very into thirty-something Sally Field."

"I was?"

"Yes. At one point you asked me if it would be a misuse of your advanced understanding of the multiverse to go back to 1977 for the sole purpose of warning her not to make *Smokey and the Bandit II*."

"I've never seen that, either."

"Nor do I think that's how the multiverse works. But you were on a mission. Until you fell asleep like ten minutes later."

He'd cringed in the direction of the island. "Sorry."

"Mmm," she'd said, shaking her head and finishing a bite of the chocolate croissant she'd gotten with her decaf. "Don't be. I was riding high—no pun intended—from locking in your tattoo. I ordered room service and had a lovely dinner out here. Besides, when I handed you those gummies, I was basically the kid the D.A.R.E. cops warned you about, so I have to take some of the responsibility."

"I liked the stoner kids. They were less put together than the alpha jocks or the National Honor Society people or whatever. I could relate to that."

"Because of your dad?"

"Yeah. I mean, they were as smart or as athletic as anyone else, but I didn't feel so self-conscious around them. Like we all had our stuff that made us not quite fit the ideal image of a high school student. It made me feel less weird that I was the only guy on the basketball team whose dad had never seen him play."

His dad had played basketball in high school too. It would've been nice to have had him to talk to after the coach, at the first practice of Will's senior year, told the entire team, "If there's one thing last season taught us, it's that Easterly's not allowed to take important shots."

Then again, his dad had left, so maybe he would've agreed.

Rachel had chewed the last of the croissant before turning to look at Will.

"You know," she'd said, "people who peak in high school aren't very interesting adults."

"Aunt Katie actually said that to me once."

"What?"

"'Don't peak in high school.' It was at my graduation, which of course my dad didn't attend, either." He paused. "Seems like we should pass that on someday."

"Yes, we should."

It'd been so unlike him to feel this serene about parenthood (at least without anything harder than caffeine in his system) that he'd almost forgotten what she'd said about the tattoo.

"You really got through z? You're not just making that up because I can't remember?"

Rachel had stood. "What a thing to ask the mother of your child. And, hey, at least with this, there's no hangover." She'd kissed him on top of his head and opened the balcony's sliding door.

"That wasn't a no," he'd said, and she'd laughed from inside their room.

She'd been relaxed all the way through them getting dressed, driving to and parking at the dock, and then joking about the casino when the boat had come into view. But it wasn't until they boarded the ferry and staked their claim to two seats on the open-air top deck that he felt like the second date on their itinerary was cleared for metaphorical takeoff.

That wasn't to say Rachel didn't have her doubts. As soon as the engines lurched to life and they were warned of the chance for spray from the lake, she started twisting a strand of hair—the one that happened to be purple at the moment—around and around with her pinkie finger in a way she did only when she was nervous. Will had mentioned this habit to her once, and she wasn't even consciously aware that she did it.

He put his hand on her free one and started to massage the back of it with his thumb. She didn't say anything, but by the time the boat started to move away from the dock, the hair twirling had stopped.

"Tell me something that will distract me," she said.

"Hmm. Oh, okay: I don't think there are any cars on the island. Like at all. It's all bikes and horses."

"I like horses."

"I know you do."

"They have the good sense not to get on boats."

"Unlike that couple across the aisle," he said, jerking his head toward the people all the way to their left at the far end of the row, where they were seated up against the boat's railing. He lowered his voice to a normal speaking volume, which was like a whisper compared to the noise from the water and the rush of the wind whipping across their faces. "I think they're breaking up."

Rachel leaned forward subtly to look. "How can you tell?"

Will explained how he hadn't heard (obviously) what the nearer of the two women had said first, but that he'd had a good view of the other's face, and he was almost positive he'd read her lips saying "On our anniversary?" before she'd proceeded to glare at her partner with equal parts disgust and disbelief. That had been followed by some angry gesturing at what appeared to be the boat itself, suggesting she was pointing out the lunacy of dumping someone shortly after you've boarded a ferry with them, let alone when the two of you are headed to an island with unusually limited transportation options for escaping one another.

Rachel leaned back. "Wow. So what's the move when you go ashore? Storm off on a mountain bike or wait around for a horse-drawn carriage to clip-clop you away?"

They debated that and whether one of the women couldn't just stay on the boat and go back to St. Ignace. It felt like the best solution, except that Will and Rachel agreed the woman being dumped absolutely should get to pick who stayed on and who got off, and neither of them trusted the woman ending it on a boat—*on their anniversary*—to be self-aware enough for that.

But as darkly engrossing as rubbernecking the end of a relationship can be, Will could feel his and Rachel's conversation starting to lose steam while they were still out in open water. He briefly entertained the idea of pointing out the Mackinac Bridge, which had emerged behind them and to the right as they pulled away from land. Then again, something that big, looking as small as it did right then, with nothing but water in between them and it? He decided it maybe wasn't the best thing to call a reluctant boater's attention to.

What awaited him a few hundred miles on the other side of the bridge in Ann Arbor would work, though.

"So tell me about this tattoo I'm apparently getting," he said when the breakup had gone unremarked upon for 30 seconds and Rachel had restrengthened her grip on his hand.

"Well, there are a number of contenders," she said, and he could feel some of her tension releasing again. "Tell me: What do you think of 'Rachel, I don't think it's doing anything'?"

She found that hilarious and proceeded to share more of her ideas, ranging from a confounding Tolkien line about hobbits to the lyrics of Carly Rae Jepsen's "Call Me Maybe" to "Rachel is a boss" written in binary code.

"I'd have to do some research for that one," she admitted.

"Why do I feel like our entire relationship was a long con all leading to you picking out this tattoo?"

Given his machinations with Creative Vices, he instantly regretted his use of the term *long con*, but she had no way of knowing that, laughing and leaning into him and briefly resting her head on his shoulder. She then sat back up, looking past the breakup couple, over the railing, and out to Mackinac Island, whose shores had come into full view off the ferry's port side.

"Whoa, what is that?" Rachel asked.

Will followed her gaze. He recognized the building from his internet searching. "I think it's the Grand Hotel." The enormous white structure commanded the coastline in a way that announced to anyone passing by that its name wasn't a misnomer. "Full disclosure, if this were actually *Date Me Now!*, that's where we'd be staying."

"That's okay, babe. Trust me: making sure we can afford to get the full Rascal Flatts discography on your upper thigh is my top priority."

He pulled his hand away, pretending to be annoyed, and she grabbed it back, laughing again. They rode the rest of the way into the bay where they would disembark, idly making plans for their hours on the island. There was an old military fort that had been used by both the British and American armies, which was supposed to be pretty cool, and they both felt like they should suggest visiting it as something they could do even as they each made it clear that they had no real desire to do so. There was also a state park and plenty of trails, and if Rachel hadn't been pregnant, they might have taken a longer look at the horseback riding. But after a full day in the car, a significant portion of which they had spent driving through forest, keeping to the downtown area with its shops and restaurants felt like just the right speed.

The ferry slid into a dock behind a two-story building with a reddish-orange awning, on the other side of which was Main Street. Out of habit, Will went to stand as soon as they were cleared to get off, but Rachel tapped his arm and nodded her head toward the women, whose moment of truth had arrived. Without the wind and water noise, their parting words to each other were easy to hear.

"Will I still see you for dinner?" the one who had dumped the other said.

"Will you still see me for dinner? Are you crazy?"

"C'mon. We've been looking forward to the Marquise for months. It might be a nice way to, you know, say goodbye."

"You're unbelievable." She got up and slung her bag over her shoulder. "Sure, Annie, see you at five o'clock. If you get there before me, the table's under your name, although if they can't find it, tell them to try looking under *bad bangs*."

The unnamed woman stormed off while who they now knew was Annie stayed in her seat, self-consciously touching her hair. Will and Rachel waited several seconds and then exited into the center aisle themselves. They did their best not to make eye contact, for all of their sakes, but that didn't stop Annie from sort of shrugging as if to say "Who could've seen that coming?"

"I want to preface what I'm about to propose by acknowledging that I'm firmly team Lady's Name We Never Got," Rachel said after they stepped off the boat onto the dock and headed for one of the signs directing them to the street. "And in no way do I mean to minimize what she's going through, even if it does seem likely she's dodged a bullet in the long run."

She paused, almost like she was observing a moment of silence for their failed relationship before continuing.

"That being said, it occurs to me that there's now a table available at this Marquise place, and we just so happen to know both the time and the name it's under."

Will slowed his pace, and Rachel slowed with him. "What are you suggesting?" he asked.

"I'm *suggesting* that at five o'clock this evening, my good sir, your wife, *Annie*"—she stopped to curtsy—"is going to take you to dinner at the best restaurant in town."

As happy as her excitement made him, his enthusiasm for the plan did not match hers.

"Can we even do that?"

"Why not?"

"I don't know. Couldn't we get in trouble or something?"

"With who? The restaurant police?"

When she put it that way, it did seem pretty low risk. Especially for someone who'd seen his way to sending fake emails from his wife.

Chapter 15

No sooner had they stepped onto Main Street than they saw a carriage—really more of an open-air wagon with a roof and several rows of bench seats—hitched to two large horses, which meant Rachel was gone. She went straight to the driver and asked if she could pet them, quickly progressing from rubbing the bridges of their noses with her hands to nuzzling cheek to cheek with the one who seemed especially receptive to her. Logic dictated that the carrots the driver gave her to feed them had something to do with their instant connection, but Will believed it would've been impossible for the horse not to pick up on how much genuine affection this human was displaying.

While Rachel loved on her new friends, he hung back and made a quick email check. Beatriz had said she'd write back that day, but with the three-hour time difference, there was a good chance she wasn't even at work yet. Still, he wanted to verify there was nothing there, no details officially confirming Rachel's interview that would officially start the countdown to when he had no choice but to tell her.

The relief he instinctively felt upon seeing that the inbox was empty made him nervous for what he'd feel when it wasn't.

He put his phone away and refocused on getting a sense of the downtown. The no-car thing was apparent immediately. Most people stuck to the sidewalks on either side of the street, but there was also a good amount of drifting out into what anywhere else would've been two lanes of traffic. Here, all you had to navigate as a pedestrian were the horses and the bikes. So many bikes, in fact, that they had their own designated parking areas along the curbs. These strips were much narrower than what you'd get for parallel parking cars, and unlike when trying to squeeze in between an F-150 and a Prius, double- and triple-parking with the bikes seemed to be not only tolerated but expected.

The ferry had deposited them on one edge of downtown, such that if they went left, the stores and restaurants would soon give way to historic homes and inns and views of the lake—Huron in this case, as the Straits of Mackinac between the Upper and Lower Peninsulas mark the transition from Lake Michigan. But if they went right, the colorful downtown buildings, no more than a few stories high, would close them in on either side. It was sunny and warm that day, but Will still thought it looked like a town you might find in a snow globe.

Rachel started back toward him, and he noticed the Marquise's sign not that far behind her. He'd missed it the first time he'd glanced in that direction, but it was right where the downtown started to thin out, probably with some sort of seating on the water that he couldn't see from where they were standing.

"Okay," Rachel said when she rejoined him on the sidewalk, "their names are Crayola and Pastel, and they're brothers, and I want them."

"How do they feel about apartment living?"

"Surprisingly open, although they were a little concerned about the bathroom situation."

There was a spot on the street a few yards away that had yet to be cleaned, illustrating the reasonableness of this concern.

"Smart animals," he said.

"Told you."

Will and Rachel began walking, joining the crowd casually making its way along Main Street, which sloped gently upward as they went. This was the first pass through, so it was something of a window-shopping reconnaissance mission as they spied the shops they might want to return to. Rachel mentioned perhaps getting a new pair of Birkenstocks, Will pointed out a small bookstore that looked cool—that sort of thing. The number of bike-rental locations per capita was predictably higher than anything they'd ever seen. But make no mistake:

This was a confectionery town.

"I feel like there's a lot of fudge," Will said.

"Like *a lot* a lot of fudge."

They kept going, eventually emerging from the downtown area on the other side at a large green space, where a steep hill to the left led up to Fort Mackinac. They remarked on what a great view it must be from up there while silently congratulating each other on being the type of people who would never subject themselves to that extreme of a climb simply to look at some water.

Past the fort, they followed the road through a mix of smaller hotels and private residences all the way down to the Mission Point District, where a resort marked the spot that the shoreline started to curve back in the opposite direction. Knowing that if they didn't turn around here, they'd end up on the other side of the island, with a state park between them and all the places enticing them to spend their money in a montage of retail frivolity, they stepped off the sidewalk onto a patch of grass under a tree and stopped.

"What do you think?" Will said.

"It really is beautiful here. And so . . . I don't know . . . chill. Even with people everywhere."

"I had the same thought. I think it's the lack of cars. It's like literally not being able to rush off anywhere forces everyone to decompress more than even on a normal vacation. You could probably walk up to a total stranger and just start chatting with them about the best place to buy your fudge."

"Nowhere should be that chill."

"Hey, with great fudge comes great potential for awkward conversations," he said, checking his phone. It was a little after 11:00 a.m., so they decided to head back and find somewhere to grab lunch.

"I can get on board with all these dogs, though," Rachel said after they'd stepped around a pack of three Labs with two humans who were chatting. Another benefit of not having any cars around was that it did seemingly bring the dogs out in full force. In addition to their shared aversion to steep climbs with fleeting rewards, Will and Rachel subscribed to the theory that the higher the proportion of dogs to people in a place, the better its mojo.

Don't peak in high school. Dogs are good. At least he knew a couple of things to teach this kid.

"You know," he said, "since the horses expressed their reservations about our facilities, maybe we could get a dog instead."

"I'd love that, but we can't have something like a GSP in an apartment." Rachel had grown up with a German shorthaired pointer. GSPs were a highly intelligent, midsize hunting breed with close to an unlimited reservoir of energy, and although her family didn't hunt, Rachel measured every other type of dog by her memories of Pedey.

"Maybe we could get something a little less"—Will knew he had to be careful—"bouncy."

"Eh, I don't know," she said, doing her best to conceal the true extent of her skepticism. "I guess I'd rather wait until we can get a bigger dog. And besides, taking one on when I'm about to have a baby doesn't sound like our best idea. Not unlike trying to reinvent our lives in California."

The thought of his emails with Beatriz exploded across his mind and temporarily halted all other brain function. He was just grateful his legs kept working and ensured he stayed upright.

It occurred to him that his panic then and his relief at the lack of email a little earlier were as telling of signs as any that the bad of what he was doing would outweigh any potential good, that he should tell her right then and there what he had been up to and pull the plug on the whole operation.

The Clemens house and the concert had already made her so happy. They'd had great—sorry, *amazing*—sex at their hotel, and he'd gotten so high in the car he'd advocated for a baby shower at the "real" Hogwarts. They'd even found little pockets of peace about what it would mean to be someone's parents. Come clean now, and hopefully, they could just enjoy the rest of this unusually cool week he had planned for them.

But he couldn't do that. It would've required admitting they weren't going to have the life he knew Rachel deserved. That she was stuck in her boring job that he was reasonably sure she had had a dream about quitting. That outside of a week like this, their life might start feeling boring too—which would give them even more time to focus on all they didn't know about parenting. And if she were going to be upset that he'd interfered regardless, shouldn't he at least have confirmed the interview before telling her about it?

"I mean, it's California, not Antarctica," he said, regaining his mental footing enough to try to leverage some of the trip's positive momentum into an acknowledgment that pursuing this job wouldn't be the most preposterous thing ever. She'd said something similar about not *reinventing* things when she'd passed up New York after college. "It's not like you'd have to figure out how to take a sled dog to the office or something."

She laughed, which was encouraging. So was her not seeming suspicious of him bringing it up.

"No work talk," Rachel said.

"You started it."

"You're right—my bad. How about pizza for lunch? I feel like I should get fish while we're here, but the Marquise sounds fancy, so I think I'm going to save that for tonight."

"Yeah, sure. I saw a place when we were walking through."

They came up behind an elderly couple who were holding hands and walking especially slowly, so they veered out into the street to go around. When they got back onto the sidewalk, Rachel put one hand over her heart and grabbed Will's with the other.

"How adorable was that?" she said. "Do you think we'll be like that when we're that old?"

"Of course." He hoped he sounded convincing. Between worrying about how Rachel was going to react to him meddling in her career and worrying about five years from now if she was still at her university job because he didn't meddle, he conceded to himself a more appropriate response might've been "Assuming we're still together." Rachel would've no doubt laughed at that, taking it as another joke. Which it was.

Except when it felt like it wasn't.

"Speaking of pizza, do you remember talking about that last night?" Rachel asked.

"Pizza? No, I think that must be in the *Smokey and the Bandit* file."

"It was actually before we got to the hotel. You were trying to explain to me how much better pizza is than hot dogs."

Will attempted, and struggled, to give his high self the benefit of the doubt. "I mean, clearly pizza *is* better than hot dogs. But it seems like a strange thing to have an impassioned opinion about."

"Oh, it was. But you were adamant. 'It's gooey *and* cheesy, Rachel; don't you see?'"

"Did I say what the *difference* between gooey and cheesy was?"

"No, that remained a mystery. But when I asked you why you had such strong feelings on all this, you mentioned a phone call."

"A phone call?" he asked once they had made it past a family reunion disjointedly debating where they could eat that could seat all of them.

"Yeah." Rachel pulled her hand away. Will looked at her. "Sorry," she said. "Too sweaty."

"So much for our undying love."

"I'll always carry you . . . in here," she said, repeating her touch of the heart but with a healthy dose of schmaltz. "Anyway, you said your dad called you when you turned ten, and when he asked you what you did for your birthday, you told him your mom and Aunt Katie took you out for pizza."

"Ha, yeah. There was an air hockey table there, and the two of them took turns playing me for like an hour after we finished eating."

"You didn't say that. But you did call him a bastard and tell me he had the nerve to go 'Pizza's no Reds dog, right?'"

Will went to respond. To remark that he hadn't thought about that in years. To marvel yet again over how awful his dad could be or dismiss him with a simple "What a dick." To reaffirm his appreciation for all the ways his mom and aunt had tried to make Will feel special even when the world was telling him he should feel anything but.

But just then, it was all a little too much.

"You didn't deserve that, Will," Rachel said quietly after he hadn't spoken in a while. "None of what he did. None of it was you."

"I know."

"And none of it *is* you."

"I know."

"You say that, but sometimes I don't think you really believe it."

He got quiet again, not understanding how she could have such faith in him. Presumably his dad hadn't set out to be a bad father. He just was.

Then there was his sister- and brother-in-law. Isa's miscarriage had been two years before. She'd lost the baby when she was six months pregnant. First there was the heartbreak, which had been bad enough on its own. They'd just put the crib together the weekend before they found out. It had taken months for them to bring themselves to take it back apart.

And in those months, something had changed between her and Owen too. It wasn't like either of them had blamed the other for what had happened. It was more that some sort of fundamental optimism about their life together, their marriage itself, had been snuffed out. Will had never thought they were a great match for one another, but they'd worked. Or at least they had. Now she was trying to convince him to go to marriage counseling, and he was refusing.

Will remembered his dad telling his mom the same thing a few months before he'd left.

The crowds were growing thicker the closer he and Rachel got back to downtown, and there were plenty of things to see and snippets of conversation to overhear. They spent several hundred feet on either side of a glittering white Catholic church looking for an opening to get around a man, in a Declaration of Independence T-shirt, lecturing his reluctant companions on the finer points of the surrounding architecture, which included misidentifying the church as a cathedral.

The group eventually turned down a side street, and Rachel and Will were able to resume moving at an average pace. Without saying anything, she took his hand again.

"I thought it was too sweaty," he said.

"It is." She looked over at him. "But you're worth it."

Chapter 16

"That has to be the Mackinac Bridge over there, right?" Rachel said, pointing off in the direction of about two o'clock. After lunch, she and Will had walked the other way out of the downtown area, following the sidewalk as it became a wooden boardwalk and started to wind past a stretch of historic homes. The houses came in an array of colors, and they had an unimpeded view of a lake that in every way resembled an ocean when you were sitting on a big white rock looking out at it, as Will and Rachel were right then.

"Yes," he said. "I actually saw it when we were on the ferry but didn't say anything because I thought a five-mile-long suspension bridge appearing that small in the distance would make you feel like we were farther away from land than we really were."

"You probably weren't wrong about that."

"Honestly, that's what I'm nervous about."

"What? Driving over the bridge?"

"Yeah. The ferry goes down, you get on a lifeboat and get picked up by the Coast Guard, no problem. But if you go off that bridge, I think you're praying for a heart attack to kill you before you hit the water."

"I bet you say that to all the girls," Rachel said, nudging his foot with hers.

"Ha, what?"

"Nothing. I just didn't expect this conversation to transition so seamlessly from 'Hey, look at that feat of human engineering' to you preparing yourself for entombment in a watery grave."

High Will, seeing the concept of time, had thought his child would help him and Rachel achieve a sort of immortality. Sober Will was back to wondering how people didn't die *more* often, which was not comforting at all when you were about to be responsible for someone's survival for the next 18 years.

"Yeah, I guess that was a little bleak," he said, thinking it best not to offer any more on the subject.

"It's cool. When we were driving last night, I pulled over in this little lookout area for you to get some fresh air by the water, and you were convinced the waves were trying to talk to you, so this is reassuringly morbid."

"Oh wow. I think I remember that."

"All things considered, I think we should eighty-six the you-taking-edibles-before-your-tattoo plan."

Will looked from the lake to Rachel, his eyebrows rising above his sunglasses, but her gaze stayed on the water.

"Don't get any ideas," she said. "The tattoo's still happening. Just not the gummified weed."

"You're ruthless," he said.

"You love it."

They sat there a long time, neither feeling a need to move. The beach was rocky and not the kind you'd take off your shoes to walk along, and they hadn't had a strong desire to keep walking in the first place. Lunch had been good—so good that they had both eaten more than they'd intended, making not moving all the more appealing. The rock wasn't the most comfortable perch, but they had taken the souvenir T-shirts they'd bought at the pizza place and turned them into makeshift seat cushions. It would've been a great spot to let the rhythms of the big lake hypnotize you for a while if you weren't waiting for a woman you'd never met to write you back about a job because she thought you were your wife.

The ferry was passing by on one of its many trips back and forth throughout the day when Rachel felt a text buzz on her watch. She was scrolling and reading for a while, and when she was done and looked back out at the water, her lips were pursed and her relaxed posture had stiffened.

Beatriz texted her instead of emailing, Will thought, only then registering that just because he hadn't seen Rachel give Rochelle's assistant her phone number didn't mean Beatriz wouldn't have it. *This is it. I'm done.*

"Everything okay?" he asked, working very hard at sounding unfazed.

"What? Oh yeah. Just texts from my mom and my sister. Mom sent me a link to an article about women quitting their jobs to stay home with their babies, which I know I wouldn't be getting if she and my dad thought I had"—she contorted her face to look as repressed as her parents—"some *serious career* worth staying for."

Will channeled what had been stress into righteous indignation.

"Do they also plan to give me a raise to make up for the very real lost income from your supposedly not real job?" Will and Rachel were comfortable enough financially that this trip, even with the occasional indulgences, was doable, but not so comfortable that they could just lop off one of their salaries.

"I know, right? And then my sister, she and Owen were over there for dinner, and Mom and Dad told her while it wasn't the way they *expected* it, how *relieved* they are they're *finally* going to be grandparents. You know, like if Isa couldn't come through for them, at least derelict daughter number two could."

"That's pretty awful," Will said. "Even by their standards."

"I mean, my first reaction is to be horrified for my sister. They talk about it like it wasn't the most traumatic thing she's ever gone through, or that it hasn't completely screwed up her marriage. And then on top of that, it's like 'Praise the Lord, Rachel may be a dippy artist, but she has opened her eyes and accepted her child-rearing destiny.' Plus, Isa was farther along than I am when she lost the baby! What if I have a miscarriage? Then what?"

The word hit Will like an icicle through his heart. He could not talk to Rachel about miscarriages. Not without telling her about the dream he'd had the night before he'd decided to paint the nursery and opening up his bigger box of fears. For that reason alone, it was a relief to have her parents' gross insensitivity to focus on.

"I don't think I ever told you this," Will said, "but when I danced with Aunt Katie at our wedding, she said something about your dad's toast, and I told her I thought your parents weren't that crazy about me. She asked me why I'd say that, and I said it was just a vibe I'd gotten."

Rachel didn't try to counter him on this, and he didn't take offense. Will knew that she loved her parents, and like everybody does at some level, she wanted their approval. But she wanted it for who she was, not for who they wanted her to be, so Will existing outside whatever straitlaced narrative they had constructed for her life was actually a source of pride for him. Especially because, in pretty much every way, he considered himself basically a run-of-the-mill, conventional person. He was an IT guy, for God's sake.

"You encouraging me to get the tattoo probably didn't help," Rachel said, admiring her arm. "Or, you know, taking my virginity—*outside the bonds of wedlock*."

"Uh, what?"

"Oh, they totally think you were my first."

"Why would they think that?"

"Because you were the first guy I ever lived with. That was also a strike against you, by the way."

"So, just to be clear," Will said, "I spent most of my weekends in high school playing Xbox while you were busy having sex with Seth on school grounds, and now your parents hate me for sleeping with you before we got married?"

"C'mon, that's not fair. They don't hate you."

Rachel seemed like she had something else to say, so Will waited.

"They do still kind of love Seth, though," she added with a laugh.

"You're the worst," he said, but he was smiling, and for the two of them, that combo was the equivalent of an *I love you.* "Anyway, when I said that to Aunt Katie, she told me everyone might be the star in their own stories, but that from what she'd observed at the rehearsal dinner and the wedding, your parents wanted their own biopic. Like, it was all about them. She said that with people like that, you can never do enough to please them, so you shouldn't waste your time trying."

Rachel mulled that over while a pack of people heading into town passed behind them on the boardwalk.

"Sounds like she could've been talking about your dad too," she said when the lap of the waves was again the only noise. "You know?"

"I never really thought about it that way. But yeah, I guess you're right."

"Do you ever wish you could talk to her about everything with the baby? I know she didn't have kids, but she always had such a good perspective."

"I mean, yeah. Her dying was like losing a parent. And you're supposed to be able to ask your parents about being a parent."

Including about all the stuff that scares you, he kept to himself.

"And Katie would've been an amazing mom," he went on. "She had this ability to cut through the noise and tell you just what you needed to hear even when you didn't realize you needed to hear it."

"Case in point: that dance at our wedding."

Despite being almost right on top of the lake, they had gotten hot sitting there in the sun, and Rachel pulled out a sparkling water she'd bought in a coffee shop on Main Street. The crack of the can opening sounded especially crisp against the background static of the waves. She took a sip and then offered him one.

"Thanks," Will said after taking a drink and passing the can back.

"So what do you think she would've told you?" Rachel asked once she'd taken another sip. "You know, if she were sitting here right now."

It was a simple enough question. One that he had parried once by saying what a great mother his aunt would've been. But whether Rachel had seen through that or was simply that curious, she had asked again, and Will needed a better answer. He couldn't tell her what he would've wanted, would've counted on, his aunt to say—namely, that his fears he'd take after his dad were completely unfounded. Because that kind of confession would also entail admitting how ill equipped he felt to be a dad and how scared he was that something was going to go wrong.

But that was anxiety Will was unwilling to put on Rachel, especially after she had expressed her own uncertainty about what was awaiting them once the baby arrived. He had a responsibility to build her up, not add to the things bringing her down. So he deflected in a way he hoped wasn't too obvious.

"She would've made sure I knew that just because you're the one having the baby, that doesn't mean you should have to do more than me once the baby is born," he said. He took a smooth stone sitting atop their rock and flung it toward the lake with a snap of the wrist, trying to skip it. It hit three times before disappearing below the surface of the water. "Oh, and if I ever referred to watching our child as *babysitting*, she would've dropped me like she did that sorority sister."

That made Rachel laugh. "She would've been right to," Rachel said. "Same goes for saying '*We're* pregnant.' But if you can figure out a way to split breastfeeding fifty-fifty, please don't hesitate to let me know."

"It really is okay if you don't want to do that," Will said. Seeing as it had come up several times in the last few days, he could tell that the decision was weighing on her and saw another opportunity to be for her what he couldn't be for himself: someone convinced they had it all under control. "No one would judge you for it."

She turned to look at him. He couldn't see her eyes behind the dark lenses, but her face nevertheless managed to convey her opinion of what he'd just said.

"Have you ever *talked* to other women about this?" Rachel asked.

"Even if I had, which I haven't, I really don't think *yes* is the answer you want to hear there."

"If I choose not to breastfeed," she said, not acknowledging his joke this time, "I will be judged nine ways to Sunday. Hell, they'll think I'm a monster if I *do* breastfeed but don't do it long enough, or don't think it's the most magical, heartwarming experience of my entire life."

"Well, you're talking about people like Gwen, who, based on what we saw in that house, may very well be a sociopath."

"It's *a lot* more people than you think," Rachel said, her tone staying sober. "Including my mother. My sister too."

"Isa? Really?"

"Oh, don't get me wrong; she wouldn't say anything, and she'd probably feel terrible that she was even thinking it. But she was so enamored with all things baby that there's no way she wouldn't feel like I was taking it all for granted or something. And honestly? There's a part of me that feels like I need to do it for her. Like I'd be insulting her otherwise."

"I mean, I love your sister," Will said, choosing his words as carefully as he could, "and what happened to her and Owen was awful. I also can't pretend I understand the pressures you're feeling right now.

"But in the end, this isn't about Isa. Or anyone else. It's about us. And really, it's about you—whatever you want to do and feel is the best decision. You're the mom, and you're going to be amazing at being a mom, regardless of how you choose to feed our child the first few months of their life."

Rachel chuckled soundlessly to herself. "I wish I had your confidence."

I wish I had it too, he thought.

"You're pretty easy to have confidence in," he said.

"Well, I'm glad one of us feels that way. But you know it's okay if you want to freak out a little bit about everything, too, right? It's pretty normal."

Since sometime around their second date at the botanical gardens, Will had known that Rachel Armas deserved far more than *pretty normal*. So he said, "Thanks, babe, I appreciate that," and squeezed her hand.

They went back to watching the water, which lasted until a college-aged guy sat down on the grassy embankment behind them to carry on a loud phone conversation. He was talking to someone named Lane, who after some unavoidable eavesdropping, Will and Rachel determined to be the kid's significant other. It sounded like Lane was unhappy that the guy sitting on the grass had chosen to spend his summer working on the island rather than being wherever Lane was.

"God, Lane," he barked into his phone, "you're like . . . you're like a vending machine that only sells bullshit."

With that, he hung up angrily and stormed back toward town.

Will and Rachel waited until he was out of earshot. "That is . . . quite the image," Will said.

"Yeah. I think we can cross Lane off the baby-name list now. I'm never going to unhear 'vending machine of bullshit.'"

She offered him one last sip of the sparkling water, then finished what was left and dropped the empty can into her bag. They gathered up the shirts they'd been sitting on and put those in the bag, as well, and began following the college kid along the boardwalk at a respectable distance. Their plan had been to do some shopping once they'd had their fill of watching the boats go by, and the conversation about their families didn't seem to have dulled her enthusiasm for that idea, so Will was glad he hadn't complicated things by opening up any more than he had.

Rachel nominated the Birkenstock store as their first stop. She'd had her eye on a pair of metallic gold ones online for the last several weeks and had so far resisted buying them, but they felt like the perfect vacation purchase if they were in stock.

While she went in there, Will hit up a nearby bookstore. He wasn't looking for anything in particular but soon found himself lingering at a display devoted to the latest Emily Henry novel. Her books were often categorized as romance, which did make him a little self-conscious. However, when you'd watched your mom have her life blown up by your dad—not to mention your sister- and brother-in-law's marriage hit the rocks and your wife's parents harbor a low-level loathing of joy in general—a well-delivered happily ever after was one of the greatest gifts a book could give you.

"Ooh, what're you getting?" Rachel said, appearing next to him at the cash register, new sandals already on her feet.

"*D-Day, Concussions, and Other Manly Things: A Retrospective*," he said as the woman behind the counter handed him his bag. Rachel gave him a quizzical look and pulled out the brightly colored paperback.

"A new Emily Henry? I didn't even know there was a new Emily Henry!"

"I know. You're slipping."

"Apparently," she said, reluctantly giving the book back to him. "It's a little disturbing. Like, that-thing-you-called-a-beard-during-the-lockdown disturbing."

"Disturbing? I thought it was rugged."

"Was it?" she said, playfully shrugging her shoulders. They left the bookshop and reentered the interior corridor lined with stores. He hung back behind her a few steps and then rejoined her when they got to the street.

"Dammit," he said after they'd gone about 20 feet.

"What?"

"I texted Ali and asked him to tell you that my pandemic beard was not disturbing."

"And?"

"He says, 'You're right. I would've called it more *appalling* than *disturbing*.'"

This time Rachel's laugh was more of a chortle.

Despite the lockdown, Ali had seen that beard a lot. It had started over Zoom, first with him and Will watching movies together and eventually, when the truncated Big Ten football season started, watching Michigan. Will was grateful to have the games to think about, but seeing them played in largely empty stadiums was an uncomfortable reminder of how upside down the world felt right then. But Ali, still laughing and joking with him like he always had, had reinjected some normalcy. Ali had even driven to Chicago to spend that Thanksgiving with them, observing a strict two-week quarantine beforehand. He'd said it was because it didn't make sense to fly home given the circumstances, but Will was pretty sure Ali had wanted to reconnect with him and Rachel in person. Although they'd hardly left the apartment, the five days they'd spent together had seemed to make everything a little less heavy for all three of them.

Whether Ali knew it or not, his texts were doing the same now, helping to relieve, perhaps only momentarily, some of the pressure Will felt to get this all right.

Enough time had passed since he and Rachel had eaten that pizza, so they decided they were ready to be around massive quantities of fudge. They picked the first place they came to of the many they'd seen. The little shop smelled like the olfactory embodiment of dessert, and they were quickly overwhelmed by the options inside the glass display case. Chocolate. Chocolate peanut butter. Peanut butter with chocolate chips. Just peanut butter. Something with caramel and sea salt. And on and on, all sliced in large, roughly semicircular chunks.

There was a sign advertising a special: FREE TOTE BAG WITH $50 PURCHASE. Such a sum initially seemed like an extravagant amount to spend on fudge, but the longer they agonized over which slices to buy—Rachel in particular did not like the idea of leaving any of the peanut butters behind—the more rational the 50-dollar threshold became, especially since the extra bag would help with the purchases they were accumulating. Five slices and a bag of saltwater taffy later, they had their tote.

"This might sound perverse," Will said once they were back in the afternoon sun, "but after seeing all that fudge, I could really go for some ice cream."

Rachel stopped in the middle of the sidewalk. "That is the single hottest thing you've said to me on this trip."

Ice cream on a summer day was a popular idea, so by the time they navigated back to a shop that had caught their attention earlier and made their way through the line, 40 minutes had passed. But when you're on vacation time and the reward is black cherry (her) and rocky road (him) in a waffle cone (both), you hardly notice.

They found a spot to eat outside, sitting on a small concrete ledge beneath one of the building's windows, and traded bites of each other's choices before digging into their own with purpose. The ice cream was good, but the cones were better, and considering the noises they both periodically made while chewing, Rachel may have been right that it was the steamiest part of their week to date.

Will was done first, and he sat back against the window with a sigh. They were in the shade, and Rachel had her sunglasses up on top of her head.

"How'd you get ice cream in your hair?" he asked.

She ran her hand through it, and her fingers came back with a dark-red residue. "Artistic license. The little dribble on your shirt is far more conventional."

He saw the spot she was talking about and licked his index finger to try to rub it off. "We make quite the pair."

Rachel nodded while taking the last bite of her cone. "You know," she said when she'd finished it, "even before we covered ourselves in ice cream, I was thinking we might be underdressed for the Marquise."

They both had on T-shirts, shorts, and tennis shoes in anticipation of a day of walking punctuated on either end by ferry travel. Those choices had served them well, but they were not the things one wore when impersonating fellow diners at a midscale restaurant.

"What do you suggest?" Will asked.

"It's three thirty now, and 'our'"—she put the possessive pronoun in air quotes—"reservation is at five o'clock. I think we should each take the next hour to shop and buy ourselves something that is classy, beach dinner appropriate, and then we meet back here fully changed, ready to go."

"You trust me to purchase classy, beach-dinner-appropriate attire on my own?"

"Only partially. But I saw some cute stores I want to check out, and you'd be bored out of your mind waiting for me. Just remember: simpler is better. There should be no, like, still life depiction of a beach scene across the back. And no silk."

"Got it. What about an airbrushed seagull?"

Rachel pulled her sunglasses back down and stood. "Ha ha ha. I'll see you at four thirty."

"Is that a no to seagulls specifically, or to birds generally?"

"Depends on whether you want to sit at the same table with me or not."

"Hmm. Okay. I'll have to get back to you after I see these shirts."

She waved goodbye to him over her shoulder without looking back, but he could tell how much fun she was having with this—with the shopping, with the island, with everything. He didn't get up right away, watching her until she disappeared into the crowd and thinking he was even more in love with her now than when they'd gotten married, as impossible as that seemed.

Will was so caught up in the good feelings and the carefree nature of his surroundings—replacing cars with horses really did do wonders for your nerves—that he didn't realize until he'd walked a way down the street and was about to try his luck in a store with a miniature lighthouse in the front window that he hadn't checked his email in a while.

He stepped through the doorway and off to the side before opening the app.

There it was, sent 15 minutes earlier.

Hi, Rachel—

Good news: We are all set! Below, I've put proposed flights from Nashville to LAX and then back to Chicago (which is where I'm assuming you'll be headed after?). You'd be with us all day Tuesday.

Let me know if these will work for you, and I'll go ahead and book them.

Thank you!
Beatriz

Will moved his attention down to the flight times, noting the Monday-morning departure and the Wednesday-morning return. As much as he had built up the moment of responding to Beatriz when he'd been in the Milwaukee hotel, this was the true point of no return. The first time she'd written back, she'd been confident but not certain she'd be able to make the interview work, and he, as Rachel, had not officially agreed to flying anywhere. Nothing had been booked.

Even now, he could write back and say something, anything, had come up, and Rachel couldn't fly out after all. It would all be over, just like that, just like he'd imagined when he'd briefly thought about coming clean to Rachel earlier. Do that, and there'd be no ticking clock counting down to when he'd have to tell her what he'd done.

And if everything that had brought him to this moment was as simple as all that, and if it wouldn't have made Rachel look like an absolute flake who kept changing her mind, he very well may have done it. But it wasn't that simple, and embarrassing her in front of these people was even more unacceptable to him than the idea of her being furious about what he'd done.

> Thanks so much, Beatriz—this looks great. I can't tell
> you how much I appreciate your help.
>
> Rachel

His finger was literally moving to send when he stopped himself.

> By the way, we're on the road at the moment, and my
> cell service is inconsistent, so if you need anything
> else, please just continue to use this email address.

Sent.

Will felt like a poker player who had just gone all in, except he wouldn't be seeing how the hand played out right away. Simultaneously nervous and amped up, he knew he was in an odd state of mind to be surrounded by so much casual wear and distressed wood, but he was glad to have the next hour to calm himself back down before seeing Rachel.

He was near that window with the lighthouse, looking at shirts, when he heard from Rachel about something else.

> So I don't forget—Isa just asked me to go with her
> to the fertility doctor the week after we get home.
> Owen's being an ass.

What day? Will typed, his stomach sinking as he awaited her answer. He didn't have to wait long.

> Tuesday.

Chapter 17

"Wow," Will said as Rachel walked up to him. "You look . . ."

That was as far as he got. She'd picked out a dark-blue sundress with white polka dots that turned sheer the farther it went down her legs and paired it with hot-pink wedged espadrilles that tied around her ankles, and she looked so gorgeous he couldn't finish his sentence. Instead, he took her in his arms, his hand gently passing over her partially exposed back, and let the people passing by them on the sidewalk fade into the background, catching a whiff of lavender as he did so.

After a few seconds, Rachel took a step away and gave him an appraising, satisfied once-over. "I have to say, you didn't do too bad yourself."

Will had gone with a lighter-blue button-down, the long sleeves rolled up to his elbows, and dark-green shorts with a wool-blend slip-on sneaker. He'd also made what for him was a bold fashion decision:

Shoes without socks.

If they were going to get found out at the Marquise, it wouldn't be because they weren't playing the part. They looked like one of those couples you see who seem to levitate just above everyone around them, how Seth and Francesca had looked when Will had seen them approaching at Summerfest. In his mind, Rachel always occupied that rare air, with or without him, but his minimakeover had given him a confidence in his outward coolness that he didn't always possess.

Internally, things were a little less settled.

Not an hour before, not only had he been attempting to change the direction of Rachel's career without her permission—not just without her permission, actually, but in direct contrast to her stated wishes while impersonating her over email—but he'd also followed that up by texting his sister-in-law and lying to her too.

Rachel told me about the doctor and Owen. I'm sorry.

He and Isa had a good relationship, so he had known it wouldn't strike her as odd that Rachel had told him this.

Thanks. He's just so difficult sometimes. I so appreciate Rachel going with me.

I know. And I hate to ask this, but I have a surprise planned for her at the end of the trip that's going to extend it by a few days, so we won't be home by Tuesday.

Oh. I had no idea.

Neither does she. He'd grimaced as he'd typed. Would you be willing to tell her the appointment got moved to help me keep it a secret?

The *I'm typing* bubble had appeared right away, disappeared for the better part of a minute, and then popped back up. It hadn't felt like a particularly happy interlude for either of them.

Yeah, I can do that. Good luck, Romeo.

Thanks, Isa. I owe you.

Will had felt awful doing it—for pulling Rachel away from her sister when he knew she was going through a tough time, for involving

Isa in what he was doing, for lying to them both. But after he had confirmed with Beatriz, what other choice did he have?

"I got you something too," Rachel said, reaching into the shopping bag where she'd transferred the clothes she'd been wearing (Will had stuffed his into the tote from the fudge shop).

Her hand reemerged holding a black hat. It was a wide-brimmed fedora. Like the one Taylor Swift wore in the "22" music video.

"I don't think so," he said.

"It's for Saturday night in Nashville."

"Yes, I put that together. And look, I love her too. But no."

"Are you sure?" Rachel asked, dipping into the bag again. This time she pulled out a new flowy purple midi dress and held it up in front of her. "Because I'm going to wear this, and I don't think your standard wardrobe can keep up."

Will didn't have to think that hard to imagine her in it. It was a striking image.

"Still," he managed to say. "You get to look like *that*, and I'm going to be some nerd trying to pull off a hat he has no business with."

"But you're *my* nerd," she said, happily putting her purchases back into the bag. "It's gonna be great."

"What era even is yours? I feel like you just got to pick out a hot dress."

Rachel's expression turned serious. "Are you saying you *don't* know purple is *unequivocally* indicative of the *Speak Now* album?"

"Uh . . . no?"

"Good answer."

They took their time walking down the street toward the Marquise, their bodies just an inch or two apart, and he didn't need to see her face to know how happy she was. They were laughing and talking, sure, but he could feel it coming off her. She was practically radiant, a far cry from the person who'd wanted to spend the week watching reality TV. He didn't want that spark to go away when the trip ended, and he believed the best shot of keeping it alive wasn't waiting for them back in

Chicago. Viewed in that light, his plan didn't appear quite so reckless. He was swinging for the fences, sure, but with good reason.

That he still wasn't revealing anything to her was more telling than he was willing to admit.

"All right," she said when they arrived outside the restaurant. "The key in situations like this is confidence. If we believe I'm Annie, they'll believe I'm Annie."

"Situations like this," he repeated. "Have you often stolen other people's dinner reservations?"

"Not at five o'clock. I mean, it's four fifty-six right now. I feel like my parents. I'm afraid it's going to affect my performance."

"Just use it as part of your backstory. We know she—"

"You mean me."

"Right. We know *you* made these reservations months ago, presumably because this place is very popular, and you probably picked five o'clock because . . . ever since you've been pregnant, you've liked to eat dinner earlier?"

Rachel weighed the merits of his lie. He hoped he hadn't come across as too knowledgeable about how to temporarily assume someone else's identity.

"I think I can work with that," she said. "Shall we?"

They entered the Marquise, the interior of which was bright and airy thanks to the white walls, the light hardwood floors, and the floor-to-ceiling windows that looked out to the patio seating and the lake beyond. It was busier than either of them had expected given the early hour, but a quick glance around the dining room suggested most of the others were indeed their parents' age or older.

"Hi, there," Rachel said cheerily to the young woman at the host stand, whose tattoo of Pikachu on the inside of her left wrist peeked out from under the sleeve of her white linen shirt. "Annie, party of two."

Like the kid from the beach, this person appeared to be working a summer-break job and offered a weak smile as she looked down at her tablet, doing her best to be pleasant and hide her boredom. She started to scroll the screen with her index finger, first up and then back down.

"Huh, I'm not seeing it," she said with a frown. The tag on her shirt said her name was Skye, and Skye seemed to come a little more alive now that she'd been confronted with a mystery amid the doldrums of her shift. "What'd you say the name was again?"

"Annie," Rachel replied, calm as ever. Meanwhile, there were two couples who could've been their grandparents waiting behind them now, and Will imagined the cracks beginning to form in their story. Maybe Annie or her ex had called and canceled, maybe the reservation was only under her last name, or maybe there really were restaurant police and the two of them on the boat had been undercover.

Their entire conversation could've been a setup from Jump Street, he thought, only partially aware of how lucky he was no one could hear how ridiculous that sentence sounded.

Okay, undercover restaurant police was a stretch, and not just because that theory hinged on a college girl named Skye with a Pokémon tattoo working a sting with Mackinac Island law enforcement. But the longer she looked for "their" name, the more uneasy Will got—never mind that he had just perpetrated a far more consequential email deception with relative ease. Given the circumstances, you would've thought he would've held it together better when the only stakes would be getting embarrassed in front of some random early birds. So it was probably just the accumulation of the various schemes. Because the threat of face-to-face condemnation from four retirees wearing *really* sensible shoes loomed bigger than it should have.

He was readying himself to grab Rachel's hand and make a break for it when Skye said:

"Oh, there it is. Right this way."

She was going to seat them at one of the windows, but Will asked if they could sit outside instead. As luck would have it, there was one table left out there, a two-top at the far edge of the patio so that there wouldn't be anyone between them and their view of the lake, which was sparkling in the early-evening sunlight.

Rachel sighed once Skye had left them with their menus. "This turned out sorta great."

"I thought the jig might be up when she couldn't find our name back there."

"Just a blip on the radar. Who's going to say no to a pregnant lady at dinner?"

"A *hot* pregnant lady."

She smiled. "So you've said."

"It bears repeating."

She rubbed her foot against the inside of his shin under the table. "Seriously. I know sometimes I tease you about your Rachel goggles"— her term for how Will had a tendency to describe her like she was Helen of Troy—"but pregnancy can have a way of making you feel . . . less than your best. So, yeah. Thanks."

Will thought back to what his mom had said again, only this time, the wisdom of her words overshadowed how awkward they had made him feel when she'd said them.

The server appeared before he and Rachel had taken a look at the menu, but they were ready with their drink order: gin and tonic for him, virgin daiquiri for her.

It took everything in them to act like they'd never seen him before.

"Oh my God," Rachel said as soon as he was gone. "Is that . . . ?"

"Vending-machine-of-bullshit guy? Yes!"

"And did he say *his* name was Lane?"

"I thought he said Blaine."

"No, I think he said Lane. And if so, that begs the question: Was he in a relationship with someone also named Lane—which, amazing—or was he calling himself a vending machine of bullshit in the third person? Which would also be amazing but slightly troubling too."

They started reviewing the appetizers while all they could really talk about was how they were going to get visual confirmation of the name via Lane's or Blaine's name badge. They landed on the spinach-artichoke dip and the shrimp tartlets—because it was vacation, so why choose one, and because Rachel was technically more pescatarian than vegetarian—and Will checking the name while she pretended to examine the menu as she ordered for them.

The server returned with their drinks, and Rachel made sure she had his full attention by pointing at the entry for the dip and asking a question about the cheese. Will scanned his shirt once, and then again, but, to his dismay, discovered that unlike the people at the host stand, the waitstaff did not wear their names on their chests. Or at least this guy didn't. Will would have to improvise.

"I'll get those started for you," the server said once Rachel had finished. "Can I get you anything else at the moment?"

"Actually, could you take our picture—I'm sorry, what did you say your name was again?" Will asked, instantly sounding as old as every other diner looked.

"Bane," he said.

"Ah, *Bane*, right," Will said, now wanting to ask him how he felt about the Batman character. "Could you take our picture with the lake in the background, Bane?"

"Sure, happy to," Bane said. He seemed so carefree. You never would've pegged that vending machine line coming from him.

"Awesome, thank you," Will said. He handed Bane his phone and scooched his chair part of the way around to Rachel's side. They leaned toward each other until their cheeks were touching.

"No name tag?" she whispered through her smile.

"No."

"Nice work."

"Say cheese," Bane said.

"Chee . . . sus, Mary, and Joseph," Rachel replied as he snapped the picture, her expression shifting midsentence from relaxed to horrified surprise, which explained the rare occurrence of the closest thing to an expletive she'd heard in her house growing up. The photo caught Will's face right as his jaw had finished dropping.

Skye was winding her way through the crowded patio, approaching their table from behind Bane.

And she was approaching with Annie. The real Annie.

"Do you want me to take another one?" Bane asked before moving to hand the phone back to Will. "I think the . . . uh . . . light might have been weird." What he should've said was that take one had captured them looking like gargoyles, but when you work for tips, you learn to blame all photo snafus on lighting.

"Oh no, that's okay," Will said, grabbing it from his hand. He glanced back at Annie and noticed it wasn't just her with Skye. There was another woman, one who hadn't been on the ferry. He didn't know how this was going to go down, and there was no escaping it now, but he was hoping to shoo Bane on his way and minimize the number of spectators.

"Um, excuse me?" Skye said, sounding as sweet as she possibly could. Once she arrived, it was clear Bane wasn't going anywhere. He couldn't take his eyes off her, which may have explained what Lane from the phone had been so jealous about. Will would've enjoyed sorting through all the layers of this with Rachel if Annie weren't also there looking like someone who had been stewing over that bad-bangs comment all day.

"I'm sorry to interrupt your dinner," Skye continued, "but this woman here—"

"Annie," Annie muttered.

"Right. Annie says that . . . well, she says that *she* had a reservation for five o'clock, and since that was the only Annie in our book for the entire night, I was wondering if, maybe, there was a chance you'd gotten your days mixed up?"

Skye advanced this suggestion in the noncommittal manner of someone who wasn't paid nearly enough to insert herself into a disagreement between tourists a decade or more her seniors.

Annie exhibited no such hesitation.

"They didn't get anything mixed up. They heard me on the ferry earlier with . . ." She seemed to be catching herself. "That part's not important. The point is, they heard about my reservation, they thought I was going to cancel it, and then they showed up here, with her"—she jabbed at the air in Rachel's direction—"*pretending* to be me."

"That's the most ridiculous thing I've ever heard," Rachel said, surreptitiously leaning down toward the table. Will was almost positive she was untying her espadrilles underneath, and that could only mean she was thinking what he was:

This time, she was ready to run too.

"Okay, then prove it," Annie said. "Show us one piece of ID that says you are who you say you are."

"That's really not necessary," Skye interjected.

"Who the hell do you think *you* are?" Rachel demanded, ignoring the efforts at peacemaking and looking at Annie like she was deranged—while also continuing to take her shoes off.

"Annie, what's going on?" the mystery woman said from behind Bane.

"Nothing to worry about, Amanda. These two were just leaving."

"Uh, it's *Manda*? Like *panda*? I told you that."

"Wait, wait, wait," Rachel said. She straightened back up, which meant she was done untying her shoes and was now barefoot, and inhaled the air of the moral high ground—or at least the moral flatlands. "You picked someone up the *same day* that you dumped your girlfriend, and now you're taking her to what was supposed to be your anniversary dinner? That's *super* classy."

"Aha!" Annie shouted. "That proves you were on the boat with me and overheard our whole conversation! I knew it!"

"You broke up with your girlfriend *today*?" Manda who rhymed with panda said in disbelief.

"Me too," Bane said, staring straight at Skye, who seemed kind of panicked by the information.

"Aman . . . ," Annie tried, turning toward her date. "Dammit, sorry. *Manda*, it's not like that. We'd been growing apart for a long time."

Rachel snorted. "*That's* your line? God. What's-her-name did get out just in time."

Annie looked back to the table. "You know, you got a lot of nerve acting like Miss Holier Than Thou while stealing people's dinner reservations."

"Didn't you stay on the ferry and go back?" Will asked. He was genuinely curious, and he figured since they'd come this far, he might as well know.

"We met at the casino in St. Ignace," Manda volunteered.

"So you took the boat back," he said, still talking to Annie, "thought 'My relationship's over, so what the hell; let's shoot some dice,' met someone new, and then took the ferry *back* to the island, like, five hours later? All to eat *here?*"

He looked at Skye and Bane. "No offense. It seems lovely."

"We had a Groupon," Annie said. "Sue me."

"The shrimp tartlets are the best on the island," Skye said, desperate.

"I think I'm in love with you," Bane said to Skye.

They all stopped. Bane looked at Skye. Skye looked at the ground. Annie and Manda looked at each other. The rest of the patio didn't know who to look at.

Will and Rachel's eyes locked over the table.

"Now?" he mouthed.

"Now."

The two of them threw their wrought iron chairs back with a clatter and booked it for the exit, Rachel's bare feet gliding across the concrete with her hot-pink shoes in one hand and her bag in the other, Will following with a tote full of clothes and fudge.

He was right behind her until they got to the sidewalk wrapping around the building and leading to the street, at which point he hit the brakes and sprinted back to the table, where the other four hadn't yet entirely processed what had just happened.

"For the drinks and appetizers," Will said, half gasping as he threw down two 20s. He looked at their bewildered faces. "Peace be with you."

He spun back around and was gone again.

When he got to the street, he didn't see Rachel right away. He looked right and spotted her two doors down outside the building that was in front of the ferry dock.

"Oh my God," she said as he jogged over, hardly able to get the words out because she was laughing so hard. "Oh my God. What just happened?"

Will put his hands on his hips to catch his breath. "I think we learned why you don't steal dinner reservations from people who break up with other people on boats."

Rachel reached out and rested a hand on his shoulder for balance as she put her shoes back on. "This might be the greatest night of my life, and it's not even five fifteen. Manda, like panda? C'mon!"

"Poor Bane, though. I couldn't let us dine and dash on him, especially not after that."

"Oh, I'm so glad you thought to pay. When we tell this story to our friends, we have to be the heroes."

"*Heroes* might be a little strong. Let's go with *people who were there*."

She finished retying the first shoe and moved on to the second. "Hey, speaking of Bane, please tell me this photo is as big of a train wreck as I want it to be."

Will got his phone out to check. There it was. He stared at it while he waited for Rachel to stand up.

"And?" she said when she did.

"It's a . . . it's a definite vibe," he said, showing the screen to her. Bane had taken the shot at the exact moment both Will and Rachel had spotted Annie. Peak Cheesus.

She busted out laughing all over again, and so did he.

"Holy shit, that's perfect," she said, wiping the tears out of her eyes. "This would absolutely be our Christmas card if we were Christmas card people."

It took a while, but their giggling finally subsided (more or less), and it struck Will how close they still were to the Marquise.

"I know it's not like we stole a car or anything," he said, "but I would feel better if we, like, fled the scene a little more definitively."

"That's probably fair. I also hate to admit it since I made fun of the reservation time before, but I am pretty hungry now."

"Must be our brush with the law."

They walked a few more minutes down the street and found a low-key place that could seat them immediately if they were okay with the bar, which they were.

"Weird," Rachel said, looking at her watch.

"What?"

"Isa said never mind about the doctor; it got moved to the following week."

"It doesn't seem *that* weird," Will said a little too defensively.

"I just meant it was kind of late in the day to be scheduling and then rescheduling doctor appointments."

"Yeah, well, we're on eastern time here. So, you know, it's an hour earlier there."

Rachel shrugged, clearly not interested in spending any more time on a subject she had remarked upon only in passing, and Will was grateful for that. They were having too much fun to let real life intervene.

It was as good an excuse as any.

He ordered a replacement gin and tonic, she switched things up and went with an Arnold Palmer, and they both got fish-and-chips. It wasn't the glitz and glamour of shrimp tartlets, but it's hard not to be content when you're dunking something that's been deep-fried into tartar sauce.

"Let's see here," Rachel said when they were done eating and had paid their bill with considerably less flair than at their last stop. "It's *almost* seven o'clock. What do you think? Should we catch the next ferry back so we can get to bed while it's still light out?"

"Actually, I have a surprise for you," he said. "Out front."

"Oh, you do, do you?"

"I mean, don't get too excited. It's just a little thing."

They got up and went from the noise of the bar to the murmur of the packed restaurant waiting area to the evening hum of the street. There, at the curb, was a horse-drawn carriage awaiting its passengers.

Will had let Rachel walk out in front of him, and she turned back, clearly smitten with him and his idea. "Is this for us?" she asked.

"I figured we could take it out to the Grand Hotel and watch the sunset," he said.

She took a step toward him and wrapped her arms around his shoulders.

"I love it," she said quietly. "And I love you. Thank you. For all of this."

Sometimes when you swing for the fences, you do in fact hit a home run.

THREE DAYS AGO

Chapter 18

"I don't know how else to say it, so I'm just going to say it."

The words were on the tip of Will's tongue, and he knew no matter how far apart he and Rachel may be on this, no matter what her reaction might be, he couldn't keep it to himself any longer.

"How could you possibly find that ferry ride scarier than driving over this bridge?"

"Oh, it's no contest," she said. "This bridge has been here for a million years and is like a four- or five-minute ride over solid ground. The ferry was twenty minutes at sea."

"I'm sorry, is the fact that the bridge is *old* supposed to make me feel more comfortable? Because apparently I've read more stories about the crumbling state of our nation's infrastructure than you have."

She laughed. "That's fun for you. I just mean that clearly it's stood the test of time."

"And solid ground? Have you looked over the edge at what's *under* it? It's a two-hundred-foot drop into the abyss."

"I told you I'd be happy to drive," Rachel said, breaking off a piece of the peanut butter fudge. It was a little after 8:00 Tuesday morning, and they had grabbed coffee and tea but foregone breakfast in order to get on the road early for the four-hour drive downstate to Ann Arbor.

"No, it would be worse if I weren't the one driving," Will said. "Having a job to do is distracting me just enough to keep me from having a repeat of the Sears Tower."

"Well, then here, have some more of this." She held out a piece of fudge to him. "It's so delicious you won't be able to think about anything else."

With his hands locked at ten and two, he glanced from the road to her offering and then back again. "No thanks, the one was good."

"Seriously, I'm going to eat the whole slice if you don't take some."

"I don't think I'm really a fudge guy."

Rachel pulled the piece back and bit it. "You're kidding, right?" she said through her chewing. "Oh my God—it's so good. It's like if they took that sunset last night and turned it into candy."

"I don't know. I always want fudge to be better than it actually is. Does that make sense?"

"No. No it doesn't. And I'm now reconsidering our entire relationship."

"I'm sorry to hear that. At least we'll always have last night."

The return carriage ride to the ferry, the ferry across the water, and then the short drive back to the hotel had basically served as extended foreplay, their bodies in constant contact with one another. The way they'd touched hadn't been scandalous, but it definitely had conveyed what was going to happen as soon as they got to their room. Rachel had ripped his new shirt yanking it off him. Neither of them had seemed to mind.

"So why'd you let me buy so much?" she asked, returning the fudge box to the back seat.

Even knowing they were within their budget, Will had started to notice their spending more while they were in Mackinac and to tally up the ways it would have to change once there were three of them. But this wasn't the time to be nitpicking the fudge or Birkenstock expenditures.

"You seemed really excited about it," he said.

"Not fifty dollars' worth!"

"Hey, don't sleep on that tote bag," he said. "And for the love of God, how much longer is this bridge?"

"Okay, here, let's put the audiobook back on. I'll back it up to where we were when you did the second gummy, and we can try listening to that for the third time."

"You don't mind?"

"Nah, we didn't make it much past that anyway. Trying to find those letters while managing you being high was a real challenge."

"Wanna tell me anything about this tattoo yet?"

"Nope," she said, smiling and pressing play.

Rachel reached out and gently put her left hand on his right, beginning to massage it in the same way he had hers on the boat. He took it off the wheel and rested his right arm on the center console, where she continued to rub her thumb on his hand in a circular motion. He didn't realize they had left the bridge until he had to slow down to pay the toll.

Her thumb eventually stopped moving, but they continued holding hands that way for quite a while, listening to their Taylor Jenkins Reid novel and occasionally commenting on how this stretch of I-75 in the Lower Peninsula looked just about as isolated as their drive across the UP but somehow felt less remote. They decided it was a combination of being back on a proper highway—even one so rural that the speed limit stayed at 75 for a long stretch—rather than a two-lane road plus the knowledge that their alma mater was now just a few hours away.

"So here's a question," Will said after they'd listened to four chapters in a row. It was a book where the main character had been married multiple times, and he was thinking again about his parents' failed relationship. "Do you believe in romantic destiny?"

Rachel hit pause on the screen. "You mean like the idea of soulmates?"

"I guess, yeah."

"Seems like a funny question to ask someone while listening to a book that literally has *Seven Husbands* in the title."

"I don't think getting divorced is a sign that there's not someone you're meant to be with. It just means you haven't found them yet.

Divorce might even be nature's way to get you to leave the wrong person to go find the right person."

Would the right person ever be keeping the secret I'm keeping right now?

The thought took him by surprise, and it sent a shudder through him that he did his best to ignore, adding:

"I mean, look at my mom."

"Exactly, look at your mom," Rachel said, taking her sunglasses off. For the first time on the trip, it had gotten cloudy for more than a few minutes. "I'll grant you that she was married to the absolutely wrong person in your dad. But she's never gotten serious with anyone in particular since, and yet I think if you asked her, she'd tell you she's living her best life."

"You usually don't have to ask her," Will said, the memory of the heavily dog-eared copy of *50 Sex Positions to Try in Your 50s* he'd once stumbled upon on her bookshelf bringing him fully (and graphically) back to what he and Rachel were talking about.

"Right. So is she just some sort of lost soul until or unless she finds her one true love?"

"No, of course not. But don't you think if she met the right person, she'd know, and she'd want to be with them for the rest of her life? I'm not even talking about marriage. I just mean a committed relationship."

"Sure. Except I don't believe there's *one* right person for everyone. I think for anyone, there are lots of people out there who, given the right circumstances, they could build the kind of relationship you're talking about with. So no, I don't believe in soulmates, at least not in a you're-destined-to-be-with-someone sense."

Logically, Will knew she was right. There were, what, eight billion people in the world and counting? It was simple math. And in reality, thinking that you had a shot at happiness with only one out of all those people wouldn't be exhilarating. It would paralyze you with indecision and commitment issues.

Part of him still wanted to believe it could be true, though. Admitting that he and Rachel were together due at least in part to chance made their tightly knit bond feel a touch more severable, which was not something he wanted to contemplate while in the midst of such a consequential lie.

"You look like I just told you there's no Santa," Rachel said.

"I mean, I feel like I should get on eHarmony just in case you're trying to tell me something," he said, tiptoeing across his sense of vulnerability. "But no, disagreeing with anything you just said would require a degree of mental gymnastics that I'm incapable of without massive amounts of THC in my system."

She laughed. "Hey."

When she didn't keep talking, he looked at her.

"I find it far more romantic to know that I have a choice, and the person I'm with is the one I choose," she said.

She was right again. That was better.

"Well, when you put it *that* way," he said in the direction of the windshield.

"I know. In addition to being correct, I'm quite charming."

"And just for the record, I am that person, right?"

Rachel stuck her tongue out at him, and he smiled.

"You wanna listen to more of the book?" she asked.

"Actually, I was thinking it might be nice to put the windows down while the weather is still cool enough to go without the AC. You in?"

"Road-tripping with the windows down? Of course I'm in."

She opened hers all the way, and he did the same with his and the two in back. Driving that way at 80 miles per hour lasted for about 15 seconds until papers started flying out of the tote bags and Rachel's hair looked like it was being teased by one of those industrial-size dryers at the end of an automated car wash.

"Maybe a little too much?" Will shouted over the gusts of wind buffeting them from all sides.

"What?" she shouted back.

He raised the back windows three-quarters of the way up. "I said, maybe it was a little too much."

"Good call." They were still almost yelling, but it no longer sounded like they were on the flight deck of an aircraft carrier. "How about some music?"

"Yes," he said. "But no playlists. If we're gonna do this, we're gonna do it right."

He pushed the button on the screen for the FM radio— an anachronism that mildly dampened his nostalgia play—and engaged in the time-honored but slowly dying tradition of pressing "Seek" over and over again to listen to two to five seconds per station until you hear something worth stopping for.

Violin concerto. Apocalyptic preacher. News talk. Ad for a used-car lot. Something with a banjo. Something with an overly aggressive guitar indicative of men compensating for something else. Cell phone commercial. Then:

Elton John, "Saturday Night's Alright."

They were in business.

Will cranked the volume louder than he would ever have reason to in their day-to-day lives, and he and Rachel were immediately rocking out despite a very limited knowledge of the lyrics. That was not a problem with the next song, however.

"Aah!" Rachel screamed over the synthy beginning of Lady Gaga's "Poker Face." "This *was* my freshman year of college!" She turned it up even louder and started moving from the waist up like she was on a dance floor, not in a RAV4. There were hand gestures and everything.

The station was a gold mine, hopping from decade to decade like a wedding DJ you didn't mind being drunk on power. Gaga gave way to a murderers' row of tracks by Madonna, Adele, Alanis Morissette, Michael Jackson, Rihanna, and Ed Sheeran. It didn't let up until they'd made it through all eight-plus minutes of Prince's "Purple Rain." They were starting to lose the station to static about halfway into the song, but there was no way they weren't going to hang in there.

Rachel turned the radio down as the static grew even louder and a commercial started playing. "That was so incredible I'm going to pretend this station didn't just age us by twenty years by referring to itself as 'continuous soft rock.'"

Will rolled the windows up and turned the air back on. His ears were ringing from the combination of road noise and music, but it was hard to believe he and Rachel weren't somehow meant to be after flawlessly lip-synching "Umbrella" together.

"There's something about *not* being able to control what comes next on the radio," he said. "I think it makes it harder to take the songs for granted."

"Whoa, be careful. You're going to start sounding like the art major in the car."

"If we make our kid listen to the radio just so they have that experience, would we be good parents or annoying old people?"

"Yes and yes."

They saw their first sign for Ann Arbor, now 81 miles away, and decided to celebrate by stopping for gas and to use the bathroom. They were making great time and on pace to get there a little after noon.

Will filled up the car, which didn't take that long because it was a hybrid and had a smaller tank, before heading into the convenience store. On the other side of the pump, the woman with the full-size SUV that could wear his like a backpack had started before him and was still going when he stopped.

"Speaking of our child," Will said when he returned to the car, referring back to their radio conversation. "How are we going to explain humanity's collective inaction on climate change?"

Rachel, who had gone to the bathroom and bought them bottles of water while he was pumping, looked up from her phone. "Humans suck?" she tried.

"I'm sure that will be a real comfort when they're swimming to a floating Trader Joe's."

"Do you worry about that?"

"No, the Trader Joe's people are entrepreneurs. I'm sure they'll figure it out."

"The environment and the future, smart guy. For the baby, I mean."

"Yeah, I guess so."

It wasn't altogether unlike the gun stuff. Climate change had always been upsetting, but knowing they were bringing a kid into the world who would have to deal with it long after they would? It magnified the stakes. In his lowest moments, during those 2:00 a.m. conversations with himself, Will questioned whether they were already betraying their future child's trust.

"I'm not asking because I have some great answer," Rachel said. "Just sometimes it helps to say stuff out loud."

She left some space to show him that he could keep going, whether about this or some of the other anxieties she suspected he was keeping to himself. He nodded to show he understood, which was debatable, but didn't offer anything beyond that. In his mind, every fear he would list—from the earth's rapidly degrading climate to the baby's health to how to pick a day care to just thinking he'd be as bad a dad as his was—would just stack on top of Rachel's own worries until she couldn't see a way to anything but staying put in a life she'd eventually outgrow.

That's why this thing with Creative Vices had to work.

"So what're you looking at?" Will asked as he started the car.

"Oh," Rachel said, returning to her phone. "Just the map. We go right by Brighton, that town where Seth's client grew up."

He rolled his eyes. "Did you know they call it U of M, Rachel?"

"I also heard that the Lower Peninsula looks like—get this—a mitten."

They both shook their heads. Rachel got the book going again while Will piloted them back to the highway, their anticipation starting to build with each passing mile. Because even if the idea that there was just one right person for everyone didn't hold up, you still had to meet the person who would become *your* person somewhere. Some place. Distinct from all the other places in the world as the spot where your story began.

The next time they stopped, that's where they'd be.

Chapter 19

Perhaps it would come as a surprise to learn that even after the incident on their second date, Will and Rachel had continued to frequent that deli. There was no denying the sandwiches were on point, and they had multiple veggie options, which wasn't always easy to come by, particularly back in the early 2010s.

The two of them just avoided the coleslaw like it was the Grim Reaper himself.

So by a little after 1:00 p.m., not only were they at the Matthaei Botanical Gardens, sitting on a plaid blanket in the same open grassy area where they'd had their picnic the first time, they were also eating food from the same place. He'd ordered the turkey (but no roast beef) for old time's sake, and she went with a portabella-mushroom-based creation.

"To us," Rachel said, raising her travel wine tumbler filled with sparkling grape juice, which Will met with his own. They'd debated whether to stop and pick those up because they didn't know the gardens' policy on alcohol and didn't want to have to explain themselves if they appeared to be running afoul of it. Then again, after having to flee the Marquise on foot, what was a little mix-up over their beverages?

Fake wine it was.

The weather had stayed cloudy, something Will actually welcomed. Rachel loved to be out in the sun, but ever since that summer at Cedar Point, he had come to appreciate overcast days because you weren't so reliant on a breeze to keep comfortable. The weather had warmed back up now that they had driven four hours south, and the sun beating down directly overhead would have been baking them on that blanket. The clouds may have also explained why there weren't that many other people there, although that could've been because it was a Tuesday afternoon too. Either way, they had the area around the herb knot garden almost to themselves.

"So I have a confession to make," Rachel said as she went to pour them more grape juice. He weighed that phrase as an option for revealing what he'd soon need to tell her. As long as you had no reason to worry that it was going to be followed by something like "I'm boning my tennis instructor" or "I bet six months' rent on the outcome of the NBA All-Star Game," it wasn't bad.

"I . . . um . . . never finished the alphabet," she admitted, her voice barely audible.

Will heard her loud and clear but was already enjoying this way too much. "I'm sorry—what was that?"

"I never got the z."

He put his sandwich down to make sure he was free to gesture with both hands like a lawyer working a jury box.

"Well, I for one am shocked—shocked, I say!" He was having a hard time keeping a straight face while trying to prosecute her over the integrity of a road trip game, and her laughter wasn't helping. "What a thing for the mother of my child to admit. And at the site of our second date, no less. A place, I would like the record to show, I was promised myriad sexual delights"—Rachel shushed him and swatted at his hands—"if just such a scenario arose."

"About that. That's not why I'm telling you. Because it's obviously not happening."

"Oh, I know," he said, returning to his normal persona. "And not just because me pushing for it would take this story to a really dark and possibly criminal place. I frankly don't think I have the sexual acumen to pull off doing it on a nature trail."

"I also saw on the sign a disclaimer about both ticks and rattlesnakes."

Will took a bite of his sandwich and looked out at the woods beyond them.

"Yeah, so maybe we just hit the indoor exhibits," he said after he'd swallowed.

"Maybe," she said, laughing again. "But the reason I'm bringing it up is because there's no way I can go through with making you get the tattoo. I mean, I wouldn't *really* have made you if you didn't want to, anyway, but I at least could've roasted you relentlessly about backing out."

"Well, I appreciate your honesty, however delayed it may have been," he said, briefly reassuming the affect of comically aggrieved guy. But hearing himself say those words, the joke quickly gave way to something else.

There, in that place, surrounded by the memories of what had started them on the path to the life they'd built together, Will was struck on a fundamental level by how much he had to lose if his emails to Beatriz didn't just fail in getting Rachel to go on the interview, if they didn't simply make her mad. What if it harmed their marriage permanently? What if she didn't feel like she could trust him the same way anymore?

What if it was this, and not some boring job, that would start to unravel everything?

Half of him wanted a way out of what he'd done as desperately as the other half was fighting to make it happen.

They finished their sandwiches and sat there amid a different kind of quiet from what they'd experienced on the shore of the lake, the lapping of the waves replaced by the calls and buzzes of birds and bugs. There was no way of undoing his lie without making a complete mess of things. Will knew that. And he still wasn't even convinced he wanted to, the potential of it giving Rachel everything she'd ever wanted too seductive to turn away from.

But he did know the idea of that tattoo suddenly felt like more than a bet to entertain themselves on a long car ride. It felt important, a way of physically cementing their bond with whatever she had envisioned—which he knew, when it actually came time to do it, wouldn't have been something goofy.

Rachel scooped up the wrappers from their sandwiches and went to throw them out while he topped off their cups with what was left of the grape juice and put the bottle back in the bag. As he watched her walking back, they smiled at each other.

"Did you know what you would've had me get?" he asked her when she'd sat back down on the blanket. "For the tattoo?"

"You didn't like the binary code idea?"

"C'mon. For real. What would you have picked? Or did you not know?"

Rachel looked at him for a few seconds and then out at a colorful kinetic wind sculpture near the garden. "No, I knew," she said, taking a sip of her drink.

"So what was it?"

"It was a date. 2-19-12."

He mouthed the words back to her. "For February nineteenth, 2012?"

"Yup."

"What was February nineteenth, 2012? I mean, I know it was our senior year." She nodded. "Was that around the time of your grandma?" Rachel had been very close to her mom's mom, so much so that even more than a decade later, Will thought saying "When your grandma died" would come across more sobering than he intended.

"Two days after, yeah," Rachel said. "A Thursday. She passed on the Tuesday, I was driving home Thursday afternoon, and the funeral was Friday."

"I remember we had lunch before you left, and I felt like such a jackass because I wasn't going with you."

"I know. You'll recall you had an exam the next day, and you wanted to skip it, and I told you that you were crazy and prohibited you from coming."

"Rings a bell," he said sheepishly.

"Anyway, we ate, I left, and you went to your next class. Or you were going to until I called you like ten minutes later, crying, and told you I just really needed to hear your voice again. I regretted it almost instantly."

Will startled back, wounded, like it was him who'd gotten stung by a botanical garden bee this time.

"Not because I *didn't* want to hear your voice," Rachel quickly clarified, "and not because of anything you said. I was just embarrassed to be so clearly falling apart, especially when you had other stuff to do. So I said I was being stupid and tried to get off the phone. But you said, 'Just talk to me until you pass the next exit,' and I said okay. Then you started telling me about this debate you and Ali were having over which Chipotle location was the best, and by the end, I was laughing so hard because they were all the same, but—"

"Uh, they were so *not* the same. The tortilla chips at that one by our apartment were consistently ten to twenty percent too salty. He said he liked that, which was patently absurd."

"My point," Rachel said, making it clear that the tortilla chips weren't it, "is that I'd gone by like three exits by the time you were done telling me that story. Not to mention I wasn't crying anymore. I thanked you and told you that you should go to class, but you said you'd rather talk to me. You said the same thing two hours later when you should've been getting ready to go to your intramural basketball game, forty-five minutes after that when it was tipping off, and then again when Ali asked if you wanted to go to the movies."

She took another drink, but it was clear she wasn't done. She also began twisting that strand of hair, so he knew whatever she was about to say would be highly personal.

"You stayed on the phone with me for that whole drive, Will. *All five hours of it.* I tried to wrap things up like half a dozen times, and each time, I was secretly hoping you wouldn't take the bait. And you never did. Even though we saw each other all the time and talked all the time, so what else could we possibly have to talk about? But it didn't matter. You just wanted to be with me.

"When I pulled into my parents' driveway, you made me promise to call again if I needed anything, and then we said our goodbyes and finally hung up. And I'll never forget sitting there for a minute in my hand-me-down Honda Accord, dreading what the next few days had in store, but feeling this peace over what was waiting for me on the other side of it."

Rachel took a deep breath to keep herself from choking up too much to get it out.

"Because that was the day I knew I was going to marry you. February nineteenth, 2012. And I wanted this tattoo to always be there to remind you that it's not just you. I have *Will* goggles too."

Will couldn't believe his ears.

He knew that Rachel loved him—and didn't just love him, but loved him so deeply that it made him want to believe in soulmates. Hell, he'd just tried to argue for their existence on the drive. But that was him. He was the wear-your-heart-on-your-sleeve romantic. Not only that, but back when he and Rachel had that phone call, he had already been busy worrying about what was going to happen to them once they graduated a few months later. He'd known he was all in, but he'd been scared he was fated to fade into her personal history as the college boyfriend and nothing more. That Build-A-Bear monstrosity wouldn't have happened otherwise.

So to learn that Rachel had known then that she wanted to marry him, and known it so definitively that she could remember the precise date when she first thought it?

"That's the most romantic thing *you've* ever said to *me*," he said, now determined to ensure this story would never be far from their minds, even if things got bad. "I think I have to get it now. Like, I want to."

She smiled softly, and he could tell that was the reaction she'd been hoping for.

"You know," she said, sniffing and composing herself, "I could've made that whole thing up just to trick you into getting it even though I didn't finish the alphabet. Like a reverse psychology thing."

"Hmm, I don't think so. You've got a tell."

"Was I doing the hair-twisting thing again?"

"Uh-huh."

"Damn. Well, you caught me. Even us coldhearted pragmatists have a soft side, I guess."

"Plus, the tattoo was technically my idea to begin with. I was planning to do it even before we made the bet. I just hadn't had a chance to come up with what it would say. But now I have that, and since you lost the bet, I get to decide where it goes too."

"And?"

"I'm thinking the inside of my right wrist. That way I can see it whenever I want, but I can still cover it with a long-sleeved shirt."

"That does seem more practical than a butt cheek."

They finished their drinks, tossed the tumblers in the bag, and stood up. Will folded their blanket while Rachel checked out the map that they had grabbed on their way in of the long narrow greenhouse-type structure known as the conservatory. It was a short walk from where they'd been sitting, and even without the sun, the rising afternoon humidity made it an attractive option for reasons that had nothing to do with snakes.

After taking a slight detour to look at the large mosaic panels adorning one of the conservatory's exterior walls, they headed inside. Admission was, gloriously, still free, and the building was broken up into three climates: the tropical house, the temperate house, and the desert house. You entered at tropical, which was fitting for the two of them because it meant they came to the orchid display almost right away.

They stood there looking at them for a minute while a brother and sister, somewhere between the ages of five and ten, raced by, trying to hide the fact they were playing tag from their mom, who was hidden behind the pineapple plants and halfheartedly imploring them to slow down. Will imagined Rachel and himself bringing their kid here someday, and the child running around and not paying attention while Will tried to tell the story of that second date, Rachel lovingly rolling her eyes at him. Through that lens, being a parent seemed like it could be . . . natural, hopeful, full of possibility.

"You really were into me," Rachel said, slipping her hand into Will's and breathing in deeply to soak in the freshness of the air. "I remember that orchid painting I did. It was not good."

"It was . . . not your best work, no," Will said, and they both laughed. "But when you're trying to plan a creative date on a budget, you look for inspiration wherever you can find it."

"Yeah, it was a lot easier to overlook that you tried to kill me with that coleslaw after this."

She laughed again, and he acted like he was going to pull his hand away, prompting her to grab it even tighter.

"Whatever," he said, smiling at the familiar shape of the way they flirted with each other.

They meandered their way deeper into the tropical house, following one of the semicircular branches off the main path and stopping to admire the coffee plants. As they went, they got closer to a small indoor waterfall that set the entire scene against a soothing backdrop of white noise.

"It's so peaceful," Rachel said. "Maybe we should get a noise machine for the baby's room."

"Forget the baby. I feel like I could fall asleep standing up right now."

In the temperate house, they passed a fragrant olive tree and followed the center aisle all the way to the koi pond and then doubled back on one of the side paths, past the black bamboo and the bonsai display. There in front of them was a wooden bench set back off the path, against a date palm tree.

"Do you remember what I said to you about that bench when we were here the last time?" Will asked.

"You told me you'd read online that sitting under that tree while you were on a date was supposed to be good luck."

"God, I was so *smooth*," he said with a self-deprecating laugh. "How long did it take you to figure out I was completely full of it?"

"Oh, I'd say almost instantly," she said. "I'm skeptical of most things involving puns."

"So why'd you sit with me?" he asked, taking a seat on the bench. She took the spot next to him.

"You were trying so hard, especially after everything that happened with the picnic," Rachel said. "It was very sweet, and I found it incredibly genuine—even though, ironically, you were lying."

The way she told it—it made him feel so warm and comfortable. Understood. Safe. Like *of course* she'd get why he'd emailed Beatriz. It was Will, and this was a very Will thing to do.

So was this the moment? Should he say something like *Speaking of being genuine while lying* and just go for it and tell her? This bench had worked once before. So had the one at the art institute when he'd proposed. Maybe benches had a weird cosmic significance for their—

"Hey, let's ask them to take a picture of us," Rachel said, nodding toward an older couple looking at the olive tree, pulling Will's attention back. "You know, so we have a nice one in addition to the one from the crime scene."

Will went over to see if they'd be willing, which they of course were. He returned to Rachel and sat back down, wrapping his arm around her shoulder and pulling her close. The man took the picture while the woman stood to the side and sighed, more to herself than anyone else. "Just beautiful," she said.

Will and Rachel thanked them and waited until the couple were at the carnivorous plant display before checking the photo, just in case they didn't like it. Their caution, though, turned out to be unnecessary.

"Oh, that's a keeper," Rachel said, still studying Will's screen. "We look *good*."

"Right?"

She kissed him on the cheek, and they got up from the bench and headed in the direction of the desert house. He was still trying to gather himself to say what he needed to and decided he'd send the picture to his mom as one final confidence boost.

Back in Ann Arbor where it all started ☺, he typed as a caption and then sent. He'd instinctively slowed down with his eyes on his phone, and when he looked up, he realized Rachel had disappeared into the new climate ahead of him.

It was the smallest of the three—and surprisingly, not really any hotter. It was also quiet, even more so than the tropical and temperate houses. If he hadn't known Rachel had gone in ahead of him, he would've assumed he was alone among the cacti.

"Babe?" he ventured while peering down at something called living rocks.

"Over here," she called back. She sounded like she was up a path that arced through the center of the room.

Will followed her voice. Before he turned the corner, his phone vibrated in his hand.

"My mom says we're a perfect . . . ," he started. "Whoa, what's this?"

Rachel was down on one knee next to a short stone wall.

"Will Easterly," she said, unable (or uninterested) in keeping the huge grin off her face.

"Yes?"

"Will you make out with me for a minute in front of this giant cactus that looks like a mushroom from *Super Mario Brothers*?"

He laughed and walked to her, offering her his hands as she stood.

"Well, *this* certainly didn't happen the last time we came here," he said.

"What can I say? All these years, I guess your love of the unexpected romantic gesture has rubbed off on me."

The window of opportunity hadn't closed. He could still tell her now.

But just as surely as he knew that, he knew it would be more romantic to do it right after he got 2-19-12 inked on the inside of his wrist.

Get the tattoo, and then he'd put it all on the line.

And besides, before he could say another word, Rachel brought her mouth to his, and they kissed like they hadn't already done so a thousand times before.

Chapter 20

Will and Rachel's run of dry weather on the trip had come to an end at the botanical gardens.

Despite their earlier hesitation regarding the animal life on the nature trails, they had always planned on walking at least one of them again, like they'd done on their second date. It had been misting as they were about to start, but so lightly they couldn't even really see it on their clothes. He'd stopped at the head of the trails to read (and then reread) the paragraph on the sign about how not to annoy the massasauga rattlesnake—something his younger, more adventurous self apparently hadn't given a second thought because he'd had no memory of being concerned before.

"It tends to avoid human contact," Will had said to Rachel, who'd been studying which path to take.

"What does?"

"The snake."

"Ah. That makes sense. I don't think they'd let people just go for walks out there if it were, like, a *Snakes on a Plane* situation."

And just as he had been telling her he'd seen that movie in high school and hadn't slept for a week after, the sky had opened up and unleashed a downpour.

It had gotten so heavy so fast that they hadn't even bothered with the performative "What's a little rain?" reaction you're supposed to have as a well-adjusted adult and instead had broken out almost immediately in the wild, full-on sprints of an elementary school field day. They'd made it inside the car in under a minute and had still been dripping like they'd just failed in an attempt to hoist the Jolly Roger in rough water.

After using the T-shirts from the pizza place on Mackinac Island to wipe down their heads and arms and then putting on something dry from their bags, they'd decided to head to the tattoo place, reasoning that going in the middle of the afternoon would mean little to no wait. Will had also liked the idea that there'd be fewer people around in case he asked for it in a font they didn't have. Or in case you weren't supposed to say *font* at all to a tattoo artist. Or was it *tattooist?*

He'd kept these doubts to himself, which hadn't been hard since what he'd really been thinking about at that point was telling Rachel about the interview once those numbers were etched on his arm. Getting the tattoo right then would mean less time to lose his resolve.

Situated between a hot dog joint and an arcade on South University Avenue, Work of Art Tattoos and Piercing looked just like they remembered. The hours on the door said it had opened half an hour earlier at 3:00 p.m., and the inside was empty except for a guy, whose left arm was already fully covered, getting ready to have something added to his right by a woman with gauged ears and wearing a black bandanna and overalls. Unfortunately, she told Will and Rachel from her chair as she got her equipment ready, she was the only one working that day, and she was booked up with appointments.

"Tomorrow afternoon might be better," she suggested. "You can make an appointment on the website."

"Thanks," Will said, mostly disappointed but also slightly relieved to have something beyond his control both keeping a needle out of his arm and his confession, for the time being, off his lips. He was also highly aware of the man with the biceps depiction of SpongeBob decapitating Squidward scanning him for any visible ink. "But . . . uh . . . we actually won't be around tomorrow. We went to school here, so I just thought I'd take a shot while we were back."

"Oh," the woman said, stopping what she was doing to look at Will with more purpose. There were no bare spots on either of her arms. "Well, what were you looking for? If it's something pretty basic, I might be able to squeeze you in that last hour before we close."

"I mean, I think it's basic?" Will replied, unsure how to answer. A few numbers separated by some hyphens sounded like the definition of simple, but under the watchful eyes of two people who clearly knew this world in literally painstaking detail, he clammed up.

"It's just a date," Rachel said, jumping in. "Like, a calendar date. February nineteenth, 2012. But written in numbers, so 2-19-12."

"And where do you want it?" the woman asked.

"Uh, on the inside of my wrist?" Will said, but again as a question. For some reason, saying that out loud felt like the tattoo equivalent of standing at the Emily Henry display in the bookstore. Like a man's man would've gotten it elsewhere. But to his surprise, both customer and artist gave slight nods of approval.

"Okay, so not that big then. Any colors, or just black?"

"Just black," he said.

"Cool. Yeah, if you can come in around nine thirty, we can totally do that tonight. I'm Clarissa, by the way."

Will thanked her and said they'd be back, and he and Rachel turned to go. The rain had let up before they got there and had stopped completely in the few minutes they were inside, and he could already feel the humidity gaining strength as they emerged onto the sidewalk. The mugginess seemed to spur on the swarm of butterflies that arose in his stomach when he heard the tattoo machine switch on as the door closed behind them, and it sank in that he would still be telling Rachel today—just not yet. Waiting around once he'd decided to do it was the one thing that could make it even harder.

"You doing all right there?" Rachel asked him.

"Huh? Why?"

"You seem a little . . . woozy."

"Just a little anxious, I guess."

"About the needle?" she asked as they started walking.

"Yeah, partly. Partly how glaringly obvious it was I had no clue what I was doing in there."

And partly because I don't know what the hell's going to happen when I tell you all this.

"*Pfft,*" she said, waving his spoken concern off. "You were totally fine. And who cares if you were anxious? I guarantee you she's seen far worse. Especially on a college campus."

Rachel's assuredness helped. Even though in reality, it was just about him getting the tattoo, and even there, she didn't know any more about tattoo-shop etiquette than he did. She just had the one, and although it was more involved than what he'd be getting, it was still relatively small and simple. There was of course the huge caveat that she actually knew what it felt like to have that needle go into your skin while he had only watched her from a distance in the waiting area. But that didn't mean she was some sort of expert on the culture around tattooing. As in many other areas of their lives, though, she possessed a natural ease that eluded him.

He could use some of that ease right about now.

"You know, I think it's late enough that we could probably check in at the hotel," Will said. "Do you want to go back to the car and get our stuff?"

They'd parked in a garage a few blocks away from the Michigan League, a student union that had a hotel built right into it. Will had thought that would be a fun place to stay that would also put them within walking distance of anything they wanted to do.

"Not yet," Rachel said. He sensed she had a destination in mind but was a little confused by it.

"It seems like we're going to the library."

"Does it?"

"Yes. But I can't figure out why."

"That's because we're not going to the library. We're going *close* to the library."

"Oh, don't tell me," he said.

Rachel's smile threatened to consume her entire face. "Did you bring your hacky sack?" she asked as the sidewalk began to cut a path through the trees to the big open area known as the Diag, the quad where he'd first tried (unsuccessfully) to ask her out.

"Joke's on you. Because it's fifteen years later, and here we are again."

She cackled as they approached the big block *M* that was set in the ground, and the sound bounced off the massive paving stones around it.

"You were lucky you were so cute," she said. "I can't believe Ali let you go out of the house with that."

"He was going through a real disc golf phase back then, so he had his own problems."

"Disc golf? Yikes. You two really were quite the pair."

"I know. But that gives me an idea. Do you mind backtracking just a little?"

"Lead the way."

Will steered them along a route he'd taken more times than he could count—but not once since graduation. When he'd walked it regularly, he'd been a college junior, then senior, who hadn't wanted those four years to end. Not just because of what it might mean for him and Rachel but also because of how much he'd loved living in that town with the guy who'd become his best friend. He'd known even back then that while he and Ali would always be tight, it would never again be like it was in that apartment on Church Street. It couldn't be.

He hoped he wouldn't someday be saying the same thing about him and Rachel after those emails. That in the event it all went wrong, that tattoo could almost serve as a talisman tethering them to before.

"Ah, Moonshine Manor," Will said fondly when they arrived outside the building's front door.

"What was the story behind that name again?"

"*Moonshine* was because of the time we tried to multiply the recipe for a Hurricane so that the resulting beverage could fill a Gatorade cooler. *Manor* was because we were distinguished gentlemen in charge of our first estate."

Rachel looked across the street. "Yes, the unobstructed view of the brick wall is rather stately."

"God, we had so much fun here." He tilted his head back and to the left. "Ours was the one with the Michigan flag in the window," he said, pointing four floors up. "I have to text him."

"Hold on. Give me your phone so I can take your picture in front of it."

He handed it to her and stood up on the wooden edge of a curbside flower box while she crossed over to the aforementioned brick wall to make sure she got their old apartment in frame. When she asked him if he was ready, he made a fist with his right hand, held it to his heart, and said yes.

"I really wish you two got to see each other more often," Rachel said, walking his phone back over to him.

"I know." Ali had taken a job with a law firm in Brooklyn about six months before Will and Rachel had gotten married. Work brought him to Chicago once or twice a year, but his schedule usually only left time to grab a dinner while he was there. That was another reason the Thanksgiving trip had been so special.

Much love from A2, old friend, he typed, and then attached the photo.

"We always talk about coming back here for a weekend for a foot-ball game," Will continued. The parking garage was about a 10-minute walk away, and they'd begun to move in that general direction. "But he and I are terrible about actually planning anything."

"Ironic given that you put together this whole week for us in, like, a night."

"True. But you and I are married, so we just sort of fall into taking trips together."

"Um, I mean this in the best possible way, but nothing about this week has felt fallen into."

You have no idea, he thought, his mental clock ticking down toward his tattoo appointment and afterward.

"But you get what I'm saying," he said. "He and I have completely separate lives and responsibilities. Not to mention men on the whole are just worse about friendships."

Was it friendships, or relationships generally? You came across a lot more examples of husbands and dads checking out on their families—whether literally or emotionally—than the other way around. Will's father was no unicorn, and Will realized the glass-half-full interpretation of that would be that his parents' divorce had had nothing to do with him. It had just been his dad doing what so many other men had done.

Half-empty, on the other hand, questioned whether Will could be sure he was any better than the rest of them. It felt like the outcome of this week would have a lot to say about the answer.

Ali's response came through. Will looked at it and laughed and then held it up for Rachel.

"'Ah, Moonshine Manor,'" she read and laughed too. "Like I said, quite the pair."

He had just turned the screen back to him when Ali's next text popped up.

Is Rachel enjoying the trip down memory lane as much as you?

Will could tell Ali had kept his question vague on purpose in case Rachel saw it, and he appreciated that his friend remembered the conversation they'd had when Will was at the Clemens house about the balancing act he was trying to pull off on this trip.

And yes, internally Will was going with *balancing act* due to its implication of precision and skill rather than manipulation and deceit.

I think so, he replied.

That's great. Keep making good choices.

Ha—I said the same thing to my mom last week.

Oh, I have no doubt your mom got up to something you're never going to want to know about.

Thanks for that.

But there's still hope for you, Ali wrote.

Will wasn't sure how he wanted to respond. He thought about it as he and Rachel came to a crosswalk and had to wait for the little light-up pedestrian to appear.

"Promise me you'll set something up for this fall," she said. "You and Ali."

"You think that'll work? I mean with the baby coming and everything?"

"We'll make it work. And besides, football season starts in August, and my due date isn't until November. We've got time."

"You're the best, you know that?" Will said. The light changed, and they began to cross the street.

"I do. Plus he flies all the time, and as long as you don't go through the Upper Peninsula first, you can do the drive in an afternoon. It's not like Chicago is *that* far away from here."

He hesitated a split second and then nodded.

Chicago wasn't that far. But Los Angeles was.

Will looked back down at Ali's last message and pecked out his reply.

Check back with me around midnight.

Chapter 21

Once they'd checked in at the hotel and taken showers, Will and Rachel were ready to head back out for dinner as the preamble to Work of Art and the sterile needle with his name on it. That the tattoo had been relegated to the role of secondary stressor came as a surprise given that he had indeed embellished a bit when he'd claimed he'd "totally watched" at his last flu shot. It had been more of a one-eye-opened-one-eye-closed peek.

However, after you'd started down that road, the whole Am-I-destroying-my-marriage-now-by-trying-to-save-it-in-the-future? debate had a way of dominating your thoughts.

They'd picked the Italian restaurant on Main Street where they had celebrated both the one- and two-year anniversaries of their dating. It had been almost a 15-minute walk, and anywhere else, they may have opted to drive so as not to get sweaty all over again. But it was Ann Arbor, their place, and they wanted to soak it in while they had the chance. Especially since the structure where they'd parked the car was like a third of the way there, anyway.

They'd been rewarded for their decision with a leisurely stroll in the warm but far from oppressive evening air. There was a little bit of a wait for a table at the restaurant, but they passed it sitting outside, watching the traffic, and reminiscing about the dinners they'd had there before and about college more generally.

"I don't think we were quite so matchy-matchy back then," Rachel observed, reconsidering their respective attire. She'd gone with a green blouse and khaki shorts, he with a green polo and shorts in the same shade of khaki, though they were looser and longer. She also had on flip-flops, and he couldn't imagine getting a tattoo in anything other than closed-toed shoes.

"Your neckline is frillier," Will said. "And your legs look better than mine."

"Mmm, not from where I'm sitting," she said, giving his thigh a squeeze and filling him with some extra confidence that he would try to hold on to for the rest of the night.

But it had dissipated again by the time they were digging into their appetizer, and Will had an urge to come clean about something. Anything. Just not the big thing until he had the tattoo.

"How do I tell her what kind of type I want?" he asked over a piece of bruschetta.

"You mean the font?"

"Yeah. But am I allowed to say *font* at a tattoo place?"

Rachel scrunched her nose in confusion. "What else would you say?"

"I don't know. That's the problem. But *font* feels like what a guy who has no clue what he's talking about would say."

"You're overthinking it again." She picked up a roasted tomato that had fallen on her plate and popped it in her mouth. "Just tell her if you want a serif or sans serif."

"A who now in the what where?" In reality, he knew what these were (more or less), but playing dumb about it felt fun and safe at a moment when he was trying to harvest calm inside himself.

Rachel had been about to take a drink of her water, but she put it back down. "How did you marry a graphic designer without knowing the difference between a serif and sans serif font?"

"Last week I had to explain to someone that two-step authentication wasn't a dance move. I've had my hands full."

"A *serif* font," Rachel said with a smirk, "is one that has those little lines attached to the ends of the bigger lines. *Sans serif* doesn't have the little lines."

"What a technically robust definition. I don't know how I missed it."

"You're the worst." She was returning his *I love you* from the big rock in Mackinac, and it made him chuckle. She took her drink of water. "Okay," she said after she swallowed, "can you picture the difference between, like, Times New Roman and Arial?"

Will looked up toward the ceiling and thought for a second. "Yeah."

"Times New Roman is serif, and Arial is sans serif."

"Oh. Okay. In that case, I definitely want sans serif. Probably just Arial, actually."

"Good choice. Nice clean lines for a date."

From there, their conversation switched back to a call Rachel had had with her mom while Will was in the shower. They had talked about it some while walking to dinner, and Rachel wasn't done venting over how what had started out as her mother ostensibly checking in "just to say hi" quickly gave way to asking whether her daughter had read that article about the moms quitting their jobs and if Rachel had given any more thought to doing the same.

"Why can't they understand that that's not me?" she asked as the server put their entrées down in front of them. "Ooh, that looks great, thank you," she said, momentarily shifting her attention to her risotto.

"Thanks," Will said over his eggplant Parmesan. "Also, why is she asking you that while you're on vacation?" he added once they were alone again.

"I swear to God, now that I'm having a baby, suddenly every one of my decisions is of pressing concern in the Armas house. I'm starting to miss them not paying attention to me. Did you know she actually said to me, 'Well, it's not like you'd be walking away from Wall Street'?"

It wasn't just frustration as Rachel told him this. It was hurt, too, and Will sensed the purpose in what he'd been trying to do with Creative Vices all over again.

"It's just such an insult to how great you are at what you do and how much you love doing it," he said. "I'm sorry."

"Thanks, babe." She looked down at her plate. "I mean, it's not like I want to work at the university forever. She and my dad are just so—this is just so typical for the two of them."

Will thought of the job in LA and all the glorious distance it would put between them and his in-laws, the buffer it would give Rachel with her parents, the opportunity it would bring to show what she could do. It was almost like a do-over for New York.

They finished dinner, and then they had gelato for dessert, but they still had some time to kill. Down the street, there was a branch of the M Den, a local chain of apparel stores that specialized in University of Michigan gear, so they decided to browse for a bit before walking back for Will's sort-of appointment. It was fortuitous, really, given how recently he had been projectile-vomited on. He'd saved his favorite tee, but he was pretty sure he'd never be able to look at it the same, and this was a great opportunity to pick out a new one.

The university's colors were maize and blue, the former of which being a bright shade of yellow that had always made Will feel like a human highlighter when it was anything more than an accent. Since they'd gone over on the fudge budget, he was committed to buying only one shirt, and he had it narrowed down to two dark-blue options: one with a cool old-school drawing of the mascot, a wolverine, and another with University of Michigan written crisply and plainly in a serif font (it looked better on a shirt).

"What do you think?" Rachel asked as he was putting the one with the wolverine back. She'd been in a different part of the store, and he hadn't noticed her until she was next to him, seeking his opinion on the maize Future Wolverine onesie she was holding up.

"Uh," he said, caught off guard.

"I thought it would only be fitting if this were the first piece of clothing we got. It's three to six months, so it will be a little bit before we can use it, but it's the smallest size they have."

Will's mind started to spin. Discussing Rachel's mom being weird about her wanting to keep working after the baby was born was both abstract and familiar, an issue for future Will and Rachel that represented a wholly predictable attitude from his mother-in-law.

But this onesie, in this store—this was concrete.

If he'd worried painting the nursery could be a jinx, buying clothes for a six-month-old before the baby had even been born seemed like it would be jabbing an index finger in karma's eye. Or maybe it wasn't buying this one item specifically. But this one would open the door to more clothes, which would open the door to bottles and car seats and toys and who knew what else. Which of course they would need. But the sooner they started that process, the more they'd have to lose if it all went wrong. Were they just supposed to act like that wasn't within the realm of possibility? That it wouldn't shatter their entire world?

And on the subject of jinxes and karma and omens, was lying the way he had—no matter how well-intentioned—and introducing that into their marriage while she was pregnant the pretext for something awful that would be coming their way as a result?

Thinking that they and their baby could be punished for actions wholly unrelated to prenatal health was the height of irrationality. Will knew that. But standing there, half-formed ideas whipping through his mind at dizzying speeds, the room seeming like it might start to spin, he felt like he'd found himself on a ride that he couldn't get off.

And yet all Rachel was suggesting they do was buy a onesie—a *onesie*, for crying out loud—so reacting with anything close to what was going through his head at that moment would make him hate himself even more than he did for panicking in the first place.

"I'm not sure about the color," he said, grateful that he could direct his doubts into something far less consequential. "Maize is a tough hang."

"They had blue too. And you know, that would probably hide stains better anyway."

"Also true."

"Okay, I'm going to go switch them. Meet me at the register?"

Splitting back up gave Will a chance to regroup, and by the time they were walking out of the M Den, he had mostly moved on, which was to say he had stuffed the anxiety back down as far as he could. He was still quieter than he'd been on the walk to the restaurant, though, listening to Rachel tell stories about herself and her series of roommates and thinking about how young the two of them had been when they met there. College simultaneously felt like a lifetime ago and last week.

However, there was nothing like the ding of the bell on the door welcoming them back to Work of Art Tattoos and Piercing to snap him back to the present. Clarissa looked up from the ramen she was finishing behind the front desk and smiled.

"Sorry, we're a little early," Will said, doing his best to sound chill. This was it. They were here.

"No worries," Clarissa said as she set her bowl aside. "It's actually good. My last appointment had to reschedule, so I've just been sitting around trying to resist the urge to close up early and go smoke with my roommate. Her boyfriend gets the best weed."

Will shifted nervously, his explanation of the Doritos multiverse still fresh in his mind. "Uh, but you're not, like, high right now, are you?"

"Oh, no way. I'd lose my license. Plus I learned the consequences of that the hard way."

She walked around the desk and extended her right arm, bare under her blue tank top and overalls, and directed their eyes to what appeared to be some sort of brown-and-yellow bird. Rachel and Will both squinted at it, trying to decipher what exactly they were looking at.

"I'm guessing that's not a gigantic pigeon," Rachel ventured.

"It was *supposed* to be a griffin—you know, half eagle, half lion? The guy who did it for me claimed he did his best work while stoned, and I was sleeping with him at the time and dumb enough to believe it."

Will found her candor comforting in its own way, and both she and Rachel laughed, but he stuck with an empathetic nod just in case. No point in accidentally insulting the person he was counting on not to turn his 2-19-12 into an amorphous centipede or something.

"So what kind of font are we thinking for this date?" Clarissa asked, hopping back behind her computer. Rachel elbowed him below the desk's wood counter at the word *font*. "What was it again? February nineteenth, 2012?"

"Yeah, good memory," he said. "And I was just thinking, like, Arial."

"Gotcha," Clarissa said. Her fingers flicked over the keyboard, and a few seconds later, the printer against the wall behind her came to life. She went over to it and retrieved the piece of paper it spit out and walked it back to him.

"If we're doing the inside of your wrist, I'd suggest something around this size," she said. He had been about to remind her that he wanted it written in numbers and hyphens, but she had already done that. For someone counting the minutes until she'd be glassy eyed, eating Cheetos on her couch, Clarissa was reassuringly detail oriented.

"Yeah, that's perfect," Will said.

"Cool. Just let me get the stencil set up, and we'll be good to go. I'll meet you over at the station on the left."

He turned to Rachel. "You're coming with, right? Back there, I mean?" He was always going to ask her, but this was about more than moral support for getting the tattoo now. He wanted them to share this entire experience before he told her what was going on—which he'd decided he would do immediately once it was over, while he was still in the chair.

"Of course," Rachel said.

"Thanks, babe."

"Besides, I need to document this moment for future generations," she said, waving her phone at him.

Will got himself situated in the chair, which was of the rolling, swivel variety. It looked like it had been salvaged from an office-surplus warehouse and immediately gave the proceedings a less ceremonious vibe than he'd envisioned. There was a table at one of the other stations, similar to what Rachel had lain on when she'd gotten hers, so he guessed his was the seating arrangement for people with only the least ambitious tattoo goals.

He caught a glimpse of the needle still in its packaging and decided he was okay with aiming low in that regard.

"So just FYI, I'm going to look at you and not at my wrist the entire time there's a needle present," he said to Rachel quietly enough so Clarissa wouldn't hear.

"Well, this certainly bodes well if I end up needing an epidural."

Clarissa came over and started setting up, asking Will to put his arm on the little rectangular table to his right, with his palm facing up so she could see the inside of his wrist. She explained that she was going to first wash the area with soap and then shave it with a razor before using petroleum jelly to transfer the design on the stencil to his skin.

"I forgot to ask," she said while she was shaving. "Which way do you want the numbers to face?"

He had to think for a second. "I guess I've been picturing them as towards me? Like, right side up when I'm looking at them?"

"Okay. And I'm happy to do that. But you should know it is considered upside down from a tattooing perspective. Is that all right with you?"

He didn't know how it could possibly matter if his tattoo was technically facing the wrong way, but it wasn't like he could ask for a redo if he changed his mind, which wasn't in the best place to be taking on additional, nonpotentially life-altering decisions, anyway. He looked to Rachel, who already had the camera raised for a photo. She gave him a subtle thumbs-up to let him know that he wasn't on the verge of making any graver a mistake than he had in hopping in the chair to begin with.

"Yeah, I'm good," Will said to Clarissa.

"Cool. I just didn't want you to leave here and have someone claim your tattoo artist didn't know what she was doing."

"Well, don't tell anyone, but I don't exactly roll with a tattoo-savvy crowd in the IT department," he said, which made her laugh. That relaxed him a bit.

"I don't know," Clarissa said, finishing the application of petroleum jelly and looking at Rachel. "I love yours. Both the quote and the lettering itself. It's beautiful."

"Thanks," Rachel said. "It's actually in my own handwriting."

"She's an artist," Will said, at which Rachel did her best not to roll her eyes.

"Wow," Clarissa said. "Have you thought about getting any more?"

"I think I want to do one on my other arm. But I'm pregnant, so sometime after I have the baby."

"Hey, congratulations!" Clarissa said to the two of them, and then backtracked. "Sorry," she said to Will. "I shouldn't just assume you're the dad."

"No, no problem—you're right. In fact," he added, settling into what he was doing a little more and flashing Rachel an I-know-you're-going-to-hate-this grin, "the date in this tattoo I'm getting is the day she says she knew she was going to marry me."

"Okay, we don't have to start telling *everyone* that story," she said, uncharacteristically blushing.

"You two are adorable," Clarissa said. "And speaking of the date, how does that look?"

In the talk about Rachel's tattoo and pregnancy, Will hadn't noticed that Clarissa had transferred the design to a spot several inches below his wrist. It looked like a real tattoo, and he briefly entertained the thought of just never washing that part of his body ever again. Despite the obvious appeal, it seemed pretty impractical.

And seeing the numbers there, even in draft form, he knew there was no turning back.

"Looks good," he said, making sure he sounded steady and over-correcting a little too much, such that the words came out an octave too deep. Clarissa then made a point of showing him the needle was brand new as she removed it from the package and told him to make sure that if he ever got another tattoo, the person giving it to him did the same. He would've laughed at the idea of doing this again if the sight of her opening the needle hadn't caused his stomach to turn over and make the eggplant do a backflip, snatching the fake gravitas from his voice in the process.

"I'm just gonna . . . ," he said, trailing off and indicating with his left hand that he'd be looking away now.

"Not a big fan of needles, huh?" Clarissa asked, prepping the ink.

Will stared straight ahead at Rachel, who was grabbing a shot of the design on his arm before Clarissa started to work. "You could say that," he said.

"It'll be over before you know it," she said.

He was about to respond "I hope so" or "No worries" or "Please— be gentle," but before he could, the angry buzz of the tattoo machine cut him off.

The needle stabbed his skin, and he winced as it sank in. But it was more the anticipation than any pain. It surprised him how much it felt like getting a normal, run-of-the-mill shot. He guessed he'd just assumed it would be much worse. So that was a positive development.

That positivity lasted a solid minute to 70 seconds.

Because unlike a shot in the bland surroundings of a doctor's office, the pressure didn't let up, Clarissa slowly pulling the tip through his epidermis like she was navigating the world's most confusing stick shift transmission under the watchful gaze of a flaming-skull-tattoo poster.

On the plus side, it was doing a hell of a job of keeping him focused on what was happening then and not what would be happening in a few minutes.

"Breathe," Rachel mouthed at him, and only then did he realize he had been holding his breath since the machine had turned on.

Will took a deep one and tried to listen to what Rachel and Clarissa were talking about. It sounded like Clarissa had also studied art, and she was asking Rachel about Georgia O'Keeffe.

"You're doing great," Clarissa said to him when Rachel had finished telling her about the time she went to the O'Keeffe museum in New Mexico. "We're already halfway done."

At that, he perked up a little. Halfway done? Really?

He was *doing* this. He, *Will Easterly*, was getting a *tattoo*. One commemorating the date the only woman he'd ever loved, the one standing here with him now, knew she wanted to be with him for the rest of their lives. It wasn't like getting one of their wedding photos etched in full color across his back. But it was something.

And honestly, it didn't hurt *that* bad. Not even when he'd been forgetting to breathe, if he really thought about it. Sure, if he were getting something bigger or more detailed, he could imagine how it would grow increasingly intense the longer he sat there. But he was already halfway done—heck, *more* than halfway done by now—and the first word that would come to mind when describing the sensation currently coursing through his arm wouldn't be *painful*. It would be *weird*.

This he could handle. And at the recognition of that, he felt the confidence Rachel had brought out in him outside the restaurant coming back. He was going to be a dad. A dad with a tattoo that *Rachel Armas* had picked for *him*. Nobody else. They *were* meant to be, and what he was about to tell her would only prove that again.

"All right," Clarissa said, "just have to do that last two, and we'll be all set. Still doing good?"

"Surprisingly, yes," Will said, turning to look at her for the first time since the ink had started flowing. "This isn't nearly as bad as I . . ."

Halfway through saying how bad it wasn't, Will saw the needle in his arm.

It was the last thing he saw before he passed out.

TWO DAYS AGO

Chapter 22

If Will had appreciated that Clarissa was detail oriented, he was nothing less than grateful that she had had a steady hand.

Because when his head had slumped to his shoulder and his whole body, including his arm, had gone limp, she had pulled away the needle without flinching, ensuring that that last part of the 12 didn't become an unintelligible squiggle. He'd come to a few seconds later when Rachel had placed her hand on his cheek. She was concerned enough that she didn't immediately give him a hard time about fainting, but it quickly became clear that the only thing wounded was his ego. Accepting the Strawberry Kiwi Capri Sun from Clarissa's minifridge before she finished the tattoo hadn't exactly mitigated his embarrassment.

He'd felt like a child, not a man capable of being a father or a partner capable of being the one Rachel could count on when she needed him. Like when she delivered the baby. They'd been planning on him being in the room, but now he thought he would probably only be in the way.

So when Ali had texted him around midnight in response to Will's cryptic message from earlier, he had simply written back:

False alarm.

Will couldn't tell Rachel there, not after that. So the secret remained his and his alone.

"I have to give you credit," Rachel said. They had grabbed breakfast at the hotel before checking out and now were on I-75 once again, this time with her behind the wheel. "You really went through with it."

Will looked at the bandage on the inside of his wrist, covering the tattoo. "Just barely."

He hadn't just ruined the moment by fainting. He'd also broken whatever spell had convinced him that some ink on his arm would be a kind of magic binding them together. Thinking about it now, his home state of Ohio rolling by outside the windows in a display of scenery as unremarkable as anywhere in the Midwest, his plan in that tattoo parlor made him feel ridiculous.

"Still counts," Rachel said. "But, yeah, of the two of us, I think it's good I'm the one who gets to look forward to having the excruciating pain of childbirth relieved by a five-inch-long needle."

She smiled and patted him on his knee but didn't say anything else since she hadn't paused the audiobook, and he wondered if he should just volunteer not to be in the delivery room so she wouldn't have to be the one to say it.

But that was a problem for another time. Right now, he had to figure out a new plan for telling her about Creative Vices. And before he could do that, he had to figure out what they were going to do when they got to Lexington.

Earlier that morning, he'd received an email from the farm hosting the charity horse show they were supposed to go to the next day inform- ing him that it was being rescheduled for the following month due to a gas leak on the property. The organizers had been very apologetic and offered anyone who couldn't attend on the new date a full refund, which Will had declined and told them to consider a donation to the racehorse-adoption program. He'd felt good about that decision and known Rachel would, as well, when he told her about it. But it hadn't solved the problem of the suddenly gaping hole in their itinerary, nor had perusing the websites of popular horse-farm tours they might go on instead. He had no doubt they were impressive operations, but learning about things like breeding practices and training regimens wouldn't be of much interest to Rachel, especially after she'd been looking forward to the charity event.

"Mind if I pause for a minute?" he asked when the chapter they were on ended.

"Sure. What's up?"

"So the charity horse show got moved to next month," he started, not wanting to see the disappointment on her face.

"What? What happened?"

"Apparently there was a gas leak in the main barn. No one got hurt, but they're not going to be ready by tomorrow."

"That's a bummer." She stopped—thoughtful, but not overly distraught. "That they had to cancel, I mean. I'm glad there were no injuries."

"You didn't need to clarify that. I operate under a baseline assumption that you're not a practicing sadist."

"That's very decent of you."

"Well, I'm a decent guy. That's why I told them to keep the money for the tickets as a donation."

"I one hundred percent support that."

"Now all we have to do is figure out what we're doing in Lexington," Will said. "I found something called the Kentucky Horse Park that has a museum and equestrian shows. So that could be cool."

The website for this one was the last he'd come across. From the bit of browsing he'd been able to do via his 5G connection, it looked a little more like horse Disney World than a farm dedicated to racehorses, and given Rachel's experiences riding as a kid, he thought the equestrian piece in particular would capture her interest.

"Yeah, that sounds fun," she said. He could hear her hesitation, though.

"Are you sure? I can keep looking for something else."

"No, it's not that. I'm sure this would be great."

He could tell her heart wasn't in it. First the fainting, and now this. All the momentum he'd been working to build with the trip had started to wane.

"I get it," he said. "It's not the charity show."

"Oh no, it's not that, either. I mean, don't get me wrong, I was looking forward to it, but I'm fine. Really."

Will was confused. "What is it then?"

"I'm trying to think of the right way to say this," she said, turning on the windshield wipers as it started to drizzle. "Because I don't want to offend you or anything."

"It's all good, babe," he said in a credible impersonation of someone who wasn't unreasonably invested in his wife's thoughts on horse attractions. "Just tell me."

"Okay. So, I've loved everything about the last five days. Up to and including you staring at your gauze for long stretches on this car ride like you have no idea how it got there. Because let's be honest, you kinda don't."

She clearly meant it as a joke, and he pushed himself to react as such. Fake it until you make it, right?

"Hey, I was awake the entire time she was tattooing. I just . . . stepped out for a few minutes in the middle."

Rachel looked at him out of the corner of her eye. "Yeah. Anyway, as I was saying, this trip? Amazing." She paused. "But we've also been going almost nonstop. And I'm tired. So I was wondering: Would it be the lamest thing ever if I suggested that we just hang out at the hotel in Lexington for a day and a half? Like, sleep in and sit at the pool and stuff before we go to Nashville? Because I'm gonna want to dance my ass off to Taylor Saturday night."

The hotel did look nice. It was more luxurious than they typically would've done, but Will had gotten a great deal since it was a midweek booking, and when he imagined trading a seat in a barn for a reclining lounge chair poolside, he couldn't help but smile.

"I think there's a spa too," he said.

"Is that your way of saying you're in?"

"I am so in."

"Yay! Here's to being lazy!" She extended her fist toward him so he could bump it, which he did.

"I don't even think it's laziness," he added. "It's more not treating vacation like you're completing a checklist so a whole bunch of people whose opinions you don't really care about anyway can 'Like' photos of what you're doing online while at the same time judging everything they're seeing."

This time she reached for his hand and squeezed it. "I know I've said it before," she said, "but this—this is why I married you."

"Well, it certainly wasn't because I'm steady in the face of danger." Getting the tattoo hadn't been dangerous, but if he couldn't even stomach that, real danger felt like a nonstarter.

"Seriously"—she stole a quick look at him from the driver's seat, sensing he needed to be pumped up a little—"best trip ever. Thank you."

Turned out the trip's momentum was unharmed.

Now if his self-image and their marriage could just follow suit.

Rather than start the audiobook up again, they decided to look for a place to stop and use the bathroom. Neither of them was particularly hungry, so they went with a gas station right off the highway, figuring they'd keep things quick. But when Will had finished topping off the tank and gone inside, he saw there was a line for the women's room, and Rachel was still third. She frowned at him when he walked by to go into the men's, and then more deeply as he approached her again on his way back out.

"Can you get me a slush?" she asked him, keeping her voice down. "I was going to do it myself, but I think I live in this line now."

"Sure. What flavor?"

Rachel looked surprised, pained even. "Red, Will. Always red."

"You're right. That was a dumb question."

He started on his way from the front right of the store to the back left by way of the salty-snacks aisle, turning at the large cardboard box filled with five-dollar DVDs. Halfway past it, he stopped in his tracks and backed up, pulled over by the copy of *It's Complicated* peeking out at him from the pile. It was a good rom-com from one of the masters, Nancy Meyers, starring Meryl Streep, Steve Martin, and Alec Baldwin, and it had come out late in 2009. He knew all this not because he was a student of the genre but because it had been the first movie he and Rachel had ever gone to together. And that was when he remembered another one of the hotel's amenities: a reservable theater room.

So that was that. There was nothing complicated about it.

They were going to the movies.

Will picked up the DVD—the possibility of streaming it felt vaguely yet definitively less romantic—and headed for the slush machine. Looking at its two porthole windows of red and blue frozen delights swirling away, he thought them to be an apt metaphor for his own brain spinning up this impromptu movie date. Then he remembered he was 10 feet away from a gas station Subway and, as such, his brain maybe should dial it back a notch. He was buying them a bargain-bin DVD, not taking her to Cannes.

As he grabbed the cup for Rachel's drink, he got a text from Ali.

Do you remember Chocsplosion! guy?

Will did a quick search for the GIF of the infamous news clip where some dude gets fired on live TV as he watches his office building burn, with a long strand of caramel from a Chocsplosion! candy bar hanging from his face. He fired off one of several versions at his disposal in reply and then added:

I think I read he was actually the one who started the fire. On accident. But still.

It wasn't the first time in his life Will had used that GIF, but it was the first where he thought, *You know who else would pass out from a tattoo? Chocsplosion! guy.*

Even so, Ali wrote back, the people in this conference room right now make him look competent. I'm seriously questioning whether any of them really went to law school.

That's why I chose the insurance industry. No idiots allowed.

At least you have funny commercials.

No, our competitors have funny commercials. We have a jingle that sounds like a sitcom from the 80s.

It was a thread about nothing, which meant everything to Will. This was what they always did, and there was a comfort in that connection when so much else was up in the air.

Unsure whether this would be the extent of their conversation and not wanting to have to root around in his pocket while holding a slush if it wasn't, Will put his phone down by the sleeve of domed lids before pulling the lever on the red side—nominally branded as *cherry*—to fill Rachel's cup. He was halfway through when he heard the phone begin to shake on the counter.

"Hey, Mom," he answered once the cup was full.

"Oh, good. I got you. I thought it was going to go to voicemail."

"Yeah, sorry," he said, snapping the lid on. "You caught me in the middle of pouring a slush in a gas station."

"Where are you two now?"

"Ohio, actually. Almost to Dayton. If we weren't trying to fit all this into a week, we'd stop and see you." She still lived about an hour and a half from there, not too far from where Will had grown up, and she would've had the opposite reaction to his tattoo than what Rachel had gotten from her parents—which would've made the whole fainting thing more embarrassing. He found himself strangely relieved not to have to deal with his mom's loving curiosity right now.

"Uh-huh," she said.

Will had been about to get Rachel a straw, but he stopped and looked up to nowhere in particular. It wasn't like his mom to be distracted on a phone call with him, especially not when he'd mentioned a potential visit, even if it were just to say it wasn't happening. But she was somewhere else, and now that had his full attention.

"Is everything okay?" he asked.

"Oh yes. Well, I think so."

"That doesn't sound too convincing."

"I'm sorry, Willie Will. Everything is fine. I'm just a little thrown off, I guess."

"About what?"

The line was quiet for a second. "Your father."

Mentioning Will's dad was rare for her. But calling her son for the express purpose of discussing her ex-husband? That was unheard of, and Will instantly braced for impact. Disappointment or frustration, anger or sadness, he wasn't sure what he expected. But he knew it wouldn't be good.

"What about him?" Will said.

"He called me last night."

His instinct to want to protect his mother, something that had become far less acute the older they'd both gotten, shifted back into high gear. He was ready to hate his dad all over again for whatever lame-ass excuse he'd used to crawl out from under his rock and contact his mom—while also loathing the persistent little voice inside his head hoping that maybe, finally, things would be different.

"What could he possibly want from you now?" Will asked.

She paused again, longer this time, and then he heard her exhale.

"He asked me for your phone number."

Chapter 23

Will's mom hadn't known why his dad wanted the number, and she had said she wouldn't give it to him without checking with Will first. Any temptation he might have had to talk with his dad, to see why he was reaching out now after all this time, had been snuffed out by the realization that his own father hadn't *had* his phone number in the first place, which only twisted the knife deeper.

Will had asked his mom not to share it, she had supported his decision with no further questions asked, and they had wrapped up their phone call before he'd gotten in line.

My dad asked my mom for my phone number, he had texted Ali while he'd waited to pay.

Shit. Why?

Don't know. He wouldn't tell her.

What did you say?

I told her not to give it to him.

I don't blame you. It's also messed up he didn't already have it.

Will had known Ali would get it.

What did Rachel say? Ali had asked.

Haven't told her.

Are you going to?

Will had thought about telling her about the call but had quickly decided against it. Not knowing quite what to make of it himself, he hadn't wanted to complicate things so close to when he would be telling her about Creative Vices.

No I don't think so, Will had written back.

You should. It's a big deal and it's clearly bothering you.

Sometimes Ali knew him too well.

That's why I told you.

I'm flattered. But I'm not your wife.

In a vacuum, Ali would've been right. But Rachel having a good reaction to learning about the interview was the top priority. Will had gambled too much to lose focus now, to open his emotional floodgates and saddle Rachel with his unresolved feelings in the midst of this trip.

It might be revealed in short order just how big a mistake he'd made when emailing Beatriz. But letting a brief lapse in his dad's long-standing disinterest get in the way of the plan's chances at success? That wasn't going to happen. Will wouldn't let it.

So when he'd met Rachel at the automatic sliding doors that led outside, and she'd noticed that he'd looked distracted, he'd said that he'd been working on something fun yet chill for them to do that evening at the hotel and had just left out the part where his deadbeat dad had attempted to reappear in his life with zero warning.

"Is the fun-yet-chill thing related to what's in the shopping bag?" Rachel had asked as they walked back to the car. Will had also picked up a box of microwave popcorn and some candy and asked the cashier to put them and the DVD in a bag to keep them all hidden.

"It's quite possible."

She'd taken a long drag of her slush. "Well, it's like I always say: you can't go wrong with a gas station surprise."

"'Gas station surprise' sounds like bad sushi."

"Or an even worse sex position."

They'd arrived at the hotel a few hours later, and Rachel had gone to check out the pool area while Will waited to check in. It had been the perfect opportunity for him to ask Steven C., the guy working the front desk, how he could go about reserving the theater room for that night.

"Oh, right," Steven had said after a moment of trying to place what Will was talking about. "You don't really reserve it ahead of time. Just come back to the desk, and as long as it's available, one of us will be happy to open it up for you."

"But what if it's not available?" Will had pressed as Steven went back to typing. The amount of information he'd been entering seemed incongruous with whatever it must take to give someone two keys to a hotel room.

Steven had stopped and looked at Will again with the impatience of someone nearing their break or the end of their shift or possibly the end of their rope with customer service as a profession.

"It'll be available," he had said.

And Steven had been right. When Will and Rachel returned to the front desk at eight o'clock carrying an ice bucket full of popcorn that they'd popped in the microwave in their room, Janelle P., Steven's more pleasant replacement, showed them from the main atrium, down a hallway, to a little side room just past ballroom *B*.

"Enjoy," she said, flicking on the lights for them and departing with a smile.

Will let Rachel walk in and then closed the door behind them, which was when he realized *theater room* was probably a touch too generous in describing the space. It wasn't that it wasn't nice; there were four puffy armchairs in a row facing a large screen on the wall and a projector in the back that was hanging from the ceiling and connected to both the digital media and DVD players sitting on the shelf below. That said, someone other than an overzealous marketing person writing website copy likely would've called it a halfway decent man cave, and a spartan one at that, provided that this someone was also in the habit of using stupid terms like *man cave* to begin with. But for what Will had in store, it would be just fine.

Rachel went over toward the shelf with the two players and inspected the second shelf beneath it, which had 20 or 25 DVDs on it, mostly of the animated and/or PG family comedy variety.

"Are we watching *Grown Ups 2*?" she asked with her back still to him. She had been into it when Will had told her they were having a movie night while making the popcorn, but she was having a hard time faking enthusiasm for the in-house library.

"Only if you veto this," he said, producing *It's Complicated* from their fudge shop tote bag, which they'd used to transport their drinks from the room.

Rachel turned around, and he saw the excitement come back. "Aww, our first movie." She walked over and put her arms around him. "Is this what you bought at the gas station?"

"It is. I'll never look dismissively at a five-dollar DVD bin in a Chevron again."

She smiled at him but didn't say anything.

"What?" he asked.

"Nothing. I'm just amazed sometimes by how much you think about me."

Will laughed. "I mean, I love you, and you're pretty great to think about, so it's not that surprising, is it?"

"What I mean is, plenty of people never get to experience what we have together. It's no one's *destiny* to find someone who loves them the way you love me. Because if it were, that would mean there were billions upon billions of people like you out there. And there aren't—there really, really aren't. I've never met anyone else like you in my life, Will, and I hope you know that I know how goddamn lucky I am to be married to you."

Her words literally took his breath away. It was hard to imagine there'd be a time this week when his stock would be higher than it was then, their foreheads resting against each other, with him bending down to reach hers. In that sense, it was the ideal moment to tell her she had a flight out of Nashville bound for LAX this coming Monday morning.

But the way she'd been looking at him, talking about him, he didn't feel emboldened. He felt ashamed for lying to her. Especially when she added:

"I wish we could just freeze like this."

If he didn't know better, he would've thought she sensed there was trouble coming. And who knew? Maybe she did.

"Just imagine if I'd gotten you some Dots too," he whispered, not wanting to think about it. "We'd probably be naked already."

Her hands were flat on his chest now, and she patted him lightly with both before heading for one of the chairs. "Guess you'll never know. I still can't believe I let myself run out."

"You should probably check the bag, then," he said as he went over to the DVD player.

He was dropping the disc into the tray when he heard her laugh.

She'd found the new box of Dots.

"Thank you," she said after he hit the lights and sat down next to her. They had switched into their sleeping clothes as soon as they had gotten to their room, and there was just a hint of embarrassment in Rachel's tone as she snuggled into her chair in her sweatshirt from Taylor's Eras Tour and burgundy leggings, holding the Dots like a beloved stuffed animal. Mostly, though, she just sounded thrilled.

The movie started, and soon, the two of them were holding hands between their chairs, Will quickly growing to appreciate the ways in which this was better than if they'd had something closer to a real movie theater to themselves. That would've had a certain wow factor, sure, but rom-coms weren't the kinds of movies that suffered much from being viewed on a smaller screen, and it still felt way more cinematic than anything they could've achieved in either their hotel room or on their couch at home. Plus the seats were more comfortable, and they hadn't had to dress for anything other than a walk down to the lobby.

It all added up to a low-key, distraction-free environment in which the movie they were watching was at liberty to dredge up feelings about his dad that he was doing his best not to think about.

It's Complicated is a divorce movie, or at least a movie where Meryl Streep's character's divorce from Alec Baldwin's is a defining plot detail. Will had known that going in, of course. But when he had seen it for the first time, he had been so focused on Rachel and their date—they were only a couple of months removed from the coleslaw, so he was still very actively trying not to screw anything up—that he hadn't invested too much in what was playing out on the screen. Now, the "will they/won't they" of two exes considering getting back together for real after sleeping with each other a few times, and the mix of happiness and confusion and hurt the idea of this reunion triggers among their adult children, was taking Will back.

Back to when he was a kid and used to stare out his bedroom window at night, wishing on anything he thought *might* be a shooting star that his dad would reappear.

Back to when he'd thought his parents would get back together once he was a little bit older and no longer so much work.

Back to when he'd invited his dad to his and Rachel's wedding and allowed himself to imagine what it would be like to see his parents dance a dance together, not as husband and wife but just as two people who had once loved each other enough to have him.

But none of that had happened. His dad hadn't thought enough of him and his mom to have even been tempted to come back like Alec Baldwin, and his mom had never met a Steve Martin who would love *her* the way *she* deserved to be loved.

Will knew it probably wasn't his place to feel that way about his mom. She'd be the first to tell you a long-term commitment was the last thing she was looking for in a relationship. But he couldn't help it, especially as she got older.

He'd gotten good at telling himself this impulse to want to see his mom with someone had nothing to do with him, that he'd let go of his desire to have a father figure in his life when he'd finally given up on his dad.

Except giving up and letting go are two different things.

It's toward the end of the movie when Meryl Streep and Alec Baldwin's kids find out their parents have been hooking up again, and they're so shaken by it that they all retreat to the eldest's house. When Meryl comes over to explain what's been going on and that the affair is over, she finds her three 20-something children have piled into one bed, reverting to their younger selves and waiting for someone to make sense of everything for them. Rationally, they'd given up on the idea of their parents ever being a thing again, but it's clear the emotional pull of such a scenario had never let them go.

This time, there wasn't anything to keep Will from crying, and he didn't want to admit to himself that he knew why he was.

His and Rachel's hands had drifted apart over the course of the two hours, but they were almost shoulder to shoulder in their chairs, and she reached out and started rubbing his back.

"I'll tell you one thing," she said once he'd wiped his eyes, her hand still on him. "Young Krasinski may be my Sally Field." She was referring to the eldest's fiancé, who was played by John Krasinski in the middle of his run on *The Office*.

Will chuckled through a nose-clearing inhale. "I thought Obama was your Sally Field."

"Obama is in his own category. But Krasinski reminds me a lot of you."

"Is it just because his character got high and was a little bit of a mess?"

"Oh no, you were a much bigger mess. Like, much, *much* bigger. It's more just that you carry yourselves in similar ways."

"I don't know whether to take that as a compliment or be worried that you're going to replace me with a better-looking version."

"You're being ridiculous. I could never do that to his wife."

Rachel's laugh filled the darkened room, and Will took what was left of the popcorn in return.

The movie ended, and they sat there for a minute. It presented a perfect opportunity to explore his emotions about his parents' divorce, so naturally, he tried to keep the focus on the story they'd just watched and away from that of his family so he didn't risk bringing up the call from his dad. It was just too much with everything else he was trying to manage.

"Is it just me," he said, "or was this movie an odd choice for two college sophomores on a date? I mean, it's great, and the cast is amazing, but wasn't there something a little less filled with middle-aged angst?"

"Probably. But I was still in the information-gathering stage of our relationship, and this was a test."

"The movie was a test?"

"Yup."

"Of what?"

"Everything about you seemed so thoughtful and kind. I was pretty positive that was who you really were, but I figured if you'd sit through a Nancy Meyers movie with me and then talk about it afterwards without getting all bro-y, I'd know for sure."

Will tried to think back to what he could've said after the first time they'd seen this movie. He was coming up blank.

"If I had known our entire future depended on the strength of my *It's Complicated* take, I definitely would've put more thought into it."

"'Entire future' might be a little strong. But you passed with flying colors."

Ice bucket in tow, Will got up to turn the lights back on. It took a little while for his eyes to readjust, and he was at the DVD player taking the disc out before he could open them all the way again. And by then, his curiosity got the better of him.

"What did I say, anyway?" he asked.

Rachel was putting her Dots box and their empty cans in the tote bag and getting her slippers back on. "You don't remember?" she said, continuing with her cleanup.

"I don't. I hope that doesn't retroactively ruin it for me."

"No, I think you're in the clear at this point."

"So, what was this extremely well-thought-out opinion of mine?"

She slung the strap of the bag over her shoulder and looked at him, and he could tell by her expression it wasn't a happy memory for her.

"You said you had a hard time relating because you couldn't remember the last time your parents had been in a room together."

He'd been trying to avoid the clouds gathering on the horizon all night, but there were his own words, reminding him it was pointless to look away.

YESTERDAY

Chapter 24

Thursday morning.

Will had woken up to The Gift That Is TS and that hat resting on his chest. Rachel had been cracking up before he'd even looked over at her.

"I'm glad you're excited," he'd said.

"So excited."

"But this"—he'd lifted the hat off him—"still not happening."

"Give it time, Will. Give it time."

He'd known then that he was going to tell her when they were in Nashville dressed and ready to go to Swift Saturday.

If things didn't go well—if she said she needed time to think or told him to call it off or yelled he was a lying asshole or took a golf club to the car like at the end of the "Blank Space" music video—Rachel's anticipation of the night ahead would still be there to bring them back together. His sins, he told himself, would be no match for the light that was Taylor.

It was a house of cards that came tumbling down the second he conceded Rachel wouldn't need him there to enjoy herself. She'd probably have more fun without him, especially after he did what he was going to do. But it was getting late in the week, and he was running out of options.

"Got my massage booked at the spa," Rachel said, practically bounding back to their table in the hotel restaurant where they'd had breakfast. The spa's online reservation system hadn't been loading right on her phone, so she had gone to do it in person when they'd finished eating. "And I did the full hour."

"That's great," Will said. "When's your appointment?"

"In twenty minutes. So I need to go up and change, like, now."

"Oh, okay. I already paid, so I'll go with you. Just let me . . ." The coffee was no longer hot, and he took two big gulps and finished it. "All right, let's go."

"You could've stayed and taken your time," she said. "I didn't mean to rush you out of there."

"Nah, I was done, and I think I'm going to go sit at the pool, so I want to put on my trunks and grab a book."

"Just don't go in the water with your tattoo."

"I know. My swimsuit is just more comfortable."

"So you can free ball it?"

The elevator dinged open in front of them, and an elderly couple walked out. He waited until he and Rachel had gotten in and, even then, kept his voice lower.

"I didn't want to say it out loud, but, yes, Rachel, so I can free ball it."

She laughed, and they rode up to the fifth floor and got changed with a few minutes to spare. Rachel was brushing her hair in the bathroom mirror, and Will came up behind her and put his arms around her waist and his hands lightly atop her bump.

"You sure it has to be *exactly* eleven thirty?" he said, kissing her collarbone above the line of her robe, craving the uncomplicated closeness he feared might be on the verge of slipping away.

She closed her eyes for a moment, breathing him in, and then reopened them. "You're trouble. And *yes*, I am sure." She turned in his arms to face him. "But we have all afternoon and a wide-open schedule. Just don't go getting sunburned at the pool." She kissed him on his nose and went to get her flip-flops.

"Didn't you say it was indoors?" Will asked.

"Yeah, but it's got big windows. Lots of sunlight. I'd probably wear sunscreen. Just to be safe."

"It feels a little ridiculous to put sunscreen on before going to an indoor pool."

"Do it, don't do it, whatever—you're a grown man. You'll figure it out." She sounded like a woman ready to stop talking about sunscreen and get to her massage, which was confirmed when he heard her open the door to the room, effectively ending the debate.

"Love you!" she called back just before the door closed with a thud.

Will looked at himself in the mirror. "Maybe I do need sunscreen," he said to his reflection.

As he looked, the similarities to his dad stared back at him. The resemblance wasn't overwhelming by any means, but it was there. In the shape of his nose and chin, and in his mouth when he smiled. (His mom had told him that once; he had a hard time picturing his dad smiling).

Will imagined, like he had countless times before, what it would be like to have a relationship with his father. When he did this, he sometimes imagined the questions he would ask. Just then, as he started to work the SPF 50 in on his face, he'd want to know if his dad had been scared when Will's mom had been pregnant with him. Had he worried about some of the same stuff Will was currently? Had he ever gone to crazy lengths to make sure Will's mom, his wife, would be happy after the baby came?

If he took his dad's call, could he ask him now?

He shook the idea from his mind. His dad's contributions to his life began and ended with that crooked grin.

Will finished applying the sunscreen and then hit the pool, claiming a chaise lounge right next to the water. This wasn't the kind of setting your imagination typically associated with the term *poolside*. There was no tiki bar or beverage service, no lazy river or row upon row of reclining deck chairs. It was a fitting complement to the theater room in every way: comfortable, but in no way over the top. One wall was made entirely of windows that ran directly over the pool, with an opening underneath that let you swim from the indoor side to a smaller part outside, where there was also a hot tub. The seating inside could accommodate about 20 people, but late on this Thursday morning, Will had the place to himself.

Before trying to escape into his Emily Henry book for a bit, he checked his phone. He wasn't expecting another email from Beatriz and had even looked before he'd left the room just to be safe.

But there it was. The subject line: "Interview Schedule."

Hi, Rachel—

I just wanted to share your schedule for Tuesday. Please see below and let me know if you have any questions.

Hope you're having a great trip!

Beatriz

9:00–10:00 a.m.: Meet with Writing and Social Media Teams

10:00–11:00 a.m.: Meet with Design Team

11:00–11:15 a.m.: Break

11:15 a.m.–12:15 p.m.: Meet with Video and Web Teams

12:15–1:45 p.m.: Lunch with Rochelle

1:45–2:00 p.m.: Break

2:00–4:00 p.m.: Sit in on Client Meetings

4:00–5:00 p.m.: Wrap-Up with Rochelle

He went over the list of meetings once more. He hadn't expected the day would be so . . . jam-packed. It didn't shake his belief that Rachel would knock it out of the park, and he supposed any responsible employer would do their due diligence, especially when relocating someone from across the country. But this didn't read like a formality you put a candidate you'd personally recruited through. It read like a gauntlet—one Rachel hadn't signed herself up for. She had even reminded him before they left on the trip that what people say at the interview stage doesn't mean a whole lot.

What had he gotten her into?

He imagined Aunt Katie, wherever she was, already knowing how all this was going to go. The last time he had seen her, which they had both been aware would be the last time, she had said she wasn't scared about dying, but that she was sad she wouldn't get to talk with him anymore and watch him and Rachel continue growing into the people they would become. Will had responded that they'd never forget her, and they had both started crying.

"I *do* think that when you die," Katie had said when they'd (more or less) gotten themselves together, "your spirit picks up some supernatural abilities when it comes to keeping tabs on the ones you love. So whatever's going on with you two, I'll know."

He wanted that to be true almost as much as he wanted what he'd done to work. Because if it didn't, it wouldn't just be Rachel that he'd be hurting. He'd feel like he'd let Aunt Katie down too.

The thought of that tightened the pit in his stomach.

"Do you mind if I sit here?" a voice asked from above him, bringing him back to the hotel pool and the subtle yet persistent aroma of chlorine.

Will looked up at the man who had asked the question and then at the chairs around them—all of which were empty. He didn't understand why this guy, who appeared to be in his 60s, had requested to ride shotgun on the same little patch of concrete and violate both of their personal space in the process. But as awkward as it was, it would've been more awkward to tell him no.

"No problem," Will said.

"Great, thanks." The man settled into the chaise, putting his feet up as he placed a small cooler onto the ground in between them. "I thought you might be saving it for someone."

Yes, that would've been a plausible lie, Will admonished himself with more than a hint of regret. "Nope, just me. My wife's getting a massage."

His new neighbor smiled kindly. Will noticed he had on some dark-gray low-top sneakers, which went well with his white polo and charcoal gray shorts. All together, they added up to a look that was not standard-issue grandpa, sort of an avatar for the type of man Will pictured when his mom said she had a date.

"Lawrence Olsen," he said, extending his right hand.

"Will," Will said, shaking it but declining to volunteer his last name.

Lawrence reached down and opened his cooler. "Can I interest you in a beer?"

"Uh, I don't think they allow alcohol around the pool," Will said, choosing not to add that it also wasn't even noon.

Lawrence did the same scan of their surroundings Will had done when he'd tried to figure out why this man had wanted to sit by him. But instead of being confused, Lawrence was amused.

"I think we're in the clear," he said.

"Yeah, you may have a point." Will didn't really want a beer, but he also didn't want to be a weenie about it. "Sure, why not. Thank you."

He accepted the can of Heineken, and they cracked them open in unison. After neither said anything for a minute or two, Will glanced at Lawrence out of the corner of his eye. The older man seemed to just be soaking in his surroundings, while Will was half wishing for a hotel employee to wander through and kick them out for drinking. At least then this interaction would have a natural conclusion, and he could go back to second-guessing his decision-making.

"You're probably wondering why I picked the spot right next to you," Lawrence said, watching the water lap in and out of that gutter thing pools have.

So he is aware this is weird, Will thought. He took a drink of his beer to give himself an extra beat to come up with an appropriate answer.

"I mean, that chair's the only other one with a head cushion, so I guess I just assumed you like neck support."

It was an environment full of hard surfaces, and Lawrence's laugh bounced around it. "You did, did you?"

Will shrugged and took another drink. A longer one this time.

"I sat here," Lawrence said, "because you remind me of my son, and I guess I'm kind of missing him today. All of my kids. My daughters are in California, he's in DC, and here I am in the middle."

Will wasn't great at placing accents, but Lawrence did not sound like he was from Kentucky. "Do you live here? In Lexington?"

"I do. For the last forty-one years. Came from Boston to go to law school. I planned on staying three years and never went back."

"Because . . . you're that big of a horse racing fan?"

This time, Lawrence's smile was more wistful. "No. Because of a girl."

Hearing a trace of his own story in Lawrence's, Will nodded in acknowledgment. "Been there myself," he said.

"You don't say."

"I moved to Chicago because the woman I wanted to marry was there, and I was hoping that one day, she'd want to marry me too."

Because he hadn't known back then about Rachel's epiphany after driving home for her grandmother's funeral, relocating from Ohio had felt a little like leaping without a net. Both Ali and his mom had pressed him on whether it was the smartest thing to do since he and Rachel weren't even engaged. But Will hadn't thought she was ready to be proposed to—they were both still only 24—and he'd been confident he didn't want to do another year away from her. So when the opportunity to take a job in Chicago had presented itself, and Rachel had liked the idea, he'd jumped and crossed his fingers it would work out.

He was noticing a theme.

"And is that woman the same one getting the massage right now?" Lawrence asked optimistically.

"She is. We've been married for about five years, and we're actually expecting our first baby this November."

"Well, hey—congratulations!" he said, seeming genuinely excited over this news. "Now I'm really glad you let me give you that beer." He raised his can. "Here's to love and to your growing family."

For someone like Will, whose father-in-law at best tolerated him and who just the day before had been regrieving his parents' divorce because it hadn't lived up to the standard set by a rom-com, receiving a heartfelt toast from someone's dad, even if it weren't his own, was wholly unprecedented and strangely moving. Will was in on Lawrence Olsen from that moment on, for however long this chat lasted.

"It's Easterly, by the way," Will said. "My last name. Will Easterly."

Lawrence looked confused, but it cleared quickly. "I gave you my full name when I introduced myself, didn't I?" Will smiled, and Lawrence chuckled. "My kids always tease me about that. I don't even realize I'm doing it. Old business habit, I guess."

Their conversation threatened to stall for a moment or two, but now that Will wasn't in a rush to end it, he tried to find a way back in.

"Things with that girl must've worked out pretty well for you too," he said. "If you've been here over forty years."

"They did. Although I wasn't quite as brave as you. I proposed to Josie a couple of months before we graduated from college. She was coming home to Lexington to teach music, and I was ready to come with her if she'd have me, but I wasn't willing to risk ending up here on my own. I wasn't even going to tell her I'd applied to law school at Kentucky unless she said yes. We always joked that if she hadn't, I would've just gone to Harvard as my backup."

"Really?" Will said, impressed. "You got into Harvard Law?"

"Oh no, not even close. I wasn't nearly a good enough student for that. I mean, I was just lucky she grew up by a state school."

He laughed at his own joke, giving Will permission to do the same.

"And clearly, she did say yes."

Lawrence smiled again. "She did. Opening day, 1983. We had Red Sox tickets, and I asked her to marry me after the game. I was so nervous by the time it got to the seventh inning. They lost seven to one to the Blue Jays, and it was the only time in my life the Sox have been down, and I was rooting for outs."

"So why didn't you two ever move back?" Will asked. "Didn't you say Lexington was only supposed to be for a few years?"

"Yes, that was our plan. And don't get me wrong; Lexington's a fine town. But we were always a little too *hippie dippie* for our surroundings, as my father-in-law used to say. So we were going to go back to Boston, Josie was going to get her master's in music performance, and I was going to get a job at a law firm, hopefully in environmental law. But the summer after my first year, we got married, and six months later, she was pregnant.

"Suddenly, uprooting ourselves to move somewhere where we'd have no family within fifty miles and that would be far more expensive to live seemed a lot less practical. So we decided we'd put Boston off, just until Justin was old enough to go to school and I was making a little more money. Then we had our twins, Chloe and Emma, and we pushed it back a few more years."

Will was rapt. He couldn't believe the parallels to his and Rachel's situation. Lawrence took a sip of his beer and shook his head.

"Josie looked at me at the girls' high school graduation and, with no context, said, 'Maybe when they graduate from college.' I smiled, and she did too. They graduated from UCLA fifteen years ago. And here I am talking to you, in the heart of bluegrass country."

Lawrence shared all this without seeming the least bit bitter. The way his face looked when he talked about Josie and their kids, even in passing, you could sense all the unseen ways in which he adored them. If anything, it felt to Will like a well-worn anecdote that he'd shared with friends over beers when they'd given him a hard time about how he'd always sworn Kentucky was only a temporary thing.

Still, on some level, Will thought it had to bother him. Bother both of them.

"Well, there's still time," Will said. He didn't know exactly how old Lawrence was, and setting aside that they were currently drinking beers at a hotel pool on a Thursday morning, he did not appear to be someone who spent his days puttering around the house, so erring on the side of him still being a working lawyer seemed appropriate. "Maybe you two will get there when you retire."

He tried to sound optimistic as he said it, but the idea of two people wanting something for that long and not getting to it until so many of their years together had passed, if they got to it at all—it sounded to Will like a cautionary tale.

And sure enough, this time, when Lawrence smiled, it didn't read kind or wistful. It just read sad.

"That is what we decided," he said. "We were going to move there when we retired." He fidgeted with the wedding band on his finger, and for a second, Will could tell Lawrence had stopped speaking to him and was talking to someone who wasn't there. "We just didn't make it, did we?"

Josie had gone out for a run one Wednesday, Lawrence explained, as she did three mornings a week. After he'd gotten dressed for work, he had made her coffee and an English muffin with strawberry jelly, timed perfectly to when she'd walk through the door from the mudroom to the kitchen, the same door their three kids had tromped through for years. But with just the two of them, this had become their ritual, a chance to start their days together before he went to the firm and she began her lessons (she was still teaching music).

That Wednesday, though, Josie had been late getting home from her run.

She was never late getting home from her run.

So Lawrence had texted her. He'd called her. And when another 10 minutes had passed and she hadn't responded, he'd gotten into his car to go looking for her. He'd known the route she'd been running that morning because he'd known all her routes, and as he'd driven, he'd imagined catching up with Josie and her laughing at his overreaction.

When he'd come up on the flashing lights of the ambulance, he'd known instinctively that wasn't going to happen.

Josie had died of a heart attack. On the side of the road a mile and a half from their house.

Will's stomach roiled, a vision of Josie as Rachel in his head, and it took everything in him to keep the mix of breakfast and beer that had risen to the back of his throat from going any farther.

"It's been six years," Lawrence said. "When the girls were in college, we started doing these little vacations where we'd just stay at a hotel in town. Josie always loved a hotel. She said they made everything feel a little more special, even if we were down the street. Sometimes when I need to feel close to her and the quiet of our house becomes a little too much"—he waved his hand in a sweeping motion around the pool area—"I do this for a couple of days."

Lawrence stopped talking and finished his beer, his gaze on a non-existent horizon, while Will sat there, scrambled from this brush with what was in effect his worst nightmare. He tried to find an explanation, something orderly, to latch on to. Josie must've been, what, 20 years older than Rachel when this happened? More? And she was exercising, not giving birth.

"Did she have some sort of underlying condition?" Will asked, knowing he should just be giving Lawrence a sympathetic ear but desperate for a reason that felt less randomly cruel.

"No, just one of those things," Lawrence said quietly.

Will didn't know what that meant. Other than that people died unexpectedly every hour of every day. That story on maternal mortality rates came crashing back into focus, and he felt queasy again in the humid indoor air.

"I'm sorry," he finally ventured, still reeling. "For your loss and for making you relive it just now. I can't—I can't imagine."

Except he just had. And it was torture.

Lawrence's kind smile returned.

"Oh no, no, no," he said. "No apology necessary. I basically steered you into it. Like I said, she was already on my mind. I wouldn't be here if she weren't."

"I know it's not my place to ask, but have you ever considered moving closer to your kids?"

"Please, I wouldn't have told you all this if I had a problem talking about it. And to answer your question, yes, I have thought about moving. Often, actually. But I don't want to be a burden on any of them, and I don't know how to pick which one to move by."

The irony of that comment helped pull Will out of his stupor.

"I'm going to go out on a limb and say that your children don't think you're a burden. I'd *love* to have a dad like you."

Lawrence gave him a quizzical look but didn't ask for more.

"That's very kind of you to say. They tell me the same thing. Maybe they're not just being nice to their old man after all."

"Yeah, I highly doubt it."

Lawrence set his empty Heineken on top of the cooler. "I suppose the real reason I don't do it is because this is where our life was, Josie and me. We got married here, we raised our kids here, we were getting older together here . . ."

He trailed off and didn't say what Will knew he was thinking: Josie had died here. She was buried here.

"Part of you would feel like you were saying goodbye to her all over again." The words were difficult to say even though Will hadn't known her and hardly knew him.

Lawrence turned away from the water and looked at him more intently than the entire time they'd been sitting together. "For being so young, you're pretty wise, Will Easterly."

"I think maybe I just love my wife the same way you love yours."

Flexing his hand, Lawrence assessed his wedding band again.

"Sometimes, I'll wake up in the middle of the night and swear for a second I can still feel her in the bed next to me," he said. "And then I'll remember, and I'll ask myself if there's anything I would've done differently. I know our life together and our kids and the way we used to grocery shop together on Sundays and how we made each other laugh—all of it was so much more than I ever had the right to ask for. And I knew her well enough to know she felt the same. We talked about it all the time.

"But she was so talented, and she didn't just like the cello. She *loved* the cello. Now, I know what you're thinking: The cello? Who gets excited over the cello? But she did, and once you heard her play, that was it. She deserved the chance to follow that dream. And if we had moved back, she would have.

"If I have any regrets about our marriage, it's that."

Will didn't say anything in case Lawrence was going to keep going, but he didn't, and a silence spread out between them. The older man didn't know a thing about what Will had been plotting behind the scenes for the last week, nor had he offered that sentiment about regret as advice.

But Will took it in. He let himself be affected by it. And he told himself in no uncertain terms:

That's not going to be us.

TODAY

Chapter 25

"You know, Steven C. could really learn a thing or two from Kevin H."

Rachel steps off the elevator ahead of Will, nose wrinkled. "Who and who?"

"The front desk guy in Lexington and the front desk guy here," Will says. "Kevin just gave me two drink coupons for the hotel bar and told me to enjoy Nashville."

"I think that's probably the hotel's policy, not his own personal code of conduct."

"Yes, but I think Steven C. actively despised me."

"In his defense, you did try to persuade him that his hotel was haunted."

"I knew it was a mistake telling you that," Will says, pulling one of the two key cards for their room out of the little paper sleeve. "Sure, was there a period of time when I thought Lawrence *might* have been a ghost? Yes."

The lights on the lock flash green, and the door clicks open.

"But it wasn't like it was a *long* period of time," he continues once they're both inside. It's early evening, and the red numbers on the clock next to the bed read 5:14.

"Babe," Rachel says, "I say this with all the love in the world in my heart: *any* amount of time you spend thinking a conversation you just had could've been an instance of paranormal activity is, by definition, too much."

It started after Lawrence left the pool and Will discovered that his new friend's AirPods had slipped out of his pocket and gotten left behind. Will was there another 45 minutes, reading his book in an effort to recover from their unexpectedly intense conversation, but Lawrence didn't come back to claim them.

"I found these by the pool," Will said when he got to the front desk, which was once again staffed by Steven C. "I think they belong to another guest, Lawrence Olsen?"

Will set the AirPods down on the counter, but Steven didn't move to take them, instead typing something into his computer.

"I can hang on to them," he said, "but there's no one by that name staying here."

"Are you sure? Maybe just try *Lawrence*. I'm not sure how he spells *Olsen*."

Steven went back to the note he'd been writing when Will had walked up, suggesting this was not the first time someone had asked him to look up a guest's name in his computer and the search had returned no results.

"I *did* just try *Lawrence*," he said. "There are no Lawrences of any kind currently at the hotel."

"Is there any way to check people who have just checked out? He could've been leaving today."

Steven's focus stayed on the longest piece of handwritten text Will had seen in years. "Sir, when we run a search, it goes through *every* guest who has *ever* stayed here, back to when we put the system in five years ago."

"That seems a little Big Brother-y," Will said, forgetting for a moment that he was an IT guy.

"Be that as it may, I can assure you we've only had six Lawrences stay here in the last five years, and none of their last names started with an *O*."

"Only six? I feel like that's low."

"Well, I haven't recently reviewed a list of the most popular US baby names over the last twenty to eighty years, so I'm afraid I'm unqualified to comment."

"Maybe try *Larry*? He didn't seem like a Larry, but you never know." Will had had a more meaningful talk with Lawrence than he'd ever had with his own father, and he felt an obligation to get these back to him.

"Sir," Steven said, finally looking up and putting his pen down—with emphasis—"I really don't have time to start searching possible nicknames."

"I mean, it looks like you're writing the Magna Carta there, so maybe you do."

Steven exhaled deeply and then typed again. "Okay, there you go," he said. "There have been ten Larrys. One with an *O* last name. Larry O'Donahue. No Larry Olsen."

"Okay," Will said, confused. "Thanks anyway."

It didn't make sense. Will hadn't known Lawrence for long, but he was sure he wouldn't have given him a fake name. And even if he had, Lawrence would've told him what it really was after that conversation—a conversation that to Will, as he neared telling Rachel what he had done, had almost felt like the universe intervening to spur him on.

A chill passed through his body. Was it something as big and abstract as the universe?

Or was it something—or someone—a little more specific?

More to the point: Could Lawrence actually have died a long time ago and contacted Will from beyond the grave to deliver a message about not missing an opportunity to help his wife pursue her dream?

It sounded like a plotline from a far-fetched movie romance.

Which someone like Will, who had cried during *The Notebook* and was looking for good omens anywhere he could find them, was in no position to dismiss without investigating.

Will took a few steps away from the desk but turned on his heel and went quickly back. Steven saw him coming and made no attempt to hide his eye roll. Will might have found a manager or someone to complain to were he not about to inquire, in earnest, whether other guests had reported seeing ghosts around the pool.

"Sir, are you asking me if the hotel is haunted?"

"That's not quite a 'No, it's not.'"

"You know that marijuana is illegal in Kentucky, right? I mean, unless you have a prescription. But you can't, like, smoke it in the hot tub."

"Hey, we meet again!" came a voice from behind them. Will instantly recognized it as that of the man he'd known as Lawrence, and that man walked up next to him and clasped him on the shoulder. "And you found my AirPods!"

Will kept his eyes on Steven. "You're seeing this, right?" he muttered. "Like, there is another person standing here with me right now?"

Steven stared at Will in disbelief.

"Here you go, sir," Steven said, stretching a smile across his face and handing the white case to Lawrence. "Found them at the pool."

"*I* found them at the pool," Will corrected.

The hotel man lingered for a second, then shook his head and disappeared through the door behind the front desk, leaving Will alone to sort out who exactly Lawrence Olsen was. He did know now he hadn't had a supernatural encounter, which was a touch disappointing.

"I told him your name," Will said, "so he could let you know they were at the desk, but when he tried to look you up, he said no one named Lawrence Olsen had ever stayed here."

"Oh, that," Lawrence said with a gleam in his eye. "Whenever we did something like this, Josie loved using the name of a famous composer to book the room. This week, I stayed under the name of one of her all-time favorites, Amy Beach." Seeing that Will had no idea who this was, Lawrence added with a smile: "You should look her up."

So there was a logical explanation after all. Because of course there was. On an intellectual level, Will had never truly thought there had been something magical about Lawrence's appearance in his life. But he'd wanted to *believe* that some cosmic force was cosigning his plan for Rachel, and for a minute or two, a piece of him had.

Able to tell that Will was a little rattled, Lawrence invited him to split some buffalo wings in the hotel bar. They did that, with Rachel eventually joining them. She picked up some of Lawrence and Josie's story in the course of the couple of hours they spent together, and Will filled her in on the rest later, up to and including how he'd temporarily mistaken Lawrence for a ghost (but leaving out why he'd been emotionally invested in that impossibility somehow being true).

"This really has been the best week," she says once they've settled into their final hotel room of the trip. It took them three and a half hours to drive from Lexington to Nashville, and he'd gotten them reservations at the legendary Bluebird Cafe that night so they could listen to live music.

Will smiles. "I'm so glad."

Rachel smiles back. "I mean it. Going back to real life could be pretty dull in comparison."

"Could be?"

"Yeah. You know."

"Know what?"

"Are you really going to make me say it?"

"I don't know what *it* is."

"Jeez, I told you how much better you are than Seth, I told you about the date for the tattoo, I told you how lucky I am to be married to you, and now this too?"

Will raises his eyebrows.

"Fine. Real life *could be* pretty dull in comparison . . . *if I didn't have you.*"

He is looking for his phone charger, but her words stop him. Of all the moments they've had together over the course of the past week, of all the ways she's shown him how much she loves him, it's this one, on the eve of his big revelation, that makes him stop looking for omens and talismans and start looking at what's right in front of him.

She would get bored. If she didn't have him.

His carefully crafted lies feel impossibly cheap next to her honesty.

"Like, getting up and going to work on Monday is going to be a total bummer," she continues. "I've got a meeting with that rationality-of-belief guy again."

It's only Friday, and they're not on their way to Swift Saturday, but Will feels that fading into the background.

"Oh, and get this: my boss now wants me to create three designs for *every* project so we can have a more *iterative* process. She's got an MBA, for God's sake. She knows less about graphic design than I know about what you do."

Her job was the problem. But he wasn't her job.

"And my mom's going to want to do that shopping trip to Old Orchard that I canceled," Rachel adds. "I'm so not in the mood for one-on-one time with her right now."

She's ready to hear this, he thinks. *I'm ready to tell her.*

"But that's okay," Rachel goes on. "All of it. And do you know why?" She hovers over the Seurat tote and looks right at him. "You, Will. You and me and the life we've built together. The world makes sense to me when I'm with you. So there you have it. And given the unending stream of compliments I've heaped upon you this week, I think the least you could do is wear that hat tomorrow night."

"I feel the same way about you," he says, his heart now thumping.

"I know you do, babe." She puckers her lips in a kiss at him before going to sit down.

"But I still wish you didn't have to do any of that stuff."

"Yeah, well, what are you gonna do?" she says, not entirely listening as she glances at the room service menu.

"I mean, I would do anything so you didn't have to anymore."

Her attention shifts back to him now. "I know," she says slowly.

Will swallows hard, what Lawrence told him right before they parted ways the second time playing back in his mind:

I can tell how much you love her, son, and how much she loves you. Love like that is a privilege. Never take it for granted, and never stop being worthy of it.

Will, for years, has been operating under the assumption that going to extremes is how you prove that worthiness. But the privilege of a love like Rachel's, so plainly yet abundantly clear as he stands there looking at her—that demands more than a list of reasons followed by a convincing speech.

It demands he hold himself accountable.

Until he looked up from hunting for that phone charger, Will had every intention of telling her Saturday night why he'd done it.

Now he knows he has to tell her immediately that he wishes he hadn't.

"I made a mistake," he says.

Rachel's attention turns serious. "Will."

"You've got an interview at Creative Vices Tuesday."

She laughs once. It's hard. Abrupt.

She sees his expression doesn't change.

"That's impossible," she says.

"It's not. I mean, I know how it sounds, and I'm not proud of—"

"Seriously, what's going on right now?"

"Here, it'll be easier if I just show you."

Will walks over to her, holding out his phone with the Beatriz email chain pulled up on the screen. His hand shakes a little as he does it, the nervous energy running from his brain, down his neck, through his arms, and out his fingertips.

She takes the phone and is focused as she goes over the emails. He sees her eyes move as she uses her finger to scroll back up and read through everything again. When she's done, she closes the screen and puts the phone down next to her. She stares at him.

"I can't believe you did this."

She's sitting at the room's desk, but with her back to it, her body facing the king-size bed, the larger of her two bags still open on top of it from when she pulled out her clothes for dinner.

"You would've done the same for me," he says, hoping for the best while squatting down in front of her and grabbing her hands. "Well, maybe not the same. You're more creative *and* more levelheaded than me, which is kinda crazy when you think about it. But you know what I mean."

He's anxious and rambling, waiting for her to say something else. Embrace him. Berate him. Absolve him. Something.

Their TV is on mute on the hotel-guide channel, and the quiet reminds him of playing high school basketball, of all things. Junior year, he had a potential buzzer-beating shot to win sectionals, and he still remembers all the sound being sucked out of the gym as he watched the ball arc through the air toward the rim.

He just hopes it ends better this time.

And that's when she pulls her hands away.

"Is that all this week was?" she asks. "Some sort of pep talk? To get me on board? To distract me while you were doing *this*?"

He doesn't move, keeps looking up at her. "What? No. Okay, kinda. But only because I knew you would . . ."

"'You knew.' Better than me. You knew better than me what I wanted."

"That's not what I'm saying."

"I think that's exactly what you're saying," she says, standing now, her voice getting louder. "So, what, you don't think I'm capable of making my own decisions?"

He stands, too, but she's already brushing past him on her way to the door.

"Babe, c'mon. You know that's not true."

"No, what I *know* is that I don't need you to swoop in and save me. That I've *never* needed you to save me. Because I'm not some damsel in distress, no matter how much you seem to want to see me as one."

"I don't—look, I know I messed up." She's at the door now, and he's ransacking his mind for the words that might somehow keep her from leaving. "Like, exponentially. I'm trying to tell you that I'm sorry."

"Oh, you're *sorry*," she says, her voice dripping with sarcasm. "Why didn't you say so? That makes it all better."

He's stunned into silence. How did he screw this up so badly?

She opens the door.

"Where are you going?" he manages to get out.

"I don't know," she says and slams it behind her.

And there, in that nondescript, standard-king room a few miles from the Nashville airport, Will realizes something.

It doesn't matter whether he takes after his dad or not. He's perfectly capable of destroying things all by himself.

The weight of it drops him into the chair Rachel had been sitting in.

He doesn't get up for a long time.

Chapter 26

Eventually—it could've been 30 minutes, it could've been three hours, Will loses track—he gets up from the chair and drags himself over to the bed. Rachel left in such a hurry that she didn't grab her bag, and he doesn't have the heart to move it, like not touching her things will somehow make up for inserting himself into her professional life in such an egregious manner. Then again, it could also be that he just wants to be close to any part of her right now.

The TV is still on and still muted. He contemplates turning it off, but grabbing the remote off the nightstand feels like too much effort, so he it leaves it alone. Several more minutes go by, and the air conditioner kicks back on. It's the only noise in the room when a text rings out from the pillow next to his head where he set his phone. Even semicatatonic, he made sure his ringer was turned up loud so he wouldn't miss her, and his head snaps up at the trumpet text-notification sound that he long ago assigned to her, and her alone.

> I took the car and checked in at another hotel. Please don't call or text.

The surge of hope he felt hearing those trumpets evaporates before it's even fully formed.

She's gone.

He stares at the phone, unsure whether to acknowledge he's received her message. She told him to leave her alone, and he is sure she meant it. And at least he knows she hasn't left the Nashville area. But it's so out of character for them as a couple to just cut off communication like this that he can't imagine anything harder than not responding.

He thinks about asking Ali or his mom for advice. Ali has a vague sense of what's been going on, but it's too much to explain over text, and it's Friday night, so he's probably out. Not to mention he tried to keep Will from making this exact mistake, and Will just ignored him. Like an idiot.

With his mom, he doesn't even know where to start.

So he responds to Rachel with the shortest, most honest thing he can think of.

Ok. Again, I'm so, SO sorry. I love you.

When it's been 10 minutes and she hasn't so much as liked his text, let alone replied to it, he discovers he was wrong again: *that*—knowing she's ignoring him—that's harder.

Will forces himself off the bed in the direction of the bathroom and the shower, leaving his phone behind like it's betrayed him by pointing out the obvious fact of Rachel's anger at his lies.

Lies. That doesn't even cut it. This was antihero stuff, except without the *hero* and without the charm of a beautiful leading man.

Will turns on the shower. Ever since he was a kid, he's found the rush of running water extremely comforting, and as he strips off his clothes, he half wishes he could just spend the night in there. Once the water is hot, he steps in and lets it wash over him, doing his best to keep the bandage on the tattoo from getting drenched. He knows it's been long enough that he could remove it, but seeing that date right now would flood him with painful nostalgia for three days ago, when he thought those numbers could somehow keep them together, somehow keep Rachel from being furious when he told her about his ill-conceived plan. It almost makes believing Lawrence could have been a ghost look plausible in comparison.

Turning his back to the spray, Will closes his eyes and finds himself flashing back to what, until tonight, had been the worst fight they had ever had.

It happened after Isa's wedding. No one was ready to go home when the reception ended, so a large contingent of them walked to a bar down the street. Will and Rachel had been living together in Chicago for almost a year, and they'd each been asked multiple times throughout the evening when they were going to be the ones getting married. Of course that wasn't ever how the question was posed, with people far more interested in knowing when they planned to "tie the knot" or "get hitched" or sundry other clichés. The most aggressive of them dispensed with the premise of a question altogether and simply declared "You're next."

It wasn't obnoxious at all.

By that point, Will had already had the idea of proposing at the art institute near the Seurat painting, but just as when he'd moved there, the timing wasn't right yet. And he was fine with that. Young and enjoying living in the city together, they were wholly committed to each other, so there was no rush. It also didn't hurt that it gave him longer to save for a ring.

So the first time one of Rachel's uncles asked when Will was "going to make her an honest woman," and she brushed it off with a "Don't give him any ideas, Uncle Gio," digging her nails into Will's palm as she did so to keep herself from punching her dad's brother in the face, the two of them laughed.

"My family," she muttered into her Manhattan when her uncle moved on, and Will kissed her on the forehead.

They had similar exchanges all over and around that ballroom. On the dance floor. In line to get drinks. Out on the terrace when they indulged in cigars with the rest of the wedding party. And without setting out to, Rachel kept responding the same way.

"Don't give him any ideas."

The two of them had both laughed about it once, and it was an easy way to change the subject, which explained why Rachel fell into defaulting to it over and over again. But with each passing interaction, coupled with each of her Manhattans and his gin and tonics, what had started out as a harmless quip wore thinner and thinner on him.

Will thought he'd be in the clear once they got to the bar, figuring—granted, drunkenly—things would start to feel more like a party and less like a wedding reception. They hadn't been there 15 minutes when Rachel's mom's younger sister, the self-appointed *cool aunt*, sidled up to them at a high-top table and asked when they were "going to make it official already."

For what a sober person would have recognized as the seventh time but that he would've sworn was at least the 20th, Will felt like the butt of a joke. Worse, it was a joke that picked at one of his biggest insecurities: that he wasn't good enough for Rachel.

And Rachel was the one making it.

"Don't go giving this guy any ideas, Auntie," she said with a dash of a slur and her arm around him.

"You need to write some new material," Will fired back, his tone wobbly, too, but still harsh. He shrugged her arm off. "Because that shit's getting old."

Rachel looked at him, confused.

"Look at that," her aunt chimed in, either oblivious or choosing to be. "You already bicker like a married couple. You're perfect for each other!"

"I don't know," Will said, not looking at the aunt but also refusing to meet Rachel's stare. "She's told pretty much everyone at this wedding she doesn't want to marry me, so maybe not."

The aunt waited to see if one of them would play that off and defuse the tension.

"Okay, looks like I struck a nerve," she said when they didn't, and then beat a strategic retreat over to a group of Rachel's cousins.

"What the hell was that?" Rachel asked as soon as they were alone.

"That was me being over you acting like the idea of us getting married is the craziest thing you've ever heard in your entire life and making me look like a fool in front of your entire family in the process."

"That's not at all what I was doing. And you've been laughing about it just as much as me."

Still huddled around that now painfully small high-top, Will finally turned to face her. "Have I? Maybe if you'd taken a break from being *so darn hilarious*, you would've noticed I haven't laughed like the last dozen times."

Rachel lifted her glass and gave him a skeptical-bordering-on-condescending look over the rim. "I think you need to check your math there, Willem."

His full name was William, but since college, she'd sometimes call him this when she'd been drinking.

"They all already act like I'm some sort of wounded animal who followed you home from Michigan," he said.

"Wounded animal?"

"Yeah. Some little, bitty baby . . . something or other you took in out of the goodness of your heart." The alcohol had sabotaged his ability to complete the metaphor, so he attempted to make his point by pretending to rock whatever the little, bitty baby thing was in his arms.

"Okay, you're cut off," she said. Which was absolutely the right call. But the way she just decreed it, completely overlooking that she was also drunk, only made him madder.

"Oh, good idea," he said, whispering in mock conspiracy. "Don't let them see me pissed at you. The whole narrative of my patheticness might break down."

There with the water beating down on him in the shower in Nashville, nine years later and his marriage currently a mess, Will understands, maybe for the first time, just how much he'd been projecting what was going on inside of him onto Rachel's family.

Also, *patheticness*? He's pretty sure that's not a word.

He thinks back to what Rachel said next.

"Uh, I don't know where you got that. They don't think you're pathetic." They'd switched to beer, and he can still see her taking that long drink before adding: "I mean, I don't know how much they *like* you. But I don't know much *I* like you right here at this particular moment in time, either, so . . ."

When they apologized to each other the next day, she would say that was the line she regretted most. His followed in response to it.

"Well, that's good, because it's not like I'm in some sort of big ol' rush to propose to you, anyway."

They stood there stewing, finishing their beers. They hadn't been loud, but their combined body language—her ripping up a coaster into ever smaller pieces, him staring a hole into the dartboard on the opposite wall—warded off any passersby who might have been inclined to stop and chat. A few minutes passed with them each waiting to see if the other would give or, short of that, say something that would set off the next round of barbs. Eventually, Will pulled out his phone.

"What, are you just going to ignore me now?" Rachel asked, seeing an opening to go at him again. "Got some email you need to catch up on at midnight on a Saturday?" She shifted into a parody of his voice, which sounded like a besotted Smokey Bear. "'I'm Willem, and my job is *so* important!'"

"That's super mature, *Fartosaurus*," he said, deploying Isa's childhood nickname for her, which Rachel had told him about after she'd farted once when she and Will were having sex. Had she not been caught so off guard, the last of her beer might have ended up in his face. That said, she was close to laughing at how ridiculous this had gotten, and if she had, maybe he would've, too, and then they'd have gotten back to their night. But that didn't happen.

"For your information, I'm calling a cab," Will said.

"Seriously?"

"Uh-huh."

"So, what, that's it? Your feelings get a little hurt, and now you're going back to the hotel? *That's* mature."

"No. I'm going back to the apartment."

He could tell this surprised her. "Well, *for your information*," she said, "I'm not leaving my sister's wedding to join you in your little, bitty pity party."

"Awesome. Because I wasn't asking you to."

Rachel looked stung, but she covered it quickly and went over to join her aunts and cousins.

He went home, to their home, by himself that night. She stayed in the hotel room she had booked for the two of them. He had trouble sleeping and was wide awake when she tried calling at 3:30 a.m., but he didn't answer. She followed that with a text that simply read U up? If it'd been an apology, he might have written back, but considering her phrasing was better suited to a booty call, he didn't. It was and still is the one and only time he has ever purposefully ignored a call or text from her out of anger.

They didn't talk until Rachel returned to the apartment early the next afternoon. She said she was sorry for what she'd said about not liking him while they were fighting and making him feel like she didn't want to get married. Because of course she did—just not yet. He apologized for not speaking up sooner about the joke and then overreacting when he did, and that obviously he had already thought about how and when he'd want to propose—also, not yet. Then came a makeup hug, followed by a makeup make out, which would've become makeup sex if they hadn't simultaneously felt nauseous as a result of how hungover they were. So instead, they curled up together under a blanket on the couch and watched *Date Me Now!* for the rest of the day. They were back to being them, no worse for wear.

It's a hopeful thought as Will, now in the midst of a fight that has dethroned what happened at Isa's wedding as their worst, turns off the water and grabs a fluffy white hotel towel to dry himself off. As he starts drying his hair, he even finds himself thinking that if history is any indicator, everything could be fine by this time tomorrow, in time for Swift Saturday. He looks at his wrist and picks at the bandage, contemplating a permanent unveiling of the tattoo that is a reminder of just how sure Rachel had been about him.

But then he spots her toiletry bag on the bathroom counter.

He remembers *how* she left, with no thought for what she was going to wear or how she was going to, say, take out her contacts, like she had to be anywhere but near him, and his optimism disappears as fast as it arrived.

This fight isn't like last time. As angry as he was then, he never felt like anything was truly in jeopardy. For one, they were both drunk, which had inserted a certain emotional distance into the argument even as it was happening, like they both knew in real time that they were each embellishing reality. Two, they'd been out of school more than three years, but it still had many of the contours of the kind of scene you might make in college, right down to the indiscriminate use of a nickname like Fartosaurus. And the fight in the bar popped up almost out of nowhere, its roots only extending as far back as earlier in the night (even if Will's insecurities themselves were deep seated). Whereas what he'd done in arranging the interview with Creative Vices had become in effect a weeklong con. There was no misunderstanding at the heart of it, no joke inadvertently causing offense. His actions had been purposeful.

Perhaps most critically, Will got hurt before. Rachel was the one doing the harm. It was questionable if a moral high ground existed in the early morning hours at that bar, but if it did, it was his. And despite turning down her phone call, he still would've answered a text from her if it had been anything more substantive than U up?

No, Rachel isn't just angrier with him than he's ever been with her; she's angrier than he's ever seen her, period.

He'd been prepared (or at least thought he was) for her to ask him how he could've been so stupid or to yell at him for an hour straight or to demand he call the whole thing off. Maybe all of those at once. Or worse: she might have kicked him out of the hotel room, told him to sleep somewhere else.

But even then, he still would've known where to find her when it was time. For the purposes of the trip, this room was their home base, their shared space in a city neither had ever visited. Her leaving him behind here and not telling him where she went?

It feels more ominous.

He leaves the bandage where it is, picks his clothes up off the floor, and heads out to the room to put on a pair of pajama pants and a plain gray T-shirt. Retrieving his phone from the pillow, he instinctively taps the screen to see if she tried him, knowing full well that she didn't.

You'd think that would lessen the disappointment of seeing nothing there, but it doesn't.

The lack of any other text on the screen besides the clock makes 8:32 p.m. feel far lonelier than he's used to. If they were at home, they'd just be settling in for a night of TV together, or maybe she'd be reading while he did a crossword puzzle. He loves that time of day, those few hours when everything that isn't them seems to matter a little less. But right now, all he has of her is the photo on his lock screen of them at the botanical gardens and the bags she left behind.

Will imagines Rachel waking up in the middle of the night, deciding she can't be in the same city as him, and driving home alone, calling Isa on the way to ask if she can stay with her. It makes him want to start flipping through all the pictures of them to feel closer, so he slips the phone into his pocket before he can start. He needs to do something productive—literally anything—to keep himself from spiraling even more than he already is.

Dinner. He should have some dinner. The last time he ate was lunch, which was before they left Lexington. Forget the fact that he isn't hungry. He *should* be hungry, and given the circumstances, that's enough to go on.

He goes over to the desk and pulls the faux-leather-bound booklet of a menu off it. His eyes go first to the 22-dollar mac and cheese, noticeably lacking a gourmet flourish like lobster or truffles, and he quickly ascertains that the meals are reasonably priced by room service standards, which is to say exorbitant in any other context.

If he had something approaching an appetite, he'd probably give the burger and *frites* a shot and wonder the whole time whether it was actually Kobe beef or just a way to make him feel better about drastically overpaying for a meal he could get at McDonald's. As it is, he sets the menu back down and decides he'll just go to the vending machines down the hall and really lean in to the bleakness of his situation.

It's a mistake, and not just because of the scant nutritional value that awaits him.

As soon as he has the thought, his mind is racing back to Mackinac and the unabashed joy on Rachel's face at the Marquise as she weighed whether their waiter was part of a double-Lane couple or instead had referred to himself as a "vending machine of bullshit." He could practically hear her laugh.

A few days ago, he couldn't have imagined a scenario where this memory would make him start to cry. But this night is proving to be full of firsts.

"What's wrong with that man, Mommy?" a little boy asks as Will stumbles toward them in the hallway, wiping the tears off his face.

"Shh," his mom says. "That's not polite." She looks right at Will. "Sorry about that. Kids, you know?"

"It's okay." Will looks at the boy. "Don't ever let anyone tell you it's not okay for daddies to cry. Everybody cries. Mommies. Daddies. The PAW Patrol probably. Everyone."

The boy nods solemnly, and Will manages a weak smile while the woman pulls her son in closer and shifts uncomfortably. "Are you all right?" she asks as he walks away.

"Peachy," he says without looking back. "These are happy tears. I effing love peanut M&M's."

Will gets to the machine and discovers it is sold out of peanut M&M's.

He stares through the glass, debating his options. It's the kind of conundrum Rachel would love. Do you stay in the M&M's family and go with plain, or do you buy a bag of Reese's Pieces for the first time in your adult life? Or maybe just blow it all up and go with Skittles?

Feeling her absence, he can't help himself. He pulls out his phone.

You know you've hit rock bottom when the unavailability of peanut M&Ms forces you to change your dinner plans.

He slips in his money and pushes the button for the Reese's. As he's fishing the bag out from behind the machine's little swinging door, he hears the ring of a text back.

Ali, fast as ever.

It went that bad?

Afraid so. You were right.

Is Rachel with you?

No.

Where is she?

I don't know. Another hotel somewhere. She took the car and told me not to call.

Will buys a bottle of water from the adjacent drink machine and then retreats slowly down the hall in the direction of his room, waiting for what Ali is going to say next. When there's still no response after he's gone back in, sat on the bed, and opened his candy, he checks to see if he forgot to hit send on his last message.

But he did send it. And Ali never takes this long.

Will assumes he doesn't know what to say, and who can blame him? Ali had tried, repeatedly, to warn him what a bad idea it was to go behind Rachel's back, but Will had gone through with it anyway. It was a little presumptuous to ask for a sympathetic ear now. Especially on a Friday night when Ali could be out in New York City. Eating Reese's Pieces alone in his hotel room is painfully fitting.

About to turn the volume up on the long-muted TV, Will stops when his phone rings.

Not a text ring. But a ring ring.

"Hey, man," a subdued Ali says, not waiting for him to speak. "I'm really sorry."

They rarely talk over the phone. That his friend chose to call him now makes Will realize all over again just how bad this is.

But he is grateful for the reminder that he doesn't have to face it by himself.

"Don't be," Will says. "I was bound to screw things up sooner or later."

Chapter 27

Will wakes up a little after 8:00 a.m. on Saturday, and for the first time since Rachel left, he turns off the TV. He purposefully left it on overnight because the room felt too quiet otherwise. He also left his ringer set as loud as it would go in case history repeated itself and she decided to reach out in the predawn hours. If something as simple as a *U up?* had come through, he likely would've knocked the phone off the nightstand down into the dark sea that was the carpeted floor in his scramble to respond. Although the need to reply never arose, hoping that it would only added to the swirl of thoughts that kept waking him back up whenever he managed to drift off for a few minutes.

When will Rachel be ready to talk?

What do I do if it's time to go home and I still haven't heard from her?

This episode of How I Met Your Mother *would be pretty funny if I weren't perched above a yawning chasm of despair.*

How long will it take Rachel to forgive me? Can she ever forgive me?

What does it mean for us if she can't?

The notion that he did something irreparable makes him uneasy. His actions were very stupid, but he isn't a stupid person. Nor is he routinely oblivious to the feelings of others. If anything, he is *too* aware of everyone around him, too concerned with what they're thinking and how his actions might make them feel. Rachel knows this. Which has to make the fact that he chose to email Beatriz—posing as Rachel!—cut so much deeper.

He acknowledged it was a mistake, that was true. But Rachel understood there was nothing unintentional about it.

"You care," Ali told him the night before. It was near the end of the 45 minutes he spent on the phone with Will, who had debriefed him in painstaking detail. "You care so much. And you show up for the people you care about."

"I don't feel like I show up for you that much."

"What're you talking about? What about that Thanksgiving? I was desperate to get out of the city, I couldn't fly home, and you made sure I had a place to go."

Will had the phone on speaker and directed a dismissive laugh in its direction on the bed's comforter. "Some friend. You had to drive like twelve hours to get there."

"Okay. What about that time freshman year when that kid in the Confederate-flag hat tried to start something with me at that party?"

Will remembered this clearly. It had been October, a year before he would meet Rachel, when his new roommate had been the one and only person who made him feel like he belonged in college.

"Yeah, I asked you if you wanted me to help you kick his and his friend's asses—which, hilarious given my lack of upper body strength—and then you told me if you got into a fight every time someone said something like that to you, you'd never not have broken bones or a black eye."

"That's not what I'm talking about," Ali said. "I'm talking about when we went out to that all-night diner afterwards, and you asked me about what I'd said, and I told you I didn't want to talk about it. And you didn't push it but told me you'd be there if I ever did. I knew then you weren't some guy I was just going to live with my freshman year and then never talk to again.

"So don't act like what you do doesn't count. Like *you* don't count. I know your dad made you feel that way, and I know I've never met him, but I'm pretty confident he's never cared about anyone enough to do what you did this week, as batshit as it was."

Despite the many conversations on many topics he and Ali would go on to have after that incident at the party, from race and religion to comic books and Chipotle, Will had never known what he'd said that night had meant that much to his friend.

The thing about his dad easily meant as much to Will now.

"Thanks, man," he said. "I needed to hear that."

"And Rachel needs *you*. Not the misterioso, go-behind-her-back you. The real you. The one who's scared about being a dad and scared she's not going to stay happy in her job. You can tell her all that. You *need* to tell her all that."

"But what if it just stresses her out more?"

"More than you creating a fake email account for her and accepting job interviews on her behalf?"

Will gave a sad laugh this time. "Fair."

"Besides, she stuck with you after that Buffalo Wild Wings date and then that rancid coleslaw from the deli, so she's not going anywhere."

This was a reassuring sentiment in the moment, but the intervening hours—first when Will should've been sleeping and now that he's getting up to brush his teeth and use the bathroom, still with no word from her—have allowed the doubt to elbow itself all the way in. It doesn't help that he's never been able to entirely shake that feeling that their ending up together was some sort of oversight, that she's supposed to be with someone . . . less him.

Going all the way back to their first Christmas together and that scavenger hunt at the bookstore, Will's grand gestures originated from how crazy he was about her. However, as he stands at the sink, changing the dressing on his tattoo bandage, being sure to never look at it, he's forced to wrestle with how quickly those gestures also became his way of guarding against her ever noticing just how underwhelming he fears he is on his own.

And now it's one of his big plans threatening to unravel it all. He gambled the relationship with the love of his life, who is pregnant with their child, on a phony Gmail and a flight to LA. And why?

Because it's easier than admitting all the ways he doesn't like himself.

His bathroom routine kills all of five minutes, and then he's back where he started, on the bed, with nothing to do. And while he could call an Uber and do nothing anywhere in Nashville, he can't bring himself to leave the room yet, hoping that Rachel might return after a late-morning checkout from wherever she stayed. So he will sit, and he will wait. It's a kind of purgatory for someone who prides himself on finding creative solutions to challenging problems, one he'd be ill equipped to handle even if the stakes weren't his marriage.

He does decide it's probably time for him to have a real meal and calls room service from the room phone, ordering scrambled eggs, toast, coffee, and orange juice.

The phone rings two minutes later, and he wants it to be Rachel so badly that he doesn't register how bizarre it would be for her to call that phone rather than his cell.

"Hello?" Will blurts out with more breathless anticipation than the room service guy is accustomed to.

"Sir, this is Jimmy from downstairs."

"Who?" Will asks, deflating.

"Room service? You just placed an order?"

"Yes. Sorry. What's up?"

"We're actually out of orange juice."

"Oh. That's fine. Thanks for letting me know."

"Now we do have other juice options you can choose from," Jimmy says.

Will's thoughts had already started going back to Rachel, so he sounds more confused than he should when he asks, "Juice options?"

"Yes. We have grapefruit juice, mango juice, pineapple juice, cranberry juice, tomato juice, apple juice, prune juice, and beet juice."

"That's a lot of juice."

"It is."

"And you have beet juice, but no orange juice."

"Well, orange juice is a lot more popular than beet juice. It goes fast."

"I would imagine so. I think I'll just stick with the coffee."

"Very good. Is there more than one person in your party? Would you like a pot?"

Such a simple question, and it slices Will in half. Logic dictates he answer no, but he doesn't want to admit that to himself or the man on the phone.

"That would be great," he says quietly. "Thank you."

They hang up, and Will feels an immediate need to interact with something besides the self-loathing in his own head. He checks the clock again. His mom and he don't usually talk this early, but she's not a late sleeper, so he knows he can call. Except he doesn't want to call; he wants to see her face, which leads to the even more unusual decision for him to use FaceTime. When he opens the app, the list of past video calls confirms that the last time they did this was in February. She had a question about her internet router, and he asked her to show him which lights were flashing in what color.

She picks up after the third ring. She's in her robe, and he can see her pulling the door on her small sunporch closed behind her.

"Willie Will," she says, her concern already evident, even through the small screen in his hand. "What's wrong?"

"Good morning to you, too, Mom," he says, emitting an unconvincing laugh. He wouldn't have dialed her if he didn't want to tell her everything, but that doesn't mean it's easy. Talking with Ali had made him more open to asking for help, though.

"Don't try to change the subject," his mom says. "You never FaceTime me. Especially not at eight thirty in the morning on a Saturday, and *especially* not while you and Rachel are on vacation. Why aren't you still in bed with your beautiful wife?"

"Too much, Mom," he says, the overly intimate nature of her question the only thing shielding him from the devastation of it. "I really can't handle a sex talk right—oh my God, there's a penis! I'm eye level with a penis!"

Unfazed by her son's alarm, his mom turns to look at the naked man in the shadow of her sunporch doorway. Among other details Will wishes he hadn't noticed in the split second before he looked away, the guy appears to be about Lawrence's age, very fit, and likely the owner of some big shoes.

Like massive.

"Oops, sorry, Trishy," he whispers. "Do you want any coffee?"

"That would be great, Glenn, thank you."

Will hears her door slide shut again and looks back at his phone.

"Trishy?" he asks. His mom's name is Patricia, and she typically goes by Trish. Katie called her Trisha from the time they were kids. And Will has heard Pat once or twice. But Trishy is a new one.

"Yeah, it's his nickname for me. He says it's because I have a nice tushy."

"Dear God."

"Don't worry, I think I'm going to end it with him. He's a nice guy but just not for me." She makes a face like she just had something sour. "Too clingy."

"It doesn't look like you're ending it."

"I know. I mean to. It's just that . . . well, he does have *some* useful qualities, is all."

"Yes, I believe I just got an eyeful of those qualities."

She smiles knowingly. "Mmm. Sorry about that. But enough about me. What's going on with you? No more stalling."

He plays with his wedding band like Lawrence did at the pool and, under his mother's watchful gaze from several hundred miles away, is forced to decide between giving her context or jumping straight to the conflict.

"Rachel and I had a fight," he says, getting the end out of the way first. She'll hear it all in short order.

"Okay."

"A bad one. Actually, the worst we've ever had. She left the hotel room before dinner last night and hasn't come back."

"Last night?" his mom asks, her voice rising as a precursor to panic, any thought of what she'd been doing with Glenn a few minutes ago now vanished. "Have you heard from her? Is she safe?"

"Oh yeah. Yes. She texted me to say she checked into another hotel." He takes a deep breath. "She, uh—she asked me not to call or text her."

His mom sits there quietly thinking for a minute. While she does, Glenn reappears with her coffee in hand and some snug-fitting boxer briefs around his middle. It's a modest improvement until he kisses her on the top of her head and then unintentionally brushes her shoulder with his bulge on his way out.

"So what did you do?" she asks Will after taking a sip from her mug. This is the woman who tends to believe in him at all costs—she encouraged him, for instance, to try walking on to the basketball team at Michigan despite the five points per game he averaged his senior year—so her presumption of his guilt, as accurate as it is, surprises him.

"How do you know she didn't do something?"

"Well, for starters, you said she said to leave her alone, which would be an odd thing for the person who screwed up to do." He notices she has a strange look, like she's pulling something from somewhere deep inside her. "For another thing, I know how much that girl loves you. She would not walk out on you like this unless you did something colossally dumb. And given the caring man I raised and that I know you to be, I'd also venture a guess that whatever it was caught Rachel completely off guard."

His mom's eyebrows arch, searching his face, and he can't hold her stare.

"Where are you now?" she asks when he doesn't respond, sensing his guilty conscience the way only a parent can. "Nashville?"

"Uh-huh."

"Okay. That's about a five-hour drive from here. So I need to warn you: if you're about to tell me that you cheated on her, I will be there by this afternoon to break every bone in your body."

"Oh my God, Mom—no!" he says, the sting of the insult whipping his attention back to the screen. "How could you even think that?"

They're almost glaring at each other, and it goes on for several seconds until she softens and relaxes her expression, convinced he's telling her the truth. He sits back a little, and she wipes the corner of her eye and takes another sip.

"I'm sorry, Willie Will. What you were saying took me somewhere else for a moment. Somewhere a long time ago. That wasn't about you."

Even though she's being vague, and even though she's referring to something they've never discussed, it's all too clear what she's talking about.

"My dad cheated on you?"

She sighs. "Yes. While I was pregnant."

"Oh, Mom. I had no idea. I mean, I obviously knew he sucked, but this is like a whole other level."

"You know, it's funny," she says with a hint of a chuckle. "You think you leave certain things behind, that you've made your peace with them, and then all of sudden, poof—you think of them when you least expect it. 'Break every bone in your body'? I don't talk like that. That was literally what Katie said about him when it happened." She wipes her eye again. "Wow, do I miss her. Talk about things sneaking up on you. And again, I am sorry."

"It's all right, Mom. I miss her too. Part of me has been wondering if she's been looking down this week trying to keep me from messing things up with Rachel."

"Okay, so tell me: What did happen?"

Will gives her roughly the same recap he shared with Ali. She cringes whenever he mentions something about his communication with Beatriz at Creative Vices but never interrupts him, letting him make it abundantly clear that he both knew what he was doing was an enormous risk and that he took it on only because he's desperate for Rachel to have everything she wants.

His mom finishes her entire cup of coffee while he's talking, and she's quiet again when he finally stops. But the look on her face this time is kind. And sad, almost pitying.

"Sweetie, Rachel already *has* everything she wants. She has her career. She has a partner she loves who she knows will support her in whatever she tries to do with that career. And she's scared about this baby, but she's also excited because she's having it with you."

"But what if I can't do it, Mom?"

"Do what?"

"Be that partner she needs. Be strong. Be a dad. It's kind of fitting you brought mine up because ever since Rachel got pregnant, I've been terrified I'm going to be as bad a father as he was. Like it's in my DNA or something."

"Willie Will, you listen to me: your mom forgetting who she was talking to and momentarily lumping you in with that SOB is the one and only time I've ever entertained you two having anything in common. You're caring and thoughtful in every way that he is narcissistic and awful, and I'm so sorry my memory of something he did to me more than twenty-five years ago clouded my judgment."

He wants to believe her. He really does. But believing he inherited nothing other than a few facial features from the man hardly seems possible. Wasn't that why his mom had just worried he might also be a cheater?

"I know why he left," he says.

"What do you mean?"

"I was listening at your bedroom door. He said if you'd never had kids, things might've worked out between you."

His mother looks not like she's been stabbed in the back but harpooned through the heart.

"Oh, baby. I never knew that. Oh no. No, no, no. Why didn't you ever tell me you heard that?"

Because I thought it was my fault. Because I thought it meant I wasn't enough.

But that's too hard to tell her without making her feel like she did something wrong.

"Because I was embarrassed, I guess," he says.

"I can't believe I'm saying this, but please tell me you heard what I said *after* he said that."

"No. I was afraid I'd get in trouble for eavesdropping, so I ran back to my room."

"I told him it had nothing to do with you and everything to do with him not being able to keep his dick in his pants."

"Wait—he *kept* cheating on you?"

"Yes, he did. With his assistant. With a waitress at a restaurant we used to go to. With some sorority girl working at the driving range for the summer."

For some reason, it stuns Will to learn all this. It's not like he's been operating under the assumption that his dad was a decent human being. And hearing that he'd had multiple affairs still can't undo the well-worn tracks of what Will's told himself for all these years about what caused his parents' divorce. Then there's the fact that if it had really just been because of the cheating, wouldn't his dad still have tried to make some kind of an effort with Will?

It changes everything while changing nothing.

"What an asshole," he says, which feels woefully inadequate.

"I promise you this: if your aunt had known you overheard what he said that day, we would've been visiting her in prison. Because hand to God, she would've murdered him."

Will thinks of Katie at *Harry Potter*, and he nods weakly.

"I'm serious," his mom says. "That woman adored you. I adore you. And most importantly, Rachel *adores* you. I've known that from the first time I saw you two together."

"Well, I hope you're right. I mean, that you're still right. Because after this . . ." He starts to tear up and, when he is unable to finish the thought, tries to wave away the emotion with his hand. Seeing him cry makes his mom start too.

"I wish I could hug you right now, sweetie. But I can't." She inhales deeply. "What I can do, though, is tell you the honest-to-goodness truth, and I'm not going to sugarcoat it."

He sniffs hard and clears his nose. "I'm listening."

"There's good news, and there's bad news. I'll start with the bad. You screwed up. Big time. Bigger than you ever have in the entire time you've known her. You ignored what she asked you to do, you lied to her, and you compromised her ability to make her own decisions. That would be upsetting to anyone, but it's doubly so as a woman since for all of recorded history, we've been told what to do. And because it came from the person she trusts more than anyone in the world, it feels like even more of a betrayal. You need to use this time apart to really think about all that."

She studies his face for a reaction. She hasn't said anything he hasn't already been thinking about, but it hits hard coming from her.

"You said there was also good news?" he eventually asks.

"I did. The good news is that this is not going to ruin your marriage. Not even close. Trust me as someone who not only has had a marriage end but who also knows what you and Rachel have."

She smiles at him. He makes himself smile back and tries not to think about how much faith she had in his basketball skills too.

Again, he wants to believe her, and mostly, he does, just the way he had Ali.

But he knows it's not going to stick until he sees Rachel.

"Now get out of that room," his mom says. "You're not doing either of you any good just sitting there. You'll think better if you walk around and get some fresh air."

There's a knock at the door, and she looks hopeful for longer than he does.

"Room service," he explains. "Can you give me a second?"

"Of course."

Will lets the woman with the cart in, she sets his breakfast up, and he tips her, the entire exchange taking under a minute. He retrieves his phone and his mom from the desk and is about to thank her and say goodbye, but there's something else he's been debating asking, and he's found again that the call with Ali has increased his resolve.

"By the way, on the subject of my dad, did you ever find out why he wanted my phone number?"

"No. I just told him you didn't want him to have it; he started to argue with me, and then I hung up. Why do you ask?"

Will considers playing it off as though he was just curious.

But then he decides he's done enough lying for one trip.

Chapter 28

After he finishes his breakfast, Will decides he'll follow his mom's advice and get out of the room. He doesn't like the idea of missing Rachel if she were to come back, but she'll call if she does. He needs to do something before he sees her, anyway.

He needs to face his dad. And he needs to do it on his own.

Based on the location of the hotel on the outskirts of the city—Will could see the skyline in the distance from his room—and Rachel having the car, he's going to have to get an Uber if he wants to do anything more ambitious than go to the Waffle House across the street.

The elevator opens onto the lobby, and he uses his phone to request the car. Three minutes. He'd remembered a bakery he saw on Yelp when researching breakfast spots before they got to Nashville. All the reviews raved about the doughnuts. He'd take the car there and then, if needed, look for somewhere a little quieter to make the call.

The sun is blazing, the kind of day where you hope your Uber driver likes air-conditioning as much as you do. When Shayla pulls up in her silver Mitsubishi Montero and he climbs in, he is grateful to discover that she does, which more than makes up for the subtle yet persistent strength of the air freshener.

"How's it going?" Will says after he shuts the door.

"Good." Shayla is probably in her early 40s but has the voice of a smoker and seems older. If he had to describe it, he'd call the SUV's scent Marlboro Meadow.

"Long Night?" she asks.

"Huh?" he says, startled.

"The bakery? That's where we're going, right?"

"Oh. Yeah."

"Good choice."

She shifts into drive, and he looks down to see if Rachel's texted, even though he's had the phone in his hand the entire time. When he sees she hasn't, he starts tapping in his passcode with the aim of jotting down what he wants to say to his father.

"You ever been to Nashville before?" Shayla asks while he's still typing in the six digits of his and Rachel's anniversary.

"Nope, first time." The screen unlocks, and he opens his Notes app.

"Business or pleasure?" Shayla follows up.

"Uh, pleasure. Vacation." He starts his first bullet point, about how much it hurt that his dad hadn't come to their wedding. Hadn't even responded to the invitation when he should've felt lucky to be invited in the first place. Shayla at first seems to recognize that Will's doing something, but the pause in her questions proves temporary, likely brought about by her needing to shift her focus to the semi bearing down on them as she merges onto the highway.

"Vacation by yourself?" Shayla looks at him with a grin in her rearview mirror once she's successfully punched the Montero past the truck. "You know, I had a lot of bachelorette parties last night. I bet you could find yourself a bridesmaid."

This causes him to look up from his phone.

"I'm with my wife, actually."

"Where is she?"

"Sleeping in," he says, realizing that he's going to have this conversation whether he wants to or not and that his newfound commitment to not lying doesn't extend to Uber drivers. He notices Shayla's wearing a Gretchen Grayson concert T-shirt, another painful reminder that while he may want to call his dad on his own, he's not alone by choice.

"I like your shirt. Rachel—that's my wife—she's a huge fan."

"Oh yeah? I haven't listened to her new album, but I need to. I just really love her for how unafraid she is to speak up. Country music has this history of treating women like props, you know? Then it tosses them out if they go off script. It's like, 'We know this is your dream, so if we're gracious enough to let you pursue it, you better be so damn grateful that you don't dare have an opinion about what you do with it.'"

Will watches out the window as Shayla blows by a slow-moving RV. A sympathetic way of reading what he did with this interview for Rachel is that it was the exact opposite of making her choose between her dream and the other things in her life that are important to her.

But he did kind of tell her what to do with that dream.

"I wish Rachel were here," he says in the understatement of a lifetime. "You two would get along great."

Shayla must have heard the sadness in his voice because, as she moves them into the right lane so she's ready for the approaching exit, she catches his eye in the rearview again.

"She's not sleeping in, is she?"

He's a little thrown that she saw through his lie, and even more that she's called him on it.

"That obvious, huh?"

"Well, when you've been driving people around as long as I have, you notice things you might not otherwise."

Will nods but leaves it at that. Shayla gets quiet, too, and he thinks his inability to mask his emotions has succeeded where his more direct efforts to kill the conversation failed. He's about to start on the list for his call again when Shayla asks:

"So how long ago did she die?"

Will looks up from the phone again, a sign for Belmont University passing by outside his window.

"I'm sorry, what was that?"

"Your wife, Rachel—when did she, you know, pass?"

Yup, that's what she said.

"Uh, no, Rachel's very much alive."

Shayla's head pops back in surprise. "Really? Wow. You were giving off some serious widower energy there."

It definitely isn't a compliment, but he can't tell if it's all the way to an insult. It also makes him think of Lawrence and Josie.

Will bet that if you told Lawrence he could have one more day with Josie, but it had to be the day following the most he had ever screwed up in their marriage, whatever that was, that Lawrence would take that deal in an instant, even if it meant Josie being furious with him in that limited time they had together.

Will and Rachel didn't have one day. They had the rest of their lives. No one had died here. They were going to figure this out. They had to.

"Nope," he says, a little pep in his voice for the first time since Rachel left. "Just a fight."

"Well, it must've been a bad one because I don't normally make mistakes like that. Reading people is my superpower."

That harshes his momentary high, and he wants to tell her that she sounds like the world's worst Avenger. And mercifully, she gets a call and starts talking to someone through her Bluetooth, forgetting about him until they pull up outside Long Night Bakery in a neighborhood called 12 South. He thinks he's going to get out without another word exchanged between them and opens his door.

"Hold on," Shayla says to the person on the phone and then looks back at Will. "Try the churro doughnut. It'll make you feel better. And good luck with Rachel. I'm sure it'll work out."

"Thanks," he says, grateful for that bit of kindness and glad he didn't say the Avengers thing.

The bakery is packed, way too crowded for a call, which is fine because he didn't make it too far on his list. He gets in line and quickly encounters evidence of what Shayla talked about in regard to her fares from the night before, a handful of women in their mid-20s in line in front of him wearing matching Lexi's Bachelorette: Day 2 T-shirts.

Even though he's just used his phone to pay for the Uber, he checks for anything from Rachel on his way to the Notes app. But this time, when there's nothing, his disappointment is tempered by his thoughts in the car of Lawrence and Josie and the realization that when he next sees his wife, he'll at the very least know once and for all where he stands with his dad.

Whether that goes as poorly as Will expects it to or not, he knows it's key to his and Rachel's long-term happiness.

"Oh my God, did you see that guy Amy was making out with last night?" a member of Lexi's crew asks about another, who clearly isn't there.

"The guy in the Hawaiian shirt?"

"Uh, yeah. He was like fifty."

The women erupt in laughter, and he feels a little bad for Amy, wherever she is. Hearing the name also reminds him of that composer Lawrence mentioned a couple of days earlier, the one whose name he was staying under, Amy Beach. Will leaves his list and does as Lawrence suggested and googles her. Turns out she was a child prodigy born in the 1860s who grew up to become the first American woman to publish a symphony. Despite not being given access to all the same opportunities a man of her talents would've had, she became a well-known composer, only to fade from the public consciousness following her death.

Will gets why Josie, the cellist who never got to pursue her performance dreams, would've said Amy Beach was one of her favorites. Lawrence said he regretted that Josie didn't have that chance.

Will wishes he could ask Josie whether she did too.

He gets to the front of the line and orders his churro-inspired doughnut, which is handed to him in a pastel-colored box, and grabs a seat at one of the picnic tables outside. It is absolutely the best doughnut he's ever had in his life, but he hardly even notices, the call that he came to make once again his focus.

The more he thinks about it, the less concerned he is about the list, which now has five items on it. Assholes, bullies, whatever you want to call them—they don't respond to talking points. They respond when they know you're not afraid of them. And Will has been afraid for way too long.

He throws out the box and takes the bottle of water he bought with him. The neighborhood is highly walkable, even if the humidity is making the doughnut feel like he swallowed a bowling ball. In between chugs of water, his gaze bounces around between all the local businesses, restaurants and otherwise, on either side of the street and the many stickers dotting the lampposts and other poles, his favorite being the one giving the patriarchy a one-star review. As on Mackinac Island, there are dogs everywhere.

Near the end of the block, he comes to a coffee shop. The boxy building is two stories, with outdoor seating in the shade under the overhang of the second floor.

He steps inside to recycle his bottle and get an iced coffee to replace it. He reemerges five minutes later and claims a two-person table at the far end of the seating area, next to one of the brick columns.

After taking out his phone, he sets it on the table. For the first time since Rachel walked out, he hasn't done this to check for word from her. Instead, he closes his eyes and takes a long, deep breath.

When he opens them, he types in the number for his dad, which he got from his mom, hits the green call button, and starts counting the rings, waiting for an answer.

Chapter 29

"Hello?" comes through the phone before it gets to the fourth ring.

Will can hear the television turned up too loudly in the background. He doesn't know if he's called a cell or a landline, but he's picturing his dad having grumpily trudged over to the latter.

"Uh, hi," Will says. He hasn't heard his dad's voice in more than five years. It sounds older than Will expected, but he can still detect a growl of disdain in it. All just from a hello.

"Who is this?" his dad asks.

Will should've known. Why would he recognize him?

"It's Will." There's a pause, so he adds: "You know, your son?"

"Ah, William." His dad is the only person who's ever called him William, and his voice softens a bit with what seems like warmth, but Will doesn't trust it. "Good of you to call. I didn't expect to hear from you."

The TV noise disappears, suggesting either his dad has turned it down or moved to a different room. Their relationship has been so nonexistent that even that level of attention tracks as significant in Will's mind.

"Yeah, well, I told Mom not to give you my number, but I guess I changed my mind."

"So she said. I don't know why she mentioned it to you in the first place. I shouldn't need permission before calling my own son."

Maybe she mentioned it because you never *call me, and she knows I can't stand you?*

Will pushes his lower lip out with this tongue to keep those words from coming out of his mouth. This conversation is almost guaranteed to go sideways at some point, but he needs to get something from it first.

"Well, I'm here now. What was it you wanted to talk about?"

"See? I knew you'd be interested." His dad's entire phone demeanor lightens, sounds happy, which is even more out of character than the warmth of 30 seconds ago. "It's actually good news. I'm getting married, William."

Will can't keep up with his thoughts.

Does Mom know? Why would a habitual cheater get married again? Did he not hate family generally but just us specifically? Why does he think I'd be happy about this? Is he telling me because he wants me to go to the wedding? Be in the wedding?

"William?"

"Uh, sorry. That's just—yeah."

His dad barks a laugh. "I'll take that as a congratulations."

Will stares at his compostable iced-coffee cup sweating onto the black metal table. "All right, so who is this person?" he asks. He doesn't really care what the answer is. He just knows he needs to say something.

"This *woman* is someone I met at my church."

"Your *church?*" His dad had said it like the devil hadn't wept the first time he touched a pew.

"Yes, I started going about a year ago. You get to a certain age, you start taking stock of your life, and you realize some things."

Will can feel a glimmer of hope creeping in. He tries to bat it away, knowing from experience that it's fool's gold, that whenever he's thought this man was about to say or do something self-aware or humble, Will has walked away more disappointed and broken than before.

Then again, maybe his dad had in fact found religion. If he had, weren't apologies part of that?

And wouldn't reaching out to say you were sorry to the son you'd abandoned be the natural place to start?

"I knew I couldn't keep living the way I had been," his dad continues. "So I cleaned up my act, and then I met Shelley. We started dating about three months ago, and I proposed to her last weekend."

"Whoa. That was—that's fast."

"It is. But when you know, you know. Especially at our age."

"Did you tell Mom?"

That barking laugh again. "Why would I tell your mother?"

"I don't know. It just seems like the right thing to do."

"You can tell her if you want. She and I just don't have that kind of relationship. I doubt she'd even be happy for me. You'd think after all these years, but no."

Forthcoming apology or not, his nonchalance is infuriating. "Well, you were pretty awful to her."

"Hey," his dad says, his voice hardening, "we were young, and she wasn't always the easiest . . ." He stops, like he can see Will's face contorting with rising anger. "Look, I'm not here to relitigate my marriage to your mother with you. That's not why I wanted to talk."

"So why did you?"

"The wedding is in a couple of weeks here in Florida."

Will braces himself. This is it. It's not an apology. It's an invitation. They want him and Rachel at the wedding to somehow whitewash all his past sins. If his dad asks him to be his best man, he thinks he might throw up the doughnut.

"Okay," Will says, committed to making him say the words.

"And it's really important that before I go into this marriage, I have your forgiveness so my slate is wiped clean. It's a big part of our faith."

Will waits for him to say more. To say that he was wrong to blame his many failures as a husband on his eight-year-old son or that he understands now he should have been there for Will even though things didn't work out between him and his mom. Or maybe that his new-found faith has finally forced him to fess up and face what a lousy father he'd been. Will doesn't know what religion his dad is practicing, but pretty much all of them have a lot to say about family.

But none of that comes.

"So do I?" his dad asks after about 15 seconds of dead air between them.

"Do you what?"

"Have your forgiveness?"

Will laughs. He can't help it. After all that time spent thinking he was the problem, the reality is that this man is so self-absorbed he can't even tell how ridiculous he sounds right now. Not even at Will's lowest—which, let's face it, is where he's been for most of his time in Nashville—has he ever displayed this type of arrogance and entitlement. His mom knows it. Rachel knows it. Ali knows it.

And now Will can see it for himself.

"Have you even apologized?" he asks.

"Of course I have. What do you think this is?"

"Telling someone you need them to forgive you isn't the same thing as saying you're sorry."

"I think that's implied, William," his dad says, the tone unmistakably condescending.

"Yeah, well, I'm going to need you to do more than *imply* it after everything you've done. Are you even inviting me to the wedding, or do you just want me to absolve you beforehand?"

"It's going to be a small ceremony, just Shelley's kids and a few of our friends, so there's really no need for you to come."

His dad doesn't say it with any more cruelty than normal. To him, it's just a statement of fact. And Will feels like he should be relieved because the last place in the world he would ever want to be is at his dad's wedding to some woman named Shelley.

His self-centered, egotistical father, whom Will thought he'd finally closed the book on not one minute ago.

But he's crushed all the same, the message he's received for so many years delivered one more time, underlined and in bold.

I don't want you. I never wanted you. You were never enough.

And that's when he remembers why he decided he didn't need talking points.

"I guess I'm not surprised. You didn't even respond when Rachel and I invited you to our wedding, so why would you want me at yours?"

"It would just be awkward. You must understand that."

"Oh, but I thought it was because it's going to be a small ceremony. So which is it? I make things awkward, or there's just no room for me?"

"For crying out loud, William. Don't be a child."

"How the *hell* would you know what I was like as a child?" Will shouts into the phone. The dog beneath the table two over looks up at him, concerned, while the woman sitting there tries not to. "You took me to a baseball game and then left forever."

"A baseball game?"

One of his only memories of his dad. A day he had played out over and over again as a kid, trying to make it come out differently. And his dad doesn't even remember it.

"Still polishing that dad-of-the-year résumé, I see."

"Please," his dad says. Will doesn't need to see him to picture the sneer on his face. "Like your life was *so* hard. I paid my child support. I saw you when I could. I'd say things turned out pretty well for you."

"You don't even care if I forgive you, do you? This was Shelley's idea. She's making you do this, isn't she? And you're going along with it because, what, you're some kind of Holy Roller now?"

That his dad for once doesn't have a response both shocks Will and confirms he's right.

"God, Aunt Katie was so right about you. You just don't get it. You never got it."

"Ha, Katie," his dad says coldly, proving his silence was fleeting. "I haven't thought about her in years. Be careful there. She's a real piece of work."

Will's tone is more measured now as he feels himself letting go of any last bit of desire to know this person.

"She's *dead*, you prick. She loved me. She loved her sister. She knew and loved Rachel. And she was more of a parent to me than you ever were."

His dad gets quiet. Dangerous.

"Now you listen to me, boy. I am still your father, and I am not going to be spoken to the way I'm sure you let that little wife of yours talk to you. Check your tone, or we're done here."

Everything Will has felt—the pain, the frustration, the anger, the sadness, the disappointment—bubbles up inside him.

But so, too, does the relief. He knows this is about to be over once and for all.

He takes a drink of his coffee to ensure he's fully present in the moment. Because it's been a long time coming.

"No, you listen to *me*," Will says, lowering his voice so only the two of them can hear it. "Because if you don't, and you hang up, I swear to God I will find Shelley, and I will tell her all the shit about you I know you haven't."

He waits a few seconds, making sure his dad is still there.

"I thought so," Will says. And then he starts.

"What I'm going to say is probably going to surprise you. Because guess what? I do forgive you. Or at least I know I should. Not because it will make me a better person or because I think God wants me to. Because to be honest, if there is a heaven, I think you and people like you are going to have a lot to answer for.

"It's not because of the two women who raised me, either. They sacrificed for me and loved me and taught me how to be a man I can be proud of, even if I get it wrong sometimes. And you were terrible to them both, but especially to my mom. I could never forgive you for that. Only they could. I think Mom maybe has. I think you'd better hope you don't run into Katie in the afterlife.

"I'm not forgiving you for Rachel. That's my wife, by the way, in case you didn't catch her name before. I don't even know if you knew it. She of course knows about you. And she hates your guts. Like, wholly and truly. She's not even speaking to me right now, and yet I know if I told her you asked me to forgive you—wait, I'm sorry, that you *implied* an apology—she would tell you to go to hell.

"Most important, I'm not forgiving you because you're sorry. If you truly were, I would. But I know you're not."

Will stops, verifying once more his dad is still on the line. He hears something clatter in the sink and thinks Shelley must be right there with him.

"I want to forgive you for me. For what you said about me to Mom when you left. For allowing me to blame myself for you being a coward. For causing me to doubt that I'm worthy of being loved. For chipping away at my self-esteem all these years without so much as saying a word. For not being a part of my life and not *wanting* to be a part of my life. For not knowing my wife and, in five months or so, never meeting your grandchild. And for making me believe I could ever treat that child the way you've treated me.

"I am going to do my best to forgive you for all of it, Andrew, because you are a small, sad, shallow man, and I'm tired of feeling like who you are ever had anything to do with me."

Will lingers for a second or two. There's no reaction, no screaming or tears or "You listen to me, boy." Just stony silence.

"Goodbye," Will says, and he hangs up.

He sets his phone down on the table and notices how quick his breathing has gotten. Closing his eyes, he rubs his forehead between his thumb and fingers, slowing himself down.

He did it. He actually did it.

The dog who looked at him earlier gets up from under her table and comes over to lick his leg. He opens his eyes and reaches down to pet her.

"Sorry," the woman says. "She can tell when someone's upset. It's a dog thing."

"Oh no, I don't mind," Will says, smiling down at the black Lab. "What's her name?"

"Well, we let our six-year-old pick, and she went with Katydid because she loves bugs. But of course the three-year-old couldn't say that and just started calling her Katy, so now we all do."

Will is confident his aunt didn't believe in reincarnation, and neither does he. But he also could imagine her saying that if she did, you could do a lot worse than coming back as a dog.

"Hi there, Katy," he says, tears in his eyes. "Thanks for looking out for me."

Chapter 30

Will can't go back and sit in an empty hotel room. He's simply too wired. You can't spend years building up to a phone call like that, finally have it, and not be. That's how he ends up spending hours just walking laps around 12 South, trying to wrap his head around it all, getting very sweaty in the process.

He feels good, although not necessarily happy, sort of like that finals week in college when he crammed for his Physics 2 exam, finished it knowing he'd done better than he'd expected to 24 hours earlier, only to have to gear up for something even harder, Calc 3, the next day.

Because it's getting late in the afternoon, and there's still no word from her.

He eventually ends up calling a Lyft—he doesn't want to risk getting drawn into exploring the call with his dad with Shayla—to take him to the multilevel bar on Broadway hosting Swift Saturday, aware that going there without Rachel might throw him back into the depths of where he was overnight and this morning. But she'd been looking forward to it so much that he can't bring himself to go somewhere different. It's early enough that the night's festivities won't have started, anyway, so he tells himself the reminders of her won't be more overwhelming there than anywhere else. He'll just grab some dinner, have a beer or two, and then go back to the room and keep waiting.

What he didn't count on was seeing Rachel sitting there in that purple dress when he walks in.

Her back is to the door, so she doesn't see him, and he freezes in place at the end of the counter. He wants nothing more than to go straight to her, but she hasn't said she's ready to talk yet. To show her he understands just how much he messed up by not listening to her about the job, he knows he needs to start by listening to her when she says to leave her alone. If she wanted him here with her, she would've told him. She's waiting for the music, not for him to come in and sweep her off her feet.

Then again, he's not sure he's strong enough to just walk away, either, or even if he should. Which is why 30 seconds later, he's still standing there when a glass drops to the floor behind the bar. Rachel turns at the sound, only to see her husband rooted to his spot.

It looks to him like she's chuckled, and he motions toward her to ask if it's okay for him to walk over. She hesitates, then nods.

A good sign.

"I promise I didn't think you'd be here yet," Will says when he gets to her table. She's sitting, some sort of frozen drink on the dark wood in front of her, and he decides he shouldn't take a seat unless explicitly invited. "I mean, I'm not going to pretend I'm not happy to see you. But I was just going to eat and go. I can leave now, though."

Rachel weighs his explanation. "No, you don't need to go," she says, swirling the straw in her drink.

Will tries to hide both his surprise and his elation at the news.

"But I'm also not sure I want to have this conversation just yet," she adds.

"I get that." He pauses. The purple in her hair perfectly complements the dress. "I'm just not sure where that leaves me. Like, physically. Should I go sit at the bar or something?"

She scopes out the dozen or so people seated there, and then maybe 20 more scattered around the first floor at this early hour.

"I don't think so," she says. "Too easy."

"Okay. What do you suggest then?"

"I think," she says, her face lighting up with whatever's just occurred to her, "I think I want you to ride the mechanical bull."

This is . . . a confusing sign.

"You're joking."

"I never joke about mechanical bulls, Will."

"What possible purpose could that serve besides embarrassing me?"

"Ah, fitting you should mention embarrassment," Rachel says and takes a sip of her drink. "Because I have a funny story about that. It involves you, actually. Would you like to hear it?"

Surprise and elation have left the premises.

Will wants to look away, to break eye contact, to say he'd like to hear literally anything else. But he doesn't. He knows he forfeited that right as soon as he emailed Beatriz.

"It starts with when I had to call Rochelle on her vacation," Rachel says, mimicking the tone you'd use to tell a child a fairy tale, "then *apologize* for calling on her vacation, and explain to her my husband went behind my back and scheduled an interview for me with her company—*by pretending to be me*. An interview I had previously turned down, and an interview I quickly confirmed she didn't know a thing about. It was easily the most humiliating moment of my career.

"So I got to turn her down, *again*, even though she hadn't asked this time. Which led to her reiterating how perfect she thought I'd be for the job, but that she agreed with me there was no way I could possibly come out for an interview after this. That in my shoes, she would find *that* too humiliating. So I have no clue what she thinks of me now.

"Then there's my *actual* job. After I left last night, I started thinking, 'Did he just expect me to go out to LA and keep calling in sick?' And then I thought, no, not Will—he's too thorough. So I log into my work email, and lo and behold, I see two messages from my boss: one asking to meet with me about a project that just got dropped on us when I'm back on *Thursday*, and another three minutes later apologizing for forgetting and spoiling the *surprise* you had planned for me. So apparently you emailed her. Tell me, Will: Did you do that as yourself, or was that as me too?"

"Myself," he says quietly.

"Well, how *honest* of you for a change. And either way, I get to figure out how to explain all this to her when I show up on Monday. But hey, at least I know I can go to my sister's doctor's appointment now."

"You told Isa?" he asks because it's the only thing he can think to say.

"Of course I told her! We talked all about it. And you're lucky Owen is such a shithead because you'd be coming off even worse if he weren't."

She hasn't been yelling, but the intensity with which she's looking at him is just as uncomfortable as if she had been, like he's being cross-examined on the witness stand, the main difference being that he has no defense. He knows he was wrong.

"All right, potential public mockery seems more than fair," Will says. "Whenever they start the bull for the night, I'll sign up."

"That's very generous of you, babe. But you know, I'm thinking it would be better if we did it right now."

He's not sure why she's giving him the benefit of a smaller audience, but he's not going to question it. "Oh. Okay. Whatever you'd like."

The smile that creeps across her face makes him rethink his relief.

"I mean sure, there will be fewer people here to witness it," Rachel says. "But there's a zero percent chance that the people who *are* here will miss it. It will be like a little private show. For all of us."

"Uh," he says, scrambling for the technicality that will save him, "I don't think you can just get on it at, like, any time. I'm pretty sure someone has to, you know, run it."

Rachel slurps the last of her drink. "Well, good timing," she says brightly. "I need another one of these, so I'll ask the bartender while I'm up there." She stands and brushes past him. "I have a song to request as your musical accompaniment, anyway," she adds with a wink.

Will watches her walk to the bar, his remorse for what he's done temporarily replaced by concern for the next five minutes of his life—and if he's being honest, a little sexual arousal triggered by the combo of her in that dress and her ruthlessness.

His mood shifts exclusively to terror when he sees the bartender hand Rachel her drink and the two of them look over at him and smile in unison.

Rachel begins walking back over to the table, where Will still hasn't sat down. She's about halfway there when he hears it.

The opening guitar riff of "22."

She wouldn't, he tries telling himself, now remembering that when they got into their room at the hotel, Rachel realized her Mackinac purchases were still in the car. And not just the dress.

All of her purchases.

"Here," she says, setting her drink down and reaching into her bag. "You'll need this."

She goes to give him the black hat, but when he doesn't reach to take it, she just places it on his head for him.

"Perfect," she says, stepping back to admire her styling. "I mean, you're significantly sweatier than Taylor, but for the most part, this is what I was going for."

Will's eyes scan up in the direction of the hat and then move back down to her, silently pleading for mercy.

"All right," Rachel says, "hop to it. Taylor's going to hit the chorus before you know it."

She's still smiling.

Okay, Will says to himself, turning to make the short trek across the bar to the ring, where the bartender has relocated to run his ride. *This isn't that bad. She's talking to you. That's all that counts. Lawrence would do this naked if it gave him five more minutes with Josie. You got this.*

Will has indeed become the focal point for the late-afternoon gathering of patrons, who are beginning to realize the flustered-looking guy in the sweat-soaked shirt and the Taylor Swift hat is the reason the music has changed and No Bull, the resident mechanical bovine, has been awoken from his slumber. The several other people who have also clearly shown up early for Swift Saturday have no more idea than anyone else what's going on, but they're here for it simply because the queen is now playing on the speakers.

"Woo, ride 'em, cowboy!" he hears a woman who is not Rachel yell as he steps over the short wall onto the padded floor encircling the bull. He looks in the direction the shout came from and recognizes a couple of members of the Lexi's Bachelorette: Day 2 contingent from the bakery. Judging by the size of the group that has moved into prime viewing position off to Rachel's left, it's the full party now. The T-shirts from earlier have been ditched in favor of a wave of Tory Burch and Lilly Pulitzer, but the presumptive Lexi is wearing a tiara that says *Bride*. And it's she who responds to the "Woo, ride 'em, cowboy!" with:

"Really, Amy? Didn't you have your fill of things . . . *past their expiration date* last night?"

All the women laugh, the one Will now knows to be Amy included, and then one standing where Rachel can't see mimes giving a blowjob while holding her nose, causing them to roar even louder.

His insecurity flares. This is how he appears to these women looking at him right now: as lame and out of place as their friend's sad middle-aged hookup. It shouldn't really matter since, present circumstances notwithstanding, he's a happily married man, but there's no way to hear that and not have it sting. His face reddening even more than it already was, he is grateful that at least Rachel doesn't know the full context of the joke. He puts his right foot in the stirrup and swings his left leg over No Bull's back, determined to avoid eye contact for the duration of his ride.

"All right, everyone," the bartender announces into a microphone, "give it up for Will and his ride of redemption!"

Nice touch, Rachel, he thinks as the Swifties cheer in a general show of support. Thank God for them. And "ride of redemption." That *had* to be a good sign, right?

The bartender turns the mic back off. "Ready?" she asks Will while the song hits the chorus for a second time. He grabs the little knob on the bull's back with both of his hands and nods.

The motor kicks on, and No Bull starts to spin and lightly buck. Will keeps his hands where they are, partly for balance, partly because he's hoping that if he doesn't grab the hat, it will fall to the floor of natural causes.

Alas, no such luck.

Five seconds pass, and then 10. Assorted whistles and catcalls mix with the music, but they're becoming less bothersome as he goes. Then the chorus is wrapping up, and Taylor's in the bridge, and he's still upright.

He's seen videos of people riding mechanical bulls, and it always looked more intense than this. Maybe Rachel asked the bartender to take it easy on him? Or maybe . . .

Am I actually good at this? he wonders.

"Do it, baby!" someone hollers over the noise, and he looks up because this time, it's not Amy. It's Rachel.

And she looks happy.

Not happy as in she's delighting in his penance, which she surely is. But happy as in she and Will are going to be okay.

It sends a surge of adrenaline through him, which only grows when he realizes that if she had the hat in her bag, she planned on seeing him tonight all along. All of it together causes him to lift the hat off his head and shout at the top of his lungs, "I *am The Matrix*, Nashville!"

Which, sure, is fundamentally confusing on its own. But in this case, it's especially misguided, as it coincides with the bartender cranking up the bull's intensity and sending him flying before the city's name is all the way out of his mouth.

The hat finally comes off as Will sprawls face first into the heavy padding of the ring. There's a smattering of applause that is a little embarrassing, but he's glad the ride is over and looks up expecting to see Rachel's smiling face, which will more than make up for anything he felt atop that bull.

"Are you for real right now?" Lexi says, literally looking down on him. "Like, why are you even here?"

She says it, Will guesses, to get a laugh from her friends, which it does. They're young, they're pretty, and they're at a bachelorette party. What do they care? Like the girls in high school with his denim vest, there's no way they could really know how hard this hits, and even if he had all night to think of a perfect comeback, he's not sure what he'd say.

So he doesn't overthink it.

"Because I want to be. Because I love her"—he points at Rachel—"and I did something stupid. And because it's really hot outside, and I wanted to stop walking around. Is that okay with you?"

Lexi doesn't say anything but rolls her eyes. The rest of the group turn their attention toward their drinks. Some look embarrassed, but not all. Will steps out of the ring so he's standing next to Rachel and sees the smile he'd been looking for.

"By the way," Rachel adds to Lexi before walking away, "it's Taylor's night, so you're the one who looks ridiculous."

Chapter 31

Will gets the same frozen mocktail Rachel has and returns to the table.

"Can I sit?" he asks.

"Yeah, I think you've earned that. I was proud of you back there."

He takes the seat across from her. "Which part? The prematurely celebrant mechanical-bull riding or the awkward confrontation with the bride-to-be?"

"Both. Just because I wanted to shake things up a little doesn't mean I want to see some chick in a tiara talk shit to you."

"That's what that was, shaking things up?"

"I think it's good to get you out of your comfort zone sometimes and remind you that you can't control everything." She makes sure he's looking right at her. "Then there's also the fact that I'm still mad at you."

"I know." He remembers what he thought up on the bull and sets the hat down between them. "But you brought this."

"Well, I figured you'd show up, or I'd call you, and either way, there was no chance you were getting out of wearing it now."

"I'm so sorry, Rachel. I know that doesn't fix it, but I'm—I'm just so sorry."

"I know that. I know you're sorry. But I need to know you understand why I'm mad. You can't just say the words. This isn't talking teddy bears in my apartment or bad coleslaw."

Will doesn't hesitate, and he doesn't try to explain it away. He just owns it.

"You told me to leave it alone, and I ignored you. And I didn't just ignore you; I deceived you. I pretended to *be* you. Over and over, for a week. Because even as I was doing it, I knew I shouldn't be. But I did it anyway. I cheapened all the closeness we had on this trip by convincing myself I was being romantic. That this was what you *deserved*. But all I was really doing was telling you what would make you happy and taking away *your* control over *your own* career. I'm supposed to be the one person who always has your back, and I failed miserably at that. Not to mention I screwed with your relationship with your sister."

Rachel stares at him with something between annoyance and confusion. "Um, yeah. Pretty much."

"Okay. What else?"

"What else?" she cries over the music, which has switched to some indistinct song about a guy and a truck. "Let's just start with that. You know all this. *I* know you know all this. So what in God's name were you thinking?"

"I don't know how to say it without it sounding like an excuse."

"Try me."

It comes out as both an invitation and a challenge, and he's not sure how ready he is to accept either. But he doesn't have much choice.

"I'm scared, Rachel."

"Of what?"

"Of so many things. Of not being good enough for you—"

"Nope, pass. I don't accept that."

"Hey, you asked. Do you want to hear it, or do you want me to make more stuff up and say I'm fine? Because I'm not."

She's not used to hearing him this forceful and can tell instantly this isn't some setup to a roundabout way of complimenting her, which is not at all what she wants right now.

"Okay," she says. "Go ahead."

"I'm scared I'm not good enough for you. That I've never been good enough for you. So I've always done these over-the-top things to try to compensate for it. And then with this job, I got scared you'd end up

regretting passing on it and eventually get tired of our life. I've seen . . .
daunting logistics keep you from what you wanted before. So I fell back
on what I always do and tried to turn it into a problem I could solve."

"'Daunting logistics'?"

"Like with your tattoo. We both knew how much you wanted it,
and it still took a year of nudging you before you'd go."

"You can't possibly be comparing uprooting our lives and moving
across the country to me getting a tattoo."

"All right," he says, hesitating over how to phrase the next sentence.
"What about the art gallery?"

"What art gallery?"

"The one in New York."

"After we graduated?"

"Uh-huh. You told me you regretted that decision and that you
only made it because your parents convinced you that you'd be making
a mistake if you went. Now you're in a job that you yourself called
boring. I mean, I'm pretty sure I heard you talking about quitting it in
your sleep when we were in Milwaukee."

Rachel turns that over for a second, and Will wonders if he's just
made things worse. But when she doesn't object, he knows it's okay to
continue.

"Plus you were also kind of sick of how your mom and dad are
treating your pregnancy, and then I saw someone like Lawrence and all
the regrets he had about Josie never getting back to Boston, and I told
myself I'd done the right thing. I don't want us to live with that kind
of regret."

"That's what you took from that story? Those two people sound
like they had a beautiful life together—one that ended way too soon,
but beautiful."

"I know. I got there eventually. That's why I felt like I had to come
clean when I did in the hotel room. But still."

"Also, I feel compelled to remind you that I was never offered a
job, just an interview. Did it ever occur to you that *I* might be scared?"

"I know you were worried that you wouldn't get it, but—"

"Not just that," she says, cutting him off. "What if they did offer it to me, but it didn't pay enough, and I had to turn it down? LA is super expensive. And as if that weren't enough, it's also a lot less forgiving about women's bodies than Chicago. You can't just cover up for like eight months a year."

Will is taken aback by that. Even with all the thinking he's been doing, not once had this crossed his mind.

"But you're beautiful."

"Rachel goggles," she says.

"I'm being serious."

"I know you are. And more importantly, *I* feel great about the way I look. But there's a different pressure out there to be a certain way. I've talked to Rochelle about it. And I'm not ready to open myself up to that, especially not when I'll be fresh off a pregnancy."

"I'm sorry," he says again. "I had no idea."

"You put me on this pedestal, Will. Sometimes it's sweet, and clearly, I'm amazing"—she does a kind of wave with her hands—"but it can also be a lot to live up to."

"So you probably don't want to hear that after you left, there was a part of me that was scared you might be done with me." She doesn't seem to be getting what he's driving at, so picking at his paper coaster, he adds: "Like, forever."

"What? Divorce?"

He's too embarrassed to say yes and just nods.

"You thought I'd want to *divorce* you over this?"

"I mean, no. Not really. But I spiraled and didn't feel like I could rule it out entirely."

Her lips smack in a disapproving tsk. "Well, *that's* kind of insulting. But the good news is that thinking I could do something like that is the opposite of putting me on a pedestal."

"I know. I'm sorry. I don't mean it that way. It's about me, not you." He tries to articulate something that's with him all the time but he's never had to put into words. "I just—it's so much easier for me to see all the reasons why someone would want to be with you than they would with me. I think about you and talk about you the way I wish I could talk to myself. You know?"

His eyes start to sting.

"I'm sorry," he says. "I've never cried this much in one day in my life."

Rachel's expression has shifted. The exasperation with him is still there, but it's now overshadowed by concern. She reaches under the table and puts her hand on his knee.

"Thanks," he says quietly.

"This isn't just about what happened yesterday, is it?"

Will steadies his breathing. "I talked to my dad today."

Shock joins her exasperation and concern. "Oh my God."

"Yeah. And yet another thing I lied to you about."

"What do you mean?"

"Remember that gas station in Ohio where you got the slush, and I bought the movie?"

"Uh-huh."

"My mom called while you were using the bathroom and said my dad asked for my phone number. I told her not to give it to him and then didn't tell you about it at all because I didn't want it to distract from getting you excited about going to LA."

Rachel had started rubbing his knee but now stops to make sure he sees her withering glare.

"I know," he says. "It was stupid. *Again*. But then I talked to Ali last night and my mom this morning—turns out my dad was even worse than we thought, by the way—and I realized I had to do it."

"And?"

"And he was as awful as you'd expect. Turns out he's getting remarried, and his superreligious fiancée wanted him to get my forgiveness first. And *get* is the operative word because he never really apologized, he's not really sorry, and he doesn't want me at the wedding. Which I had no desire to attend but made me feel like absolute crap regardless."

Rachel gives him a minute to compose himself again.

"How did you leave it?"

"I told him all the rotten shit it wasn't my place to forgive him for and all the rotten shit that it was, and that I'd do my best, because he's incapable of being anything other than a terrible human being.

"Then I said goodbye. For good. It's done. *I'm* done."

Now she looks impressed. "Based on everything you've ever told me, I can't believe you got him to sit there and listen to that."

"Well, I may have threatened to expose his past to his bride-to-be if he hung up before I was done."

"I have to say, for as much as I don't like the lying from the past week, I support the light blackmail."

"At least I got that right."

"And you really think that's it with him? Like, forever?"

"I think I need it to be. It's the only way I have any hope of eventually moving past everything he did."

She still has her hand on his knee, and he leans in over the table, their faces now close enough for him to see the specks of amber in her brown eyes.

"It's not just thinking I'm not good enough for you. I'm scared I'm not cut out to be a dad."

"Why? Because of your dad?"

"Partially. But also because I still don't have a good answer to the God question. Or how to blow your nose."

"*No one* has a good answer to the God question. And he or she will just be a nose picker."

"I'm not kidding," he says.

"Me neither."

"No, really—I live in perpetual fear that as soon as I stop trying to control things, as soon as I let myself get comfortable, that's when something awful is going to happen."

"Like nose picking?"

"Okay, that was a bad example."

"Give me a good example then."

This is it, the tightest of the tightly kept secrets. He closes his eyes because he doesn't even want to look at her while he says it.

"I'm scared that something will go wrong with the baby, and it will do to us what it's done to Isa and Owen. I'm scared of losing you if something goes wrong with your delivery. And I think this Creative Vices thing was something big for me to focus on instead. Something I could try to solve."

He opens his eyes to see her considering this, and she takes her time before responding.

"You've never said anything like this. Why have you been keeping it all to yourself?"

"You've been worried about your sister, and I was worried about you, especially after you came home so upset last Friday. So I didn't want my stuff to stress you out even more. And honestly, I think I was also just scared to say it out loud because speaking it makes it feel more real. Like me even putting it out there is tempting fate."

Rachel moves her hand from his knee and takes his next to their drinks.

"For one, I'm sorry if anything I said or did made you feel like you couldn't talk to me. That was never my intention. This"—she points back and forth between them with her free hand—"this is always open. It has to be. We've seen the consequences when it wasn't this week, and they were not good. No damsels here."

"I admit telling you does feel good."

"Two, you're not tempting anything, Will. Just like I don't believe we were destined to be together, I don't believe everything happens for a reason. Was there a reason Josie died the way she did? Or Aunt Katie? Was there a reason your dad left you and your mom? No—other than sometimes, life sucks. It can't help itself, despite any of our best efforts.

Lawrence and Josie didn't do anything wrong. Neither did Katie or you and your mom."

She senses his emotion working its way back up to the surface, and it makes her tear up too.

"You've got me crying now," she says. But she presses on. "I really truly believe everything is going to turn out well for us with this baby. Just look at how we tried to take care of each other this week."

Will's eyebrows raise, and he feels like he's missing something.

"I didn't hatch some elaborate plot," Rachel says, "but I did try—and succeed—in getting you stoned when I could tell the weight of everything was bearing down on you."

"I thought that was about relaxing me for my tattoo."

"I don't think you're in a position to judge me bending the truth at this point."

He sighs. "So, wait: We're going to be nurturing parents because I lied to you and you got me high?"

"In a manner of speaking."

"How very Gretchen Grayson of us. I also told some little boy at the hotel to never let anyone tell him men or the PAW Patrol don't cry." Rachel looks confused, so he adds: "It was by the vending machines."

Still confused, she smiles at him.

"Now," she says, "can I absolutely, one hundred percent guarantee everything will be okay with me? With the baby? No. Can we control that? No more than anyone else can. But if the unimaginable were to happen, it wouldn't be because it was supposed to. It would simply be because it did. And the idea of that scares me too."

She squeezes his hand tighter. "But we would survive, Will. *You* would survive. Just like you survived your dad—devastated for a long time, changed forever, but still a person anyone would be lucky to spend their life with. Because I didn't fall in love with the stuff you did. I fell in love with *you*, and I wouldn't trade this version for anything."

They're both emotional at this point, so it's a minute before she adds:

"Okay, maybe I'd trade you for a version who didn't impersonate me to try to get me a job despite my explicit instructions to the contrary. But everything else I'll keep."

He laughs, shooting a small piece of snot out of his nose, which makes her laugh and him laugh harder.

"Does this mean my request to find out whether we're having a girl or a boy is back on the table?" he asks.

"Not unless you're going to start growing her or him in your uterus."

"God you're stubborn."

She rolls her eyes in a way that concedes she knows he's right. "I know. I'm going to try and work on that. Hopefully with slightly less unfortunate results."

"Again, I am so, so sorry," he says. "I hope this goes without saying, but nothing remotely like this will ever happen again."

Rachel shakes her head. "Seriously, how could you have possibly thought it would work? Rom-coms aren't real for a reason, you know."

"Too much *Date Me Now!?*"

"Oh no, don't you go dragging that fine American institution into this."

She smiles at him again.

"I love you," Will says.

"You're not bad."

She winks and sets his hand down.

"I think you can take that off now," she says, looking at the bandage still on the inside of his wrist.

"I know. But it was too depressing to do it last night."

"Can I do the honors?"

Will extends his arm toward her, and Rachel carefully peels off the dressing. Once she does, they both look at the date inscribed there together.

"What did you say I said to you when I called after our second date?" she asks.

"'You're you, and you let me be me.'"

"Ugh, it's still so cheesy."

"But it's kinda perfect," he says.

"Yeah. It kinda is."

ONE YEAR LATER

"So when is Rachel leaving again?"

Will looks at Clare, his therapist, through the computer screen. He had brought up the idea of him starting therapy again—he'd gone for a year or so as a kid after his dad left but nothing since—on the drive home from Nashville, and Rachel had of course supported him. He's been going to Clare for about 10 months now. They normally do appointments in person, but he knew today was going to be a little chaotic around the house, so the week before, he asked to do a virtual session.

"Tonight at eight o'clock," he says. "My mom is getting here in an hour to help me with the baby while Rachel's gone, so she and I are going to go out to an early dinner first, and then I'm going to drive her to the airport."

"That'll be nice for the two of you. When was the last time you did that?"

"Dinner, just the two of us? Wow. Sometime in March? I think? My in-laws watched him, but they texted with questions so many times it kind of felt like we never left."

Clare smiles. "You've come a long way. When I first started seeing you, you were so nervous about becoming a dad you said you were scared you wouldn't know how to *hold* a baby. Now you're making jokes about Rachel's parents asking *you* questions and about to take care of a seven-month-old while she's on the other side of the country."

"Well," he says, looking off camera, "her parents were texting her, not me, and I'm not going to be on my own the next few days, so I'm not sure how much credit I should take."

"Will," Clare says. She doesn't proceed until he's looked back at her. "You're doing great. And one of the things we're going to keep working on is getting you to allow yourself to see that. Okay?"

"Okay," he says. "Thank you."

"Of course. See you next week."

He hangs up the call, and before he's even shut down his computer, the door to his and Rachel's room is being nudged open from the bottom.

"I promise we weren't eavesdropping," Rachel says, pushing it all the way open now that she's sure Will is done. "But someone is *very* excited to see his daddy. I think we set a new land-speed record for crawling from the kitchen to the bedroom."

"Hey, buddy," Will says, closing the laptop and walking over to pick the baby up off the ground. "How's my guy?"

Taylor William Armas-Easterly was born in early November, three and a half weeks early and two weeks after Rachel had been put on full bed rest due to high blood pressure. She spent 30-plus hours in labor, Will next to her all the way through the delivery (but looking elsewhere during the epidural), and the baby spent a few days in the NICU. Nothing was ever dire, and everyone came through it healthy, but for all the joy, it was not an easy month. Will was grateful he had already started with Clare, and Rachel was grateful to no longer have a human being residing in her stomach.

They had chosen the name Taylor, his mom and Katie's maiden name, in September, right around the time Will and Ali took that trip back to Ann Arbor that Rachel had suggested. Michigan beat Colorado State in football, they got drunk in a bar afterward, and Will asked Ali to be the baby's godfather. They'd hugged and then toasted it outside Moonshine Manor.

In addition to the tribute aspect, Will and Rachel liked *Taylor* because they knew it would work equally well for a boy or a girl. Will did second-guess it briefly right after Rachel delivered and she was holding the baby in her arms, worrying that people might assume he'd been named after a certain famous musician.

"So, what's your point?" Rachel cooed without taking her eyes off her newborn. "I just spent over a day pushing him out of me, and I'd be *thrilled* to have people make that connection." Nuzzling her nose to his, she added, "Yes, I would."

Will loves watching Rachel with Taylor, particularly when she's bopping around the kitchen with him, listening to the music of his official unofficial name twin. Rachel is a natural, just as he knew she'd be.

She says the same thing about Will, who's now closing his eyes while the baby plays with his nose. When it feels safe, Will opens them again, and Rachel is grinning lovingly at him.

"What?" he says.

"Nothing. Just you two. Like there was ever any doubt." She takes a step closer and kisses them both on their foreheads. "Do you have him while I take a shower?"

"Yup, we're good. We're going to read."

He carries Taylor to his room, and they settle into the blue glider chair where Will and Rachel take turns rocking him to sleep before naps and bedtime. In a typical week, Taylor goes to day care three days, with Rachel working from home with him on Thursdays and Will on Fridays. Today, though, they're all home on a Tuesday as Rachel gets ready to go.

She's heading to Los Angeles for an interview at Creative Vices.

The person they had hired for the associate creative director position the year before had recently accepted a job somewhere else, and Rochelle wanted to know if Rachel would be interested in interviewing to replace them.

"So, what do you think?" Rachel asked, burping Taylor after his bottle. This was less than two weeks ago, so coordinating everything

323

with their jobs and the baby even just to get her out there for the interview would be a lot.

"What do *you* think?"

"I told Rochelle I was interested but that I needed to talk with you first."

"And are you really? Like, not because you think I'd want you to do it, but because you want to?"

"I mean, it's still intimidating. But, yeah, I really am."

"Then you should go for it."

Her eyes narrowed in on his. "That was fast."

"It's what I think. As a wise woman once told me, it's not a job; it's an interview for a job. We'd have all kinds of stuff to figure out if it goes further than that, not to mention how you'd feel being that far away from Isa right now." She and Owen had been on a trial separation since the spring.

"But Rochelle clearly loves you," he continued. "So since you are interested, I think you should at least check it out. If nothing else, it's a free trip to LA and a couple nights of uninterrupted sleep."

"I think that sleep thing was about you," she whispered to Taylor as he spit up on the cloth on her shoulder. Then she looked back at Will. "We've come a long way from a year ago, haven't we?"

"In some ways, yes. Then again, I think I still might be high from those Cannabis Queen edibles."

She laughed. "I love you."

"I know."

That made Rachel smile, and Will smiles thinking back to it before opening *Dogs Can't Go to the Zoo* and starting to read to his son.

Acknowledgments

If you're reading this because you read the book, thank you. Authors write to tell stories, but we couldn't do that without people to tell them to. It's a privilege to have had that opportunity with you.

Jessica, it's certainly not a requirement that your literary agent become your friend, but I'm glad we've never let that stand in our way.

To Erin and Tiffany, your notes on the initial drafts of this story allowed me to develop it far better than I could have on my own. And to the entire team at Lake Union, thank you for giving my books a home and working so tirelessly to ensure they reach readers as the best versions of themselves.

Chris W., you gave me my shot, and I'll never forget that.

To Addison, for believing in the potential of my writing beyond the page.

Kevin, your friendship helped me know how to write Will and Ali's. Dixon, Moonshine Manor doesn't happen without you. Thank you both for always showing up for me.

Mom and Dad, your marriage is the opposite of Will's parents, going strong for more than 50 years. You both put your all into raising me so that I'd one day have the chance to do all the things I get to do now. That's a pretty great gift.

Sheila, Rein, Kate, and Susan, I almost can't remember what it was like for you *not* to be my family. (And yes, Rein, before you ask for clarification, I meant that as a compliment.)

To Joey, Kevin B., Aunt Lia, Uncle John, Ryan, Molly, Brian, Mallory (my friend), Mallory (my goddaughter), Sam, CeCe, Josh, Pat, Cidni, Warren, Chris A., Chris E., and Katherine. I'm impressed I know this many people, as well. I hope the association has been as worthwhile for you as it has for me.

To all the family and friends who took the time to send me encouraging emails and texts after my last book was published. Writing is in many ways a solitary pursuit, but so, too, is knowing your book is out there in the world and wondering how people will react to it, if they notice it in the first place. Your kind words helped keep me going as I worked on this one.

They come and go in terms of intensity, but anxiety and depression are an all-too-familiar part of my life. I mention that here because, in whatever small way I can, I hope to help reduce the stigma around them—and because it gives me the chance to say that everyone who struggles with things like these deserves access to quality, affordable mental health care. Thank you, Alexandra, for being my therapist.

To Liz at the Georgia O'Keeffe Museum, for helping me give Rachel such a rocking tattoo.

Buckner and Roxy, my beloved GSPs. (Okay, one of you is beloved, and one of you may be plotting my demise.) My main characters still don't have a dog, but there was at least a meaningful dog cameo this time. I'm making progress.

To Henry and Caroline. Like the characters in this book, I was pretty anxious about becoming a parent. I don't know how much less anxious I am now than I was back then, but I do know that I've learned as much from you two as I've taught you, if not more. I love you both for being you.

Jenny, if you had only succeeded in making me an honorary Swiftie, you would've left a lasting impression (even before I got the tattoo). The fact that I get to wake up next to you every day boggles my mind. None of this happens without your love, support, and patience.

And finally, to Will and Rachel. When I knew I'd have the opportunity to write a second novel, I have to confess I pitched a different story first. Now I can't imagine having written this one about anyone else.

About the Author

Photo © 2021 Erin Ponisciak

Ted Fox is the author of the novels *Date Week* and *Schooled* as well as the jokebook *You Know Who's Awesome? (Not You.)*. Having once solved the *New York Times* crossword puzzle forty-six days in a row (not a joke), he lives in the Midwest with his wife, their two kids, and two German shorthaired pointers who are frankly baffled there aren't more dogs in his books. More information about Ted is available on his website, www.thetedfox.com.